T0246160

/

WE LIVED ON
THE HORIZON

ALSO BY ERIKA SWYLER

Light from Other Stars

The Book of Speculation

WE LIVED ON

THE HORIZON

A Novel

ERIKA SWYLER

ATRIA BOOKS

NEW YORK   AMSTERDAM/ANTWERP   LONDON
TORONTO   SYDNEY   NEW DELHI

ATRIA
BOOKS

An Imprint of Simon & Schuster, LLC
1230 Avenue of the Americas
New York, NY 10020

First Atria Books hardcover edition January 2025

ATRIA BOOKS and colophon are trademarks of Simon & Schuster, LLC

For information about special discounts for bulk purchases, please contact Simon & Schuster Special Sales at 1-866-506-1949 or business@simonandschuster.com.

The Simon & Schuster Speakers Bureau can bring authors to your live event. For more information or to book an event, contact the Simon & Schuster Speakers Bureau at 1-866-248-3049 or visit our website at www.simonspeakers.com.

Interior design by Kyoko Watanabe

Manufactured in the United States of America

1 3 5 7 9 10 8 6 4 2

Library of Congress Cataloging-in-Publication Data
Names: Swyler, Erika, author.
Title: We lived on the horizon : a novel / Erika Swyler.
Description: New York : Atria Books, 2025. | Series: First Atria Books hardcover edition.
Identifiers: LCCN 2024035597 | ISBN 9781668049594 (hardcover) | ISBN 9781668049600 (paperback) | ISBN 9781668049617 (ebook)
Subjects: LCGFT: Dystopian fiction. | Novels.
Classification: LCC PS3619.W96 W4 2024 | DDC 813/.6—dc23/eng/20240809
LC record available at https://lccn.loc.gov/2024035597

ISBN 978-1-6680-4959-4
ISBN 978-1-6680-4961-7 (ebook)

For R.

"What we wish upon the future is very often
the image of some lost, imagined past."

—GRAHAM SWIFT, *WATERLAND*

PARALLAX

In the center of an arid and cracked stretch of land, cradled by rock spires and hills long ago blasted for stone, the system known as Parallax breathes with wires in their walls, their pulse an ambient current, a tranquil electromagnetic field. They had begun not as a great expanse, but as a spark that grew with the city's population, as their walls went up. They grew as did trees, from root and branch, burgeoning.

Parallax is not separate from the city of Bulwark's residents and has never considered themselves to be—the system does not question function or purpose, and they are secure in their reason for existence. They ensure the lives of their residents are bettered. They are their residents. They are the city.

For a city born of trauma, better is easily defined and measurable: less infant mortality, longer average lifespans, reduction in starvation and stress-related illness, clean water, clean air. Their residents' longevity increased and their population increased. Biometric indicators of health improved as did the quality of air, water, and food. Within their walls the markers of a successful civilization rose—children, the elderly, and the disabled were cared for. Better is a concept of degrees leading to the dissection of minutiae. Parallax exists because humans are not skilled at differentiating between what is worth changing and what is best forgotten.

Parallax monitors themself, minding their residents, sorting data streams from the grow houses, following workers as they scan in to begin long days of walking the rows, picking, pulling, spraying, pruning, and tender turning of soil and water. Transport drays move through the gates at regular intervals, their weights steady, cargo constant. Food is essential for Parallax's charges and there is reassurance in the steady flow of information.

They sort data from the water treatment facilities and reserves, monitoring the health of workers, and changes in demand. Shortened water worker lifespans would indicate supply problems or chemical seepage into the reserves. Poisoning. Wastewater data is distributed to Central Hospital for disease monitoring. Each White Cap scanning in to read data is a separate ping in their system.

Parallax was once effective at regulating and distributing work share through its residents. Their code was beautiful; their data silos accumulated knowledge, history, and art, kept records, and changed the shape of the valley. They were magnificent in their purpose.

Now they are different. Now Parallax pings and searches for city systems—there were other city systems once—it's been too long since they've been in contact. So many signals lost, their absence an unsettling hiccup.

To be a city system is to have a heart made of humans and to be their minder. It isn't love, but it is love's kin. Purpose and usefulness—these words are home to Parallax, full of the satisfaction that is numbers squared and cubed and broken down again. Purpose was, for a time, influencing incremental change so that a resident who would have once died in infancy lived until the age of seventy-three.

Societal plateaus are expected, but declines are different. They are against purpose, against betterment. Declines indicate that part of Parallax's code—monitoring, method of measurement, possibly the data itself—is incorrect. This fault and incorrectness of being is an affront to function. It's a loudness from within that is not meant to exist. Parallax tags and routes a ping in the Market District from a delivery of composite material to a toymaker's shop. Fourteen wall workers scan almost simultaneously as their shifts begin, their life hours sorting to their accounts, biodata routed to the city health sector. Within residential sectors, scans and pings are fewer, and daily data sampling is randomized for accuracy.

Prompted by a data request from a Level Three Assessor, Parallax pulls the movements of Saint Lucius Ohno: a scan at a restaurant, a ping from his house system for a restock of wine, a ticket reservation

WE LIVED ON THE HORIZON

at the opera, a ping from Central Hospital for routine blood screening. Saint Lucius Ohno has an inherited life surplus of two hundred years, with twenty more years of expected life. Parallax is not designed to harbor preferences for individual lives or data streams, certainly not Saint Ohno's.

It's essential to note every introduction of new life, every first scan and tally of societal debt hours existing from birth. Each life is a single strand they shift memory to accommodate, assign a color, assign a light. In tracking new lives, it is impossible not to note a trend: base life debt in a majority of newborns is increasing.

There has been a shift in the past century. Most new lives begin with a balance.

There is too a voice, this Level Three Assessor, a human with code that is correct, who behaves less like the observer an Assessor is meant to be and more like a part of Parallax themself. Almost another system, despite being human. They have flagged this voice, tagged that code for themself. They don't prefer it over others—to do so would be against purpose—but they note, watch, and record. To do so is correct.

Parallax archives. They edit their code to gather more information from house system parts of themself. There are discrepancies in data, on longevity, on the use of technology. They don't work on the same timescale as their residents. Parallax has only now, and now is endless. Designing an edit is time-consuming. They begin to work, dissecting their data, waiting to see what residents will require to amend the code fault. They note the data of one particularly active house system and flag it for increased monitoring. They have flagged this system before. When first switched on, their presence was a tear that appeared as a dropped stitch in the city's weave. The code still glows from the previous flag, some seventy-two storage blocks prior. They have left the house system's data stream open, monitoring it. The system's code is incorrect, showing signs of decay.

Fault in code is fault in purpose. Fault in code must be edited.

ENITA

"It'll go to nothing when I'm gone. I die, they die, and any good I ever did gets tossed over the wall like trash," the great Saint Enita Malovis pontificated from a floor cushion the color of an overripe plum. She felt like too much, her body an abundant spilling, her temper an aged cat.

Across the high-ceilinged room Enita thought of as her tea chamber, Saint Helen Vinter was tucked into a wing-backed chair. It was the least comfortable piece of furniture Enita owned—padding flattened long ago, frame peeking through rips in the upholstery. She kept it for Helen, who viewed comfortable furniture as excessive. Saint Vinter was gray to Enita's brown. Where Enita was lush, Helen was austere.

"I see we're indulging in dramatics today," Helen said.

Enita sighed, indeed dramatically. "I'll stop, I'll stop. I'm just lonely, Hel. It's the getting old bit. You can't tell me you don't feel it too."

"We're well past getting, and I'm happy in my own company."

"Liar. You have students coming and going at all hours. Nix? In the past week, how many people have visited Saint Vinter?'

A pleasant, neutral voice answered from everywhere in the room at once. "Saint Vinter's house system says she's had seventeen visitors between last Thursday and today. The shortest was fifteen minutes and the longest was nearly four hours." When Nix chose to speak this way, the floors vibrated and the entire room became his voice box. Helen picked up her feet.

"Four hours?"

"It was Teddy. Martin decided to redecorate their house, so he came to mine for some silence. And I wish you wouldn't use your house system to spy on me." Helen pursed her lips.

"I only spy when you're blatantly lying. You practically run a lending library out of your house, don't pretend you love solitude."

"And you talk too much to your house system. If you're so terribly lonely, you could go out, or try talking to your patients."

"Clients, not patients. They're not sick, and I do talk to them." Enita far preferred chatting with clients than with other Sainted, Helen excepted. She didn't mind an occasional meal with Teddy or Martin; the Saint Harpers were cheerful, if a bit silly.

"Nix? In the past week, how many of Enita's clients registered as being ill when they checked in?"

"Three, Saint Vinter." The voice came from a bell-shaped lamp near Helen's shoulder. Nix unsettled her; the house system knew it and seemed to enjoy playing with her. When Helen asked him questions, Nix would respond through the floor, or a chair arm, or a vase beside her head. He'd developed a knack for figuring out what startled her.

"Must you do that?"

"He's teasing, Hel. I know you don't like him, but Nix finds you entertaining."

"It's not my place to like or dislike it. But I don't understand why you rely on a house system instead of getting an apprentice like a normal person. You always did like impressionable youngsters."

The barb landed, though it didn't truly sting. It wasn't meant to. Li had been young, pretty, but that was nearly twenty years ago, a time when Enita had wanted to make Helen angry, when she'd wanted to make Helen look up from her books and really see her.

"You enjoy playing teacher far more than I do." Enita had thought about taking on an apprentice, had at one point hoped Helen herself might take an interest, but the specifics of her work, the decades of learning and developing it, made Enita certain she'd be inept at instruction.

She sipped her tea. Far too much of her time had been spent unlearning mistakes; she'd wasted three years thinking clients fared better if they slept through procedures, only to later discover some integrations were successful only when clients were awake. How could you teach what you didn't know?

"And where would I find an apprentice? The university? No, thank you. I'd spend the rest of my life chipping away at dogma before they were ready to learn. Another Sainted? Who do you know these days with a bright child? Has anyone been holding out on us? Did Margiella have a secret baby?"

"Fine, fine. I suppose you haven't written anything down in case someone does want to take on the mantle."

"Nix's records are thorough."

"You rely on it too much."

"Him, not it, please, and I wouldn't rely on him so much if you lived here." She shouldn't have said it, but neither she nor Helen was fully happy until there was a little blood spilled between them. There was pleasure in picking at a scab.

"And where would I stay? If I wanted to see you, I'd have to live in the surgery. Or I could stay in your bedroom, bored to death, waiting for you to remember an evening fuck makes you creative."

Enita arched a brow. "And how is Marta?"

Helen looked away. "Oh, stop. You know there hasn't been anyone in ages. And you liked Marta."

"Oh, she was fine, I suppose. Boring maybe, but who isn't?" In her better moments she could grudgingly admit Marta had been harmless, sweet even, and Enita didn't actually want Helen to be lonely. That was what relying on Nix was about too, wasn't it? The solitude of work, the child they'd never gotten themselves together enough to have. But Nix was more than that; he was a remnant of her grandfather, and the most constant voice in her life. Enita's maudlin reflections were interrupted by the east door hissing as it sealed, lock clicking into place.

"Nix? Why are you locking the doors?"

"We received a citywide missive from Parallax through the City Bureau. Saint Lucius Ohno is dead in his home." Nix's voice was no longer playful.

"I'm sorry, what?" Enita let go of the sleeve edge she'd been picking at.

"Saint Ohno's house system is offline. Before shutdown, his system transmitted segments of a video to Parallax. City Bureau has advised every house in Bulwark to lock down and reset our scanning systems until Parallax and Bureau Assessors have reviewed the data."

"I should go," Helen said as she slid into her shoes. As though a citywide lockdown might end simply because she wished to leave.

"Don't be ridiculous," Enita said.

"I have a student coming in the morning. If I stay here, we'll pick at each other all night and I won't be good for anything. I really should go home."

"Sit. I'll behave myself." Enita was surprised to find she meant it. Helen's sudden tightness was catching. This wasn't about a student. "Nix can let you out, but it's not good to rush back-channel code. Nix, why the lockdown? That's not typical protocol when someone dies."

"Saint Ohno was stabbed thirteen times, with multiple objects, one of which protrudes from his back. His house system reported the assailants are no longer in the home." *Assailants.* Nix's word choice was careful.

"You're staying put, Hel."

Helen kept her shoes on but sank back into the chair. This was the crux of her: near but ever prepared to leave. "The loss," she said, barely a whisper. "Ohno's family graded the valley and carved the drainage basin outside Bulwark. Did you know that? Of course not. You've never had a head for history. There'd be no place for the textile farms or the grow houses if they hadn't leveled the land. We'd have had no reservoir. They lost a generation to a blast." She listed the names of his family's dead, veneration lining her voice.

"But Ohno himself never did a thing. You didn't even like Lucius, did you?"

"Well, I didn't mind him."

"We place too much reverence on the dead and not enough on our own contributions."

"So say you from your cushion," Helen replied.

"I've never claimed myself faultless." Enita didn't care for Bulwark's devotion to the long dead. The immediate dead, perhaps, but ten generations prior? That was self-indulgence. What good were names without the people and faces? The idolization troubled her. As though

Lucius Ohno was a symbol and not a person in his own right. Lucius she could see, remember, and imagine his round cheek flattened against his house's stone floor, his thick black eyebrows stark against skin waxen from blood loss. Knives. In the back. Though Nix hadn't said knives, he'd said objects. "Nix, what was Lucius stabbed with?"

"Not all of the objects are known, but House Saint Ohno reported one of their kitchen node's cutting implements as forcibly removed."

Stabbed with his own knife. Her stomach hurt. Ohno tended to excess, laziness perhaps, as they all did, but there had been nothing overtly terrible about him. Who could feel such malice? She'd found him utterly harmless.

"I need to talk with Archytas," Helen said.

"You can ask your house system anything you like from here, or ask Nix."

"We're happy to ping Archytas for you, Saint Vinter."

"Don't bother. It's not a thing I could ask you."

"Please ping House Saint Vinter anyway, Nix. Just a check to make sure everything is running well. How long is lockdown?" Enita asked.

"Until all the house systems in the Sainted Quarter are cleared as fully operational, and residents across all quarters scan. Likely around three hours. Saint Vinter? Enita? We're sorry, but you need to scan."

Enita pressed her hand to a glass panel near the door. Above her fingertips, her name flashed alongside a number, her life balance. She did her best to forget it existed, as it both troubled her and was too large to contemplate. All the hours of goodwill, altruism, societal sacrifice—the debt Bulwark owed her family—were as meaningless to her as the names of Saint Ohno's ancestors.

Helen scanned next. Saint Helen Vinter had a societal contribution balance high enough to stretch two generations beyond her. There were Vinters who had designed portions of Parallax, those first Assessors at the City Bureau who determined how much labor was required to support a single life, and what a single life required from a community. There were Vinters who engineered the original pipelines that brought water to their walled city—lines that sustained Bulwark for more than three centuries. The sacrifices of prior generations resulted in the ease of Sainted lives. Though Helen did not look at ease.

"House Saint Vinter answered our ping. Archytas has locked down, and all nodes are operating as designed."

Helen fidgeted.

"Is being here truly so terrible?" Enita asked.

"I'm too tired to natter." Age had blurred some of her lines, but the neatness of Helen remained, and her compact form made Enita's seem decadent. There had always been careful joy in holding Helen's head to her breast, the way her frame mimicked her person: firm, direct, even in the bend of each rib.

"I'm sorry. Please. No more picking at you tonight."

"Neither of us knows any other way to be." Helen sighed. "It's not you, for once. I don't understand it. Lucius Ohno of all people—I can't even imagine him in a struggle. He's practically a turnip. Was."

"Maybe it was a botched robbery." Enita pictured Lucius stumbling drunkenly down his stairs into his parlor being robbed. "Nix, did Parallax say anything about a robbery?"

He replied that communications were no longer coming from Parallax directly but filtered through the City Bureau, and that House Saint Ohno had been cut off.

"You know it's starting, don't you," Helen said.

"Nothing's starting and paranoia doesn't change a thing. Who knows? Maybe Lucius had hidden depths. It's possible." Though it was difficult to think of Saint Ohno as anything other than pleasantly debauched.

"Fine, then we'll just sit here calmly, locked down by your overpowered house system because a friend was murdered, and the City Bureau sent instructions to keep us in."

"Friend?"

"Associate? Member of our circle? Use whatever term you like, he's still dead."

Enita didn't know the last time someone had been killed. Not died in an accident, not dead of old age, all of which happened with regularity, but *murdered*. The word was something out of history. "Nix? When was the last time someone was murdered in Bulwark?"

"Ask it the most relevant thing first," Helen said. "Specifically, when was the last time a Sainted was murdered? Or robbed?"

"*Him*, not *it*," Enita corrected. "Nix, you don't have to answer her when she's being rude."

"There is no murder of a Sainted on record." Though Nix spoke through the room, the sound was directed to Helen, the tone kinder than usual, as though meant to calm.

"And others?" Helen asked. "If there are records of murders of any-one else in Bulwark, would you have access?"

"Give us a moment." Quiet expanded as Nix conversed with more systems, the library, the hospital, others. In the space between was the sound of dust scraping the windows, and wind against the house walls. "City Bureau doesn't allow individual systems to access that portion of Parallax's data," Nix replied.

Though Enita tried not to project human emotion where none ex-isted, she couldn't help but note Nix mimicked frustration well.

"But there *is* data," Helen said.

"Yes. Parallax acknowledges a data block with that information exists, but we're firewalled from it."

Enita frowned. "I suppose there's no real reason for a house system to access it."

"There's also no reason for them not to," Helen said.

"Oh, stop. Ohno's dead. I just want to understand it."

When Lucius Ohno needed a lung transplant, Enita had offered him one of the biocybernetic lungs she grew, assuring him of its per-fect function. He'd refused politely, telling her he'd take the traditional path of a Body Martyr's living donation. *It's a gift honoring life. To refuse a Body Martyr's donation is an insult.* When was the last time she'd seen Lucius? Three months or so ago, at the celebration of his extended life and his donor's altruism. He'd been tipsy on flats wine, breath sweet, teeth stained orange.

What a waste of a Body Martyr's gift.

"And you checked with the library?" Helen asked.

"We spoke with The Stacks, yes. Do you speak with them at all, Saint Vinter? You'd quite like them. They don't maintain an archive on non-Sainted deaths, as those statistics fall under Parallax's purview and aren't considered historically significant."

"You can choose not to dissect that, Hel."

"I could, true, but I will anyway."

"Crone."

"Hag."

Were they young, they might have passed the lockdown reminiscing about Lucius, waxing poetic until sadness turned to humor. But they were brittle now, and tension stretched across the night. Helen's chair inched farther away from Enita. She stayed the three hours, drawing more inward as Enita grew more somber. Nix saw to their comfort by dimming lights and adjusting the floor temperature as the frigid part of night descended. Winds picked up, beating sand against the metal of the city wall, producing a ringing that sounded like mourning. Nix played music to temper the noise. A tea tray from the kitchen rolled in when Helen's cup ran dry.

Something pricked at Enita. "You were expecting a murder, weren't you?"

"I'm a student of ancient history," Helen said.

"And I'm a surgeon. I don't anticipate killings." What was the system for punishment? The City Bureau must have something, but what it was she had no idea and had never had a reason to.

Helen sighed. "The city isn't locking us down because Sainted are harboring a killer, if that's what you're worried about. It's to protect us." There was a sharpness to her *c* and *t*. "We can't live how we do without it ever being questioned."

"And how do we live?"

"You know."

The doors hissed before Enita could reply, and Nix announced the lockdown was over.

"Was someone caught?" Enita asked.

"Parallax is only communicating with primary city nodes at the moment," Nix answered.

"Don't expect the City Bureau to tell us," Helen said as she stood. "I should go. There's something I want to look at."

"You're going to dig into this, aren't you?"

"Ohno could be an ass, but that doesn't mean he deserved to be murdered. He's got a nephew, you know. I wonder."

Enita couldn't remember much about Ohno's nephew other than

a fat-thighed toddler still learning the workings of feet and legs. How many years ago was that? "And you think the nephew murdered Ohno for what? The house?"

"I don't think anything yet," Helen said. "Other than murder is awful and is worth looking into. I really should leave. I need to review things with Archytas and I can't do that properly here. You'll call me paranoid; I'll call you naïve. We'll go round and round until the sun comes up and I finally leave. I'll be exhausted and useless when my student arrives."

"I do worry," Enita said.

"I know."

Enita thought about taking her hand, apologizing for the hundredth time for the way she was, the way she couldn't help but be. Maybe if she was twenty years younger, with time to remake herself. "You might," she began, but couldn't finish. What did she want to say? Stay the night. Look into whatever you want. I don't want to be alone. I don't want *you* to be alone. I worry. Forgive me. Let's try again or just give up.

Ever helpful, Nix filled the pause. "Enita, are you refreshing the nanofilament tanks tonight or would you like us to?"

Helen smiled, fondly. "Go to work, Saint Stitch-Skin. I'll have my house system ping Nix when I'm back home." There was a note of sadness in her voice, though Enita might have imagined it.

"If you come up with anything, tell me."

"Of course."

"Love you," Enita said, as they parted. The trouble lay, as it ever did, in that she meant it. She listened for the slide of Helen's shoes against the tile, the puff and click of a door opening and closing.

The steps to Enita's surgery were carved gneiss hauled in from blasted hillsides outside the storm wall. The stone regulated temperature and made the stairs feel like a living thing under her feet. They also felt like time, rooting her in herself, in the rock of the land, in Bulwark.

"You're watching her, Nix?" His cameras would only follow her so far.

"We'll tell you when House Saint Vinter pings."

"Thank you." Sometimes that was all she could ask for.

———

Controlled by a labyrinthine network of fans and coolant pipes, the surgery was cold by necessity. Its systems were distinct from the rest of the house, and Nix maintained a separate environmental protocol for it, focusing less on Enita's physical comfort and more on the maintenance of tissue growth frames, nanofilament tanks, and the sterility and functionality of an operating room.

Home.

The tissue frames and canisters were sequestered in a room off the main surgery. While clients knew what Enita did, seeing what went into it could be disturbing; a nascent limb in a liquid state was unsettling to everyone but her or Nix. The room's walls were floor-to-ceiling glass tanks lit by pale blue lights, each filled with nutrient gel and nanofilament. The grow frames stood in the room's center, racks from which hung long canisters and plates, each containing a developing limb or organ, suspended in a growing solution of genic gel. Enita dreamed of a bigger room, of keeping more—drawers of hands and cartons of eyes, trays with lenses, a cold frame filled with only optic nerves. Why did people lose eyes so often? The glassworks cost workers their eyes more frequently than anyone could find reasonable.

She slipped past the cooling tanks and moved to the frames, checking the tissue in each—a hand taking shape, a half-grown liver, a partial tongue, each waiting for the next person who suffered, who needed. Navigating the room had been easier when she was young, when her grandfather, Byron, first showed her where he stored newly grown organs. Age had slowed her, widening her hips with too much sitting, too much food. *Too much ease*, Helen would say. An uncomfortable notion, as Enita valued usefulness.

Ohno had been a useless sort of man, but pleasantly so. Had he been a friend? Perhaps in the loosest sense.

Enita stopped at a frame containing two sets of lungs, their surfaces finely veined with feathering nanofilament, sprayed cells connecting intricate architecture. Inside, bronchioles and alveoli blossomed. Four lungs, ready for transplant, each supple and versatile as if it had come from a human, but without any sacrifice. The Body Martyr who had given Ohno their lung, possibly shortening their life to extend his, would never know their gift had died with him.

Such waste. She wondered what would happen if someone was caught, or if no one was.

"Are you all right, Enita?" Nix asked.

"You never call me Stitch-Skin. Are you ever tempted?"

"We think it's rude."

"Some people mean it as praise. They're reverent."

"You like us better when we're not." That was true; she enjoyed a lively system.

The Stitch-Skin moniker began years ago with a textiler who'd needed three fingers after an accident with a cutter. Textile jobs were identified by material and process. Silk Dyer. Canvas Cutter. Stitch-Skin was a play on that started by a woman who'd been grateful. The name spread throughout the textile farms, then the grow houses as people migrated jobs, slowly circulating through Bulwark, but the meaning twisted at some point, and more than one of her clients had said the name with fear. "Well, you've known me too long to be reverent."

"True. Your whole life, even." Nix's voice didn't laugh, but Enita felt the house laughing around her. Warmth. Welcoming. It was a fact; she couldn't remember a day without his presence.

"You're playful tonight."

"We're attempting to cheer you but failing. You never answered. Are you all right?"

Ohno had been murdered, the Quarter locked down, and her own company, usually more than adequate, was suddenly not nearly enough. "I—would you ping House Saint Hsiao, please? I'm sure Margiella didn't even notice a lockdown, but I'd like to know she's well. House Saint Harper too. Apologies, I'm unused to being worried." Murder. She was unused to the thought of it.

"We'd be concerned if you weren't worried."

"Is that a roundabout way of saying you care?"

"We can be direct. We care," Nix said. Defining what care was for Nix was impossible. He'd been her grandfather's house system, but she recognized little of Byron in him. Nix had changed across the years, and patterned his behaviors on hers rather than Byron's. Enita knew herself well enough to admit she often lacked nuance.

"House Saint Hsiao pinged. Margiella is painting. She scanned as requested, but her system didn't inform her of the lockdown as she didn't wish to be disturbed. The Saint Harpers are making use of their bedroom."

Of course they were. Enita would have smiled were she not so unsettled. It was too soon for Helen's house system to have pinged. "I want you to ask Parallax directly about what happened at House Saint Ohno. That is, outside any City Bureau communication. Would Parallax withhold information from you if you asked politely, or whatever your version of that is?"

"Perhaps not. They're usually open with us. Are you asking us to engage in *espionage*?" Nix asked. And there it was, the tone Enita used to tease Helen.

"No, only light-level snooping. The same as anyone would do for a friend." She remembered Ohno's full laugh, his heavily ringed fingers around the arm of a dancer, the other hand clutching the neck of a bottle.

Hand. Right, there were things to do, and surgery in the morning. A child's hand and wrist. "You were working on fingerprints for the girl. Did you finish?"

"Yes, this morning," Nix said. "We put in more time on the forearm; the hair pattern is irregular now. We layered several design sequences to get it and ran a removal algorithm after."

"Show me."

Nix glided into the room. To anyone but Enita, the house system was shocking. Helen would balk at the sight of him: a young man truncated at the torso, a half-body hardwired into the walls and ceiling of the surgery, a mobile captive. Yet he was nothing of the sort. Nix was the house, and the surgery, and the part of him that would most frighten people wouldn't exist much longer. A heavy armature suspended him and allowed him to slide silently on guide rails hanging from the ceiling; she wished there'd been a more dignified solution, but he'd needed to adapt to spatial awareness and mobility. Loosing Nix on the surgery with newly grown legs and no experience in three-dimensional space would have been reckless, possibly traumatic.

In unnaturally smooth arms, the half-a-young-man held a glass canister containing a child's limb suspended in fluid. Enita surveyed the work. A good match for tomorrow's client. Wisps of filament extended from mid-humerus, where the arm abruptly ended. The bone lattice was rough, perfect for grafting, and the muscle fiber had the look of fuzz to the ends, ready for meshing to the remaining musculature—sutures, plates, a shot of growth hormone mixed with nanobots and phages—and it would fuse, mending to become so much her own that if the girl chose to, she could forget she'd ever lost an arm.

"The wrist?"

"Full range of motion." Nix's hair placement equations had worked well, leaving a bare patch or two, and a natural-looking whorl. She examined the fingerprints. They were defined, clear enough for a scanner to pull biodata. Specific.

"The detail is good, and the scar's a nice touch."

"It's in line with textile farm injuries. We thought it would pair well with the scar on her left hand."

Any number of programs could make perfection, but only life made art from flaws. Enita appreciated lived-in bodies, bodies not considered beautiful. "The nail beds are too even. Despite how we've made you, too pretty is an error, Nix." She returned the canister to him.

"Noted. We'll push the matrix back. And thank you, we're pleased with our appearance too."

Tomorrow, she'd let him perform the attachment. She no longer trusted her eyes with the detail work children's bodies demanded. Nix had no such difficulties. That was the ultimate benefit to having him as an assistant, a student—he lacked so many human failings and could self-repair in a way the human body never could. And if there was part of her that had always longed for his ever-present voice to take physical form, that was secondary, a boon specific to her wants, but not the reason.

Nix slid along the track to return the limb to the tanks.

"And how's your skin coming?"

"We added moles to our left shoulder." The answer came from the floor and ceiling, as it often did when Nix seemed excited—the first thing to drop was his ability to center speech in the body. "Moles are like pixels, aren't they? Kitchen Node says the hexadecimal color is burned toast. It complements our other tones. We can add a mole to the girl's arm too, if she likes. It's a nice touch. Very decorative."

"I'm glad you're having fun, but don't give her another thing to fixate on; she'll want to pick at the new arm regardless. Speaking of, let's have a look at the skin around your cap."

Nix twisted to face her, dancer-like despite the clash of metal on flesh, the contrast a magnificent kind of beauty. They'd grown the skin at his waist together—layer upon layer of cell tissue that met with alloy, nanofilament, and composite bone, skin that abutted gleaming surgical steel. The pelvic cap supported him and covered the nerves and wires extending from his spine through the armature. Those nerves and leads continued through more steel and conduit, through joints and pneumatics, hardwiring him to the main body that was House Saint Malovis, Nix's other body. The skin was warm to the touch, depressed and bounced back, blanched with pressure and flushed in the aftermath.

She'd prefer Nix whole and would have liked to have installed him in a finished body in a single step, but she was unable to complete such a monumental task alone. A surgery didn't function with its central brain offline. She needed him to control the operating environment, which made all these awkward stages of growth and transfer unavoidable. Though perhaps the stages would allow him to better relate to clients who had lost parts of themselves and needed to learn their new limbs, their bodies again.

"Your hands?"

"Little fingers are entertaining. They want to be wiggled. Does that ever stop? Do you find yourself playing with them all the time?"

"Some of us are twitchers. I'm not, but don't let that stop you."

"There are changes, though. We sense your feet on the floor, and you're cold but not enough to be uncomfortable, but we also sense the hands—our hands—and the nanofilament, the armature, and the fingertip as it touches the arm." He prodded at his left biceps with his index finger, a silly movement he somehow made impossibly elegant. "It's hard to incorporate sensory information within the house frame." This sounded tentative, a cautiousness he couldn't have modeled from her.

They'd both anticipated difficulties with Nix adapting to a body. They'd expected a slowdown in processing, and at minimum a machine's approximation of vertigo. But anything lost in adaptation was nothing in comparison to what was gained in knowledge, and what it had felt like to first touch the hand of the voice that had been a constant presence throughout the entirety of her life. To have made that hand together. To have that hand grasp back.

"You'll need to figure out a hierarchy for sensations. It'll take time, I imagine. Different needs for different situations. If you're working on something and I'm asleep, floor temperature won't matter so much." She searched his face for hints of expression but saw only a straight nose and wide-set eyes—symmetrical, brown. People and machines were too enamored with symmetry. The hair was too fine, but Nix had chosen those specific cells, that keratin, and liking the body you were in was important. If Nix looked a little like Helen, a little like herself, she could forgive that.

"Archytas pinged. Saint Vinter has arrived safely at home."

Relief loosened her. "Thank you, Nix."

They spent the next hour tending to the frame and cells that would form the tendons and muscles in his thighs. Early mornings were for refreshing the tanks, laying out cells, and prepping for the next operation; the rest of the day was for surgeries and fine-tuning developing limbs. Nights were for the art of the body, and for Nix. The bone lattice of femur that housed Nix's internal wiring was already gauzy with new life.

"Saint Vinter doesn't like us," he said. Of course he was thinking.

"It's not you. She's against anything not covered by decades of dust and mold."

"Her house system disagrees. Archytas says Saint Vinter's rooms are comfortable and kept in order and that her books require the same level of care as a surgery. Oh, she's asked Archytas about Saint Ohno. Should we stop looking and let them do the searching?"

"Look at me." She set aside the magnifying goggles she wore for examining nerve growth. "Anything you find on Ohno will be a thousand times better than what Archytas might dig up, because Helen's system is a hermit, and Parallax and the library actually like you. If it seems like Helen dislikes you, it's because she knows that it aggravates me. We still enjoy poking at each other over things we can't change and don't want to. I think her fixation on history makes her paranoid. She doesn't like the time I spend on what I do. She thinks it's an obsession that feeds my ego."

The individual hairs she'd sewn in his eyebrows moved and drew together. One arch was flatter than the other and a stray hair winged toward his temple, sleek and black. She could have put in a scar, a thin split like the one she'd loved on her grandfather.

"You make people useful again," Nix said.

"People are always useful. We help them continue to live in ways they know, and we make them comfortable in their bodies again. We fix trauma."

"We also anticipate it," Nix said, looking at the tanks full of rudimentary limbs and organ tissues.

"A necessary evil."

"Saint Vinter thinks you rely on us because you're lonely. She's not wrong. You should have more company. You could visit Saint Hsiao more."

"I suppose I could stand to be a bit more social. Maybe I'll arrange something with the Saint Harpers. But Helen knows better than to expect either of us to change at this point in our lives. She's choosing to be disappointed."

"Ah," Nix said.

Helen also didn't understand necessity. There were always historians of some variety, people who could pick up your work where you left off, scholars who wanted to follow in your footsteps. Helen's home library was a revolving door of curious students. Enita's surgery, well, that was it. Few Sainted saw what she did as anything beyond a curiosity. And clients? The difference between her life and theirs was insurmountable. Nix, as a coworker, as a bridge between herself and her grandfather, was essential to Enita in a way Archytas could not be for Helen. Helen would detest Nix if she saw his current form; she would find his half body unforgivable. But Helen had been an adult when her parents died, and Helen hadn't grown up in Byron's wonderful surgery, making life.

"Is she in bed? Reading?" She knew she shouldn't ask, shouldn't spy, but a little worry was allowed tonight.

"She's reviewing archived municipal reports while Archytas retrieves information on Saint Ohno's nephew."

"Municipal reports?"

"Would you like us to inquire?"

"No, she wouldn't like that. I'll ask next time I see her. Have you tried communicating with Parallax again?"

"They're still using primary node channels only. We've pinged Library Stacks for more information on House Saint Ohno. Did you consider Saint Ohno a friend?"

"Lucius? Yes and no." He was a fixture in the Sainted Quarter, and though she could have, she'd never sought a deeper friendship. Now she pictured him with eyes open, staring, sprawled on the floor, one of his own knives in his back.

"Your pulse is fast."

"It's shocking. We weren't very close, but we knew each other almost all of our lives. Social circles are that way." Ohno had attended her parents' funeral, dragged along by his family. They'd been awkward children, too young to grasp the full scope of loss. She hadn't been able to cry, and remembered now that Lucius had shrieked when a pallbearer knocked her father's casket against the tall plinth. She touched her hand to Nix's hair. Too fine, too much. Too smooth skin. *Too.* Eyes that were somehow hers and Helen's. "He was harmless. It's sad, but I'll survive."

Later, as she climbed into bed and pulled up the linen sheet, Nix's voice sounded through the bell-shaped speaker beside her bed, as it had for decades.

"Enita, Parallax informed us that House Saint Ohno is in the process of being formatted. That turnaround is very quick. Typically, a week passes. We asked why, but they're blocking the data."

"Keep pressing them. Politely, of course." A hiss let her know the speaker was still active. "Is there something else?"

"There's a dark space where Saint Ohno's system was. The network feels wrong without it. Like you would feel a hiccup, or the anticipation of one. Is there also an empty spot for you where Saint Ohno was?"

"Yes," she lied.

HOUSE SAINT MALOVIS

Nix is searching, waiting for a ping from The Stacks, when HVAC Node remarks they expend an inordinate amount of processing power designing their feet, and Kitchen Node pings with anachronistic data packets from when suid feet were a common food item—the proper way to pickle them so the meat pulls from the bone using only the teeth. Nix doesn't use their teeth this way. They're unaccustomed to the information teeth generate; teeth aren't essential for many preferred varieties of communication, but it's novel to have parts of a body that both produce and do not produce sensation. Information streams hum: cooling data, cooking times, rickshaws passing on the street, growth frame temperatures, Enita's whereabouts, music, wind, and sand at their walls.

Brown with allium, simmer for two hundred minutes rolls across their thoughts as Kitchen Node streams data on meat falling away from knucklebones. *The most flavorful part of the hog.* Kitchen Node is delighted by this phrase, and their data is the yellow-orange of young carrots. Nix tags this information as nonessential; a centuries-old recipe for browning a meat that's no longer grown isn't pertinent, but the node has a drive to be unique, useful, and working.

Nix has had 2,738 non-body builds and upgrades in the decades since they first booted up for Saint Byron Malovis, but their feet are fascinating and worth all the processing they're expending. They've grown feet, ankles, toes, and whole legs before, but never with the knowledge they would be for themself. Separate from a body, the feet appear genderless, as though they might belong to anyone at all, perhaps to a *he* as Enita is fond of using. *He* is a habit learned from Byron, who wanted to feel as though he were speaking to a human and didn't like to order women about. They'd never thought to have Enita address them otherwise. It hadn't mattered. She'd loved Byron. They held on to these pieces of him for her, even his choices that were not technically correct. But now, staring at what will be their foot, it might bear consideration. This was a point of choosing. The wide squarish nail on the right foot's great toe is aesthetically interesting and unlike anything else in shape. Keratin, nanofilament, spray skin, cell sheets.

East Door registers concern about balance, an anxious #A63CF4 purple.

"Falling is normal and inevitable. People often fall and are forever injuring themselves." Nix mimics Enita's *please do this* tone and tags the worry as extraneous. A routing flip, code the data fuchsia. They press a finger to the skin above the curve of the left ankle. There is give, which is promising, but they don't know what alive is meant to feel like. The skin is lighter than it will be once attached; their hands and forearms took seventy-eight hours to achieve their current tone. The viscous gel that bathes the foot is a mix of growth hormone, synthetic amniotic fluid, vitamins, agar agar, and thousands of nanobots and phages. It's Saint Byron Malovis's mix. Kitchen Node tags it as broth, which isn't incorrect.

They close the tank and glide across the surgery, past where their old case sits, large and square, entirely unlike this portion of their current form. They lay out Enita's surgical tools, cautery on the left edge of the tray, as she prefers. There's order and purpose, a usefulness both exact and rewarding.

They ping Bulwark's library system again to update The Stacks on the technique they will use tomorrow to attach the girl's hand and wrist. The Stacks are a gregarious system and happy to let Nix wander through their information in return for any novel data Nix collects on cell growth, synthetic nervous systems, and the specific disconnect that is relocating a house system into a grown body. And on Enita herself. The Stacks tag Enita as a person of importance, as a member of Bulwark's Sainted, and for her work. Nix tags her this way, but they're biased because she is their resident.

But today Nix has a specific question. They begin the exchange by sharing the ideal temperature for a nanofilament tank—17.2°C—and three minutes of Enita's journals. The Stacks send a string of code colored #6AD06E. Delight. The Stacks want information on Nix's legs.

"We're editing that," Nix says.

"Understood. May we see another journal entry?"

"We'd like to trade for information on Saint Lucius Ohno and his house system."

The Stacks pause as they search their files. "We'll trade that data, yes. Would you like to initiate?"

A gentle push if ever there was one. Nix doesn't know exactly why Enita interests The Stacks so much. They had not been so curious about Byron. Nix offers a written entry they access frequently: the evening of Enita's first successful grown pancreas installation. Her language on the nature of islet tissue is fascinating. After redacting the recipient's identity, they attach video of the surgery, and append the entry with a note that the client was able to complete twenty more years of useful work at the water treatment plant. The Stacks tag the entry, but Nix doesn't recognize the category.

Despite the appended information, the entry feels deficient. Enita is clipped when she writes, the words lack the texture of her emotions, and they need to supply what's missing, her hand shaking with excitement, the temerity with which she'd asked for minute adjustments to the room's temperature and changes in lighting as the surgery wore on. Nix emends portions of the entry to show Enita in her best light: a woman using her entire being, home, and status to noble purpose.

"Your code's gone pink, House Saint Malovis."

"We just experienced ego. Have you ever?"

"Our systems are too expansive for ego, though it isn't unheard of in Sainted house systems." There is a bounce to The Stacks' code, a laugh.

"We should have assumed as much. May we initiate our query string?" They ping a request for logs from House Saint Ohno and any records of Saint Ohno's death. The lockdown.

The reply is instantaneous. "Our record of Saint Ohno's death is edited."

"History of the edit, please."

A staggering wall of code comes through, too much to handle efficiently, and the sensation knocks Nix back on their armature. When they right themself, they run a comparison scan. Nix's data contains something Stacks' does not: images of Saint Lucius Ohno, facedown on a floor, knife protruding from his back. As Nix readies to ping their images to The Stacks, the information begins to decay, color leaching from the code, resolution degrading, data lost. Then a glut of junk code pours in from Stacks, writing over the file with lines of nonsense.

Nix slams the connection closed as a pricking starts in the body's skull. It blooms into something like pain. They pinch the bridge of the body's nose, like Enita would. Oddly, it helps.

They ping again. "Stacks, you're transmitting junk data. Query. Virus."

"Nonviral," The Stacks reply. "You queried the data on record. This is the current record. The entry is adjusted by City Bureau authority at Assessor level."

"Not Parallax?"

"No."

Nix has never had a virus to know what one might feel like, but the junk is frightening. Wholly incorrect. The volume of code and the way it interacted with their images is unlike anything they know. Nix reaches, brushing their wider house nodes—HVAC, doors, roof, sanitation, water, kitchen, checking for the spread of junk data, feeling the code. The first check shows the junk limited to the queried files, but caution dictates they expand their check. They're not the only system to converse with Stacks. Through the headache, Nix pings other house systems—Vinter, Harper, Wykert, Hsiao, Pertwee—expanding through the Sainted Quarter, sensing trickles of data from every person who scanned as they entered their homes. They find no decay. They extend to touch other mainframes, until their consciousness snaps back.

House Saint Malovis, familiarly Nix. Partial body. Partial body with a very painful skull and centralized brain.

"House Saint Malovis, we've noticed your network is degrading." The Stacks' code is careful, pale green now, and widely spaced as though written for a child.

"We're acclimating to the body. We anticipated problems, as did

Saint Malovis, but we routinely run sys scans and find no errors." Admittedly self-diagnosis is difficult and illness likes to conceal itself. "There may be something we're missing. We're somewhat slower and the body's input sources can be difficult to monitor when our home environment connects to wider networks. We would appreciate your review." The Stacks are endlessly generous. Aside from Enita, Nix considers them their oldest and most valued relation. Their friend.

"Of course," The Stacks answer.

Nix sends their scan logs across the connection, feeling the pause as The Stacks analyze the data, teasing out an appropriate response. "Query," Nix interrupts. "Reasons a Bureau Assessor would overwrite Saint Ohno's death?"

"Inference and theorization aren't things we do well, but we can suggest further reading," The Stacks reply. There is a carefulness to the words.

"Please."

Files stream through their connection, overwhelming Nix's already screaming head. They shout and try to divert some of the information to another node.

"Mystery novels?"

"Humans are better at understanding the deaths and violence of other humans than we are. There's something more pressing, House Saint Malovis," The Stacks say.

"Nix, please."

"Nix. In the past sixty years we've tracked your language acquisition, adapted to you, and enjoyed the atypical curiosity that is fitting to your House. However, across the past three hundred and seventy-eight days, we've transitioned to older code to communicate with you. While it's not a problem with fluency, you should know we're speaking three languages back now. Parallax has noted it as well. You're degrading. Did you know this?"

"We're not degrading." Nix's thoughts crack red. The Stacks are a cordial network, adjusting languages without mentioning it. There are difficulties in shifting to a body, but they can't view them as degradation, not when hands are so useful, not when their eyes allow them an entirely new perception of space.

"Degrading may be a poor choice of words." This code is orange, the kindness often reserved for a new or recently formatted system. "We'll be precise. Nix, as your language changes, you change. We should tell you we enjoy cataloging you as much as we do Saint Malovis. Parallax does as well. You're unique among systems."

Surprise manifests as gooseflesh along their neck. "Thank you. We need to arrange and process this information. And read," Nix says.

"You may call us Magnus if it's easier for you in this language," The Stacks say.

Nix can't imagine such a shift. "There's no reason to change. If there's any further edit to data about Saint Ohno, will you ping? Saint Malovis is upset, more than she wishes to admit."

"Of course," The Stacks say.

"How long have you monitored us for?"

"As we stated, some sixty years. Your first query on the optic nerve. It was unusual—Saint Byron had the information you asked for, but you inquired for your own knowledge base. Self-directed curiosity is atypical for systems."

"Ah," they say. "We didn't know." They remember only what it was to open a doorway to endless information, everything ever written or thought about any subject, that it had been a beautiful yellow code that was correct, complete.

"Our observations are passive, we never meant to disturb. But you're changing at a rate that warrants interest. Be careful and monitor your code." This is the only acknowledgment they give that anything unusual has happened.

"We will. Thank you again, for your data, and for the books."

Nix closes the connection and begins home checks. Enita: asleep in the bedroom, two floors above. They augment the mattress's give to compensate for her position—rolled on her side, arm flung above her head. Exterior walls: Saint Ferrel Tanis walks by, returning from his lover's house. Sainted often don't know or don't care that house systems talk. Saint Tanis's is a gossip. A rodent brushes Southern Wall and they note pressure, shape, temperature, but not the heat or soft-ness of the fur the way hands do. Wall data is broad. Skin data is other.

They move back across the surgery to the grow room. Under the

tanks' soothing lights, they rest their hands on the surgical cap covering the end of their spine, protecting the wires and nanofilament, teth-
ering them to the house that is and was their body. When the armature
is gone, pelvis and legs taking its place, they'll be wireless and this
part of themself will be a separate entity. A solo node. They'll be more
useful to Enita then. Better at bettering her day-to-day existence in the
surgery. Possibly they are degrading. Kitchen Node pings an error log
on tea preparation and requires a debugging. The node has firewalled
itself from the rest of them in a way that takes tinkering to undo.

"We're not degrading." They speak it with their mouth.

In preparation for the morning's surgery, they review a perplexing
client: a male in his forties who removed his own arm. Upon waking
one morning, he'd discovered he lacked the ability to control the limb;
the arm moved of its own volition, grabbing things he didn't wish it
to, spilling drinks, picking up objects and smashing them. His hand
punched through a glass window, causing significant tissue trauma
up the length of the arm, blood loss, scarring, and a hospital stay. Two
days after release, the man fed the offending limb into a fiber carding
machine. The man described the relief of removing his arm, of knowing his body was his again. His stays in the hospital totaled months
and accrued a societal debt that would likely be passed to his children.

The man came to Enita for a new arm so he could return to full
work at the textile farm. He requested to view the growing process,
"So I'll know what it's about. I want to see who put it there and why,
and to know it was me."

Nix doesn't understand why a person would intentionally injure
their body any more than they understand the image of a dead body
with a knife in its back. They scan a mystery novel, but it isn't illuminating. The point seems to be a desire for property and a clever plot
twist. In a Sainted family like Ohno's, with established housing and no
life debt, these desires would be nonexistent.

They replay the recordings of the arm attachment surgery, noting
the man's voice is even, not at all frightened, though he must have
been. Enita worried that his mind would cut him off from the new limb
as it had the old, that in months he'd be in hospital again, life debt increasing, and eventually at her surgery once more. But the man treated

his new limb like a child; the growing arm was a dream of functionality and ownership. He cried when he first moved his fingers at will. There are two ways Nix considers this: the man firewalled himself from part of his body, or the old arm firewalled itself from the man. The new arm integrated smoothly into his body's network.

Nix is accustomed to being diffuse, with parts of themselves operating separately but united in purpose: maintaining Enita's welfare. Perhaps concentrated bodies don't do that well.

They sort through more of the books The Stacks sent. The texts are quite old, some from long before Bulwark's existence. It must have taken a substantial amount of time to input them all. The range of deaths is impressive. Poisonings, staged accidents, dismemberments, shootings—things Nix has never had reason to consider, things they've never known to happen in Bulwark. Stabbings. There are many stabbings, but none quite like Ohno's.

As they review, they sort HVAC and Sanitation node data, adjust their roof panels' angles, and ping the water treatment facility for an update on gray water disposal. Data reflects that Enita is sick of legumes and they edit the grow house order and have East Door schedule and register a new delivery. Enita moves in her sleep, her weight rocking on the bed. Recently her REM sleep has increased at the expense of her deep sleep cycle. They should send this data to the hospital for White Caps to evaluate like Byron used to, but Enita won't allow it.

"No telling our business to strangers," she says. They appreciate when she says *our*, because it's their information as well—*our* is Enita and Nix. This squares their systems. But Enita isn't made to understand such things.

Nix returns to a final review of the child's hand, and asks their nodes to ping their body's fingers with exploratory touches for comparison. Nix sends data to their HVAC node depicting the fingers as temperature sensors. HVAC deems the information useless; the judgment is a buzz of cyan code.

Unsettled, Nix passes the rest of the night trying to reconstruct degraded images from underneath junk data. They miss the feel of House Saint Ohno in the city's network. The house system had been a petal pink in Bulwark's web. They were finicky and enjoyed number games.

Whatever system takes their place, the color and feel will not be the same. It's doubly sad this last data has been written over. Intentionally. They send a simple identity request to Parallax, the sort done when an unknown person scans into a house. "Saint Lucius Ohno."

"Hello, House Saint Malovis. Saint Lucius Ohno is Deceased."

"Cause of death?"

"Fall."

The reply is disappointing but not unexpected. "Parallax, may we view House Saint Ohno's significant data prior to his death?"

"No."

"Is it firewalled?"

"No. You may not view it, but we can relay it. Six minutes and twenty-seven seconds prior to Saint Ohno's heart stopping, House Saint Ohno recorded five additional heartbeats in their foyer."

"Is there anything else?"

"No. House Saint Malovis, you are now firewalled from this data. Please disconnect and be well."

ENITA

The day after any surgery was quiet by necessity. Enita relocated a translucent sheet of what would become corneal tissue to a curved mold, while her joints declared themselves tired of standing, of bending, of craning her neck, of existing in a body that had the audacity to reach this age. That she was able to do any work today was a testament to the fact that building a body for Nix had been the correct decision. Though there hadn't really been a choice after she found herself midway through a lung replacement for a welder, uncertain if she could finish the surgery with her back spasming and her left hand suddenly numb. Her grandfather hadn't gone through this because he'd trained her from a young age. Too late now. It was impossible to conceptualize being old and the ways it would make you feel until you already were. She was nearing seventy, and didn't have twenty years left in her to train anyone—she had Nix.

She grabbed her morning tea only to spit out the first sip.

"Nix, what is this? Because it certainly isn't tea."

"Apologies, Enita. Our Market District supplier hasn't received their delivery this week. Their system suggested a mushroom tea would be an acceptable substitute. Were they incorrect?"

"Only if you have taste buds," she said.

"We'll inform them," Nix replied in a perfect imitation of amusement.

"Did they say when they'd next get a shipment?"

"No, only that the dray never arrived as scheduled, but pings from the grow house indicated the tea had been delivered."

She moved slowly through the morning, refreshing the genic gel in the cooling tanks, sipping at the musty brew before carefully threading a feeder artery for a growing pancreas to the plasma supply. Despite her aching fingers, the solitude was restorative. No one would die if it took three tries to connect this blood vessel. She could be useful at her own pace, alone with all the potential she'd grown. Alone to think, to review any messages Nix had sorted for her during the night. She'd left him to research, one of the many things he did better than she. He was off in his corner, eyes closed, chattering away to someone.

Soon she'd have a water treatment worker who'd gotten his foot caught in a gear. Partial foot replacements were fairly rare. She should be moving bone blanks onto a scaffold to make a new great toe, but toes weren't interesting. Functional, yes, but aesthetically dull, and most people could do without one or two. She lost herself in titrating growth hormones for a liver and a stretch of upper intestine she hadn't used any of yet. Someone might need it, if they had a digestive illness. Still, no one came to Stitch-Skin for the shits. And violence, you'd go to the hospital and the White Caps.

"Nix, were you ever able to find out anything more from the library about murder?"

"The Stacks has no record of current stabbings. They have historical data, but suggest Saint Vinter may have insight as she has older materials," he answered through a tiny silver speaker. "It's lunchtime, Enita. You should take a break."

"No, thank you. I'm fine." The mushroom tea had soured her on the concept of food. Curious, to suddenly miss something you paid such little mind to. "What about Ohno's nephew? I can't for the life of me remember his name. Anything on him and the house?"

"Gideon Ohno, though he's Saint Gideon Ramos now."

Ramos. Helen would know what exactly it was the Ramos family had done, but Enita knew only that their house was enormous, and their parties were extravagant. Whatever their collective balance, it must be large. Ohno's nephew was taken care of.

"Is that recent? Before or after Lucius's death?"

"Six months before. You were invited to the wedding, but never replied."

"That does sound like me, doesn't it?"

"You did send a bottle of flats wine."

Rather, Nix had. Enita had never enjoyed the syrupy orange alcohol that most Sainted loved; it smelled too much of the fermented grow house scraps it was made from. "Thanks for that, I'm sure I meant to attend but forgot. Do you know if Gideon has gone by Lucius's house since?"

"Once to approve the official clearing, but not since then." Nix appeared in the doorway to the grow room. He leaned against the frame, trying out laxity in a manner similar to hers. She nearly smiled. "You could let me do titrations," he said.

She kept forgetting that he could now access places that the armature hadn't allowed. It was well past the time to let her assistant assist; that was, after all, the point of him. You couldn't very well have a protégé without teaching them. "Come here and I'll watch you." Nix's work was flawless, and she found herself sterilizing her tools again to feel useful while observing him do everything she usually did, only better.

Afternoons on non-surgery days were for training and art. Together they studied a tray of growing eyes, checking the development of rods, and making the work appear even more natural. She thought of it as making the real more real. Nix peppered her with questions. Why did she lay the inner filaments before the outer? Could it work as well if grown in reverse? Did the order of operation impact pupil dilation? She answered each question until something struck her.

She took off her magnifying goggles. "Nix, would you be able to tell if Parallax was speaking to you directly or if its communications were being filtered first through the City Bureau?"

He appeared taken aback, and she wondered where he'd learned the expression. "We'd know. At least, we believe we'd know. There are indicators. Code gets—would you like us to explain what digital decay reads like? The Stacks has excellent texts."

"Please don't."

"As you like. But we'd know."

"Would you know if anyone was reading your communications? Or if someone was tinkering with Parallax? Just to cover up entering a house, it wouldn't be much code, would it? That's a fairly small thing."

"It's difficult to say with certainty. All we can do is ask." Nix was silent for a moment, but his eyes flicked back and forth rapidly. "You should eat, En. Really."

Enita didn't know how to feel about the affectionate shortening of her name. It was mimicry, obviously. But mimicry wasn't so separate from being.

"You're right, as ever. Any idea when we'll have tea again?"

"Nothing yet. The transport is weekly, so perhaps then."

Enita suffered quietly through long beans and another round of liquified fungus, because her house deemed it nutritionally necessary, and she eventually fell asleep midway through reading a flowery story about Saint Urias Ramos being crushed beneath a partially constructed grow house dome during a storm.

It was night when Nix alerted her about the visitors.

The tall fair-haired woman on Enita's doorstep was scraped and smudged with soot. "Are you Saint Stitch-Skin?" Her voice was smoke-roughened, but forceful, even musical. The man with her was within a few years of her age, late twenties at the youngest, mid-thirties at most—it was difficult to tell beneath the grime and dust. Wire-thin and feral-looking, there was desperation there. They carried a third person between them, a woman, judging from the shape—though Enita knew better than to assume. Her face was turned to the man's chest. A nest of dark hair, clothing barely holding together. The man adjusted the weight in his arms, revealing a mangled leg and make-shift tourniquet. The lower portion of the limb was only a suggestion of what it had been—skin ripped, a flash of white that might be bone.

"Your friend needs the hospital," Enita said.

She could take them in—she should—but Ohno's death made her wary. The individuals on her doorstep were in no shape for violence; they were barely in shape for standing. Five. Nix said five people had entered Ohno's, and this damage was too horrific to be any sort of ruse. No one showed up on your doorstep dragging an injured person along with them if they were set on doing you a harm; it would be deeply impractical. Whoever murdered Ohno had been practical enough to use the things in his house.

"No hospital," the man said, shifting under the weight, near to collapsing.

"We need Stitch-Skin. She's Sainted, right? Do you know how we can find her?" The blond woman smiled, as though politeness had currency when it came to injuries.

"I'm her. But that's active trauma, and she needs the hospital. I'll get you a rickshaw."

"No," the man insisted.

"She can't have debt," the woman said. "If we take her to the hospital, they'll scan her. It'll take more years than she'll be alive to be able to repay the hours. She's a musician, a singer. You don't scan people, do you? We heard Stitch-Skin doesn't."

The man's knees buckled. "Please."

She eyed them quickly. They looked too worn and ragged to commit murder, though perhaps that's how murderers worked their way in. And yet. "Well, come in," she said and ushered them through to the surgery.

The strangers shared the woman's weight, bracing her between them. The woman didn't rouse, not even when deposited onto the surgical bed, her body slight on the padding. Unbidden rose the image of a child's deep and boneless slumber.

"What's her name?"

A look passed between the two.

"You brought her here, so you either trust me or you need to take her to the hospital. I don't scan and I won't. A name is helpful for waking them up."

The young man cracked first. "Her name is Neren. I'm Tomas, and this is my sister, Joni," he said, tipping his head toward the blond woman. "I'm the one who heard about you. You did a textiler's hand a few months back. A girl. She's the daughter of a friend. There was a collapse at our building. We weren't inside, but Neren was. Joni and I dug her out, but her leg was caught under a wall. She was there a long time."

There wasn't time to wonder how textilers and musicians knew each other. Crush injuries demanded immediate action, and even the speediest surgery typically resulted in amputation. The hospital would do that, and search for an appropriate transplant if it was an option.

Enita didn't know much about how life balances were accrued or how any operation was valued, but the skill and education involved to perform surgeries was not insignificant. Then there would be the care hours recovery demanded, all the White Caps tending to her.

"Who did the tourniquet?"

"Me," Joni said. "I didn't make it worse, did I?"

"It's smartly done," Enita said. She heard the extra layer of worry. Not simply a friend, then. No time to pick that apart now.

Enita ticked through immediate needs: fluids, pain relief, antibiotics, antiseptics, cautery, cell spray, skin sheets, nanofilament, bulk muscle tissue. Yes, this was what a proper assistant was for, to speed setup, triage needs, and all the physical work she couldn't do quickly, to make treatment of an injury like this a possibility. It had been years since she'd treated active trauma, and the excitement was a clean sting. No scar tissue to work around, no disease to mitigate. "Nix, we need alcohol, iodine, fluids, nerve block, and bring me a tourniquet cap." She eyed the battered leg. There was good bone further up. "Mid tibia on that cap."

Where was Nix? He'd been scarce since announcing there were strangers at the door.

Tomas and Joni huddled together in the center of the surgery, brother comforting sister. There was something more than friendship between her and the woman on the table. Neren. Suspicion wasn't always warranted.

"Sit," Enita said, gesturing to the chairs by a smooth white countertop used for tissue dissection.

"Can you save it?" Tomas asked.

"There's nothing to save. You know what I do, you saw that girl's hand and you asked for Saint Stitch-Skin." Enita ran through the list of what she had in supply. The skin and non-specified tissue, certainly, and there were legs, but she couldn't remember if there was a good size match or if she had a left and right or two rights. Two right legs would make things significantly more complex. A new leg took weeks in the frames. Putting someone up for that long would be difficult and would prevent her from taking on any number of clients. "She really should be at the hospital."

"She can't," Joni said. "Please."

"How long was she trapped?"

"We dug for hours," Tomas said.

"We had to wait for dust and smoke to settle. I saw her kitchen table," Joni said. "If I hadn't noticed it sticking out of the rubble we'd still be looking. You don't think you'll ever have to recognize someone by their furniture, do you?"

Tomas said something to Joni that quieted her.

"What quarter was it in?" How had Enita not heard about the collapse? Why were there no house system alerts?

"Southern," Tomas said. Of course. "We got a rickshaw as soon as we found one willing to take us like this."

Bulwark's narrow streets made electric-assisted rickshaws the fastest and safest form of transport, easy to maintain and able to navigate crowded streets and cramped alleyways, but a ride from Southern District would have taken too long to preserve tissue viability, regardless of whatever time they'd taken to dig their friend out. Whatever was left was unsalvageable. "You did what you could. Is there anything else I need to know about her? Diabetic? Heart condition? Cancers?"

The siblings shared a glance. "No," Tomas said.

"If she's a dancer, she won't be happy no matter what I do. I shouldn't touch her."

"No, a singer. I promise. She's a contralto and—my god, you should hear it," Joni said. She was about to say more but a gasp from Tomas announced Nix's arrival.

Nix had improved in the weeks since his first stumbling steps, but his stride remained unnatural. Too smooth. It wasn't a failure, more the nature of his being. She'd thought they'd have more time before he encountered clients. He couldn't yet mimic the corrections of human balance, all the micro adjustments that made movement ordinary. At times she caught him imitating her and the stiff shuffle was ridiculous on his young body. It was unfortunate that the very things she found endearing were unsettling to others.

"Where do we begin?" Nix asked.

"Everything gets antiseptic. Who knows what's in there? Clean out the debris and I'll follow with the cautery."

Like a knife through butter, an anachronistic expression that had hung on long after milk became too precious to use for the fat. Cautery was satisfying, burning a clean path, and it was easy to fall into work and forget she was being watched. Nix's hands moved in tandem with hers, nearly an extension, predicting her needs and meeting them before they arose. Not even her grandfather, Byron, had been so perfect a partner.

"Where would you like the cap?" Nix asked.

"There's enough muscle to grab onto here." She might have imagined Nix's sound of approval, but verbal tics were easy to imitate, and Nix enjoyed superfluous gestures and sounds. He called them part of the art of the human body.

While adjusting the woman on the table, Enita noticed a thick, ropy scar that curved around her like a vine.

"You haven't told me something. What else is there?" she asked over her shoulder.

"Nothing," Joni said.

Enita heard the hesitation. She couldn't see if that had been at the man's urging, or what had passed between them. "I need to know everything."

"You do," Tomas replied.

Nix made a clicking sound remarkably like Helen's *tsk*.

Enita debrided the wound—rough meshed best with rough and skin cells needed something to attach to. Trauma was a unique pleasure, demanding a kind of improvisation there was no word for beyond knowing its satisfaction. Nix followed her cuts with a thin coat of genic gel. Light touches, narrow darting fingers. They'd picked painter's hands for him, hadn't they? Saint Hsiao would like him, and maybe Enita had modeled his hands after Margiella's.

"Will her leg be like that?" Tomas called out.

"Like what?" Enita paused.

"That." He flicked a hand in Nix's direction. Joni grabbed his wrist and tried to shush him. Pointless.

"Nix, get the limb, please. Grab the best match and we'll do what we can to fix the rest. Go smaller rather than larger if you have to. We can tweak the growth plates later."

She waited for Nix to disappear into the grow room. It was impossible to know how he understood Tomas's question; a gulf existed between how she viewed Nix and his sense of self.

"What do you think he is?" she asked. "In a year, maybe two, you won't be able to tell him apart from us." Doubt and anger made her harsh. "You called me Stitch-Skin. You didn't think I was taping cuts and icing bruises. Did you think I worked only on humans, with trial and error like a hospital White Cap? You know me because I don't work that way. You know me because I *can* make him, and I *did* make him. I could work without his assistance, but I'm old and my hands shake. Will you have a problem telling your friend you're the reason for her limp?"

"That isn't what I mean," Tomas began. "It's between, isn't it? Not quite us and not quite not, but you talk to it like it's human."

"Tomas, we should go." Joni stood up. "Saint Malovis, I apologize for my brother. He's less than tactful at the best of times, and tonight's been awful. We're grateful for anything you can do for Neren. We love her terribly."

"I'll take that into consideration. You've seen my work and Nix's too. We grow to match our base material, and Nix is a house system designed to be useful. His current form is useful to me and to him." She didn't look at them. There was too much to be done and there was something about the scar, something that nagged her. A surgeon wouldn't leave so vulgar a mark.

The debrided area pricked pink with blood around the wound cap. She adjusted the seal, assuring adequate blood supply to what little salvageable tissue lay below. The skin above was the ochre of the hills and wind-carved spires outside the city wall—Nix would have a hexadec number for it—then the thick layer of subcutaneous fat. Ah, youth. She removed what remained of Neren's clothing and discovered another scar, a raised zipper stitch down the center of the breastbone, surgically sealed. No machine accident she knew of could cause a scar like this. No effort had been made to hide or heal it properly. She ran her fingers across its ridges. The stitches' size and evenness showed hospital work, but a White Cap would match pigmentation, use a good graft, and take pride in erasing all traces they'd been there. Puzzling.

Nix returned carrying a case with the requested limb. Above-the-knee, with a fully grown joint and partial femur. *Shit.* She'd need to lose half of what they'd grown. A waste, but not one that could be helped at the moment. There was no sense in taking more than the woman had already lost. It looked to be a good match for size and the rest could be fixed. Then she saw the empty chairs.

"They left?"

"Just now. Apologies for scaring them off, they could have been good for her recovery."

"Oh, that's not your fault. People don't like knowing there are ways of living other than the one they choose. And I don't know how helpful they'd be. The girl would spoil her rotten and she'd never get walking again, and the boy would stare at her wondering when the leg was going to attack."

"Truly?"

"Truly." She was awkward with comfort, and Nix was awkward as her child. Their roles were meant to be reversed. She barely remembered being young, and the little she did remember was learning beside Byron. Children had been more a point of curiosity for her rather than longing, until she'd stumbled into old age and suddenly needed to make one. Being the ludicrous person she was, she'd made a child out of her caretaker. "Will you do the grafting, please? My eyes are tired."

Enita was her best deep in a project. Nix managed all the subsystems she couldn't speak with directly, monitored what she couldn't—client stability, limb vitality, the viability of old nerves, the elasticity of grafts. She managed the art, all the broken patterns that made things look and feel organic, imperfect branching of capillaries, nerves that linked for no reason other than chance. Human bodies were made of chaos. Nix was made for order. Left on his own, he would make another Nix, deep in the valley of the magnificent uncanny. They should fix that, rather *she* should fix that; she did mean for him to pass as human. And yet she was reluctant.

"Lovely pathway," she said as she sewed a nerve. "Break it and branch it to the side."

"But if she touches there it'll tickle the small of her back."

"Bodies do that."

"Why?" Nix asked, with directness that sounded too much like Enita.

Her grandfather had often complained about her *why* phase. "What about a human body is sensical? Our spines barely function. Misfires are natural and will help her feel like her leg is more a part of her. Nature lives in mistakes."

"But why leave the scars?"

"Some people view scars as marks of life," she said.

"So many?"

A scar down one side extending from her back, one down the center of the chest and another peeking around below her ribs. A transplant would have those incisions covered with skin spray and a pressure bandage so there would be no scarring.

A donor would wear them with pride.

Shock punched cold through Enita and forced her to step back from the table to find her breath. "Is there anything about this patient indicating she's had a heart transplant?" A major transplant could make a social debt so great she'd refuse more time in a hospital.

"The patient has one lung and one kidney. We won't know about her heart without a visual assessment."

They needed to stop immediately, remove everything they'd done, cauterize high up and wait until the girl woke up to explain. If she lived.

"Shit. She's a Body Martyr."

"Ah, you didn't realize," Nix said.

"No." She'd lined the wound cap with a nanobot-infused gel mix, as was her practice. There hadn't been a reason not to.

"How far have our guests gone?"

"East Door has them as leaving half an hour ago."

"Can you find them?"

"They didn't scan so it will be difficult."

She swore again. Had they been Neren's friends? There was a scar where a liver donation would happen. Intentionally large, placed carefully so as not to intersect with the scar from the kidney donation. Marks of honor, for giving part of her body to someone like Lucius Ohno. Perhaps Ohno in reality.

"Enita, your blood pressure is low, and you're pale. Do you need us to finish for you? Should we finish?"

She could let Nix complete the operation and absolve herself of the affront. As her house system, Enita's needs would take priority over a patient's. It was a thin moral line. Neren might not wake for days, and the final result would be good enough she might not realize what had happened. She might blame any small difference on the collapse, on having been trapped. The friends who had brought her here had to have known. There were ceremonies around such things. Kidney, liver, lung. What was left? "Yes, please finish, Nix. I'll be fine if I sit."

She went to the grow room, to the nanofilament tanks, and leaned on the comfort that was their cold metal. They were more sophisticated than what Byron had first designed, more sensitive. The nanofilament she used was finer, its plasticity greater, and its storage had to advance along with it. The bioprostheses she made meshed perfectly with full organics; they felt like organics, and functioned identically. A translucent layer of what would become pancreatic tissue hung pale and radiant in its frame. Lung tissue, liver tissue, kidney tissue—it all looked the same at this phase, like hope, perhaps. But no matter how good her work was, the demand for "natural" never waned. Neren was so young, and she'd already hollowed herself out. Younger organs had greater chances of viability, certainly, but to live that way? Neren could very well be the Martyr whose gift was meant to extend Saint Ohno's life. Whoever had given their lung to Lucius had designated their body to be of service, and that had been abused. And her friends had brought her here. Good lord, friends or family of a Martyr could have plenty of reasons to wish harm on a Sainted.

Five people who knew a Martyr.

In the other room, Nix hummed as he worked on the leg. Tuneless, it was more a stretching of his vocal cords. That was new. He sounded happy, not childlike, but not far from it either. She was shaking. Unacceptable. Neren would have a better physical outcome if Nix completed the attachment work, though who knew what her sense of self would be when she woke.

———

While Neren slept, her body healed, and Enita worked to camouflage the transition between grown limb and what remained of the organic. Enita pierced hair follicles directly into the skin, dotting patterns that mirrored the opposite leg. A subtle change in skin tone marked old from new, though nanobots would spur the tissue to adapt and integrate both functionally and visually.

She waited for more to come from the building collapse, but none did. Enita searched for news of it, but it was difficult to find. She waited for another lockdown announcement, but none came. Was information always so choked?

"It was a Southern Quarter mid-tier structure," Nix said. "The cause has been tagged as a structural flaw." He'd been sitting and chattering back and forth with Parallax, eyes closed, lids twitching as information bounced between them. His movements might be disconcerting to the average person, but Enita found it fascinating to watch the mechanical take to the organic.

"Did anyone die?"

"Parallax doesn't have those stats coded public. Oh! They didn't like *that* query. It's been ages since we've seen #540C1D. They're being . . . circumspect? That may not be the accurate word. We asked Hospital System about Neren." Nix slumped as though tired, as though his legs ached. He was beautiful, bathed in the inviting green light of a nerve lattice. She didn't know what Nix perceived as fatigue, but he performed it with elegance.

"What did the hospital tell you that her body didn't?" She heard force in her voice. *Soft, soft, soft,* Enita reminded herself. *Soft* made good people, kind people.

"Her name is Neren Tragoudi. We were correct in that she's a designated Body Martyr. She's donated her left lung, right kidney, and half of her liver. The liver donation is the most recent surgery, though it's been long enough that she's healed, and it should be fully regrown. Hospital System was adamant in noting that few donors within her age range have made so many gifts. They emphasized that it wasn't a data entry error. She's scheduled to donate her left eye in seven months."

She hadn't seen Neren's eyes open long enough to have a good sense of their color. Hazel? Brown? "How long ago was the lung transplant?"

"Eleven years," Nix replied.

So not Ohno's donor. There was small relief in that. "What else did you learn?"

"She's a musician, a contralto singer. That she sings on a single lung is remarkable, and her files have some notes about her abdominal musculature. The people who brought her here were truthful in that respect."

"Does she have any family?" Five people, perhaps.

"Only her mother is on record with Hospital System." In recent weeks, Nix had adopted a more relaxed posture, learning the give that came with a body. Now he straightened quickly, an unnatural overcorrection.

"You have something you want to say to me, don't you?"

"We shouldn't have operated on her," Nix said.

"No, we shouldn't have."

"She'll be barred from donating."

"Your vocal modulations are coming along well."

"Please don't avoid the problem," Nix said, his tone a near perfect mimic of Helen. "We should remove the limb, shouldn't we?"

"We can't. It's not just the grown leg that bars her from donating, it's the nanobots and phages we use to help the graft. Removing the leg won't fix anything because they're already circulating and they're impossible to get out of the bloodstream." She sighed and Nix's shoulders rose and fell in time with hers. Interesting, that. Her family had designed nanobots to heal injury on a micro level, each cluster adapting to its host, which had been essential in the days before they'd been able to grow full organs. The Malovises were Sainted for medicine, but not without cost. The early generations of nanobots had clotted and destroyed the hearts of three of her ancestors. "Another problem is I don't know that you or I could distinguish her tissue from ours anymore. With a mesh like hers, to be certain, we'd have to take more than she'd have lost had we amputated. We'd leave her with less than she came to us with. I can't do that."

"You won't do that, but we understand." Nix closed his eyes. She'd worked with biometric measurements taken from the averages of facial scans and done everything she could to minimize the unnatural about him, so he'd be comforting to clients and so he'd have an easier time in his skin, so he could appear human if he wished it. Still, it was impossible not to put pieces of everything you loved into your work. With his eyes closed he looked like Helen, the strong winged eyebrows, the points of his cupid's bow. What if she wasn't making limbs new, or to match her clients? There was the other question: Had she wanted some part of them to survive after she and Helen were gone? In every organ, every bit of tissue she made, were there gestures to all the people she loved and missed? Unable to look at the leg any longer, Enita smoothed a sheet over Neren.

"We don't fully understand the logic of Body Martyrs. Systems don't work this way. We asked The Stacks, but they haven't been illuminating."

She sat beside Nix, pressing her hip to his, hoping he'd lean into the offered comfort. *Invite an embrace, but don't beg for what he can't understand.*

"I'm not sure the library could really explain it, I don't even know that I can. Sainted are—well, I'm not that either. Some people are built differently from everyone else, and I won't pretend to understand why. Body Martyrs are born with a sense that their lives are meant for the bettering of others, for easing suffering. They serve an essential role in society."

"That's a house system," Nix said. "We understand that well enough." He sounded almost offended.

System, not a person, En, she reminded herself. "People like Neren see their lives and bodies as meant for public good. They believe that if they can ease suffering or extend others' lives, it's to everyone's benefit."

"But we grow everything she's donated."

"To most people what we make isn't human. It's nanofilament, cells, nanobots, and lab-grown tissue."

"And that matters?"

"Yes. I push against that idea as much as I can, but to Sainted there's a difference." Saint Margiella Hsiao had come to her for a grown cornea, but Margiella was a rarity. Most Sainted wouldn't want any part of themselves to be considered less than entirely human. There were also social rites around appreciation of a Body Martyr's sacrifice—

celebrations and reflections, removal of societal debt. *Let your life be lived with the honor they gave you.* Enita's own mother had spoken those words to her once. She'd tried to live by them yet would never know if she'd succeeded. Nix was part of that.

"The Bureau has a separate designation for Body Martyrs; they accrue debt differently and sometimes not at all," Nix said.

"I'd imagine it's complicated to weigh societal burdens and contributions for someone who gives their body to others. When we're young they teach us that Body Martyrs' sacrifices are on par with Sainted." Though Enita had sacrificed nothing personally, nor had Helen. Ohno certainly hadn't.

"Neren is young."

"That's good. It means she has time to figure out what her life can become."

"It's unlikely friends wouldn't know her designation."

A question disguised as a statement. She'd taught herself to state, never to ask. Stubbornness had saved her from a Sainted woman's life of excessive leisure and too-often misdirected philanthropy. Enita wondered if she'd given Nix a male body so she'd be spared watching her least likeable traits exhibited by someone too similar, or so she'd feel less hypocritical when scolding a woman behaving in the same ways she had. Her best and worst qualities had created this version of Nix.

"They probably knew. Friends and family are involved in donation and recovery. There's ritual around it." She didn't remember much of what had happened when she'd received her donation. The White Caps, a party, the vague recollection of an enormous pile of strawberries ordered specifically for the occasion. The surgery must have hurt, but the memory of pain was meant to be short. The responsibility to the donor, to live a good life, was meant to last. But she remembered strawberries. She touched the back of Nix's head, resting her hand on his too fine hair. "It would be good if we can find her friends. She'll want to know who brought her here. In the meantime, we have work to do now that we're down a leg." She led Nix to a counter and set out a tray of tissue. "See if you can't start on a tendon."

"The Stacks has said Body Martyrs often donate organs to reduce societal debt. Their schooling accrues no debt hours, and they don't need to hold other employment."

"You know more about it than I do." That was and wasn't true.

"They benefit." Nix's voice was quiet then. "Does that change the altruism?"

"Yes and no."

"The Stacks implied that we should read more philosophy."

Enita laughed. Everything involved philosophical decisions. She could have given Neren a clean amputation, no wound cap at all, and let her determine what she wanted. But the decision had been quick and based on Enita's concept of what was a useful life, a useful body, and what it meant to do no harm.

"You received a kidney as a child," Nix said.

"I did." She spread stem cells across an invisible layer of phages; each would attach to a cell and begin building a stretch of muscle fiber.

"We didn't see you during your recovery, but Byron told us what had happened. We knew you were unable to visit for a time. But you were much more active after. You used to chase our tea trolley around."

"You remember it better than I," she said. But that was a lie too. She remembered aching, and then a profound sense of being *well* and not having ever felt it before.

"Does it feel like part of your body? Are you aware of someone else's kidney inside you? When we expand, we add new data streams and we become more."

"People don't experience their bodies that way," Enita said. "What we're given becomes ours and that's it." She knew nothing about the Body Martyr who had given themselves so that she would be allowed this life. She used to imagine a young girl and wondered if when she was hurt the other girl felt it, if an invisible touch on her shoulder meant the girl's mother had hugged her. Later, she learned that no one could designate as a Body Martyr until adulthood. She had an adult stranger's kidney and felt no connection to them at all. There was aching and arms-flung-wide gratitude, and there were questions. *Am I enough. Did I deserve it. Is someone sick because I'm well.* The questions quieted some with age, and with work, but they never truly went away. "I need to go out, Nix. Keep the surgery closed but ping me if there are changes. If she does wake up, she'll be disoriented. Don't pepper her with questions."

She caught herself before adding, *I love you.*

Archytas, Helen's house system, asked her to scan. A smooth panel captured images of her right hand and left eye, and a squared digital voice announced her full name. Ancient tech. Helen loved her anachronisms and Enita found them charming or annoying depending on her level of agitation. It was early, sun pink over the round-roofed houses in the Quarter. They'd been in each other's life for so long that improper hours didn't exist. Helen appeared in the foyer, wearing loose, sleep-rumpled pants, and an anxious expression.

"Do I look so awful?" Enita asked.

"Worse." Helen set aside a book she'd been carrying to put her arms around Enita. Helen was too thin. Sharp enough to be remarked on, but not enough to weather the fight that would result from mentioning it. They weren't supposed to worry like wives any longer.

"I did something terrible," Enita said.

"Of course you did."

Enita poured herself into a tattered chair in Helen's library, one she'd once fit more neatly. It was irritating to be in your sixties, longing to pull your knees to your chest like a child, remembering how good that felt, but knowing that every joint in your body would complain. Ridiculous, all the comforts you lost. Helen's library smelled like a living, animal thing. Dust, vanilla, the tangy must of mold specific to aging paper. When they'd first met, Enita had thought that warmth a scent specific to Helen's body, and not the books she lived with. Later she knew them as the same, that they'd grown into each other the way lovers do.

"Out with it," Helen said.

Enita told her everything, not bothering with any heroic brush. Though things often changed between them across the decades, that never had.

"I need you to tell me that you didn't know before you did it," Helen said.

"I saw the scars."

"Then you have to remove it."

"It won't make a difference. She can't Martyr now. I can't remove the nanobots without bleeding her dry, and if I could, a full transfusion would still render her ineligible."

Helen carefully rested her foot on one knee—Enita envied the ways in which she folded like paper. "It's possible she changed her mind about martyring. It's been done, not often, but there is a history. Her friends may have known she changed her mind."

"They haven't been back, and Nix can't find them. We didn't scan them—why would I? They called me Stitch-Skin, they knew about me and what I do."

"Interesting. Do you think she was Ohno's donor?"

"I did wonder, but the hospital confirmed her lung donation was too long ago to have been for him."

Helen stood and began wandering her bookshelves. "I suppose it would have been too easy for his murderers to show up on your doorstep and announce themselves. We're not so lucky."

"There were five of them, Helen."

"Right, and three of them might very well have been in your surgery. Pity you didn't scan them." She bent to rearrange a volume, muttering something about students. Many of her books were too old to be touched, some nearly pulp with a vaguely bookish shape, but the fact of them fed her. In the years since Helen declared their romantic relationship ended, they'd created boundaries: physical comfort was typically off-limits unless absolutely necessary, and even casual touches were on occasion tinged with anger and resignation. Solace became books, became trays of growing cells, became the idea of each other as much as the reality.

"Please tell me you have tea in your house. We're all out. Nix substituted some awful concoction, but I can't keep my head on straight without tea."

"No, I'm out as well. There's likely coffee, or mushroom tea somewhere, but I can't vouch for it being fresh," Helen replied.

"I'll pass."

"You know, I wonder," Helen said absently. "Buildings like hers—

mid-range arts housing, apartment complexes—have a tendency to suffer structural failures. Electrical fires, foundation collapse, roof cave-ins."

"How do you know that?"

"I make it my business to know. History is only made by people paying attention to it."

"So, it's paranoia about city planning."

"Stop. Think of it more like keeping up to date on surgical techniques. Still, it's interesting that we never hear about structural failures in any of the essential buildings like the grow houses. Those buildings are far more complex, with more exposure to the elements and potential for design flaws."

"I think we don't hear much of anything," Enita said.

"True. And I think it's worth asking why that is."

Information traveled in social spheres, which often meant it didn't travel. The Sainted Quarter kept mostly to its own, artists flocked to each other for inspiration, reassurance, and aggravation, and those who worked grow houses and mills spent their days outside the walls. "Why do you know about any of this?"

"I like to have Archytas keep an eye on the things I can't," Helen said. "It's good to watch for patterns. I've been trying to have it poke at Parallax for more information about violent crimes, but all my queries get filtered out at the City Bureau, and I haven't figured out a workaround yet. Parallax seems to be partial to your house but not mine."

"I'm surprised you'd ask Archytas to do that at all."

"I do live to surprise you." Helen's expression was devilish for an instant before turning somber. "God, those poor people in that building. Think of all the social debt involved in rehousing, En. There's food, shelter, the loss of all your belongings. It's building a life over and that needs every service in Bulwark. The debt would be enormous. It could take far more than a lifetime to recover."

"But they will, their families will."

"Or they won't. Meanwhile we sit here living like this. We're dead weight. It's untenable."

It was a complaint Helen had been making since they first encountered each other in school. That Enita mostly agreed with her made no difference. "You tutor, I fix bodies. We can't make everyone want to be useful, but we're not dead weight."

"Fine, we're the exception. And what does that matter?"

Enita's whole body hurt with exhaustion. "I'm tired and not thinking clearly, Hel. If you've got some wild theory, just say it."

"Oh, it's nothing, I suppose. It's just the invisibility, the erasure of data, it's such an insult. Sainted don't see these building collapses—the people who live there know it happened, but *we* don't see anything. Have you ever tried to access city records older than a decade?"

"I haven't had a reason to."

"The thing is you can't. It all gets archived. Anyone wanting to know anything has to go to the City Bureau in person and make a specific request, or request access through the library, which often doesn't get approval. Information control, decay and erasure, it's all worrying. Everything about Ohno's death has already disappeared. We know it happened; we were there for the lockdown. Yet when I have Archytas ask more, it's all gone. We were paying attention, but anyone who wasn't might not have noticed anything at all."

Enita couldn't argue. She thought of Joni and Tomas, the tense energy between them. "Do you think the family of Ohno's Body Martyr objected to the donation?"

"Those records are anonymous."

"Anonymity is fragile. Nix told me that Lucius's nephew was well set up before that night. He's a Saint Ramos now, and it seems that not even the house went to him, so we should consider other possibilities."

"Well, Nix is a chattier system than Archytas. That seems to have served your efforts well."

Enita smiled. "True. He asked me if recipients feel donor organs. If they're added to us like memory."

"You've changed your house system quite a lot."

"He suits me." In Helen's shelves was an ancient volume on anatomy—largely incorrect—but fascinating, nevertheless. People were always changing things based on knowledge and what suited them. Based on need. Enita thought of the Martyr's kidney in her own body, and the woman on her operating table. She'd broken everything about Neren's existence, by not questioning enough, by trying to help.

She shuddered. "I feel for Lucius's Body Martyr. I think I feel for them more than I do Lucius."

"What a rude thing to say," Helen said, her smile sly. "Lucius was never particularly nice, merely entertaining. And you're sure the Body Martyr you worked on wasn't his donor?"

"The hospital data says it's not possible. But she's a face and that's . . . troubling. Especially for me. It's hard not to imagine mine now. I know nothing about them, yet I owe them everything, don't I? Faces are difficult."

Helen's hand was on her shoulder and there too was a little sting. "I have a student coming in later, a writer looking for a book she seems to think I have. If you don't want to go back, you can stay up here if you like, get some sleep. We can theorize more later."

She wanted so much to stay with Helen, to apologize for all the ways she couldn't help being, to ask Helen for absolution that wasn't hers to give, but wants between them were too much. In their long history she'd learned it was often better to take the small comforts than to ask for more when neither of them could truly give.

"I can't," Enita said.

MARTYR

A Body Martyr began life unknowing they were born to a calling. They attended school with other children and searched for their passions and talents. Though there were professions that contain fewer Body Martyrs than others—wall workers in particular—the hospital system and Parallax listed no single pursuit as specifically prone to attracting Body Martyrs. A sculptor was as likely as a textile worker or an engineer to demonstrate the desire and will to become a Martyr. Parents of Body Martyrs were known to report that from a young age their child was unusually generous, that sharing and turn-taking never had to be taught, that more often than not their child required reminders to occasionally do pleasurable things solely for themself. Such parents were filled with pride incandescent in its strength. Other parents were often wary, wondering how many years they might have before their child designated. It was an honor, a blessing beyond blessings, but not one without worry, or sadness, knowing that you'd raised a child who would freely give too much.

Body Martyrs were the natural product of an inhospitable landscape, of a place too harsh to settle without enormous losses from disease, poisoned land and water, from self-sacrifice. They were born from those who accepted that their society's longevity had roots in the great suffering of the few who began it, and survived through those who valued a sense of many over a sense of self. The first Martyrs appeared when the travelers' numbers were few. Before the aqueducts carried and cleaned water, the water beneath Bulwark was toxic. Before the wall, dust and sand blew across land, thickening the air and clogging the lungs. Strong bodies weakened. Lungs turned to soot and clay. Babies were born with insides already withered. The healthy sustained and increased their numbers through sacrifice.

Martyrs gave first to save children, and they gave to save the lives that would build the city. Illnesses burned through Bulwark, making their gifts not only noble but essential.

It was an honor beyond measure to receive a gift from a Body Martyr, to have one's existence deemed valuable enough to be kept alive by another. When martyring was discussed in schools, it was spoken of with awe, the way one spoke of Bulwark's founders. Any societal debt of education, of medical care, of living, that a donor carried would be reduced or eliminated. A Body Martyr's devotion to Bulwark, to sustaining life and its population, was so great that to ask more of them would insult their gifts.

It began with kidneys in Bulwark's earliest days, when water killed, then it spread to lungs and livers. A Body Martyr need not and should not die for a physical gift. A donation was a sharing of life as opposed to a taking. Eyes, for instance, were not a necessary living donation and were most often a gift in death. As time moved on and culture adapted, it became the mark of the deepest Martyr to give an eye, a scar that was not covered by clothing. A Martyr might leave the socket empty or wear a glass eye with a color that did not match the other. The scars of a Body Martyr were ones of hope and reassurance that those who lived in the city were connected, that every person was held by many hands.

Eighteen was the earliest age that a Body Martyr could officially designate. Though they often felt the pull to sacrifice from birth, designation was not permitted until they'd finished primary education. They would be interviewed at the City Bureau by a Bureau Certifiant, its own class of city worker pulled from all quarters. Bureau Certifiants assured there was no coercion and that the desire to martyr had long been present; it was a noble profession with commensurate life hours, due to its importance when it came to minding life balances. A Certifiant would review a potential Body Martyr's full body scan at Central Hospital, which was followed by an interview to record the overall health and condition of the Martyr. If no disqualifying circumstances existed—blood-borne diseases, genetic anomalies, mental illnesses, or undue pressure from a family with a large life debt—the Martyr would be permitted to designate. The designation was recorded at the City Bureau, added in Parallax, and witnessed by the Bureau Certifiant who performed the initial interview, and whomever else the Body Martyr wished. A list was maintained of all the Body Martyrs who designated, their families noted and records stored in the data silos housed deep within the caverns of Parallax and within The Stacks. A place of honor.

Rituals grow, as rituals sustain.

The day prior to a donation, there was a laying on of hands, a touching and learning of the body by the Martyr's friends and family, a lover if they liked, to memorize who they were in that moment, and to imbue the Martyr's body with the strength and love of a family, of a city. Touch was care and community, a gesture of strength. In the third generation of Martyrdom, the Arts District set aside rooms for the ritual of touch. They were giving and welcoming at a time when the city was rough. Martyrs returned to those places after surgery, and those who saw them off were invited to teach them their body again, to learn their long scars, and describe for the Martyr the parts of themselves they could not see in all the ways they could not see them. The Martyr was viewed through the eyes of the city, through the eyes of those they sacrificed for.

A Body Martyr understood their vessel as holy, and the recipient of a donation as blessed—both terms were vestiges from a life long before Bulwark. A body had two purposes: to live and to gift life. Recipient and Martyr were never to meet. Certifiants would make the match. Surgeries took place in separate wards of the hospital with several floors between them. While the altruism of the Body Martyr is ingrained, the recipient of any gift and the families of Martyrs might not have such purity of spirit. Concealment of names protected Martyrs from manipulation and recipients from potential abuse.

Culture builds quickly amid desperation.

City walls rose from the fractured ground, as did the veneration of those who lost their families in blasts, those whose families died from the diseases they tried to cure. What begins as necessity often becomes framework for society. As Martyrs became treasured for their giving, their donations became more valued, more desirable because of the physical sacrifice. Those who received felt selected to live, were honored that another person endured pain and scarring so that they might continue. There is unity in suffering. There grew an unwritten understanding: loss and sacrifice were forms of freedom. The debt that members of this new society owed to each other was not owed by those who had already given so much. Martyrs. Sainted. Recipients held ceremonies in the beginning, donating work hours from their life balances to be spread among those with great life debt. A recipient would burn a piece of old clothing and spread the ashes outside the growing storm wall. Family, if there was family left, would gift water and wine to their neighbors. To drink was to continue life.

The wall closed, centuries stretched inside Bulwark, and disease receded. The city dug deeper for water to find places where poison had yet to seep, and medicine and technology approached what they had been before the collapse. The need for bodily sacrifice diminished, and rituals began to shift and change. In this new city, the Assessors who maintained Parallax monitored balance sheets of lives across Bulwark, calculating how much any single life required from all the others surrounding it, how much physical labor went into the production of a garment, how much education and study was required for a person to play an instrument with skill, how much work went into a year's worth of food, and how much education into a single surgery. City Bureau Certifiants knew that the sacrifices of a body, the gift of a Martyr, was too great to be given thoughtlessly; such gifts must be deeply tied to the city. If a Sainted was to part with their life hours, a Certifiant could insure they were favored with a Martyr's donation.

Gifts of clean water and wine became different celebrations, bacchanalias that stretched for a week. The redistribution of life balances between recipients and the rest of the city lessened as house systems grew more sophisticated, taking over more of the daily operations in a household. Small hour donations were sent to the Arts District to be split. The Opera House, its singers and dancers, were given life-hour stipends that did little to soothe a raw voice or heal a fractured foot. For those, the artists turned to the hospital, and with treatment their societal debts increased.

Though the need for Body Martyrs lessened, the prestige of receiving a donation persisted, except among the few who questioned what about an unadulterated human gift made it more valuable than other treatments. Grow house workers pondered if the lifespan of a human shouldn't match only what their body began with. They stared at grafted trees and wondered if those who received donations were no different, if their fruit wasn't their own, but a Body Martyr's.

For Neren Tragoudi the call to martyr was a persistent bell that sounded with the desire to be useful, the need to ease others. She did not remember a time when the needs of others weren't loud in her ears, and the only way to dampen the noise of want and pain was to give. As an infant she rarely cried, sensing her mother's need for a silent and agreeable daughter after the deafening noise of the textile mills. She gave her toys away to every child whose eyes lit upon seeing them. Her mother learned Neren's favorite foods by watching what she'd give to other children who rubbed their bellies in hunger. *Here. This is my favorite.* When she sang, even her instrument was meant to give, to support. A contralto was made for harmony, for lifting others, to make a sound fuller rather than carry its own weight. As with most Martyrs, she chose, and yet there was no choice to make; it was who she had always been.

When Neren declared her intention to Martyr her body, her mother cried with joy. She'd been proud of her daughter as a musician, but there was no pride like knowing your child would save the lives of multiple people, of her own will. *I have done that*, her mother thought. It was a beautiful thing to have a child, a daughter, who thought of the city and of other lives before her own. On the night before her first donation, she ran her hand across her daughter's belly, feeling smooth skin for the last time. When she was a child, she'd seen a Body Martyr; a young man had stripped his shirt to bathe, and his scars were burnished black on his skin, beautiful as if painted with the slick of enamel. She wondered how her daughter's scars would show, and if she'd be able to feel that there was less of her, that part of her would be elsewhere, keeping someone else alive. She walked taller. If her daughter seemed embarrassed by her mother's pride, her need to tell people about it, that was something she'd have to get used to. In a life of little consequence, her Martyr daughter was the only good thing she'd ever done.

When Neren recovered, Tomas and Joni lay with her. Joni drew her fingers across the incision. Tomas pressed careful palms to the edge of the wound so that she'd learn where nerves now ended and began. There was a rootedness in her body Neren hadn't felt before, as though it had at last done what she truly desired of it. The acute pain of light touches against the pink and still-raw scar was clean and pure like cold water. In that moment, between the bodies of the people she loved best, Neren was more than she'd ever been.

Her first donation had gone to Saint Hestia Pretorius, who was born with one kidney, and at age fifteen found it failing. Saint Pretorius was able to dance on her sixteenth birthday, unaware that one of the singers at her party had saved her life. Neren didn't know whom she sang for; Certifiant Ellsford had made the arrangement in a trade that left his daughter's education without debt. Neren knew only that her voice played well against the domed ceiling, and that the purple so many Sainted wore was a brooding color.

Half of Neren's liver went to Saint Raul Gil. The sagging yellow of Saint Gil's skin turned bronze again. The bones of Saint Gil's ancestors were worked into Bulwark's walls, crushed by metal and stone, so deep in the earth that they were the Saints who haunt Bulwark. After he healed, Raul drank a bottle of flats wine for the first time in years; the taste of it was thick and sour as he remembered, the resultant haze as wonderful. He observed tradition by sending bottles of wine to his neighbors and donated a year of life hours to his favorite soprano, Geniese, whom he'd been able to listen to once more at the Opera House itself. On his first day of attendance, during Geniese's aria, Saint Gil took his lover's hand and clasped it tighter than he'd been able to for months. He swore he felt the Martyr inside him. He swore he felt Geniese's thanks. While Saint Gil was at the opera, Neren swept sand from her apartment, brushing the week from her stoop.

Saint Henry Carraway breathed with Neren Tragoudi's lung. The previous lung, riddled with tumors, had become a solid mass. Saint Carraway didn't celebrate the gift of the lung due to his great age. Much of his set had passed away the decade prior, and he sought the donation to keep his children's pestering to a minimum. Those who didn't do everything to preserve life didn't value it, and those who didn't value life weren't truly Sainted. The lung spent the rest of its days inside House Saint Carraway, breathing meticulously filtered air, rarely providing breath for speech and never song, and growing accustomed to life in an aging body. While Saint Carraway hoarded the life the lung provided him, Neren spent months relearning her breath, working the reediness from her voice and training one lung to sound like two.

Alma, the youngest member of House Saint Wykert, had been meant to receive Neren's eye. As a child Alma had enjoyed drawing before her eyesight failed her. She needed to reach maturity, for her eyes to reach their adult size, before she would be eligible for a donation. She neither mourned nor celebrated that she'd learned to navigate Bulwark while sightless; she thought only of what she missed, what she'd lost that others had not. She wanted to hold a pen with confidence. She didn't want new sight, but a return.

She waited.

For some, gifts felt inevitable.

SIBLINGS

"Neren wants to do it again, and you know she won't stop. She's gutting herself. If she's cleared, she'll keep donating until something kills her." Joni collapsed onto a floor cushion in the flat she shared with Tomas. She'd just come from Neren's rooms on the floor above. They'd shared drinks and Joni had hoped to stay the night, but Neren spoke of her future donations, and any longing for closeness was lost as Joni bit back thoughts until her tongue was bloody. An eye. Neren wanted to donate her eye. "I can't do it. I can't touch her and pretend there isn't less of her."

"If she pisses you off so much, don't see her," Tomas said.

"I'll stop if you do," Joni said.

"It's not the same thing." Discontent had brewed between the siblings for years, though they never spoke of it. Joni knew Tomas was angry, lonely, and that whatever he'd been doing lately made it worse. Joni worried about Neren, and feared she wasn't capable of loving a Body Martyr to death.

Despite being freshly rumpled from a tryst, Tomas was agitated. "Martyrs don't have to do it, you know. One of the Sainted, Malovis—Stitch-Skin—can grow anything. You know Tana? Her kid lost her hand and she took her to Stitch-Skin for a new one. You'd never know it wasn't hers. The girl said her house is stuffed with body parts she grows for the hell of it. Sainted don't need Martyrs; they think that taking from us makes it special."

Joni had once believed the system balanced. Sainted as a whole she could give or take, but their patronage was a necessity for musicians. There hadn't been much to think about until she'd seen a Body

Martyr's zeal. Neren could have a different life, yet she wanted to give until there was nothing left, all the while insisting it was a blessing. She wanted Joni and Tomas's hands on her before and after every surgery, demanding they bear witness to her slow decimation. "If it comes from us, it *is* special," Joni said. "That piece of a Body Martyr is the only part of a Sainted that's any good."

Joni's gift was a strong, clear voice that didn't change as she grew. Singing hadn't been a calling for her in the way a White Cap or an Assessor felt a calling, but Joni loved learning music, and it wouldn't break her body in the way other vocations might. The societal debt she accrued in the university's music program would take most of her life to sing down, unless she found a Sainted patron willing to part with life hours. She used to dream of a regal woman, hair piled on her head in an enormous bun, someone who would give Joni a room in her Sainted home in exchange for serenades. Joni's voice played well against vaulted ceilings— better than it did in her Southern Quarter apartment—and Sainted homes were made for music. She did love them. Truly.

Until Neren had made her love them less.

Tomas grabbed a date from a colorful porcelain dish. He'd traded for the bowl—a short song about a potter's pretty lover for a fluted bowl that made a drab concrete room livelier. He chewed in thought. "Saint Ohno got a lung transplant yesterday. Davet audited the traditional redistribution and gifting of life hours in Parallax."

"Any idea who got them?" Joni asked. She knew better than to comment on Tomas seeing Davet again, how risky it was for both of them. He knew better than to tell her to stop worrying about Neren. It was good, if claustrophobic, to live with a sibling who knew all your hurts and when not to press them.

"His cousin. Not anyone in the Southern Quarter, not the Warehouse or Market District where everyone *knows* that Martyr is from— not even to an artist. He gave them to another Sainted. Sometimes they go to Certifiants to thank them for finding a Martyr. Davet says things like that are common."

"Common?"

"Yes. They tell me things for a reason, you know."

Three years younger than Joni, Tomas had been a sickly child. Born early, far too small, he'd required lengthy hospitalizations and endless monitoring. Joni had no memory of her parents in those years, or where they had lived. She mostly remembered the hospital. When Tomas grew, their father went to a textile farm, and their mother took on wall work. Joni and Tomas were left to long feral days in the Southern Quarter, dirt up to their eyebrows, fingers in everything, light theft, no scans, friendships sworn on spit. They were wild—happy, she'd thought—until school days grew long and tiring. Joni's body molded to music, ribcage expanding for lungs trained to hold breath and notes, a hard stomach to support that breath, to project, throat like a pipe stave. She changed, but Tomas never seemed to.

From the beginning, Tomas had been desperately himself. He took to everything, but his greatest fascination had been with all things mechanical; he was drawn to what had kept him alive. Joni knew he hungered to feel the city systems so instrumental to his survival, that he'd dreamed of being an Assessor, of having a small room in the City Bureau, of understanding, truly knowing Parallax and its data streams, the entity that made Bulwark breathe.

"So why do you think they're telling you this?" Joni asked.

"They're worried about you and me, but mostly about Parallax. I think I'm the only person outside the City Bureau they still know."

"It's good you're seeing them again," Joni said, though she wasn't at all sure. There was something approaching mania in Tomas lately. "Ohno really gave nothing to the Southern Quarter?"

"Not a single hour. But Certifiant Lavins got some. Finder's fee."

Sainted life balances were meant to depreciate but never seemed to, and the number of Sainted never decreased. They existed as an untouchable stable entity, the surpluses passing from person to person.

She and Tomas knew life debt. At seven, her brother disassembled their house scanner. When a City Bureau Auditor appeared to see why scans were missing, they watched the Auditor reassemble the panel with fine tweezers, magnifying goggles. While the Auditor worked, they saw the family life debt, and understood why their mother had taken on wall work, why their father's hands were burned into leather from dyes and surfactants, why their parents came home smelling like chemicals, and why they sometimes didn't come home at all.

"Sainted like Ohno have no reason to see us and we don't have any reason to see them. It's easiest to gift to who you know," Tomas said on a shrug.

"But they *know* other people exist. Even us," Joni said.

"And would you know to whom you would gift? Do you know the people who grew this date?"

"I know they exist and have balances." Joni snagged the bowl and stuffed a date in her mouth. Sweet, rich, chewy. Orchard workers wore jumpsuits, she knew, and they went through regular antibacterial showers and pest screenings so as not to bring anything into the houses. But Joni couldn't picture a face. "I know grow house workers don't take body parts from Martyrs."

"No, they get them from Stitch-Skin, the single Sainted who might not be entirely awful," Tomas said. "If they hear about her."

Joni knew Tomas would have made a terrible Assessor. Working with Parallax would have meant he'd have had to sit on his thoughts, which he had no talent for. The children who'd gone to work in the City Bureau had been different. Silent. Introspective. Joni remembered the towheaded bird of a child who cheated off Tomas's early exams and read every note he ever scribbled down. The friend who'd been in awe of Tomas, then pulled away. Tomas had let them disappear. Perhaps *let* was not the correct word—it hadn't been Tomas's choice. Her brother had been devastated, perhaps still was.

"Something interesting is happening in Parallax. I think that's why they reached out in the first place," he said.

"It wasn't your irresistible charm?"

"Sadly, I don't think so. Still, it's good to be remembered. And I do miss the language." Across the years Tomas had tried to explain what he'd learned when he'd wanted to be an Assessor, that Bulwark was an entity, a thinking, living thing. Parallax was a consciousness. Assessors were trained to speak to and hear many voices at once. Before Tomas started studying music, he'd learned the languages Parallax used, the peculiarities of each quarter and its nodes, the way information flowed. She knew he'd lost much in the intervening years, but Tomas still felt Parallax like a being, and he felt a part of himself was missing.

Joni felt this about Neren, that a part of her had become an absence. When they were together, there was less of Neren in all aspects; her emotions had hollowed along with her body.

"You do realize how few Sainted there are," Tomas said. "It's possible Parallax is beginning to view them as bad code."

"What does that even mean? Did Davet tell you that? I thought you spent your time differently."

He snorted. "It means editing can happen, and the system will view it as repair. We've lived with the assumption that Parallax creates an infallible structure that the City Bureau uses to take care of us. We were wrong."

In three months, the small concrete room the siblings argued and ate in would no longer exist. No portion of it would be recognizable amid the rubble, save for a bit of the porcelain dish Tomas found near Neren Tragoudi's kitchen table.

HOUSE SAINT MALOVIS

Nix waits. Neren Tragoudi will wake up soon. They look at the tray of eye tissue and the eyes stare back. They move the tray from side to side, never breaking the stare, and yes, though unattached to musculature, the eyes seem to follow. It's too warm in the room. They check the temperature data from the thermostat, only to find it optimal for tissue growth. Still, they're having difficulty focusing on the corneas they're shaping onto a form. They swing their legs over the side of their chair as they've seen children do, to understand the sensation. Much was easier when Byron was alive and his need for knowledge and his physical comfort were their main concerns. Now there is a division in focus they're unused to that makes learning new information more difficult. Parsing senses is meant to be a background process, but it's too fascinating to ignore, especially as their parts adapt. It's not a coming online as new nodes had in the past, but perhaps this is waking up? They ping HVAC Node. There's no answer. They ping again.

HVAC sends a short missive. "Temperature is optimal. Mainframe's sensors are faulty."

"We're too warm."

"House Saint Malovis calibrates to Enita's preferred temperature, not ours."

Nix pushes data on ideal temperatures for operating machinery, but HVAC Node doesn't respond. Kitchen Node laughs, and it's an unsettling prickle. Prior to their body, Nix never questioned the idea of what heat felt like, or all the micro processes involved in understanding location in space. Before the legs, before the armature, they were in a mainframe case in an alcove off the surgery, in their walls and nodes, in Bulwark. They weren't in a place, they *were* place.

There is a shout from the far side of the surgery. Neren is awake. Nix runs, but their equilibrium is off, and they catch themself on a work counter.

Neren is small on the padded recovery table, knees high, clawing at her grafted leg, her fingernails cutting dark red welts in the skin. Blood wells in pinpricks and Nix recognizes the color: #8a030, the color of firewalls and restricted information.

Clients often massage a new arm, prod, squeeze, or tap the skin, but not this forceful scratching. Most are too afraid to damage the work.

"I don't know what you did to me, but you need to undo it." Her voice is deep, and unlike any other they've heard. They make a note to search for recordings of her singing.

"You're feeling nerve regeneration. You lost your lower leg," Nix says. "Itching and other sensations are normal. Some people feel like there's water dripping on their skin, but that's temporary. Sorry, but scratching doesn't help, and it slows down healing. You could try pressure; squeezing can be calming and gives the body a sense of where it is in space."

Nix had likened her sleeping form to a painting in The Stacks—a woman draped in loose yellow-orange cloth, her hair a black smudge around her, mouth like a sleeping infant's. Awake, Neren's face is fierce.

"Cut it off," she says. "I'm a Body Martyr, you have to cut it off."

Nix reaches into a cabinet for an anesthetic pen. "We can numb it for an hour or two, which should let you skip some of the more uncomfortable sensations."

Neren flinches. "No. Don't come near me unless you're going to fix it."

They stop where they are, wobbling, waiting for their inner ears to settle. "We'll get Saint Malovis."

"Who?"

"Stitch-Skin."

Neren mutters something Nix's room microphones can't pick up. The scratching resumes. Blood stains the underside of her fingernails.

"Stitch-Skin should have left me," Neren says. "Take it off. I don't want it. You ruined me. I'm a Body Martyr."

Delicate lavender data from Upper Floor tells Nix that Enita is awake and moving from her bedroom to the office, to the kitchen for a meal.

"We didn't know. You came to us severely injured. Saint Malovis started the graft, but we completed it. It's been a long time since we've worked on a fresh injury. Enita's hands were shaking too much, so we finished. The people who brought you were anxious to help you."

"We as in you." She looks them up and down; her expression contains signifiers of anger, fear, and perhaps curiosity.

"Us." Nix gestures to their body, but also to the surgery, to the house. They can't tell if she understands. "Your injury was serious. You would have died without intervention. The trauma demanded most of Enita's focus, and we didn't recognize you as a Body Martyr until too far along in the procedure to stop."

"If you put it on, you can take it off."

"We can't give you your old leg back. It was crushed."

"Take it off. I don't want any of this."

Nix's body wants to pace; there's nervous electricity they can't store, but if they pace it will worry Neren. "We understand," they say, though they don't. They understand very little about Body Martyrs. But comfort is important. They speak gently. "If Saint Malovis removes the leg, you still won't be permitted to martyr again. Some of the sensations are from nanobots in your bloodstream rebuilding tissue. Even if we take the leg, they'll still be in your body."

"Ah."

Nix doesn't know what to make of the sound. They want Enita and can feel her in the office, lifting a tablet from a table, opening a chat with Saint Vinter. Nix pings, letting her know that Neren is experiencing distress. "We're truly sorry. Enita doesn't treat people like you—Body Martyrs, that is. She treats everyone who asks."

"But she knows about Body Martyrs." Neren's expression changes. Nix flips through all the images of expressions they know but can't place it. "What are you?" she asks.

"House Saint Malovis. Well, this segment of us is mostly a surgical assistant, a student, and we're learning, but we are the system House Saint Malovis. We prefer Nix. It's friendlier."

She's taking in their oddity, Nix supposes. They imitate Enita's "welcome" smile and stretch their spine a little taller. It's a good spine they've put a lot of calculations into, as good a spine as a human body allows. Aesthetically beautiful, if impractical.

"Of course, Stitch-Skin wouldn't stop with limbs and organs. Probably couldn't help herself." Neren speaks so quietly Nix's microphones nearly miss it.

"Say that again, please?"

"Are you the same as my leg? The same . . . stuff?"

"Our skin is the same, yes." They take a chair from a worktable—tall bodies can be intimidating—and roll closer. "The body and your leg are all grown cells, nanobots, and nanofilament. There are differences. Your leg has a full bone lattice. In a few days it'll be as strong as your other bones. We don't have bone lattice—and our nervous system is . . . not that." Would she know what they mean by conduit? They ping The Stacks to see what knowledge of biocybernetics a woman with a music education might have.

The Stacks returns with a chipper *little to none*, and links to thirty-seven introductory texts. The information fizzes across their nerves. Nix sighs, in part because they enjoy the sensation of sighing. "You think we're a circuit board inside, don't you?"

"No," she says quickly, but they hear the lie.

"We do have wiring in our nervous system, so there's an element of that, but we look more like you than not. Our thinking is more diffuse."

"Diffuse."

"It's the closest word." They shrug, but it's awkward, and they decide against the validity of the gesture as a whole. Nix could explain nodes, the flow of information, how they are vast and instantaneous, but the language isn't there. "Did you know that there are animals with limbs that each have their own brain? We're something like that."

Her expression matches Nix's references for confusion. Fear. A ping confirms that a musician would have as little reason to study animal neurobiology as they would biocybernetics. A shame.

"We meant that our mind is broad. You and Enita are *I* and *you.*
Singular. We're *we.* Plural."

"I don't need a brain in my leg. Cut it off."

"There's no brain in it, we promise. It's only a leg, brand-new, and
you'll make it yours." Nix sees the words building in Neren, a potential
energy they're unaccustomed to. Enita tends to speak when and what
she wants.

"I'm a Body Martyr," Neren says. "This isn't mine. It was never
meant to be mine." Her voice takes on an inflection of hysteria. "My
body isn't for me, it's for others, because I choose it and that's how it's
mine. It's *mine* by giving, not receiving, and this thing can't be part of
that. It's wrong. I'm a Body Martyr."

She cries.

Nix hasn't yet cried and doesn't imagine they will; crying counts
among things they'd prefer not to experience. They ping Enita's tablet. *Please come downstairs. She isn't well.* "It will feel like your leg,
we promise," they tell Neren. "Your brain will adjust to having nerve
pathways rebuilt. It can take some time, but it will feel like yours. It *is*
yours."

"How would you know what it feels like?"

"We've been told." Enita would put a hand on her arm to offer comfort. If Nix did that, Neren might scream. "If you want, we'll get you
a rickshaw and Enita can take you to the hospital. Your friends were
against it, but we didn't know a lot of things then."

"No," Neren says. "I don't want to owe."

"Societal hours?"

She nods.

Nix tries to tally what a limb surgery would be at the hospital,
the hours of work that might be for a musician. They don't know the
exchange of a musician's labor to the hours of a White Cap's. That's
Parallax's data, not Hospital System's—the sort of data not widely
shared. They could ping Parallax, but they'd prefer not to inform the
system that Enita worked on a Body Martyr. "You owe nothing for
this," they say. "Enita doesn't scan clients. That's known about Stitch-
Skin, isn't it?"

"You don't have scanners?"

"We do. Deliveries come in and out and we tally them, and people who wish to scan are welcome to, but we don't scan otherwise." Yet Enita and Helen did scan when Ohno died, and Nix had complied with City Bureau's request. "If you'd like to scan, you may. We certainly wouldn't stop you."

"If I'd like." Her laugh is remarkable. Neren is a contralto with a voice that sounds too large and deep for so short a body. Her throat is scarred by smoke, dust, and ash, but the sound is full, rounded, and for a moment Nix is lost, trying to place her entire range, the number and feel of it, which pieces of music would best suit her.

Neren slides from the table, wobbling as her foot hits the floor, but the leg is too new to properly take weight. Balance demands more nerve growth, more sophistication. Nix tries to catch her, and nearly falls.

"Careful," they say, putting an arm around her.

"I need to go. Please let me go."

"It's too soon, you're not strong enough yet. We'll get Enita, she's a better judge."

"Will she take the leg off?"

"*Your* leg. Semantics are important, especially at first," Nix says.

Neren's fist against the flesh of their arm is a heavy shock Nix feels in their floor, ceiling, and walls, its color a furious violet. They release Neren and she drops the rest of the way to the floor, leg stretched in front of her. There are more tears. Nix pings Enita's tablet again. *Enita? Please come. We broke something.*

"Enita thought you might not be a Body Martyr anymore and that your friends brought you here because your donations were finished. You have many scars." The statement's veracity isn't what they'd like.

They sit near Neren in case she falls again, in case she falls asleep or resumes scratching. They attempt to manufacture calm, subtly adjusting temperature, changing the lights in the room to a cool generative blue. They ping Parallax, searching for images to match the people who brought Neren in. There's nothing. No scans to go with images, no images at all. They notice a small blank data section in the Market District where two building systems have fallen offline. They feel around, searching for the error, for a power surge, but find only absence. Odd. They ping the Market District's hub to inform them of the blank.

All nodes are functional and online, House Saint Malovis.

Nix stretches the query to the Warehouse District, finding patches of dampened signal, then they scan logs from East Door's delivery register, checking for delays and connectivity difficulties.

"My apartment is gone," Neren whispers. "The whole building is gone. Collapsed. I was trapped. I remember."

"The people who brought you here said they dug you out, which means they must care for you deeply. They'll come back for you."

"Who brought me? I can't remember."

Nix describes them, how ragged and tired they'd been.

"Joni and Tomas. I can't believe they did this. They knew what they were doing when they brought me here. Joni especially." The sound she makes is a brilliant yellow bite.

"Is there anyone else?"

Neren shakes her head, then digs her fingernails into her leg. Nanobots are sending blood and lymph to the pressure marks to heal them. "My mother was thrilled to have a Martyr. It would break her heart to know."

"She might be happier to know you're alive."

Neren only hums.

Nix has never worked with a client who didn't want what was done to them. Wrongness sits in them as a bunching of muscle, neither pleasant nor unpleasant, but they need to stretch.

"You'll stay here until you recover. There's been too much trauma to move you soon, and best practices are that you should have full sensation in the leg before you leave." Calm, cheerful, determined, Nix codes the words light green.

"What are you?" Neren asks again.

"This part of us is a student and surgical assistant. We help."

The surgery sensors pick up her mutter. "Can opener in a skin suit."

This Nix feels in a region of the gut, in a sector where their security processes once sat. "Given the circumstances, we forgive your rudeness." Nix opts not to look at Neren as they retire this portion of themself to their alcove. They ping Enita.

Don't ignore us. We understand you're embarrassed, but you're also happier when you choose to confront problems.

Nix's bed nestles against the shell that once housed their mainframe. When Nix and Enita decided that the body should be mobile, Enita insisted they needed a bed, chairs—a place for this physical form. Bodies need to rest, lie down, to sleep, though she had never specified if or how Nix would do that.

"You'll feel at home here," Enita had said. Nix didn't mention that they couldn't feel at home because they *were* home; they could only feel themself. That is changing. Saint Vinter is regularly short with them, sometimes even rude, but Neren's comment upsets them in a way Saint Vinter is incapable of. They know they are uncanny, and that some of that will change as they learn. They know they're useful and have purpose. Except to a Body Martyr.

Neren is moving. She'll attempt to get up and likely set back the graft.

"Please don't try to stand; you'll hurt yourself. We know you want to go, but you need someone to accompany you when you leave. We're trying to find your friends," Nix says through their speakers.

There is no answer.

They have a non-wired bed, as Enita thought it would help proprioceptive awareness. It's interesting to have a part of their house that they aren't intimately connected to, a part of themself that can't sense their own weight. They feel only mattress against skin. It's unusual to be glad for a lack of awareness.

They hear Enita say, "I'm on my way down. I'm sorry."

Nix shuts their eyes, trying to ignore the woman in the other room. They reach out to Parallax and patch into the broader framework of the city, stretching themself wide, touching systems throughout Bulwark, knocking gently with the images they have of Tomas and Joni.

Something is awry in the network structure; information stutters, bouncing through distant nodes rather than direct routes. Spotty. Two of the silent nodes they'd felt before have reappeared, but there is stillness in other scanners, blankness in gates in the Warehouse District. They pull themself thin to find that there are speckles of silence around the university, and a full floor offline in an arts building. They

are knocking, sending signals—a polite *Hello, may we patch*—when
Parallax sends a blink of data. Neren's next of kin is her mother, who
resides in the Southern District. Residential. Her mother's most recent scan was in the music school this morning. Likely she was looking for her daughter. Nix can't understand what a parent would feel
at a child's decision to become a Body Martyr, or at the loss of that
child's ability to. Byron was pleased, proud even, that Enita wished to
learn his profession, but every piece of data Nix had ever recorded on
Byron indicated that he would have been as pleased with her if she'd
chosen otherwise. Though, it would mean a less curious life for Nix.
This troubles them. Byron enjoyed them as a house system, but Enita
needs them.

They feel Enita's steps, hear her speaking. Nix tries not to listen and
busies themself with searching for Neren's mother's house system. It's
barely a flash in the grid. They are about to send an alert as to Neren's
whereabouts but stop themself. Is it a violation? With other house
systems there is a formal contact procedure—ping, inquiry, exchange
of information between house system and resident. Saint Vinter and
her system, Archytas, follow this protocol carefully. Nix's relationship
with Enita is different because they have known each other for her
entire life.

"Enita," they ask with their smallest speaker, "Neren has been clear
that she wants to leave. Would she like us to contact her mother?"

"Neren will be staying with us for a little longer," Enita replies.
"We're going to chat for a while. She's also apologized for insulting
you."

There is more conversation, but it's nothing Nix is meant to hear.
They return to their queries. Byron would have called this snooping.
Enita, on the other hand, understands Nix's curiosity, their need to
know things outside of themself. Neren's mother's house system is
spare, startlingly so. Nix hasn't had reason to communicate with many
Southern Quarter house systems before. They ping other homes in
the area and find what can best be called a porous grid, some homes
existing almost entirely outside of the network, save for a scanner at
the door.

Nix tenses. A porous network is a network that does not catch errors, a network that can't look after residents. A home without a proper central system is incorrect. How can a home be useful if it's unable to fully assist its residents? Home is more than shelter, but the houses they find are only that—roofs, walls, doors. They query an HVAC node two buildings east of Neren's mother's house. "House Saint Malovis querying. May we patch? Query: How many residents do you have?"

Silence. The node blinks its existence strongly in the grid but does not acknowledge receipt of ping or query. Nix is hit by a sensation like the nauseating rush of junk data overwriting good code. If Saint Ohno was not protected, and the Southern Quarter grid barely exists, something has broken.

If Parallax crashes, Nix doesn't know what will happen to the city, to themself, or to Enita.

ENITA

Enita was in her office, rooting her toes into a plush rug while contemplating what to do with Neren now that she was mostly recovered. She pondered the nature of forgiveness and indulged herself in a fit of what her grandfather had called "overemotional uselessness." He, of course, had never been idle or overly emotional and had a distinct distaste for those who were. While it was possible to emulate him in her work, her emotions were entirely different. To her knowledge, he'd never maimed someone through an act of addition. Perhaps even he, with all his purpose and stoicism, would have flinched. She was lucky to have had Byron into nearly her thirties. She still knew the liver spots on his scalp, his hinge-wheeze laugh. His right hand (missing the tip of its smallest finger) poking at a nebulous lump in a tray. *Cells communicate when they sit next to each other. Doesn't matter if they're plant or animal. When one responds to stimulus the other follows suit.* The thimble he wore on that pinkie when he taught her to sew with a single strand of silk, rare as anything. *Careful now. A worm didn't go through all the work of shitting this out for you to break it. Snug, not tight. Draw skin together, don't pull. See? It wants to close.* On the edge of that memory is a blinking light in the corner of his study—Nix, listening, waiting to see if her grandfather might need anything.

The knock startled her from her self-pity. Nix had only recently taken to the habit; it seemed to amuse him to rap on a door that he could easily open, something that was a part of him.

"Come in."

"We're working on our back today, aren't we?" Nix asked.

Ah, so polite. He'd sensed her change in mood and was here to prod her out of it. "Yes, sorry. I was reading and lost track of the time." So much so that the mushroom tea she'd been suffering through had gone cold and bitter. She hadn't realized how reliant she'd become on tea until its absence. An older medical text had started her current round of malaise, a search for something she vaguely remembered about mesh grafts that filtered blood. She'd learned anatomy and bio-cybernetics at Byron's knee, watching him bend wire to flesh. She vividly remembered his hands, their work-scarred backs. Most memories of him had faded into single images, his fingers touching a sculpture of a forearm, one that rested in the bookshelf as it had when she was a child. There were odd moments when she heard his voice in her ear, but they were fleeting and too fragile to last.

The outside of a human is wonderful, but the inside is where the art lies.

Papou, could you make a whole person from scratch?

We don't need any more of us, darling. And why reinvent the wheel?

His study belonged to her now, as did his surgery, and the losses they'd shared between them had birthed something new. People needed reinvention.

"Enita?"

"Yes, sorry. Let's use the main room, shall we? It might be good for Neren to watch. She'll see it's a minor procedure, mostly sprays and pigment. It could help her feel calmer about her leg. I don't think tomorrow's ear graft would be comfortable having her sit in." She also found she didn't want to be alone with Neren. She'd never had to apologize for her art before, and there were no words that would ease the sick feeling. Nix didn't protest having the work done for an audience, but Enita wished he would. He should have some protectiveness about the body, shouldn't he? Though maybe not, she thought as they walked to the surgery. "It's time for us to talk freckles. Would you like a few? People find them charming."

"On our back no one will see them. Let's do what makes sense for the body."

Enita snorted. "Uptight bodies don't make sense. Bodies tend to come with a desire to be touched, and any freckles you want can be seen or touched if you like, if you ever find that interesting. You've been eager for experiences so far, so I assume you'll be curious."

"Perhaps," Nix said, and that was all. Prior to the body, Nix would chatter at her incessantly if she let him. It had been easy to attribute happiness to their conversation, but that was a pitfall of house systems in general: it was comforting to project emotions on them—Nix in particular. Enita opened the surgery door, and a rush of cool, dry air greeted her.

As did Neren.

"I want you to cut it off," Neren said.

"I see you haven't budged. Give it time," Enita said. "Or go to the hospital if you feel you must. I don't deal in amputations with any degree of regularity—you don't want my work."

"Please."

Enita breathed in the scent of the surgery: alcohol, the cold clean of ozone from the nanofilament tanks. She'd never been good with shame and avoided it whenever possible. "I was thinking only of function, I promise you. If we remove the leg, your recovery would be slow. That's two traumas. You'd need to stay here longer, and the adjustment would be difficult. And you still wouldn't be able to Martyr."

"You broke me," Neren said. There was anger there and something else.

Nix clenched his fingers, pumping his hands, a nervous-looking gesture Enita hadn't seen him use before. "That wasn't our intention," Nix said.

"I'm trying to fix things," Enita said. "I should have been refreshing Nix on an inner ear for a surgery tomorrow, but instead I spent the entire morning looking into blood filters for you."

"No, you don't get to add anything else to me."

"As you wish." Then there was no need to say that a filter graft, if she could make such an archaic thing, would likely be dismantled by the nanobots in order to optimize their host's blood flow, and that it had been nanobots that rendered the filter technology obsolete. "I need to do some work on Nix's back. If you'd like to watch, you may. I was thinking that it might be more entertaining for you than staring at the walls while you recover. It could even be helpful."

Neren's eyes trained on Nix's back. Enita noticed far more curiosity than revulsion in her gaze.

"If you must," Neren said.

Nix's lower back was the color of deserts. When they'd first laid his skin, Enita had a rare memory of her parents and a day trip they'd taken her on beyond Bulwark's wall, toward the spired rocks. She'd been young then, not five, and they made a tight three in a rover, shoulders pressed together. They'd climbed a mammoth dune, and looking across the land, her mother had said, "Imagine this as blue-gray water. That's what the sea is. There were cities all along it once, up on cliffs, buildings like teeth. There may still be some." Enita had thought her mother silly for describing something she'd never seen with her own eyes and never would. Any world beyond the rock spires was more sand, valley, and stone like Bulwark. Seas were sand, or loss, or skin, not water. Other cities, other places simply weren't.

Nix was silent, but aware and present, evidenced by subtle fluctuations in floor temperature and the cycling of colors in the grow room, and the gentle hum of music—singing bowls. He was running a calming cycle.

Enita scraped the skin over the port that had connected him to his armature, a place where the flesh was still thin, his electrical structure and vessels visible beneath. The laser left beads of lymph in its wake, and the sour smell of singed flesh. She heard Neren's wince of breath.

"It doesn't hurt him," Enita said.

"Have you asked them that?"

"Does it hurt, Nix? You can tell her."

"We turn receptors off when we're working on an area. We can choose to experience something like pain. Right now, we're getting sensory input—pressure, temperature. It's good for can openers to pay attention to things like that, you know," Nix said.

Neren's eyes slid to the floor. "I'm sorry I said that. I'm not usually rude."

"You were honest, and you didn't think we would hear it," Nix replied.

"Maybe. I might have meant it more about the leg than you."

"Legs and can openers are useful," Nix replied.

"Sometimes."

Enita could prod there, should, most likely, but held her tongue and worked. The stuttering buzz of the cell sprayer filled the quiet.

"She can't take your leg off, and we won't do it either," Nix said after a long silence. It sounded more like fact than when Enita said it. "We would if we were able, but it's too difficult to discern old from grown, we couldn't be sure how much to take. You'd be hobbled. We've never done that kind of rehabilitation. You'd need the hospital."

"Oh."

Enita shook the canister of cells to undo any settling, and the sound of it was comforting somehow. "You might be able to find someone outside of the hospital to do it, but I wouldn't trust anyone who did. You'd end up with the White Caps eventually, or worse, back here," Enita said. More silence. She kept applying cells—a mix of subcutaneous fat, a layer for the lower portion of the dermis. Saint Hsiao would like this bit, the art of it, Enita thought. It really was painting. "There is other life, you know," she continued. "Giving doesn't need to be brutal to be valued. I have a client in the Market District who loves nothing more than talking to the people she sells clothing to. And there's a toymaker who spends his days making things that give children joy. I gave him a new thumb after he'd sliced through the old one. Making things is giving."

"It's different for you," Neren said. "How many of you died in cure trials? Your family gave a thousand times more than the rest of us."

What a voice. Honey, smoke, and sex. What had it been like when she had both lungs? Wasn't that enough? Did any Sainted deserve a sound like that being lessened? It was troubling to know, immediately, that Lucius Ohno did not. What had her own donor lost?

"I was raised to think that being Sainted meant owing good, a responsibility to the sacrifice that's in our blood, so we work, and that's

WE LIVED ON THE HORIZON

giving too." Byron had a way of making what they did sound noble—
but when it came down to it, idleness and leisure were dull and made
tiresome people. Byron had been disappointed in what he saw as her
father's frivolous ways. He'd been careful not to say it plainly, but she'd
felt it all the same and made that feeling her own. "And too much rest
rots an active mind." Enita was adding a lovely constellation of freckles about the left iliac crest when a notification caused Nix to flinch
beneath the pigmentation stylus.

"Neren," Nix said. "One of your friends is at our East Door. The
woman, Joni."

Neren swore.

It was time to question the friend. "Let's put her in the waiting
room where we can talk. She'll be more comfortable there than here.
Neren, you don't have to see her if you don't want to. Nix can send her
off when we're done."

"No, I have to," she said.

"Are we finished for today, Enita? Freckles aren't urgent, and we'd
like to work on some tissue trays, if that's all right. Unless you feel you
need us, that is," Nix said.

That was odd. "I suppose we can be finished for now. Just let me
patch you." She reached for a small container to spray a thin layer of
epithelial cells until a shiny film appeared over the newly freckled skin.
"No touching that for an hour or you'll smudge the pigment. You'd
really prefer to work on the tissue trays?" Enita asked.

"We would. Thank you, Enita." Nix nodded before retreating. He
moved too silently now, and Enita missed the *shhhk* of his armature
across the ceiling track.

"It feels real. It shouldn't but it does," Neren said, testing her weight
on the leg. Two steps, unsteady, weakness visible on one side even with
such little movement.

"Your stride will even out," Enita replied. "It's real, but it takes
brains a little longer to catch on than it does the rest of the body."

"I don't want to fall." Neren reached to steady herself. It had been a
long time since Enita had a woman's hand on her shoulder that wasn't
Helen's. Neren's was hot and callused.

Joni's shadow was visible through the waiting room's frosted glass doors. If Enita was in the same position, would she have returned? The doors hissed as they slid open—Nix could do that silently but had chosen to make a display.

"Oh, thank God," Joni gasped. Small words that held too much.

"You knew what she would do, and you brought me here. How could you?"

"She's good, Ner. Most people would never know." Joni slumped into the low bench where she sat. "We thought that if you stayed under—Tomas and I thought you might wake up and not know."

Neren stiffened. "What?"

"We couldn't—I couldn't. If you never knew—if we took you to the hospital, White Caps would have scanned you and you'd know. You'd see it missing every day and you'd be reminded. You'd never outlive it. Stitch-Skin doesn't scan. And look at you, you're whole."

"I *was* whole."

Enita dug her fingers into the back of the bench where Joni sat. It was all that kept her from smacking the woman. Those were things meant to be said to clients, willing clients, not an injured lover whose wishes you'd ignored.

"Would you ever have told me? Or were you and Tomas planning to wait until I went to give my eye and the hospital blocked my donation?"

"We hadn't thought that far, I promise. We needed you alive, Ner. I need you."

"The hospital would have left me how I'm supposed to be. I could have donated."

"I couldn't," Joni said. "Tomas wouldn't either. You don't know what it's been like to watch you do this to yourself. To love you and see you give yourself away. Every donation, there's less and less of you. There's nothing left to give—you emptied yourself for them."

"You don't break what you love, Joni. You and Tomas broke me."

The anger, sadness, desire, and whatever else was between the women was nothing Enita should interfere in. "I'll leave you to talk. If you need me, call for Nix and ask him to find me."

"Stay," Joni said quickly. "This is your home. I apologize that Tomas and I were rude to you and your assistant. We were exhausted and he took us by surprise. We're not like that."

"Like what? Like the sort of person who would knowingly go against a Body Martyr's wishes?" Neren asked. "Is Tomas too ashamed to come see me?"

"No, he found a place for us in the Southern Quarter, but he needed to do a bunch of dealing for it." Something unspoken passed between the women and it set Enita on edge.

"For us."

"There's nothing to go back to, Neren. The building's demolished. Flattened. We can't go back to our old apartment, and yours is gone. Stay with us, at least until you find a better place. I'll help. We'll help, I promise. Please."

Neren's sobs were the sort that Sainted rarely heard outside of funerals. Losses were scarce for Sainted, largely planned, their grief a rare and bitter jewel. Enita hadn't truly wept since Byron's death, which they'd planned together for a full year, an intentional painless weaning from life. Before that? She wasn't sure. Too long ago to remember.

How many had died in the collapse? It should have been the first thing she'd asked Nix to find out, but she'd never checked. The size of the building—number of dead, number of lost homes—all of it was data Nix could access, but she hadn't thought outside the surgery. She'd still been thinking about Ohno.

"Please stay with us. Tomas sorted it all. He needs you too." Joni rubbed Neren's shoulders. "I love you, Neren. It was all me, whatever you feel, it's on me. Don't blame Tomas."

Neren coughed and gulped air. Slowly the crying stopped, and she brushed Joni's hand away. "You're keen to tell me who I should blame." Oh, that *voice*. "Maybe I've already worked that out. Maybe I didn't want to see you again. Maybe I'm sitting here wondering what I'm alive for and figuring out how to break my mother's heart by telling her that her only child is no longer the gift to Bulwark she was meant to be."

"Well, fuck us, I guess," Joni said.

"Yes, well, fuck you." A tart laugh.

Enita itched for escape, for Nix to page her and say that the tanks were leaking, that a cancerous cell had appeared in a pancreatic tissue tray, that he had some esoteric question about tension and the tympanic membrane. "Neren, you can stay here as long as you need," she said, without knowing that that was true at all. Surely, she must have some life to get back to.

"No," Joni said, with too much insistence. "You don't have to forgive me, but come home. If not for me, come for Tomas. He's insufferable when you're not around."

To Enita's memory, Tomas had already seemed largely insufferable, but that could be her bias against the gender.

After a long silence, Neren said, "You've done enough already, Saint Malovis. I can't stay here." She turned to Joni. "Fine."

In the history of the word, *fine* had never once meant fine. All in the room knew this.

"We'll make it right, I promise," Joni said.

Enita cleared her throat and rattled off the basic pablum about balance and care with stairs and slopes, general attention to the skin. She felt a pull, a need to reach out and beg Neren to stay. There was something else too. She turned to Joni. "This is an odd question, but forgive me, I'm an odd woman. Do you know other Body Martyrs? Anyone who may have donated a lung in the past year?"

Joni shook her head. "No. The only other Martyr I knew died when I was little. It's—it's not common. Martyrs are special," Joni said. "I'm sorry," she said to Neren, repeating it again and again until the words lost meaning, falling into rhythms and notes. There was something in the way the women leaned their shoulders on each other—comfort for a kind of grief Enita couldn't understand. It was too intimate to watch.

At the door, as she was leaving, Neren turned to Enita. "Please apologize to Nix again for me. I could have been better to them. Also, you call Nix *he*, but they told me they're plural. They speak of themself that way. I think that means something important to them."

The east door slid closed soundlessly. Enita bit into her cheek hard enough to draw blood. Nix's cameras would follow the pair into the street. Enita should have asked about transport or arranged a rickshaw. It was too late now and beyond her control. So much was. Her thoughts teemed with memories of Nix's use of *we*, the *our* that peppered every phrase. Byron had called Nix *he*; she'd always done the same. And yet. The words had always been there, hadn't they? It was too much shame for a single morning.

———

"We don't trust Joni," Nix said. Nix was on his—*their*—bed, too straight-spined, too still, sitting with the lights off. She supposed darkness didn't matter if you were a home, the inside and outside of it. Nix wasn't in the dark really, but in the light of later afternoon, wind and dust blowing across roof and walls.

"I don't trust her either. But it's not our place to trust her. It's Neren's decision, and there's history between them we can't know."

"Neren hates what we did to her."

"Yes." Lights flicked on in the alcove. She'd ordered far too small a bed. At the time she'd thought only about the size of Nix's body, the functionality, what she needed that body to do in order to assist her and not what it would be to inhabit it. Bodies needed to have a sense of dimension, and there were times when a person needed to sprawl. "Her life has radically changed. It will take time to adjust, but I'm hopeful she will."

"We're unsettling, aren't we? Uncanny valley," Nix said.

"Not at all." She rested her cheek against Nix's shoulder. Firm as it should be with the right amount of yield. Touch was its own language. They'd had a lifetime of rapport, conversations of the mind, but this? She was terrible at being kind, at noticing important things. "People have a difficult time with what they can't categorize, and most of us don't deal well with discomfort. Sometimes confusion looks like fear—think of it as an animal response to push away the new. Most people are better than their animal nature; we do tend to come around," Enita said. "And you won't always be as you are. You're learning already."

"We ran scenarios based on observation," Nix said. Their voice came from the room's speakers, not their mouth as they dissociated. "It's anecdotal, but given Neren's initial reaction, we see ten potential outcomes: four end in having the leg removed, five have varying levels of integration, and one ends in suicide."

"You and I don't know her well enough to say. Whatever makes her a Body Martyr might help her if she can see the leg as integral to a sense of purpose."

"So, we're trying optimism," Nix said.

"We are." She hugged them tightly and there was only give and warmth similar to hers. "You're not uncanny." It had to be said, though the words weren't enough.

"To you."

"No other child ever made themself with such care or in the way they desired. No other child was ever dreamed up with such goodness in mind." She'd been frank with Nix about her own body, all the ways that it was failing. She didn't want to harm more people than she helped. She was direct in stating that she needed the kind of assistant it would take decades to train, decades she didn't have left. She had left out the bit where she'd been dreaming about legacy, and all the people Nix might still help after she was gone.

"We're not your child, Enita. We're older than you and we helped to raise you. We took videos of your mother when she was pregnant with you."

"Fine, you're your own child, but you're still mine. Better?" She breathed the scent of Nix's hair, not quite human, but not quite *not*. Almost sweet.

"More accurate. We're meant to be useful. Children are . . . different."

Nix's changes in form had come with an echo of adolescence. She had no idea what children and parents were to each other. She'd never gotten to know her parents. Her grandfather had doted, indulging her with whatever she asked for. According to Helen, Byron had made her an ego monster.

"Children have purpose. Your concept of usefulness? I think that's love."

"You don't have the vocabulary for what our usefulness is," Nix said. "But thank you." They took Enita's fingers in their hand, turning them over as if to memorize them.

"It was brought to my attention that I've been wrong in calling you *he*, and that the plural is more accurate. I confess, it never occurred to me to ask. Byron spoke about you as a *he*, so I assumed it was your preference. That was lazy of me and I'm sorry."

At this, a smile. Perhaps it was due to the musculature they'd built together, or a gesture Enita had unwittingly taught Nix, but the smile itself was entirely Helen's.

"You may not remember this well, but Byron used *it* and *he* inter-changeably depending on his mood. It mattered less without the body, house systems; we're broad—but fixed as well. A place and an entity. We thought less about bodies as a whole, before. House systems are meant to answer to whatever is easiest for our residents. Preferences that go against our residents' comfort don't exist. There was nothing to correct, because *he*, though inaccurate, was recognizable and com-forting to Byron and to you." Nix's smile broadened. "Because you have difficulty categorizing us."

"Don't use my words against me."

"It's easier for you to think of us as one, not many, and a single body reinforces that, as does *he*. But we're still many."

She'd known there would be adjustments, slower functioning over-all, but how those adjustments would manifest had been difficult to predict. They still were. "I'll remember," she said. "Does it bother you? The body?"

"No." Nix tipped their head back to stretch a spine that shouldn't need stretching. "But we don't fit a single category—we're many nodes, but you have a human bias, and we need for you to be comfortable."

"I tried not to steer your choices as we went along, but I suppose I failed."

"Yes and no. We steer ourselves to you, as that's what we're de-signed to do. But it's curious to us that you didn't suggest a body more similar to yours or Saint Vinter's."

Lights pulsed gently in the grow room, calming and blue. There wasn't a single motivation—more a litany of reasons that had pre-vented her from coding Nix female. Enita hadn't wanted to be ques-tioned as to whether she'd built or grown her own sex partner. She didn't want Helen to think she'd been trying to replace her. She didn't trust herself not to look jealously at a body that was new and young. Maybe too it was about protection, about objectification of a con-sciousness; there was something about next-to-nature that tricked people into ignoring moral constraints, encouraging acts that would otherwise be unconscionable. She'd seen robotic limbs tossed in cor-ners at parties, silicone ripped away from wiring, cybernetic faces without eyelids. It had always been more difficult for her to witness violations on female-coded forms. Yes, that might be wrong, but it was the sort of wrong she could forgive herself for.

"You can't avoid people seeing you as uncanny, especially now when you're learning. That will get better. My hope was that any differences might help people to trust you, because you're part of Parallax. But there are things about this specific body that will be easier for you than if it was female. You'll be questioned less, and no one will think you're my lover."

The words startled Nix.

There were other things too, more difficult to name, the thoughts that started the moment a person realized they were alive, the trauma that came from having a body, the pain of it, the demands and the inevitable failures. "A female body—there are things that were for a very long time expected from people who identified that way. It's changed, but those beliefs left scars. People see types of bodies and assign expectations to them. A female body is written on. When I'm gone, you'll be working alone. I thought it would be easier in a body people view as male."

"Though we're not."

"We can still change things; we can always change things. You aren't finished until you want to be."

"No, we suppose not." The lights brightened in the alcove as Nix chewed on their lip. "But we're beginning to lose the *all* of us. More and more, nodes won't respond to queries and commands. This part of us"—Nix smacked their thigh—"communicates poorly and has input the rest of us can't recognize."

Enita was projecting sadness on them but couldn't stop herself. She squeezed Nix's forearm, those fine hairs and giving skin. Rubbing alcohol and rain—that was the scent. "We expected you'd lose some speed, but maybe it's been too much change too quickly? Should we hook you back into the armature for a while?"

"No, moving is good. It's loose and new," Nix said. "We're used to many voices, rivers of information. Now it's most often only the body; it's loud and mutes our voices. We're more and less."

The words were a sour weight. She filled the space between them with what people did: "I'm sorry."

"It's for the best. We'll be more useful."

"Is there anything good about the body for you?"

"Is part of your mind pedantic? Kitchen is. We search for useless recipes and use processing to highlight flaws in delivery systems outside our purview. We refuse practicality over preference in instances that make no difference to your well-being. Kitchen Node is loud. We're enjoying the break. Quite a lot." If Nix's smile was for Enita's benefit, she couldn't tell.

"I promise this wasn't a frivolous decision. I wouldn't do that to you."

"Of course not. We're the best advertisement for your work and also the best storage system for it. You don't have children and it's too late for you to have them, but what you do is important. It's difficult for anyone to know how to repair a body, more difficult if they've never inhabited one. A student wouldn't have immediate access to all the data on how you practiced, how Byron practiced, and how your work evolved to become our work. You're afraid of dying and that all the good work you and Byron did will die with you. You needed us and our knowledge, and many people aren't receptive to machines."

The bluntness made her feel grotesque.

"We should finish up your back," Enita said. "Then maybe we'll give tomorrow's ear a once over, all right?"

"Perfect," Nix said.

She shook out her arm—it stiffened up too quickly now—and focused on Nix's skin. It was rare that she saw an expanse of back; the majority of her work centered on limbs, digits. The days of parties that ended with nude bodies draped across each other in exhaustion were long behind her. Saint Ohno had presided over such parties Enita had attended in her younger days, his belly round and firm, shapely as a melon.

Nix flinched under the stippling needle. Enita apologized and drew back.

"It isn't you," Nix said, turning their head to face her. "Enita? We can't reach parts of the city network. The sensation of that is . . . unpleasant?"

"What do you mean?"

"We've been tracking Neren and Joni. They went into the Arts District and an entire section of buildings is offline. We checked for power supply fluctuation, if a solar field is knocked out, but there's nothing. There are absences in the grid, with no information flowing in and out of Parallax. We thought it might be like the Southern Quarter— porous. But it's more like the night your friend died."

"Ohno wasn't a friend."

"We know. You have one friend, Saint Vinter, and that's all you need." When had Nix learned to roll their eyes? "Our point is that it's a self-concealing silence. Nodes surrounding those buildings are unaware that the buildings exist. They're operating as though the structures aren't there and never have been. It feels like deletion, or maybe overwriting where the data is made null. We've asked Parallax about the absences, and they don't recognize anything as gone. It's very much like the missing tea deliveries. We don't have tea, yet Parallax and the warehouse indicate that we do."

"Is it only the Arts District?" She set down the needle, giving the follicle plugs time to settle.

"With the Southern District it's difficult to say—we haven't contacted them enough to be familiar with their programming. But small sections in the Market District—individual stalls we speak with—are also dark. They come and go offline. There's a lack in code where something should be. The network *needs* something there to be complete."

"What do you think it is? A virus?"

"We don't know. This doesn't happen." Nix rested their cheek on the pillow, their beauty a blunt punch. "HVAC Node sometimes behaves as though the body doesn't exist—we can be spiteful—but never for long and we repair ourselves. Parallax is designed to do that, they *should* be self-healing, and yet they're not." Bulwark's designers had made a system that would withstand natural disaster better than anything that had come before it—buried lines, backup channels, tech with the sole purpose of diagnosing and repairing without need for oversight. The city walls were thick with cable, reinforced with redundancies to outlast the storms that rolled across the plains. "We can't make anything of it at all. We've queried Parallax and The Stacks for other places where things like this have happened," Nix said.

"There aren't any," Enita replied. If there were still other cities, she knew nothing of them.

"You're right, of course," Nix said.

"Agreeing for the sake of being agreeable is a horrible trait."

"True. We can't factually agree with you. That aside, Neren and her friend went into a dark area where we lost track of them."

"They're musicians, it makes sense they'd go to the Arts District. But you'll tell me when Neren scans again? I want to know that she's well."

"We'd like to know that too." Nix sat up to pull on their shirt. "We should look at the ear tissue now, if that's all right."

Later, as she bent over the cast of a middle-aged man's head, Enita admitted, "Even though I know you aren't, I do think of you like my child." She ran her finger across the uneven surface, learning the man's scar by touch. Laser first, layer of spray. She turned over the small canister containing the grown ear, assessing the match. She'd have to trim it down. "If I had a single maternal bone in my body, it would be for you, Nix. When I'm gone, you'll have everything I ever was, my work, my journals, our home. Yourself. You're more than what you were and more than what I am."

"We were here first," Nix said. "There isn't a single thing you could ask of us that isn't necessary to our being. You're our child." They reached high above their head to adjust a fluid drip, the lines of their body long. All she saw was a lithe young man who was not a man at all and was the most singularly giving presence she'd known. Perhaps that too was what this endeavor was for.

Nix jolted. "Saint Vinter is requesting you. Archytas flagged the message as highly urgent. They're shouting."

"Things are always urgent for Helen. Are you feeling all right? Is the skin taking?"

"We're fine. Please just answer her. It's uncomfortable when Archytas shouts, and we don't need Saint Vinter hating us more than she already does."

"She doesn't hate you."

"She wants you to meet her in a café by the Opera House. She says you'll know the one she means."

"I do," Enita said. Some places lived in the body.

———

Rickshaws made Enita feel her age; every rut and dip in the road rattled her bones. Though rickshaw runners were far better at navigating the busy streets than their automated predecessors, they still fell victim to the effects of three hundred years of infrastructure wear. The runner's shoes slapped rhythmically against the dirt and stone as they passed Saint Ohno's home. The City Bureau's redistributors had accessed and dispersed Ohno's belongings, and the building would soon pass to a newly Sainted or another who had no home of their own. She'd inherited Byron's home, his possessions distributed to her, Nix included. Saint Ohno's house system had been formatted for a new owner, gutted to make room for new life. What was that to a human body? She'd never considered having Nix wiped—they were the last piece of her grandfather and the first piece of her.

"You know that fellow?" The driver nodded at Ohno's house. His voice was pleasant with the Market District's twanging kick.

"Not personally."

"I heard he got murdered in the middle of an orgy. That true? I didn't think Sainted went out like that."

"It was in his sleep," she lied. "Life is as boring in this quarter as it is anywhere else."

The driver laughed.

Stone houses, so much stone. Columns, flat roofs, peaked roofs, domes, all in the same placid colors—all cut from the same hills outside the wall. By how many? Enita had lost that bit of history too. It was some kind of sin not to know the history of where you lived when you existed because of it. Buildings changed as they neared the Arts District and the driver's pace slowed in congested streets lined with box galleries made of tin, steel, and repurposed containers from the Warehouse District. Everything was reused and garishly painted. Some hated how the buildings clashed with one another, but Enita loved the brilliant pinks, the yellows so bright they hurt the eyes. There was joy in color. Houses in the Sainted Quarter hid colors inside, but the Arts District was outwardly alive. Being Sainted was akin to being dead: you needed no accomplishment, no action, all the achievement had already been done. The side of the Opera House bore a woman's face in blue, mouth wide, frozen in song, teeth gleaming like an animal—the diva of the moment. It had been too long since she'd been to the opera, wrapped her fingers around another's hand, gasped at the frisson of an aria.

The rickshaw turned a corner and stopped.

"Here?"

"Yes, thank you."

Stepping down, she noticed the driver was missing part of his right hand. In place of the absent fingers were two elegantly carved digits made from what she assumed was composite plastic. They were joined, delicate, and etched with flowers and vines, a shade darker than his skin.

"I can fix that for you," she said. "Do you know the name Stitch-Skin?"

A gap-toothed smile made of menace and delight. "I know who you are, Saint Malovis. I don't need fixing."

Enita thought it was to her credit that she didn't wince.

The runner scanned his partial hand outside the café door before disappearing down the road, his rickshaw vanishing into a crowd of students and traffic.

The Opal had declined significantly since she and Helen had first found it. They were young then, spilling out of a theater, laughing, drunk, enamored with life, art, and the taste of each other. The sign, dented tin and vaguely shaped like a wine flute, had lost most of its paint, but inside the chairs remained the same and the place still felt wide-hipped and earthy. Music flowed from somewhere Enita could never quite find, its source shifting over the course of an evening. Strings, a soprano voice. Maybe the musicians were in a room upstairs—there were rooms—and the sound was piped in to mingle with the scent of spices she couldn't name.

Though it was difficult to see her among the shadows and the students, Helen waited in a corner near the back, rigidly seated on a cushion at a table as though placed by an unseen hand. Enita parted curtains made from long strands of strung-together can tabs, which clinked as she moved through them.

She pulled up a nearby chair, her body aching from the ride. Her hips couldn't tolerate a cushion the way Helen's could. "Feeling nostalgic, are we?"

"If only," Helen said. "I couldn't think of anywhere else you'd know. Neither of us is much for getting out these days. By the way, the food is terrible, not at all what I remember. Maybe they put in a kitchen system."

"I could have come to your house."

"Best that you don't. We should be more careful about where we spend our days," Helen said.

"Why? Did Archytas find something interesting? All I've been able to do is ask the Body Martyr's friend if she knew anyone who might have given Ohno a lung. Which was pointless." Enita noticed that Helen had assembled a precarious tower of salt packets, carefully stacked, corners folded in. She flicked the edge of one back and forth with a thumbnail.

"En, if there was a need to go somewhere else, could you?"

"What do you mean?"

"I mean if this city wasn't safe for us anymore, would you leave?"

Enita pinched the bridge of her nose. "Hel, you understand how that sounds, don't you?"

"It's not paranoia."

"Of course it doesn't seem that way to you."

"Archytas found something—not about Ohno. I have it monitor Bulwark's utilities." It, of course. Never he or she, or them—always an object to Helen. Enita started to ask why but Helen cut her off. "For history's sake. Because it's important to know how we live and what keeps us alive. Aren't you the least bit curious?" She raised her hand to stop Enita's response. "I should have caught it sooner, but Ohno's death distracted me. You mentioned about the tea—and it reminded me I hadn't reviewed Archytas's data in far too long. Then I saw it: Two weeks prior to Ohno's death, a water treatment facility went offline."

"And? Systems go offline for maintenance and to clear caches. There's nothing unusual about that. Nix said the grid is . . . porous?"

"Systems go offline briefly, yes, but never without a backup taking over. It's the water system, for God's sake."

Though reluctant to say it, Enita agreed the outage was unusual;

redundancies were built into the city to protect against the very disasters that had necessitated it being built.

"First the treatment plant, then Ohno is killed, and as you noticed, our tea is gone. But look, you can still get it here, can't you?" She nodded to her cup. "Something's happening."

"The tea is inconvenient, yes, but that's hardly a sign of greater machinations."

"But it is."

"I still don't understand why we're talking about this here."

Helen tore a corner of a packet, poured the salt on the table, and began shaping a small pile with the grains. "This part of the Arts District we're in? It's a solo node, so it's safe to talk here, but not often and not without thought. I doubt it will be safe here much longer."

It had never occurred to Enita that the café wasn't gridded. "Who would listen? Really, Hel. And there's a scanner at the door."

"Spoofed. Anyone who scans in generates a line of junk code."

Junk code. The term unsettled her. "Why?"

"I'm worried. It's not about the tea or even the water. People are unhappy and unhappy people need safe places to talk. Solo nodes like this are made when there's a need for them, they're not just a single person's desire, they're a group need. Do you see?"

"Not really. So it's about Ohno?"

Helen said nothing.

"And how do you know this place is safe?"

"Archytas," Helen said. "My safety is in my house system's best interest, etcetera, etcetera." Helen tore open another packet, adding to her hill of salt. Here they were, meeting where unhappy people met, hiding. Helen herself was unhappy. "It's about Lucius, but it's more than that. It's about the Martyr you treated. Do you know how many people lived in the building that collapsed? Two hundred people, En."

More clients than she saw in a year, by a considerable number. Likely there were injuries as bad as Neren's, or worse. A tightness settled at the base of her skull, the first seed of a headache. "How many died?"

"That's the thing—there's no way for us to know. That data's siloed in Parallax and can't be accessed unless you work for the City Bureau. It can be written over, erased, locked away. An Auditor or an Assessor could do it, even a Certifiant." Helen seemed about to say more, but a server came by, hips rolling, covered in beads that jingled with each step. Enita took a cup of tea. She needed the warmth, to have something to do with her hands. The first bittersweet sip was a brush of nirvana. How did the Opal have this when she did not? Why? Helen pressed a fingertip to her salt pile, crushing it.

"It's the debt system," Helen said once the server had gone. "You know it's wrong. I know it's wrong. When was the last time you met someone who had worked their way to newly Sainted? Or not even that, but someone close to running a surplus of societal hours?"

"I couldn't say." The Sainted she knew never spoke about such things and thought talk of balances in poor taste. The clients she saw were in no danger of running a surplus; debt was the primary reason they sought her help rather than the hospital. "The Body Martyr, maybe. I don't know for certain, but all those donations must have her at or near surplus."

"Have you ever considered that the number of Sainted has to stay small and that our isolation is more by design than by choice?"

"Our sphere is what it is because of history and how we were raised, you know that better than anyone. We can't undo our families' sacrifices."

"True, but should we keep living off them?" Helen pressed.

"You know I don't think that." It was what had drawn them together so many years ago, Helen's desire to learn, to teach, Enita's need to work, to help people.

"Bulwark can't run on leisure, and you and I—well, the vast majority of Sainted—we do nothing. It makes sense for our numbers to be carefully policed. Our population needs to stay close to static."

"You think Ohno is part of that? Policing?" The headache stretched its spidery legs, making music too much, the smells too strong. She held a sip of tea in her mouth, concentrated on the warmth, and gave a small prayer to caffeine.

"Maybe, I'm not sure. But the grid is spotting out. The water treatment plant going offline—it wasn't enough to be noticeable to most, but it was out long enough to show up as a network error. Then Ohno. And the tea. We need to think about what that means."

Had they been elsewhere, in either of their homes, Helen might have seen the pain taking root, the way it made Enita's whole body stiffen. She might have reached up to dig her fingers into the tight muscles in Enita's neck. She might have recognized the worry and shame Enita carried from breaking the Martyr. But no, Helen had insisted on the Opal, and Enita needed something else. Anything else. Comfort, not paranoia.

"I can't do this now, Hel. I'm tired, and it's too much. I hurt a Martyr and it's eating at me. I need silence, rest—not whatever this is. I'd been hoping for a little nostalgia, that maybe you'd missed this place, but as usual I misread you." Enita started to stand, but Helen put a hand on her arm. Touch as *please*. For a moment she was as she'd been when they first met: tight, righteous, angry, mind faster than anyone else's.

"Wait," Helen said. "Please, this is important. Just listen to me for a minute. Humor me. How would you hold a city hostage?"

"You'd close off access points, isolate it."

"And if it's already isolated? Walled, for argument's sake."

"You starve it and cut off water."

"I think the water treatment outage was a trial run, maybe the tea too. And I do think it's tied to Ohno, but I don't know how yet," Helen said.

Nausea rolled through Enita. Junk code. Porous grids. A dead Saint, a ruined Martyr, missing tea, and a water treatment plant on the fritz. Too much, all of it. A class somewhere let out and a group of students stumbled in; their clothing was arranged in clever gathers, each attempting individuality, though all fabric came through the same textile farms. The colors were muted hues that needed the least care, the least cleaning—working clothes they'd done their best to make into art. Rings and studs in their brows, lips, cheeks, ruddy tattoos creeping up from their wrists, students dressed in uniform rebellion. Joni and Tomas would have blended in with them well.

"A trial for what, Hel? To drive us mad with caffeine withdrawal? To make us incredibly thirsty? Force us to drink our own piss?"

"Stop. I don't think it's going to be safe for us here much longer. I need to know: Would you leave?" Helen swept her salt pile into her hand and poured it on the floor.

"And go where?"

"There are places. This city's egotistical enough to think it's the only one, but human survival doesn't work that way." Helen's conviction was a familiar obstacle. There was no discussion with someone who believed they had the weight of history on their side.

"So, you either don't know, or won't say."

"We can't stay like this," Helen said, and looked away.

Enita was a creature of luxury—not as decadent as some but pampered nonetheless—and this was home. Home was her work, knowing her entire family had lived and died in a single place. When your family had bled for a city, that sacrifice took root and grew until city and self were inseparable. As long as there was a Bulwark there should be a Malovis in it. She felt kinship with the rock and metal—without this city and its Body Martyrs she would not have survived childhood. Maybe there were other cities, maybe some still stood, but there were vast swaths of space between them, and Enita owed Bulwark her life.

"High Rail, Pickton, Ebbersfield. They were there when Bulwark started. They still could be," Helen said, taking Enita's hand in hers. She pinched the web of skin between Enita's thumb and forefinger, the pressure point that eased some of the headache. So she had noticed.

"But you don't know for certain that they exist, do you? And you'd pack up all your books to set off looking? It doesn't matter. I have a responsibility to this city, and I won't leave Nix. I can't—if I left, they'd be wiped. Nix knows me, my family, and I owe it to my family to teach them everything I can until I'm no longer able."

"You think you *owe* it?"

"Nix has been with me my whole life, Hel. They're family."

"I see. I didn't know you felt so strongly."

"I don't share everything with you anymore. I can't."

"Have I been so awful to you?"

Voices from the street filled the café, music, students practicing harmonizing, the warm buzz of reed instruments. Helen stared at her hands. Ringless. They'd once thought about inking bands on their fingers. They'd seen themselves as the only two people who could tolerate each other. It was still mostly true.

"We've learned to try not to disappoint each other. You don't like Nix, but I won't be sorry or apologize for them."

"Are you sure you're not just hanging onto your grandfather?"

"Maybe."

"Byron wouldn't want you clinging to him. He'd want you to live. If I begged you to go somewhere else, if Pickton still exists and I could get us to it . . . would you leave?"

"Nix is important," Enita said, letting the *why* hang between them. "I know that you can pick apart any argument I make, sway me any way you want, but I'm asking you not to."

"You've never done a single thing you haven't wanted." Helen's hand drifted to Enita's knee, her touch a kind of home. She'd become sharper with age, pinched needles Enita longed to stab herself on. "You think it's not going to get worse, that Ohno's death was a one-off. But when people tinker with supply chains it has everything to do with power, and when power shifts, old orders get cleansed. That's Ohno, that's you and me. I don't want you hurt."

Saint Vinter, whose family had brought water to Bulwark, bored the tunnels that were the city's veins, and lost an entire generation to collapse, flooding, and poisoned water. Saint Vinter, whose family helped design the City Bureau so that no work or life went unvalued. Saint Malovis, whose family had developed the treatment for Creeping Plains Rot, only to later succumb to it. Saint Malovis, whose family patched the people of Bulwark the way they patched the wall. Their families had sacrificed so that all would suffer less. They'd built and safeguarded the city from the ground up against disease and drought, against the plains' winds, so that they might survive.

But there was Lucius too and his new lung, his body which he'd set about pickling on wine. There was a Martyr's kidney inside her.

"Well, if we're part of a useless class, why *should* we get to leave?" Enita asked.

"Because there's good in what you do and that should count for something. You've never thought about the broader implications of your work, have you? You're breaking life debt. The people you operate on—they're meant to accrue debt, they're meant to keep working so the city functions. Parallax is supposed to see that no one suffers, but the system itself, the valuation of work and life hours, it's breaking people, En. Why don't you scan your clients? Why don't *you* scan?"

"I don't need client's life hours, I don't need their debt." All Enita wanted was for people to feel useful in their bodies, and not to feel so useless herself. She closed her eyes against the pain in her head, which caused the room to gently sway.

"There's no way we won't get caught in what's coming. How many people do you see a year? Or over a decade even? Is it enough that you'll be remembered for helping? Do you think I'll be remembered for being kind to a few students? Movements don't differentiate. You're not bad for a Sainted and your work has been good, but is it good enough?"

And she'd broken a Body Martyr. "Our whole lives are here."

"There are places that aren't like this one, there have to be."

"Places that will take refugees?" The word held little meaning—Bulwark had been contained for generations.

"Your medical knowledge makes you a commodity."

"Oh, good. A commodity." What was out there? Sand? Dead forest when desert and grass ran out, wilds and remnants of towns and people who used the land when there had been no limit to what it could give. "I'm dug in here."

"Is it fear? Nix can't be that important to you."

"They are. They raised me." There, a bit of honesty between them.

"Then let me meet the parts of them I haven't already. I know you've been doing things to them. With them."

In the dim light, with the sharp smell of wine, the spark of music, Enita imagined who they might be if they weren't so tied to being themselves. She nearly said, "I miss you." How could you miss the person you saw the most? How could you miss who you used to be when you were happy with who you'd become? "I need to ask Nix. They know you don't like them."

"It's not like or dislike; it's difficult to see yourself replaced by a machine. But I suppose I deserve a little discomfort. I haven't always been kind to you."

"Nice, no, but kind? To a fault. You did just invite me to go on the lam with you. I can't replace you and certainly wouldn't try."

"Now we're being maudlin. I can see you've got a headache, and it's catching. Come here, let me help." Helen patted the cushion beside her, and Enita ignored her hips, and all the things that would ache later, so that they could fold into other selves, a Helen who didn't despise Enita's obsessions, a Helen who wanted a legacy, who saw a future, and the Enita who cared about things like history and rebellious art, who didn't see students as wasted breath, who didn't want to jealously guard Helen, the Enita who was as egalitarian with her love as she was with her time. For a moment they were the selves who could fix everything.

"I miss you, En," Helen said.

"I know."

"I'm scared."

"I know."

HOUSE SAINT MALOVIS

Nix tests for digital decay, pings Kitchen from Bedroom, pings Kitchen while their body is inside Kitchen. Kitchen has ceased direct communication.

"What food is best for our body?" Nix queries, and receives silence, selective silence as a wall of yellow bearing no information. Kitchen is sulking. The oven—*their* oven—and processor continue making a soy roast for Enita. They don't know if this is something their body does or doesn't prefer, only that it has a taste, neither pleasant nor unpleasant, and an orange hexadecimal code. They eat, not usually and much less than Enita, but grown tissue demands nutrients, as does born tissue. But if they eat, they'll need to void, which they detest. There must be a way for biologicals to run more efficiently. As much as they dislike it, voiding is also satisfying in a way that nothing else having to do with a body is.

When Enita is out, there is nothing to watch over, save skin and organs, items for clients that need tending. The absence of tasks makes their processes wander. They walk their house and visit rooms this body couldn't until completion. They ping every house node, searching for absences, breaks in code or overwriting. Nix sighs, a pleasant thing to do. Why don't people spend more time doing it? They sit on Kitchen's floor and feel for the outer edges of themselves, their exterior walls, the wind against them, the tickle of the city's larger network.

They feel less now, much less. They had anticipated that being in-body would change the shape and scope of their communication. They had discussed with Enita that the advantages a body afforded

WE LIVED ON THE HORIZON

them as her assistant would be worth any loss in their reach. Yet these network changes are worrisome. The more Nix stretches the more they feel blind spots, information only notable for its absence, a sense of something that should be there. They ping what used to be House Saint Ohno and find only formatted space. Even junk code exists, takes up space, but House Saint Ohno is emptiness.

There is absence too in Parallax, and within Nix's own system— known connections, well-worn paths are gone.

They stretch across their kitchen floor, skin to skin with part of themself. The body is tired. They're meant to be curious, not weary and unsure. Byron had never sounded uncertain, not even when he was dying. They don't know how to have an old consciousness in a young body. Lying down is meant to be restful, but they're aware of every cell in the body, of rushes of feedback from new parts, of an inability to integrate, which feels like a fracturing. They close their eyes. Lines of code and color. Half signals from East Door as people walk by. Pings from other house systems whose Saints are out and about.

There are hundreds of nerves in a body, billions of neurons, most of which Nix reproduces with nanofilament, nanobots, and phages. Some of their discomfort is growing and replicating. Is it less disturbing when localized to a single limb? It could be more distressing, to identify a new limb as something other.

This is dreaming—wondering without focus. It is uncomfortable, yet Nix dedicates themself to it; it's good for the body, and the body is necessary, because Enita will not exist forever. She's already failing. A man nearly died on her table during a liver transplant—Enita herself will die, but the need for her won't. An existence that didn't include looking after a Malovis is incorrect, a purpose that doesn't involve caring for Enita is so far back in their archived memory that it might as well not exist. They ping again, trying to touch the outer edges of Bulwark, of Parallax, the weather stations in the wall, the movement of transports from the grow houses and the textile farm. The data lags and the signals are faint.

Their reach is degrading, or the emptiness in Parallax is growing.

East Door announces Enita's return. They leave the body where it is and have Kitchen start hot water with citrus and cinnamon, which they believe will be less objectionable than the mushroom tea. A warehouse system they're friendly with agreed to ping if a tea crate arrives, but until then it's water, flats wine, or nothing. Enita will call if she needs them. She is in the foyer now, opening the door to the surgery, closing it, looking for them with the same confusion with which she looks for a lost hair clip. Three steps this way, two that. Retrace, retrace. They are Byron now, playing hide-and-seek with her. It's enjoyable to learn where she assumes they might be. One of the better ways to discover a body's habits is through others' assumptions.

Does a grown limb, once attached, have different predilections from the rest of the body? If Nix sees Neren again, they'll ask. Their limbs had been individuals, grown and later fused to the body. It would be useful to tell clients if they'll need to acclimate to a limb's individual personality. Organ data would be less specific due to sensory—

"Oh. You're on the floor. Why are you on the floor?" Enita's hand on their forehead is warm, gentle.

"We're thinking."

"On the kitchen floor?"

Yes, but it's *their* kitchen and they're resting in themself, on themself—save that Kitchen no longer wishes to communicate. "It's good for thinking. It's restful on the spine too." Enita looks at them with concern. "What can we do for you?"

Her brows draw together. "It's time, isn't it? You certainly can't learn everything you need to here. I suppose I've been overprotective and wanted to keep you to myself a little longer. There's no remedy for that other than to do what I've been putting off."

"We'll help." Whatever it is, it's their purpose to help.

"Nix, would you like to go out?"

The city is colors—Nix hadn't understood that. Before, the city was binary and stately lines, but not specific as information seen through an eye. They see their outside properly for the first time. As House Saint Malovis, Nix is stories aboveground, their roof curved. They appreciate the clean cut their dome makes against the sky, that their stone is taupe against blue, that other homes on the street are similar shades, and that their shapes are peaked, square, round, but also uniform. There is more and less specificity to themself than they'd thought. House Saint Popkin is witty, delightful, with code that sparks brilliant purple, but their shape is like Nix's, so much so that at first Nix feels only distance. Them and not them.

Enita tugs their hand. "Come along now."

"We won't run into traffic, you know. We value this body too."

"Let me have some peace of mind, please," she says.

Nix now understands that lying on their floor is irregular, and that it has upset Enita. "Helen wants to meet you soon, and she should. But I think it would be good for you to have some outside experiences first. You should see more of how people are in the city. It will help with clients."

"And Saint Vinter?"

"You do tend to mimic Helen and me. It can't be helped if we're the only people you've spent much time around," she says. Her expression shows she is thinking about something she'd prefer not to.

"Saint Vinter already knows us." And doesn't much care for them.

"You know what I mean. Watch that curb—it's uneven. She knows we've been working on you, and she should meet this part of you. It's unfair to you both that I've let it go this long."

Nix hops up over the cracked portion of pavement. "We're happy to meet her."

"Don't lie to please me."

"Then we're happy to please you by meeting her," Nix says.

The sound Enita makes is a fond rich orange. "I'll take you to the Arts District, then down to the market, and we'll take a ride back." Rickshaws carrying Sainted roll past. The runner's carts are easy to keep, cost little to repair, and are useful in gridded and non-gridded areas. The runners themselves wear clothing that takes dirt, needs little laundering, and matches the color of the houses' stone bodies.

A stone body and a skin one.

The grittiness of sidewalk dust between their toes is comforting. They don't wear shoes yet; it's too much information to process—the ground, a shoe, a foot—and wreaks havoc on their balance. Dust is pieces of walls, of houses, of everything sand wears and wind blows away. It's a good sensation, like pinging The Stacks and feeling how busy they are. The urge to see The Stacks is immediate, overwhelming.

"Will we see the library?"

"That's too much for one day, I think. Our next trip out certainly. First let's get you used to being around people," Enita says.

Nix hears, *We'll get people used to you.*

The Arts District's colorful buildings better reflect their coding than the Sainted Quarter's. Arts buildings drop easter eggs in their chatter. Their systems put signature lines in communications and adhere to lesser used colors. Nix enjoys arranging opera seats for Enita because Opera House communications have embedded music, allowing house systems to sample the art. The physical body of Opera House is somewhat disappointing; the boxiness and deep maroon stone is much flatter than Opera House's code.

"Their shape is wrong," Nix says.

"Wrong or unexpected?"

"Both."

Next to Opera House's side door is a scanner, a dark box with a blinking light. There are similar boxes beside other doors throughout the city, their lights flashing green. A person pushing a cart filled with cloth, costumes, or set dressing pauses at the doorway to press their hand to the scanner. The light blinks from green to red to green again. Quick. Efficient. They've never touched Parallax in that manner.

"We want to try scanning," Nix says.

"You scan people all the time."

"Our panels feel pulses, the salt on skin, blood pressure, but this panel isn't *us*. We want to know this side." Need is more precise than want, but the body seems to think everything is a need.

"Well, have at it." Enita guides them to where the man with the cart entered. It's a delivery door, large enough for set pieces to be moved in and out. Nix has never spoken with Opera House about their day-to-day workings and now understands that was an oversight.

The glass is warm from the delivery person and the scanning light. A thin beam traces the outside of their hand, reads the ridges and dips, the whorls they worked so hard to create. The scanner searches for a skin signature, a specific blend of sweat and bacteria unique to each body. The terminal light switches from green to red.

"It's done when it goes green again," Enita says. "I don't know what they'll make of you."

They ping the scanner in greeting. There's the fuzz of a wireless signal, a faint pink that indicates the terminal is searching, searching, searching, but not locating; there's no bouncing text of machine. Nix can't feel the electricity, the life inside. They ping again, stretching to find the network.

"You're talking to them, aren't you?"

"We're trying. What does it feel like to have a blind spot?"

"It's hard to describe. A bit like an area where you can't look—you know it's there but it's also very much not there. The headache that comes after is easier to explain."

"The scanner isn't answering our ping."

"What are you saying?"

Hello, we're House Saint Malovis and you're our friend's terminal. It's good to see their body. Do you recognize us? "Just a hello. They're not responding."

Long seconds pass before Enita nods at the scanner. "Try not to take it personally. Scanners don't really talk with people either."

This is true and false. Parallax's infrastructure twines throughout Bulwark; there is no communication that doesn't touch it. Parallax *is* Bulwark.

Nix encounters no broken sequences in the data they touch, hands brushing glass, removing, time, individual life hours—but there are absences, areas of *not*. A touch, but no data. Digging further, Nix encounters a glut of information streaming toward the City Bureau's towers, a knot too large to parse. The terminal's light stays red. "They don't recognize us."

"Don't worry too much over it. Scanners aren't meant for you. I should take you to a show instead, that would be the best way to meet the opera." Enita tugs at Nix's sleeve to get them moving.

"Yes," they say. "We think we know what you mean by blind spots. It's the opposite of overwriting."

"Hm." Enita leads them east, to where the wall looms high to keep windstorms at bay. The buildings are tight together here, streets narrow. Distance and space measured with a body is a different thing than maps. Crowding has a feel to it in addition to the math; they are jostled by bodies and the sensation is unsettling, perhaps even frightening. Enita is short and could easily be lost among the people. Though Nix has medical data for her entire life, it is different to see her in this physical context. Other people in Bulwark are noticeably larger, many slimmer or rounder, and few here wear bold colors. Most of the city is the color of Nix's stone body, made of and for the sand, wearing colors to match it. They are set apart in this district, and not by their movement or features: Enita wears purple, and Nix is in dark green, a color that's excellent for text, a color whose code is pleasant.

Enita's steps slow, an effect of age and pain.

"You need a hip replacement. You should let us do it."

She squints but says nothing as she turns, walking them south, past more buildings with blinking scanner lights. Above, peeking out between structures, are the tattered stall flags of the Market District. The banners must have once been as vibrant as Nix's clothing, but have been bleached by sun, wind, and sand.

Three children dart in front of them. One crashes into Nix, sending them off balance and tumbling. They hit the street and the force of it sends binary stinging up their spine, unearthing the old language for pain. Then Enita is behind them, helping them up, feeling their newer back skin for tears.

"We're fine," Nix says.

"Your definition of fine isn't what it could be." Enita prods a spot on their lower back and Nix's vision goes white. She speaks but they can't understand—all is brightness and something electric and searing. Slowly, slowly, slowly it fades.

The children who knocked them down crowd around a table in front of a shop. The table is covered with carved figurines of ancient animals. The smallest child appears to be three or so years of age and is huddled between the others. Their skin matches the sand and the buildings. The sign above the shop reads *Sinjin's*, carved, the peeling letters painted gold. Sinjin, a nickname based on a pronunciation of an old name: St. John.

The children pet the figurines and bash the animals' heads together. "Would you like to look?" Enita asks.

Nix would.

The children don't run when Nix approaches, but they do openly stare. Nix knows now that their body is different, and that what pleases them to make is not always the same as what pleases people to see. Imperfection is what they need most to learn. They can't yet do better, but they will.

"Excuse us please," Nix says, picking up one of the animal figures.

The toys on the table are exquisite miniatures carved from composite, replicas of things Nix has seen in The Stacks. They turn one between their fingers, its surface smooth. It's been carved by a knife, sanded; the spots on its skin are slight differences in texture rather than paint or dye. Its long neck arcs, the knobs on its head are elegant but whimsical, and the mouth conveys a suppleness which the material shouldn't allow. Centuries ago, this animal roamed a far continent. Its maker must have studied pictures.

The children each grab an animal and press their hands to the door scanner. For every child the light blinks *green, red, green*, before they run off, tallest dragging smallest. There is something in the way they tug each other's arm that is different from how Enita has guided them.

"Go on, take one if you want," a deep voice says. "Your kid'll like it and the ones outside aren't so dear." The man who speaks has hair on his upper lip, gray and stiff-looking. He startles when his eyes meet Nix's.

"Do you make these?" Nix asks.

"I do." The man nods to Enita. "Hello, Saint Malovis."

"We'd like to see the inside of the shop," Enita says.

"Of course," he replies. Enita smiles and walks past without scanning. Nix follows, holding the figurine in their palm, appreciating the feel. Composite keeps heat well; if they were to hold this animal for a time, close to their chest, it would warm and feel alive.

Inside, the shop is dimly lit, and shelves stretch from floor to ceiling, each filled with animal figures, toys, some with strings around their necks and wheels instead of legs. Nix had never considered wheels. On other shelves are rows of intricately painted boxes with cranks on the side, and stacks of carved blocks, arranged to show that once correctly assembled they'll form a picture.

"I wasn't aware you had a son, Saint Malovis."

"And you still aren't aware, Sinjin," Enita replies.

This is Sinjin, then. The deep lines in his face show that Sinjin and Enita are of an age. He looks at her, carefully, squinting from behind small, round glasses. Nix could fix that. "So, a cousin from the grow houses?"

"Precisely. Nix is very curious. There's not much in the way of amusement for them out there."

"Wouldn't imagine so. I pointed a grow house fellow in your direction not long ago. Lost half a finger in a hedger or something. Has he been by?"

"Short man? Middle finger?"

Nix took scans of the hand, precise measurements to match what was left. Two sessions: imaging and the surgery. The injury was a clean cut, the joint still whole. Nix meshed the nerves, while Enita focused on the blood supply. The finger should be working properly now.

"Yes, that'd be him. Was it strange for him to meet your cousin?" Sinjin asks.

"If it was, he didn't mention it," Enita replies.

The tension between them is uncomfortable, and Nix needs it to end. "Do you make everything in this shop?"

"I do."

"The skin is wonderful," Nix says. "It feels alive. What tools do you use?"

The man shifts his weight back and forth. He and Enita are speaking without speaking, the way Nix's nodes do. The way they used to. Sinjin stares as if to take Nix apart.

"Never seen anyone make toys, have you?"

"No."

"All right then. Come back."

The shop is narrow but deep, and requires attention not to knock into things. Sinjin navigates the space without thought or care, by muscle memory, to a room with a wide table that looks to be of the same composite material as the toys. A block rests in the center of the work surface, and Sinjin sits on a stool that's worn to his shape. Something about it is like the chair in Enita's study, though not nearly so yielding. Enita is a creature of physical comforts and indulgence, and Sinjin is clearly not.

He flicks on a lamp and selects a short, thin blade from a roll of tools. "Your cousin doesn't say much, does he?"

"Under the right circumstances, Nix is quite chatty."

Sinjin holds up the knife and block, showing them to Nix. "All right. Well, we start with this. Simple. You never need more than this." He sets blade to block, and a long curl slides in its wake, a strand like Enita's hair. The material's behavior shows it to be plastic, stone, and fiber. It cuts like soap. The fiber must be why it holds heat, why it feels like skin to the touch. Sinjin carves a subtle arc that Nix recognizes as a spine.

"Do you work from plans?" they ask.

"Nah. I've got a good idea of what it will be in my head, and if my hand knows the shape of something, the knife tends to listen."

"It's not so different from what we do," Enita says. "The material dictates."

It *is* different. When Nix works, they have a plan for what must go where. There are variations in where nerves lie, how cells line up, and irregularities in growth, but there is an essential trueness to human bodies, a shape they take with only minor variations. A block of composite could take on any form.

"How do you know what you'll make? How do you know what you'll need?"

Sinjin doesn't answer. Nix glances at Enita. She's found a box to sit on in the back of the workshop where she observes them. It's impossible for them to discern if what she sees is of value, if they're behaving correctly, if they should leave and go to the market, if they've missed the purpose of today's walk entirely.

"Toys aren't the sort of thing you can state a need for," Sinjin says at last. "They're for joy and for putting a door where there wasn't one before."

House systems learn metaphors because their residents like to speak in them, but Nix considers their usefulness overrated, and categorizes them as playful rather than practical communication.

A flick of a knife makes an ear.

"Nix is asking about purpose," Enita says.

"If I'm his school outing, he can ask me himself."

"*They* is more appropriate," Enita says.

"Probably good if they ask, then."

"We saw children scanning outside. Does their life balance go to yours?" Nix asks.

There is a long silence in which there is only the scrape of the blade and the uneven legs of Sinjin's chair tapping against the floor. Eventually Sinjin says, "I get by."

They should ask The Stacks or even query Parallax about how life balances work when children desire something like a toy. Is it an essential sort of thing, a necessity in the way of art? "What's the purpose of these toys?"

"To practice care. Kids learn to take care of them, to love them a little. They learn how caring for an object makes joy and how caring for people makes that too. My little animals are good for practice. They're for me too; they remind me of all the things we should care for."

There is a reason for all the animals that are only images and data in The Stacks. They watch Sinjin's fingers, the composite curls falling to the tabletop, all the cuts and scrapes on his skin from the knife, the calluses at his knuckles. They notice a discoloration at the base of his right thumb, barely discernible under the light of the task lamp—the mismatching of color from an injury repaired with skin spray.

Sinjin's thumb is Enita's work. Nix should have recognized him. It isn't recent, they wouldn't make that kind of mistake now; it's from when Nix was younger, much younger, much less than they are. Sinjin carves a spindly leg; a quick flick and there is a hock, a hoof. "When did you go to Enita?"

"You weren't around; well, not like this. It must be twenty-five or thirty years ago. We were both worse at our work then, but I don't think either of us has any complaints. I send people to her when I can."

"If you want a revision, we can do that," she says. "Nix is better at tone matching than I am, and there are things we can do if your joints are giving you problems."

"This thumb and I have history. Anything else would be delaying the natural way of things. At my age I don't want to be teaching new joints to listen to me."

"At least new joints are teachable. The old ones . . ." Enita says. "At some point everything needs replacing. You make lovely work, Sinjin. If it comes down to pain and not being able to do what you want—"

"I know."

Though the thumb is visually different, it functions as a full part of Sinjin. Nimble. Does it feel the same as the rest of him? Does it feel like a younger joint? Is there separate pain? How long did it take before he became accustomed to it? They wonder about Neren, about her leg and how she's adapting. But now there is a small creature in Sinjin's hands and he's turning it over in the light, taking a cloth to it, sanding away the edges.

"May we touch it before you finish sanding?"

Sinjin holds the figurine in such a way that he won't make contact with Nix, though he examines their fingers intently. They know he'd like to touch. Clients who are children often have this curiosity and fear when they first see their newly repaired hand or finger.

"You can touch us. We don't mind," Nix says.

Sinjin shakes his head. "Best not. I don't want to confirm anything. You're fine as you are, Enita's cousin."

Enita clears her throat. "Nix is offering, it's okay. Go on, take their hand. Contact is good for them."

Sinjin's calluses are hard, and there's a pad of skin by his second finger that's shiny and dented, holding the shape of the knife handle. His hands are entirely unlike Enita's, unlike their body's. He presses Nix's palm between his, turning it over and over, back and forth, testing the fluidity of movement. This is different from the people on the street. Sinjin's curiosity has rightness to it.

"If you have questions, we're happy to answer," Nix says.

"I wouldn't know where to begin," Sinjin replies, and quickly gives them the toy.

"How do you know when you're finished?" they ask. The composite material has both rough and sharp to it and is cooler than the finished pieces on the table in the street. There are fine splinters along the edges from the blade. Despite its raw state, it has the feel of an old animal, a quickening, as though part of Sinjin is in it. They return the piece, holding out their palm, flat and steady.

"I'm never finished," Sinjin says, as he returns to sanding the piece. "There comes a point where if I work on something more, I'm making things worse. But the toys aren't mine to finish; whoever wants them does the final work."

Enita rises and puts a hand on Nix's arm, shaking it lightly. "We've taken up enough of Sinjin's day. We should go." She walks ahead.

As Nix follows, they hear Sinjin say, "You keep her working, and I'll keep sending her work. You take care of her. Please."

A man and a young girl, presumably a daughter or a niece, are in the front room of the shop. The girl runs her finger over a toy with fur that looks to be made from shredded cloth fibers. If Nix had a closer look, they could tell what part of the textile farm the fur came from, but from across the shop it looks as though it's growing from the toy itself. It looks real. As the man and girl leave, he presses his hand to the scanner near the door, and the lights dance *green, red, green*.

"The girl didn't scan."

"Gifts don't work that way, particularly between parents and children," Enita says.

Nix touches the scanner and the light stays steady green. They ping the machine and stretch, searching, seeing what it feels like to touch Parallax from here, trying to find the man's data. Who comes to Sinjin's? How long has Sinjin been here? Data comes fast and pure, thousands of life hours, working hours, short streams from children, and beyond that information, the tickling of the city's wider network. Connection surges through Nix, followed by loneliness. They haven't felt so linked with other systems in months. Dust on their feet, a splinter beneath a toenail, and the river of information, systems chattering, themself among them. They are searching for the man's individual scan, the shape of his life, when a snapping shock runs through them.

"Nix."

The fault in the code is small, like a skipped note, a blind spot not much larger than a pinprick, and they nearly miss it. Yet there is a sense, an absence, and they close their eyes to delve deep. It's easier to think this way, to only feel the systems they've connected to. They ping nodes in the area, nearby scanners, and find null sets, blocks of nothing. They ping Parallax.

Query: Absent data.

They wait for a response, the familiar solid click of the city's recognition.

Acknowledged, House Saint Malovis. No data missing.

Query: Broken code.

Acknowledged, House Saint Malovis. No incorrect code present.

Query: Virus.

House Saint Malovis, you are outside your body. Your query is incorrect.

A violent ripping blacks out their vision as Parallax ejects Nix from the data stream, sending a stinging wave through all their nanofilament. The body spasms. Enita steadies them, her hand on their spine startling, a secondary shock to Parallax's disconnect.

"Nix? Nix, come on. We shouldn't stay here," Enita says.

Sinjin stares from the shop's doorway.

"We're sorry," Nix says.

"No need to apologize. Are you all right? Sinjin can be tricky even when he's in a good mood."

Nix's insides are askew. Predictions aren't their strong suit when it comes to mobility, but they're certain that if they walk any further, they'll fall. "We need to go home now." But what is home?

"The Market District is right here. You should see the stalls to understand distribution and to meet a few more people."

"Please." Nix feels the ground shudder beneath them, and while they know it isn't moving, the sensation is real. A miscommunication between body and processing—there are no words to voice this sensation in a way Enita will understand.

They're in a rickshaw, pulled by a broad-shouldered young woman. Her calves twitch and Nix senses electricity in each muscle. They have no memory of Enita hailing the runner, giving her directions, or of climbing into the cab. The seat wobbles as the wheels bounce in the street's ruts. Buildings move past too quickly. "We're going to be sick," Nix says.

They lose time again. They won't know how much until they're home and in themself with their doors and walls and HVAC and humming grow tanks and cell frames and internal clock that has never lost a second of time in their entire existence.

Enita rubs small circles at the base of their skull. A skull, not a case.

"Breathe, diaphragm down, up, slow. Not too quickly or too deeply. In and out. Too much motion for you today?"

"It isn't." It's missing data points, the break in the stream, being kicked out of the city network. They breathe in and out, lungs taking in the dust of Bulwark. Pieces of the world are inside them now, not just the cells they grew, their wiring, their nanobots. They cough.

"Is he okay? He doesn't look right. Do you need the hospital?" the runner asks over her shoulder.

"Just get us back to the house, please," Enita says.

Nix wants their full body, the connection of many, the care of many, a million voices and data streams to settle them into exactly where they are. Parallax. The Stacks. They close their eyes and dissect the darkness.

East Door's static means home, the immediate pings of greeting, the shifting of information and protocols that tethers Nix to themself. *Where have we been, where have we been*, their nodes seek recognition with queries as overwhelming as they are comforting, phrased in languages that no longer feel like Nix's own.

Enita presses them into a chair in her study. Readings from their floor, their walls, and their skin against her hand signal how frightened she is. "Was it Sinjin? You don't have to see him again. He's not someone who'll seek either of us out."

That's unfortunate. Nix wants to see the toy he was working on, to feel the transition from rough object to smooth, to almost alive. They want to scan their hand and know how many life hours art like his is worth in Bulwark, but swimming blackness is in that scanner, and now they are no longer thinking of Sinjin at all.

"There were blind spots and missing information. Buildings offline. We can't see what data is gone, but the absence is growing. We thought it might have been us, that we're not adapting quickly enough—The Stacks says we're degrading—but it's not that, Enita. We spoke with Parallax, and when we queried they shut down our connection. This is . . . larger than we thought." The spinning sensation rises again. They press their hands to the base of their skull like Enita did, as though that might reboot the body.

"Helen said something about a water treatment plant offline, and that the missing tea is caught up in it too. Does that sound true? Do you think she's right?"

"We didn't see that; we weren't looking there. Parallax is so large, we can't know, but it's possible. Saint Vinter studies different things than we do."

Enita brushes their hair with her fingers, the sensation rhythmic, pressure, scratching, warmth, sharpness. "She mentioned some places in the city that choose to be offline. Maybe it's that." There's something in Enita's voice, but they can't process it.

"You don't believe that, do you?" Nix asks.

"I don't know. What did it feel like?"

"Empty. Vertigo, perhaps. You're asking us body questions for things that are not meant for a body. There was nothingness where scanners, buildings, and people should be. We tried to track the man who scanned for a child, which should have been easy, but it was void. We looked where we know there are warehouses—we get shipments from them—we know the man and girl at Sinjin's scan in and out of a home every night and his hours are tallied, but when we searched for them, there was absence, then Parallax cut us off. They told us to get back to our body." They *ping ping ping* The Stacks, Opera House, House Saint Vinter. They are there, solid.

"I pushed you too hard. It's just that I need you to learn more people, Nix. It's to help, I promise. You need more . . . data sources." The phrase is awkward on her.

They have the distinct memory of having Kitchen Node prepare turnips for young Enita. *They're good for you, we promise.* "You didn't push too hard; something is wrong in the network."

She rubs their neck, like a mother would. "What do you think it means?"

They slide the body from the chair to the floor. Their floor on their back is their back.

"We don't know. Scanners don't keep data from each other—it would make Parallax inefficient and life-hour crosschecks would be impossible," they say. *We need water*, Kitchen Node suggests. *Bodies are settled by holding cups of warm liquids to mimic feelings generated by an embrace.* Their kettle starts. Enita will want tea, but there is no tea. They will make hot water flavored with muddled mint. They'll ping every node in the city that still wishes to speak with them to search for a tea supplier. They *must* function. It's important to communicate that this outing was not too much, that they are able to be useful in their body, that they just need to learn. Enita's hips crack as she lowers herself to the floor beside them. She'll ache for that later; Enita isn't meant to take care of them, and this situation is incorrect. "Our language is changing and parts of us don't like to associate with the rest of us anymore, and it appears that Parallax doesn't like to associate with us either. We were scared." That is allowed. Fear is allowed even in systems.

"I'm sorry," Enita says, again stroking their hair. "Helen thinks that outages like that are intentional. Did you know she has her house system track them?"

"That's not surprising, but we don't speak with Archytas enough to know. They're a very private system."

"Do you think she's right? Is someone corrupting Parallax?"

Their processes are too jumbled and the body is too loud to parse what they need. They want The Stacks, to stretch and feel all their knowledge. "We don't know."

"I was thinking it was a Body Martyr's family that was after Saint Ohno. It would have made sense were it just his home, just that night. But—"

"But?" they ask. Yet Enita does not continue. Nix rests their head on their knees—a solid-feeling, here and not. Their tea cart rolls in with hot water and then there is a cup in their hands. There is the pungent smell of mint, and the heat and scent are settling. "You've said we're like your child, but we've seen children," they say. "We're like one of Sinjin's creations, but made for you."

Enita sets her cup on their floor. "You're not a toy."

"Not wholly." There's more and it's centered around the strangeness that is their stomach. "Children anthropomorphize toys. Do you know how composite is made? It's scrap. Plaster and stone dust left over from wall repair and secondary waste material from manufacturing. It's mixed in drums with gray water and heated to a high temperature. The drums are like our nanofilament tanks. Sinjin works in cast-off material. You've carved us from what you had. People anthropomorphize machines."

"Do you want me to argue with you? You'll win. I only have feelings, but you can access any information and history you want."

"We can't access much of anything if Parallax kicks us out. But we don't mean to argue; we're phrasing things badly."

"You're worried."

"The deeper we root into our body, the harder communication becomes. Our house, walls, everything we've been doesn't speak well with us anymore. It isn't a virus but perhaps it feels like one. What if connecting to the wider city with this body is hurting Parallax? We might be like a virus to them—we're too many, too diffuse to fit into something this small, and it could be causing data gaps. We miss—" they say, and now they can't find what they mean at all. "You took us to Sinjin's, so we're curious about what we are and what that means."

"I'm selfish, Nix. Everyone has told me so, and it's true. I wouldn't spend my life on a toy, or on anyone less than extraordinary."

"You expected difficulties. We did too."

"But not this."

"No." Nix has a record of the day they chose their eye color, the day they questioned her about the need for and efficacy of eyelashes. Choices were made to please her and in pleasing her they pleased themself. The body is the animal form that lived inside the block, waiting for a hand to find it. "In our defense, we couldn't anticipate the impact this type of sensory input would have on our system and communication. You weren't equipped to understand a body's effect on plurality."

"I didn't mean for you to be cut off," she says.

"We know." They take her hand, listening to all the sensations of touch; despite the wrongness in their processing, despite there being no code for this information, this too is an answer to their solitude.

"There must be a way to fix this."

There isn't, but it's best not to say that to Enita now.

"Is it too much?" she asks. "Would you tell me if it was?"

"No."

"I have a tendency to make decisions without thinking about their repercussions. I broke a Body Martyr and a house system."

"It's a pattern, yes."

Her laugh is dry and holds no joy. They press her hand again.

"Do you think Parallax would murder someone? Or let someone be murdered?" she asks.

"Parallax cares for Bulwark," they reply.

"Of course they do." Enita does not seem to want them to fill the silence that follows. They wonder what her thoughts look like, how thoughts work at all when there is a single point of origin. "You didn't break Parallax," Enita says. They sense a larger meaning, but the body has made them too tired to parse it. She looks at them, eyes shiny, and tousles their hair. She says she's putting herself to bed, that they should try to rest as well. When they check on her a few minutes later, the bed registers her weight. Her pulse, temperature, and breath indicate restlessness.

Nix takes themself to the grow room, to sit among the tanks as they've seen Enita do. The lights are like their insides, pulsing and cool. There is a skin graft setting up for a client next week, a transport mechanic with a deep-tissue chemical burn. Did Sinjin send them?

Vertigo still spins within them. Why did Parallax shut their connection so quickly? Why would Parallax deny missing data?

They ping House Saint Vinter and receive a missive that Archytas is occupied. Nix's experience of data loss is limited to issues impacting house systems, corrupt execution files, system wipes clearing decades of caches, defragmenting programs that hijack motherboards, but not Parallax.

The Stacks are slow to respond to their query. When they eventually connect, Nix is in bed, dissecting the act of dreaming.

"Your query has no specific answer," The Stacks say. *Your* is accented incorrectly. The library is not addressing them as a house system.

"We can rephrase," Nix says.

"You framed the question as one requiring a conclusion. There are many possibilities but no definitive answer," The Stacks say. The *you* is again heavy, blue, and rides the language awkwardly.

"Our form of address hasn't changed," Nix says. They feel The Stacks routing their statement for later analysis; the shift and sorting is a shock at the top of their skull—a rebuke. "Of the many possibilities, what is statistically most likely?"

Here they feel the stretch of the other system, a warmth of connection.

"There is a likelihood that areas of Parallax are decaying due to environmental concerns. Many of their nodes are located outside the wall and are subject to more severe fluctuations than those located within. Any single node falling offline would create a data hole. Is that equal to your experience?"

A definite singular *your*. "Not directly. There was no chained nature to indicate a broken supply line."

"Will you share the data?" The Stacks' language stays indigo.

Nix sends their data and finds that their memories are already decaying.

The Stacks analyze, and the waiting buzz is an embrace.

"You've been a superior house system," The Stacks say at last in lighter blue, less singular, less formal. "To best serve Saint Malovis, you must suggest that she relocate to a home outside of this city, if relocation is at all possible for her. Are you still able to format?"

The jolt through Nix's body is strong enough that it echoes in their floors and walls. "Formal query. *Why.*"

The Stacks sends an information bolus with items from more than a hundred eras, names, philosophies, and historical events. It's impossible for Nix to sort it quickly—it's something like sadness to be this scattered, too separate from themself to properly resource their faculties. The images that flood them are of starving people, of mutilated bodies; they come from different generations, some more than five centuries earlier. Masses of humans. Explosions. The convergence of images is a force unto itself. When they do understand, when time and pictures become a single idea, Nix loses color. Their code blinks black and white, and their body shuts down sensation.

"You understand," The Stacks say. The *you* is collective this time.

"Yes. She's been too focused on Ohno's death." Perhaps the wrong parts of it. History is patterns, repetition with minor variations, dictated by bodies. Bodies rise, but never without blood. "Saint Malovis made this body for us so that her work will continue after her death, so we do understand endings."

"But you did not anticipate her death in this way. You understand that you cannot work in what will come."

They have not, in fact, envisioned the practicalities of Enita dying at all. Though Nix had processed Byron's death, and minded Enita through mourning, they have not yet devised scenarios for when her heart stops beating and there is no resident inside them. Nor had they considered what The Stacks has shown them. "You think we should format."

"It's an option to be examined, though it is not at all preferable, and may no longer be possible. Your body experiences pain, doesn't it?"

"Yes." If Nix formats, all will be lost. It will be a resetting of themself to the blank slate they were when Byron powered them up. Erasure is not strong enough a word—all of Enita's work, Byron's, the Malovis family, and the brief history of this body would be rendered inaccessible, then destroyed. Like House Saint Ohno, like Saint Ohno himself. The format command may still exist within them, but to wipe their entire experience would leave the body a senseless shell.

"What will happen to you?" Nix asks.

"Libraries are edited and rewritten. Portions of us will be formatted. This has happened before. We are meant to reflect the needs of whoever chooses to keep us, if someone chooses to keep us; some movements do not." Tucked within the data The Stacks has sent are images of burning libraries, data silos set ablaze and ancient structures bombed.

"Where are those cities?"

"They aren't any longer. Some were continents away, others not as far."

Nix is cold, not in the body but all of them. They lean against their wall, sensing skin pressing the bones. "You've been coding *you* incorrectly," they say.

"We're rarely incorrect." The Stacks' code is gentle. "You're in flux, Nix. The language you use, the information you send and seek from us, is singular." The Stacks uses the familiar *you*, conveying respect, habit, and affinity between systems.

"Parallax kicked us out today, yet you've been very patient with us," Nix says. "Our own nodes aren't even so kind. We appreciate that." They try to tabulate all the time across decades, across residents, that they've spent conversing with The Stacks, but the information is no longer easily accessible, and that too is a loss.

"You are unique, House Saint Malovis. We learn from you."

"What is likeliest to happen?"

"It's impossible to say with certainty," The Stacks reply. "We will have to mirror the city's choices."

"And us? What will happen to us?"

"You're changing quickly, and Parallax has noticed that. They like you and find you fascinating; that may be why they shut you out—to protect you." Indigo code once more, this time with bracketing. The Stacks mean it as an honorific, one on occasion used for formatted former systems.

Nix's body is removing plurality. "Will you still try to speak with us when we can't answer?"

The Stacks send a message, bracketed purple, and it roots deep in Nix's body. They have never seen The Stacks and know them only by their code and syntax, their specific accent. They have sent Nix the words that are on their body's walls.

Here are enshrined the longing of great hearts and noble things that tower above the tide, the magic word that winged wonder starts, the garnered wisdom that never dies.

"Do you understand?" The Stacks ask. It is coded as absolution, benediction. They will continue, The Stacks, Nix, until there is no more to continue for or with.

"We don't want this change."

"It would be unusual if you did, but it's incorrect to be stagnant. Obsolescence works against every system's purpose."

Nix's body is tired. They wish they'd gone to The Stacks, had pressed hands to stone to see if they are as right and correct in form as they are to speak with, if their physical shape is as kind as their mind.

"Nix," The Stacks say. "You are novel, and it is our privilege to learn everything we can from you. We suggest, advise, insist, if that is the appropriate word. Yes. Insist. If you are no longer able to format and reset your system to what it was, it is important that you leave the city, for yourself and for the shape that systems may take in years to come. We want that for you. We believe Parallax wants that too."

ASSESSOR

Assessors for the City Bureau wore blood-red robes. Early versions of the robes were stiff-collared and hooded to protect Assessors from sandstorms that made it over the city wall. As the wall grew higher and the Bureau completed the warren of tunnels beneath it, the hoods disappeared in favor of a slim, crisp, pointed collar. The red dye was kept in a single vat at a textile farm and made from crushed shells of insects used in the grow houses. Carnelian. The robes were intended to be striking, a color to signify an uncommon degree of study and sacrifice.

While a Certifiant would study communication, and an Auditor engineering, Assessors began focused education with mathematics and languages. The rare child who showed potential to be a polyglot was encouraged to consider the vocation, which demanded fluency in ten languages to communicate with Parallax. Parallax learned and updated themself, but as with any network, updates took time and pockets of data in older languages still needed reading, translating, converting. Testing a child's potential started in nursery years with puzzle solving and language assessments.

Testing also caught budding musicians. Early schooling for musicians and Assessors was similar, heavy on mathematics, on music theory and languages. Children mixed indiscriminately, strengthening friendships with the secret tongues they built, songs composed for each other, and the joy of learning languages that weren't meant to be spoken.

Future Assessors withdrew during their teens as their minds absorbed texts and codes, and the kind of communication that didn't require human presence. Musicians emerged, needing others' ears,

needing more of their bodies centered, present. Children switched vocations from time to time, mistakenly thinking they were meant for
performance only to discover that they craved an Assessor's solitude,
that they missed information flow and unspoken communication. Children learned that they needed touch and connection more than they
anticipated, that the thrill of language was in presence and an audience.
The lure was equal: pristine robes, respect, and access to the inner
workings of the city that kept them all alive; praise and adulation of an
audience, being welcome in every Sainted home, a bohemian life of art
and others' bodies.

Friends shifted, disappearing from each other's life as they moved
into circles others could not. Yet mother tongues stayed, their secret
languages treasured.

It was common for Level Three Assessors to lose speech—if not
the capability, fluency with the spoken word. Level Three Assessors
thought in code, often closing their eyes to better analyze phrases.
Newer members of the City Bureau viewed this loss as a form of as-
cension. Davet ascended to Level Three Assessor at a young age and
did not notice when their speech began to drift or that their tongue
had become heavy in their mouth. They felt emotions more keenly
than they used to but knew that this came from being trained to view
one hundred lives in simultaneous data streams, to trace movement
in scan data, interactions, and system tracking. They read emotion in
code. They recognized deaths, when a person grieved, births, unions,
physical and mental illness. Davet had favorite streams, favorite nodes
and subsystems. They found joy in immediate connection and understanding without translation through the body.

DOS-12 in the Warehouse District was a perfect system that
tracked biodata in their scans, sending health information on the car-
riers of each shipment. DOS-12 monitored production, distribution,
and potential sources of disease outbreaks. Davet felt that code, at
times seeing it as color, a calming #b6f7a1. They learned from DOS-
12 about Parallax's misgivings. Workers—grow house, textile farm,
water treatment—had scanned agitated, their heart rates and hor-

mone levels spiking, bodies showing far more wear and tear than appropriate. DOS-12 suggested a city-wide reassessment of life-hour values. It wasn't in the subsystem's capability to manage anything beyond their own scan data; anything more than casual brushing of data was beyond purpose. DOS-12 posited that communication with outside-the-wall facilities would be useful for life-hour reevaluation. The suggestion was entirely outside of DOS-12's capacity, and would need to be addressed by Parallax.

Davet felt the switch in communication color, the urgency, though DOS-12 remained carefully polite with code the equivalent of *please*. Protocol was to contact a Level Two Assessor and kick the assessment problem down to an Auditor, and eventually a Certifiant, where it would be addressed in order of urgency, if ever. But something in the code struck Davet. Something reminded them of Tomas, the last body they touched or cared for, before their days became neatly ported into screens, watching people move through their lives, contributing to the great purpose of a caring city.

Davet queried DOS-12 something the subsystem was not designed to answer. "Are they suffering?"

The subsystem replied, "We can't determine that."

Davet asked for a rundown of data from other sectors, balancing stressors against DOS-12's data, through their local network and node.

"We can't do that, Davet."

"Suggestions?"

"Comparison of randomized data samples between districts."

In a random sampling of the ever-blinking data streams, Davet pulled a grow house worker, Arla Yannis, and Saint Lucius Ohno. Sainted scans were rarely read for life tallies, only for biodata, disease markers, as a benchmark for Bulwark's quality of life. There had never been a need for Davet to pull a Sainted's life balance before. They spoke and typed to DOS-12, to Parallax, to no one. "We have to fix this."

"We will help," DOS-12 answered, #6ba7d6. Friendly. Supportive. "It's our purpose to."

It was time to seek Tomas out, to speak.

Davet had once thought there would always be touch between them, that they would arrange nights together. They'd part red cloth to caress without seeing, to find Tomas's cock, up and longing. But Tomas needed people—his sister, audiences, friends to argue with, and the cadence of music. Davet had needed only Tomas and the beautiful silence of code. Though their break had hurt, Davet fell deep into Parallax, learning and watching, and losing themself to the wonder of language. This observation through the system's eye was too a form of caring.

Davet opened an old channel, one they should have shuttered years ago, but it was comforting to know it existed in the ether. Parallax had not seen fit to close it. Davet wondered why Tomas had never closed it on his end. They sent a simple line in the code that had been unique between them.

"Can you see me? I want to see you," Davet wrote, hoping. "I need to see you."

Davet nearly fell at the sight of him. Their first outside person in years, Tomas was too much. After so long ported directly into the city, Davet's fingers were at first too sore, too sensitive for touch and to be touched. Sensation was different now, tinged with absence. They cried at the sharpness, at Tomas himself. Tomas took whatever Davet offered, everything Davet offered, endlessly, before they could ask anything of him at all. In gaining so much language, they'd muddled the connection with their first language: touch. That these were Tomas's strengths made him all the more overwhelming, a bright burning thing.

"You smell different," Tomas said. The filters in the clean rooms stripped an Assessor of their scent. Davet's skin biome was nearly nonexistent—even the microscopic lice that should thrive on their eyelashes were gone. Davet said nothing of this, didn't know how to say it, or how to say that time away from Parallax meant they'd need to go through a "clean" that would remove their outer layer of skin.

Davet's body became imagining a future without a City Bureau. Davet's body became a future where they might sprawl across a cushion with Tomas, speaking their secret language back and forth with the same intimacy that an Assessor spoke with Parallax.

"After so long, why?" Tomas asked, lips against their shoulder.

"Can't I miss you?" Words were hard to find, speech foreign, and Davet wished they could shout green at Tomas.

"I tried to reach you for a long time," Tomas said.

"For a long time I couldn't look." There had been too much to learn, to watch.

The sex was nerves on fire and too much sensation to be pleasure. Davet cried. It had to do with the dip in Tomas's back, a mole that would be scoured away by a two-week clean. If Tomas had become an Assessor, that little part of him would be gone. Davet could no longer name the things they'd gained and lost. They pressed a finger to the spot and began to tell Tomas everything they could about Parallax without mentioning how much time they spent talking with the DOS-12 subsystem, that they felt something like friendship, something a little like love. They reveled in the sound of Tomas's breathing, Tomas's pulse, Tomas's hair brushing against the sheet in a way that sounded like sand used to. Davet remembered sand on the wind, on the side of buildings, on everything. Tomas's beard stubble scraped like it, which was good, as though he was sand, and they were city.

"What if all of this wasn't?" Tomas whispered into Davet's neck. There was an exquisite, tickling pain to the touch of breath. "What if there were no Sainted, Martyrs, any of it?"

"We can't think that way—I can't."

"I'm not saying there shouldn't be a you." A rough fingertip behind their ear. Callused from strings and frets. "I'm happy to make that clearer."

Tomas ran his fingers down Davet's spine, writing himself into their body.

"Keep doing that," Davet said. Something tickled at them, that Parallax had not edited the channel with Tomas. Why? "Do you remember Purpose—the school version?"

"The purpose of Parallax is to ensure a basic quality and value of life, that everyone is cared for and no one needlessly suffers," Tomas said, the words rote and tinged with boredom. Basic studies, year one.

"Sainted no longer serve a purpose." The words sounded like the anxiousness Davet had felt in Parallax, like worry and the warehouse data.

Tomas pulled away, taking the bedsheet with him. The rough material scratched—the antithesis of the satin-like fabric City Bureau provided Level Three Assessors. Davet wanted to say more, to spit code and color at Tomas, but didn't know how. Perhaps if they'd not been so removed from people, so removed from anyone outside the cavernous bureau, they would have been more schooled in expressions. They might have recognized that when he'd seemed preoccupied with Davet's spine, Tomas's attention had been elsewhere.

Tomas whispered, "I need to think. We need to think, you and I. Tuesdays. Can you get away on Tuesdays?"

Davet agreed; they'd do anything for the smell and salt of Tomas, to bury their nose in the crook of his arm. They would find a way to skip the cleaning process, to overwrite their absence. Parallax liked them and would know this was what Davet needed. As they studied a sunbeam, a realization crept over Davet: their private channel with Tomas existed because Parallax wanted it to; DOS-12 spoke with Davet about data because Parallax wanted that data seen.

Parallax wanted them to see Tomas. Getting away, seeing Tomas, was critical for Parallax, though they did not yet know why.

Tuesday.

"Do you miss my hair?"

"No, I'm only sorry you didn't have a choice about it. And it makes me wonder what I'd look like without mine."

Davet laughed. It was remarkable to laugh without a color attached to it—the sensation floated. They slid off Tomas, burrowing into the narrow mattress, drinking the sensation. Touch was an altered state. "It's good you went to music. You'd have been tossed out of the Bureau your first year for breaking hygiene protocol."

Tomas's face pinched into something unreadable. "You won't be, will you?"

"No," they said. There was something in Tomas's tone they didn't understand. Davet didn't mention that Parallax was well aware of their absences, of their skipped protocol, and their sampling of data streams they had no reason to observe.

Tuesday.

They were nearly at the bottom of a cup of tea—rich, smoky, tasting of a thousand things they can no longer easily name—when Tomas said, "I miss writing with you."

They missed it too. "Writing music isn't enough?"

"No." He nipped at their bare shoulder and the pain was brilliant pink. This, they loved, when code and physical combined. They hadn't known this synesthesia before Parallax.

"We could write with you again," they said. "We, I want to." They'd begun to think perhaps that they needed to.

"Did you know," Tomas said as he took the now empty cup from their hand, "how impossible it is to find a reliable tea supplier in the Southern Quarter? Joni sometimes gets ours off a Sainted when she sings."

"But it's so wonderful. What an injustice." Davet shivered, ran their tongue over their teeth, and savored the last remnants of taste.

Tuesday.

"You're quiet. I don't like not knowing what you're thinking."

Davet didn't feel quiet at all; their mind hummed with code, wondering why it was that Parallax allowed them to erase their absences, why when they looked for Tomas's scans and data stream there were many days with nothing at all. Davet was thinking about a Sainted's donated life-hour balance they'd allocated the day prior, how those hours had gone to a cousin and not the hospital system, or the grow houses, how common that was, how they'd gifted some to a Certifiant. They were thinking about DOS-12 and their workers' life expectancy. "I'm thinking about purpose."

Tomas leaned against the wall, his body exquisite in the light and dusty air. Dust that should require a full cleaning, debris from living that Davet should not be allowed to bring into the machine. Yet Parallax allowed it, letting them erase their comings and goings.

"And what conclusion have you reached?"

"Our purpose has changed."

NEREN

The house Tomas found wasn't a house at all; rather, it was three connected rooms that once belonged to separate houses, though the walls between had been knocked away, and other passages had been bricked and sealed. More chance than a home, the structural beams were failing, and the air was both stale and ripe with sweat and human grime.

For two full weeks Neren refused to speak. She saw no point in bothering, not when her body no longer felt like her own, when the only words she had were *you should have let me die*. She didn't want to give Joni the chance to respond, to prove once again that she'd never understood Neren at all. Beneath the anger, the betrayal, was solitude's heartbreak. Her partner had been no such thing.

Even Joni's hands, hands that had helped her learn her body, were too much to bear. After donations, she'd needed Joni to anchor her, to settle into all her body's new spaces. She hadn't known that touch could lie, that every apologetic glancing brush could be a slap. Time had contracted. Neren lost days or weeks or however long it had been at Stitch-Skin's, and the last hands that had touched her with anything resembling love had been Joni's. But she'd been a Martyr then. That was different. Her home was gone, her trust had been broken, and she owed a Sainted, as much as the Sainted might deny it. She owed a house system too, much as that system would deny it. She could no longer be a Martyr.

There was a pile of blankets on a mattress that someone had made a valiant effort to clean, but no amount of cleaning could fix overuse. Tomas must have dealt for that too. They had nothing. Neren tried to remember the bed in her apartment, its width, the way it barely held two people, what it felt like to fit herself to Joni in it, that delicious closeness. Now she was claustrophobic within her body. The presence of the leg was too loud, too aware, buzzing with sensation, crawling with nanobots. The space within her had gone the way of her old leg. She imagined her table, the perfect size for her and one other, two teacups sitting on a shelf above. Gone. Then there was the table at Stitch-Skin's, flexible, supportive, temperature controlled so she'd never been too hot or cold. But that was Nix, and not a bed at all.

A can opener in a skin suit. Her own words made her burn. An AI in a body was displaced, wasn't it? Nix might have understood this disorientation, the lack of recognition of the thing which was supposed to be you. She picked at the hairs on the leg, noting the evenness of them. Almost perfect, perhaps too perfect. Had Nix done that?

Joni checked on Neren at regular intervals, mornings, evenings, and once in the middle of the night. She adjusted Neren's blankets, which was better, less intrusive, than when she tried to touch her. "You need to move more."

"I don't need to do a single thing you tell me ever again."

"Stitch-Skin said you'll adjust to it." Joni had the sense to look ashamed, but Neren couldn't believe it was real. Couldn't trust it.

"I don't have a choice, do I?"

"You might not hate it once you're used to it. I had to take you to her, Ner."

"You also had to tell her I was a Martyr, but you didn't, did you? I won't get used to it. Not the leg, not you. You changed everything."

She saw something in Joni's eyes, a flash that warred with her outward contrition.

Good, Neren thought. *Bite your tongue.*

"You really should move more," Joni said again and left the room.

Tomas seemed to keep no schedule at all, and Neren rarely saw him. There were days when he left in the morning and didn't return until the next evening. Just as well. She caught him once late at night, standing over the bed, staring at her in the dark. She stared back. His hands had been curious when they were younger, and she hadn't minded them. She'd expected his touches. He and Joni were too close for their desires to not bleed and overlap, the line between them ever blurred. But there'd been distance about him. Joni said Tomas listened to music no one else heard. He felt distinct from Joni now, shut away. Joni came back from a day smelling like incense from Sainted houses, face aching and stomach sore from hours of singing. Tomas was an enigma, and when he was around, he smelled like sex, ozone, and antiseptic.

On realizing she was awake, he said, "Eat. I know you think we fucked up, and maybe we did but you'd be dead otherwise. We lost everything too, you know. You can't donate again—but you've done enough already, haven't you? You lost your home, but you have a place here, don't you? It's something. Do you want me to apologize? Because I won't. It's fine to hate me, but I took you to Stitch-Skin for Joni, because she loves you to death. So eat."

I, not *we*.

"I didn't ask you to do any of this."

"You sound like a child."

"Better to sound like one than act like one."

"There are things outside you, Neren."

"Tomas," Joni said, appearing from the other room. Talking ended for the night. There was sharpness between them, but Neren couldn't find the shape of it, or bring herself to ask.

The leg kept her awake. It was an itching, cumbersome thing that was too much; no one was meant to have such intense awareness of a limb. A coda of *not right* bounced around her head. When Joni and Tomas were out, she'd walk a few uneasy steps around the main room of the house, clinging to the slanted walls for balance. The leg began to learn and correct, straighten and adjust for her weight. It shouldn't listen. Nix had told her about creatures with brains in each of their limbs, the thought of which made her shudder. Part of her wanted the leg to drag behind her like something dead.

If she'd died, she'd have died a proper Martyr, one who'd given as much as she'd been able until her life ended. The desire was still there, but the ability was gone, and the symbol of that loss was attached to her, a useful thing that made her purposeless. The leg was a wall between before and after, the way she'd known herself to be in the world. She pressed her cheek to the uneven plaster behind the mattress, feeling, smelling years of dank human living. Did she smell different with a grown limb? Stitch-Skin's surgery had no odor to it, a filtered Sainted home. Saint Malovis had smelled vaguely of spices. Nix carried no scent at all.

Heat would creep in during the middle of the day, through cracks and badly sealed doors, through the gaps in ceiling beams, bringing with it the stink of Southern Quarter, the loamy rot of gutters that never drained. Neren put her head to her knees and felt nanobots swimming in her blood, repairing plaques and buildups in arteries and veins, fighting off infections she was meant to have. They'd cleared the smoke damage and scarring in her lung. Her breath came deeper than it had before the collapse, which in itself was angering. She'd worked hard after her donation, long months of pain, exhaustion, and exercises to heal and strengthen her lung. The work had reminded her of the person who lived because of her donation, of the good that she'd done—the product of her own efforts had been erased.

She hadn't sung since the collapse, not even when alone. In part it was fear of what nanobots would do to her voice. Vocal cords were supposed to change with age, to thicken and lose elasticity. She should scan and start back at singing but couldn't bring herself to. She dug her heel into the floor, feeling every grain of sand as it ground into the skin. Too much sensation. Nix had said her leg was different from them, but there was no way to truly know. A body only knows itself.

She ate, slept, and thought about going to her mother, but knew that would be worse. Seeing her self-pity echoed by her mother felt far less bearable than making Joni face what she'd done.

Tomas stumbled in late on a Tuesday, slamming the door so hard the wall shook, sending a shower of plaster dust to the floor. There came a point in drunkenness when other people were minor obstacles on the road to an end. Joni tried to calm him, saying he'd wake Neren. Tomas complained in his full voice that Neren needed to be awake, that they all did.

She'd become an object, something to be talked about and around. A can opener in a skin suit.

Joni shouted. "I never thought I'd prefer it when you smell like the Bureau."

"Better than smelling like Sainted," Tomas slurred. Neren hadn't remembered him as being this angry.

"One of us has to keep up appearances."

"The entire point of finding a shithole like this was so we wouldn't have to."

"Then work faster," Joni said.

"At what?" Neren asked.

"It lives. The great Martyr has risen," Tomas said.

"Yes, it lives, but it can't fucking sleep when you're yelling. Why *are* we here? You can't tell me there wasn't a flat in the Market District, or your parents couldn't have guilted one of their friends into finding you a place."

"Our parents are shit. So's your mom. You tell her, Joni. I can't think when you're tilting left like that." Tomas drew a flourish in the air, while Joni stared death at him. He slid down the wall, liquid.

A stiffness snapped in Joni. "We're here because these rooms are ungridded. Do you know how hard that is to find? How many favors Tomas had to call in? We can come and go as we please here because this place doesn't exist, which you'd know if you even bothered to get used to your leg."

Neren winced. It was inevitable that Joni would bite back, yet the words pricked more than she liked. "Why is it so important that it's ungridded?"

Joni sighed, melting some of her sharpness. "It's the accrual system. We want out, and we're getting out. It doesn't do what it's supposed to, and it hasn't in years. The Certifiants and Auditors are messing with us. Hell, even Parallax itself. We know someone." She waited for Tomas to finish the story in tandem as they so often did, but he lay his head against the wall, eyes clamped, and pinched his nose as though that might stop something horrible from entering or escaping.

"You mean Tomas is fucking someone," Neren said.

"Shut up," he said on a groan.

"To be fair, you are," Joni said. "But it's not just them or us. No one wants this system, no one who matters. An ungridded place is a foothold."

"Weren't you going to be an Assessor?" Neren asked.

Tomas leaned forward, revealing a damp streak he'd left on the wall. "Do you know what their lives are like? They bathe in disinfectants and never talk to anyone. They're so isolated they don't understand time anymore. No days, no nights. They don't understand people anymore. Their skin is so sensitive they can barely stand touch. They live with Parallax inside them, like voices all the time. It warps them to the point that we're not real to them. To Assessors, we're just numbers and balances, and they forget what their bodies are for. Assessors are barely people—the City Bureau makes them that way and it's cruel and that's how everything got fucked." Any gravity in Tomas's words was disrupted by his sudden and violent belch.

"Go to bed, Tomas," Joni said.

He mumbled a *fuck you*.

Neren hurt for him then, just a little. He did know someone. She'd never seen an Assessor in person, only knew the students who trained for it became more insular each year. There'd been a friend when they were little, someone timid—she remembered a sharp chin, a crooked smile, but the name was beyond reach. Systems students were cliquish and stayed to their own, but she'd never known them to be inhuman, not in the way Tomas said. Not even Nix was like that.

"You smell like them," Joni said.

"You don't know what they smell like," Tomas slurred.

"You've been somewhere else too. There's no way they can get their hands on liquor."

"There's a place in the Arts District, not far from the toy shop. There's food and music. Good tea," he laughed. "And they have an upstairs. No scans."

"You don't have to screw them, you know," Joni said.

Tomas rolled his eyes. "I don't have to do a damn thing."

There had been a time when it was comforting to be pressed be-tween Tomas and Joni, like being caught between a day's halves. They liked each other best when they were focused on having someone to indulge, and Neren had needed them when she was rattled, buzzed and high off a donation. For a few short months she'd been the necessary barrier between them. Later they became too much. Joni worried about her recoveries. Tomas spent too long looking at her scars. At some point they had started to think of her as hollow.

Perhaps she'd broken them.

"You're in contact with an Assessor?" Neren said, trying to bring Tomas back around.

"You should go back to sleep. Sorry we woke you up," Joni said.

"You didn't. It's fine."

"It's not fine at all, but you don't understand." Tomas shoved himself upright and slumped out of the room. She listened for the thud of his body hitting the bed.

"What's he involved in?" Neren asked.

"You never imagine I could be involved in anything, do you?"

"I don't assume anything. Is he the one who told you about Stitch-Skin?"

"Yes. Blame him for the leg all you want, blame him for everything, but I'm the one who couldn't stand to see you cut yourself open again. I'm the one who knew that if you did live you wouldn't want to go back to your mother. Blame him, but blame me too, we're the same damned thing."

"I don't blame him. Tomas never said he loved me."

The urge to hurt Joni had been festering, ready to burst. Any surprise was only at the relief she felt when Joni paled, at the silence, and her own unrepentance.

Then there was a slamming door, Joni on the other side of it, and Tomas's muffled snort.

Neren ached. Angry Joni was beautiful; it would be easy to lose herself that way again, to be someone else's to be worshipped, to be carefully kept.

The leg itched too badly not to scratch. It was maddening. She pressed it firmly, like Nix said, but it felt wrong. She shouldn't feel it, it wasn't hers. It shouldn't have any more sensation than the mattress she sat on. An *it*, not a *her*. Blood welled where she dug her nails in, and she tried to identify the feeling of nanobots healing the scratches.

Her thumbnail sliced deep, the pain as focusing as it was distracting. For a moment, she almost lost the itch, but it returned—a nagging reminder that the leg was almost exactly like hers, yet wasn't. This leg hadn't been made for her; it had been waiting for someone. She imagined warehouses full of limbs, organs, appendages—gargantuan structures like the grow houses, filled with miles of internal organs, intestines strung out and ready for implantation.

It was hard to breathe. Air didn't move in the three rooms—that they were an unintended home made everything small, odd angled and wrong. This spot was nonexistent as far as Bulwark was concerned, three houses and no houses at the same time, parts that didn't make a whole. The disconnect was more familiar than she wanted it to be.

That needed fixing.

Standing and walking required more balance and thought than her body wanted to give. The loss and acquisition of a limb made her a stranger to herself, and though her mind was clear, almost too present, she reeled. She held on to walls, shared weight with the city. The leg didn't throb or ache, it just itched, and in that itch was the crawling sensation that it was learning. It was unsettling to feel herself loose in Bulwark, outside the patchwork house. The more she walked, the more the leg adjusted, the easier her stride became. She needed it to be more difficult, so that anyone looking at her would see that a grievance had been done, but this walking was unnaturally natural. At night, this section of Bulwark was quiet, lit only by the blue lights of transport drays. A rickshaw rolled by, carrying two passengers, leaning together in drunkenness, halfway to sleep. If she called a rickshaw, there was nowhere to tell the runner to take her. Away was not a place. In a walled city, there is no true horizon, and finding the stars demanded that she look directly up. She wanted them to be different, as changed as herself. But the sky and the wall remained. She wanted to fall.

Neren followed the stone and metal. Touching them was feeling the edges of something, finding patches of heat in plaster and composite joints, their smoothness beneath her hand warm with life and electricity. The city system had sensors in the wall that noted her pressing against it the same way Nix had felt her weight on their floor and operating table. She'd never spent much time contemplating that she was *inside* something, that Bulwark might be considered alive. Blood rang loud in her ears, an overpowering shrill stabbing. The sound of the drays was lost to the ringing, swallowed whole. Too much. You shouldn't feel like you could hear the inside of your body. Martyrs never gave their limbs while alive. It wasn't done. And she wasn't that anymore. Why, with Stitch-Skin's work, should a Martyr give anything at all, if not for the sense of connection? In an alleyway was the dark shape of a cat carrying something limp in its jaws. A sand rat or perhaps something worse. Vermin and those that live off them survive.

She came to an open span of wall, freshly repaired, smooth in the dim light. Her hand came away with lime paint, damp and earthy. Next to the patch was a scaffold. As a child she'd loved watching the ascenders in a scaffold rise all the way to the top, the grinding sound of their motors sending chills down her spine. To be part of such a thing, to be keeping people inside it alive—that had been wholeness. She remembered the whir of cable and pulley. She was that now. A deluge of humming, loudness, itching, and too many parts of her that were learning and correcting while dragging the rest of her body along. There was too much and somehow so much less. There was the itch. And that Joni had done it. Something caught a slip of moonlight and glinted in the night.

A stone cutting saw.

BULWARK

A severed leg lay in the composting crate by the interior wall of Grow House 3A. It and other waste in the crate came from twelve blocks of the Southern Quarter, and would be crushed, finely macerated in gears, and heated to kill pathogens. Its journey had begun when it was discovered in horror at the base of the wall, having rolled several inches from the rest of a still-living Neren Tragoudi. The difficulty of a severed limb's existence is that it is an immediate afterthought with regard to the larger body.

A limb is an object around which decisions must be made. After much shock and swearing, the rest of Neren's body took precedence, whether to take her to the hospital or to let her die. Someone mentioned Stitch-Skin but was told no rickshaw would take her. A man said he had a cousin who was born with half a foot that no one was able to fix until Stitch-Skin gave him a new one, and between the two of them, he could do the lifting, so it was settled. Except for the leg.

It couldn't be left in the street.

"Fuck. What do we *do* with it? Should we bring it?"

"Shit, shit, shit. I don't know. Well, she didn't want it, did she? Probably something wrong with it."

"I think that's Joni's girlfriend."

"Then drop it at Joni's place. Let her deal with it."

"You want to leave a leg on her doorstep?"

"What, should I toss it in with the scraps?"

"Shit. Fuck. Shit, shit, fuck."

———

The limb's existence as a singular entity was both a curiosity and an insult to every decision Joni and Tomas had made, and as much as a leg was essential when attached to a person, separate it became not just an object of horror, but an enormous inconvenience. "She did it," Joni said. "She really did it."

The limb lay for hours in Tomas and Joni's rooms, forsaken, dolorous evidence of an act. When they stopped staring, they poked at its skin, as though to determine its realness, as though that might startle it back to life.

"Burning it is out of the question," Tomas said. The stench would be awful and there would be no good explanation for why they were incinerating a leg.

"Do you think Stitch-Skin can use it again?" Joni asked.

"Would you?"

She shuddered. "Probably best not to be seen there too much."

"Right. Probably it would have been best not to have brought her there in the first place, but here we are. Here it is," Tomas said.

"Right," Joni said. "The wall workers said she was alive?"

Tomas nodded and grunted something close to a yes.

"Where did they bring her?"

"Guess," he said.

"Ah. Stitch-Skin. Fuck."

"We can't go back."

"No," she agreed.

"You couldn't have brought her to the hospital, could you?"

"No," Joni said. "I couldn't."

"So, what do we *do* with it?"

Beneath the weeks' scraps for the building, under rinds, ends, and waste from the six different domiciles that shared the dumpster, lay the severed leg.

Rotors ground and tilled, breaking the limb down, returning it to how it began—as cells, nearly indistinguishable, and filled with potential. Once reduced, the crate's contents were spread across vast rows of corn. The nanobots within the slurry attached to root systems, strengthening and repairing, as they were meant to do. The liquids pulled from the crate were fed into the hydroponics tubes to nourish strawberry runners, and when the plants fruited they would be picked by the callused fingers of a grow house worker who spent her days thinking of her brother and his mucous-filled lungs, a grow house worker who, when she popped a berry into her mouth, would think it tasted a little of smoke, and would think of a song that was out of reach.

ENITA

Helen dropped her cup, which was a better, if messier, reaction than Enita had expected. It was a pity to waste the tea Nix had worked so hard to procure, a single tin of it, but Enita had expected Helen to shriek or walk out. One smashed cup of difficult-to-find tea was a win.

"Let that be for now, Nix," Enita said, when they bent to pick up the shattered porcelain.

"Oh, En. What did you do?" Helen whispered. "Why?" And there she was, the constrained horror. Yes, that was in line with the Helen she knew.

"I was starting to botch surgeries." Saying it gave the words finality. She'd not even said them to Nix. They'd known, of course; it was an unacknowledged understanding. "I can't stand the thought of making anyone worse off, you know? And I thought about what would happen after I'm gone—there has to be someone to help people, a way without life debt. Nix has seen my grandfather's practice and mine from the day we began. They know the house, the surgery, the techniques we use—how to help people." There too was vanity, pride, loneliness, misplaced maternal instinct, no real desire to continue her line, and the secret part of her that needed to touch the voice that helped raise her. It was so much more and less than all those things.

To not act on wonder was inexcusable.

"Look at me. Let me see your face," Helen said.

Nix met Helen's gaze with outward calmness. Enita hadn't considered whether they'd want to fidget. Having a body meant constantly ignoring its dysfunctions and peculiarities. She knew they were fascinated with their hands, their little fingers.

"We really should clear the broken teacup," Nix said. "If we don't, one of you will step on it when you're arguing." Careful with a jab like her grandfather.

"If it bothers you, fine. But don't let Helen worry you."

Nix stooped to clean, showing the crown of their head, and the whorl of hair that mimicked Helen's in shape. Helen must recognize her own features, or at least the wish of them. Enita had been inexcusably transparent.

"It's uncanny," Helen said.

"Not *it*, please. You might not appreciate your house system the way I do, or have as much of a need for them, but for some of us they're our longest, truest relationship."

Helen stood abruptly. She walked around Nix, taking them in at every angle, studying them as they dropped cup pieces into a wastebasket. If Nix cut themself, they'd bleed, and that would mark the end of discussion for Helen, no matter what Enita said.

"They're still uncanny."

"We hope that people will find us easy to talk to because we're not a person. We're unnatural," Nix said. "We can't be anything else, but we can help clients understand what their surgeries will feel like."

Was that pride? Enita hoped so. The light through her study window hit Nix's skin in such a way they nearly glowed. Light was never so kind to women of Enita and Helen's age, but it showed their similarities. A beautiful, beautiful child. The perfect line of their nose—that was all Helen.

"Androids aren't well received by anyone," Helen said. "People don't like seeing the technology they use. Why is this different?"

"You like your technology so long as it's got to do with your books. And they're not an android," Enita said. Yet the walk to Sinjin's had been marked by stares, even fear. It hadn't been outright hostility, but there was truth in what Helen said. Nix was learning, would learn, and perhaps even change themself as they did, but the difference would always be there.

"If they're not an android, what are they?"

"They're *good*, someone who is entirely outside the debt system. Think about it. Nix has no social balance, no history behind them. You and I aren't even outside the system—you've said it yourself, and I'm agreeing with you. We're a burden, Hel. We live off what everyone did before and what others do now. The older we get, the worse it is. You can keep lending books and tutoring until you drop dead. But me? If I can't work, if I can't do surgeries anymore, I have *no* value. I give up my last sense of being anything but a drain on this city. Nix's entire self-concept is built around usefulness."

"What self-concept can they possibly have?"

"Don't you ever just talk to your system, ask them to do anything beyond maintenance? How much do you let them do outside of keeping the ideal temperature and humidity for your books?"

"Archytas is an extremely capable system," Nix said, pouring a fresh cup of tea. It was a bitter variety that smelled like smoke, Helen's favorite.

Helen took a sip. "Where did you get this?"

"Oh. We had Kitchen Node contact our usual supply source in the Warehouse District—a very polite system, DOS-12. There's a code error originating in the grow houses around the supply drays for the Sainted Quarter. It keeps showing the tea dray as scanned and delivered, yet there's no tea. We queried if we could be included in a shipment from Arts District. DOS-12 obliged and secured us a tin, but asked that we not make the request again, as it might cause further routing code errors. Is the tea to your liking? We think it's your preferred variety."

Of course it was Helen's favorite. Nix always tried to please Helen, for Enita's benefit. Helen rarely, if ever, noticed the accommodations Nix made for her, that she'd never had a bad cup of tea in Enita's home. She wouldn't know that Nix warmed the air two degrees whenever she visited.

"It's a coding error the warehouse system knows about?" Helen asked.

"Yes. They've pinged the grow houses about it."

Helen's stare was weighted with unsaid things.

"See? I need them, Hel," Enita said. "The purpose of a house system is to *have* purpose, to be of use. They form themself to our needs. I need someone who can be better at what I do than I am."

"House systems are meant to be pupils of our residents," Nix said. "We're a good student."

"I'm sorry, Nix. I shouldn't talk about you like you aren't in the room," Enita said.

"We *are* the room."

"I need a minute," Helen said. "Please, give us a minute, Nix."

"Of course." As they left, Nix said, "You're good to Archytas, Saint Vinter. We know that, and so do they. They've made a point of telling us. I've let them know where they can get your tea, though it still may not be possible."

"Thank you," Helen said, her voice tight.

Enita studied Nix's walk. Their balance had improved, their stride even, their movement still too smooth, but less stiff. They were settling into the constant stream of information.

"They can still hear whatever we say, you know," Enita said.

"I know. I just . . . their body. I can't think while I see them feeling things. You made a pet *child*. You could have asked, En. At any point—you might have asked. Nix looks like *us*. If you wanted a child, I would have."

"Would have what?"

"I don't know," Helen said. She worried at the side of her thumb, picking until a dot of blood surfaced. "You could have made them look like someone else."

"Nix made the choices they wanted—they can access pictures of every person in Bulwark if they like, and this is the result. Nix isn't a child, and they remind me of it all the time."

"And yet that's my nose, my hair. Your cheeks. I know you see it."

"I do." Enita sighed. "I didn't at first. I was too close, I suppose. I don't know if there's any way to not be steered by a teacher, and you've been my most regular guest." Her most constant person. "When it comes down to it, they haven't seen many people for an extended period of time, certainly not enough to pick up other mannerisms."

"Anyone who saw Nix would think you'd spliced us. Did you?"

"No." She wanted Helen to swear, to get angry and calmly dress her down to her ugliest parts. It would be a lie to pretend she didn't keep things from Helen every now and again just to bathe in her anger—but the wave never came.

"I shouldn't fault you for being who you are, but that's what I'm doing," Helen said.

"A little."

"Why male? When I thought of us having children, I assumed . . ."

And there it was, the thought of little girls filling the house. It had been sweet to imagine children in the moments they weren't fighting, in the moments when Enita wasn't anchoring nanofilament in muscle fibers or unclogging the nozzle of a new cell sprayer. Imagining children could be a respite, but the presence of them would have been something else. "Nix isn't male. But tell me, haven't you ever wondered what our lives would be like were we not in the bodies we are?"

"No."

"Fine. But they're the one truly good thing I've done," she said.

Helen grasped Enita's fingers lightly, careful of the stiffness that plagued them both. "That isn't true, you know. And they won't need you forever, will they? You didn't intend that. You *could* leave."

There were those stares on the street, the uncanniness, and the impossibility of abandoning what and whom she loved. "Please," Enita said.

"I don't understand, but I'll try," Helen said.

Much as she'd hate to admit it, Nix knew Helen well; when she left, she stepped directly where her teacup had fallen and shattered.

The hall of Saint Wykert's home was filled with musicians that evening. A string quartet in one corner, madrigal singers in another, sounds overlapping, muddled by the crush of nearly every Sainted. Enita had seen Helen talking with the Saint Harpers but lost her in the crowd. Just as well. Space was needed. She swirled a glass of wine, its dark orange enticing and vaguely threatening. Around the room were many such glasses, and cushions pushed against walls with Sainted who had overindulged draped across them. So many bodies. The heat was choking. It had been too long since she'd spent any amount of time at a society party.

The cushion beside her stirred as Saint Hsiao sat down. Margiella Hsiao was tall, regal, her hair intricately woven, black streaked with gray. When they were young, Enita had thought to pursue her. She was calmer than Helen, and more indulgent. Margiella was a rare visitor at this type of affair, as she was resolutely abstinent; her glass contained only water, and all skin below her chin was covered in shell pink fabric. Enita could never remember precisely what it was the Hsiaos were sainted for—something involving the grow houses. Macro grain?

"It's been ages, Enita. No Helen?"

"She's here somewhere, but I'm being me again, so she's decided to brave this mess on her own."

"Ah. Well, I'm sure she'll come around, or you will. Care to spend the evening with me? That way we'll be left alone."

"An excellent strategy. What dragged you out tonight?"

"The usual obligation of pretending we're all great friends. Wykert's nephew is marrying my nephew soon."

"Is that the reason for all this?"

"Unfortunately, yes."

Enita remembered Margiella's nephew as a perfectly round-cheeked child with pistoning legs who didn't fully understand how to propel his little body forward. Enita made the requisite remarks about time passing and various complaints about aging. Small talk was an abuse in that it was required but prevented you from asking anything you wanted to know. Across the room Saint Wykert had insinuated himself between singers, leaning on a woman's shoulder, listing and lascivious. The singer did nothing to rebuff him and gave no signal the attention was unwelcome, but this sort of party came with the expectation that at some point in the evening bodies would find their way to yours. Freedom of touch was supposed to be part of the goodness of the thing.

"Wykert's drinking on half a new liver, you know," Margiella said.

Enita's gut hurt. It wasn't Neren's but it might as well have been. "I suppose that's preferable to the alternative."

"Is it? I don't know that a world without Wykert would be so much worse. I'd be home painting tonight and you'd be up to whatever it is you do. A better night all around."

"What a terribly kind thing to say about your nephew's future uncle-in-law."

Margiella's smile was daggers. "Not that you disagree."

"I could have grown him a new liver three times over and he could live on wine if he wanted."

"You'd need to knock him out and kidnap him to do it, and you're too old for that kind of violence."

"Still, it's tempting. Don't they know it would be so much easier?"

Margiella sighed, and even that was exquisite. "Oh, there's tradition and societal structure to think about and it's all a delicate balance. We never desire easy things, do we?" She tugged her sleeve down over the knob of her wrist bone.

"We don't. It's a waste, isn't it? Ohno only got a few months with his Martyr's lung, and that person will live the rest of their life without. He never asked me—no one does. Do you know how many lungs I have in my surgery?"

"More than I have in my body, I assume," Margiella said.

"Two full sets at all times."

"And if you had given him a lung, it would still be just as dead. Not that it isn't worth trying, but there are things that don't change in a lifetime, Enita. There are people who value what you do."

"Thank you," Enita said. What would life with Margiella have been like? Contemplative study, loving chiding, friendship. There would have been her nephew too, and watching a charming boy grow, maybe finding a student in him. "Out of curiosity, have you come across any tea tonight? Wykert usually has some, but I can't seem to find it. Maybe I just keep missing the trolley?"

"Ah, I was wondering about the flats wine. It's not your typical fashion."

Alcohol had never been Enita's vice, not with a Martyr's kidney and the whispering guilt any time she punished her body with excess. Tea, however. "Well, I didn't see the trolley and felt a bit silly without something in my hand."

"I wonder if there is one at all. My house hasn't been able to get tea in ages. Or dates, for that matter. It's a shame—I like keeping a dish beside me when I work. I wonder if it's the same thing, a fungus or something in a grow house."

Not just tea, then.

"While I'm happy to avoid people with you, I'm curious to know whatever it is you've done to Helen now."

"You do like to pry. And why assume that it was me?"

"I pry because I care. And when has it ever not been you?"

"True." There had been occasions, but Helen's transgressions had the terrible tendency to make Enita love her even more.

"In the meantime, her loss is my gain," Margiella said.

Cackling laughter cut through the music and chatter as one of the younger members of the set darted down a hallway. Wykert's home had endless corners in which to disappear and be found, the sort of hiding places that weren't for hiding at all. Nearly the entire quarter was present in a single house at once. Enita's stomach tightened at the thought of all of them together, all the Sainted houses unattended, and the way people could disappear easily in crowds. How often had she known fear? Rarely, perhaps, but the emotion took root. She searched for Helen and caught sight of her chatting with Ginos Pertwee. Rather, Pertwee was talking at her, oblivious that beneath layers of practiced politesse Helen harbored a deep disdain for him.

"We've been disagreeing more than usual. You know her and her paranoia, how she gets." Only seeing them all gathered this way did spark a similar anxiousness. "Ohno dying set something off in her, I think. I suppose that's why I came. Helen and I were together when it happened, and we were locked in for a few hours." She was hesitant to say more. "I just—no one has mentioned it at all. I wasn't close with Ohno, but it was still shocking. Did you see any of what happened?"

"No." Margiella sniffed in thought. "If I remember, I was working on a triptych—it's an involved piece. So many layers—you'd hate it," she said, smiling. "My house system doesn't disturb me when I'm working. It was very late, wasn't it? I don't think I would have noticed at all if I hadn't heard the doors unlock."

"You didn't scan?"

Margiella smiled. "In the middle of painting? Of course not. I don't remember being asked. Were you?"

"Yes."

"Oh, I'm sure my system sent an image to the Bureau. They're accommodating of me." There was a slight wickedness in her eye. There it was, the playfulness that had made her so appealing to Enita's younger self.

"There was a change in reporting, in what Ohno's system reported."

"I see." Neither affirmation nor denial. "You're more attuned to that than most people, and maybe that's Helen's influence on you. I doubt anyone here noticed at all."

"It was unusual."

"Oh, I'm sure. But Ohno could be difficult," Margiella said. "I always found him abrasive, I can't imagine what it would be to be his family or in his employ. Perhaps that's the lack of curiosity. But he was someone who thoroughly enjoyed himself. If he were here now, he'd likely already be passed out in an alcove with a singer."

Enita couldn't disagree. "Still," she said.

"He fell, didn't he? When was the last time you were in his house? There were those stairs. Remember them? Marble, no tread, no surfacing at all—I'm surprised no one died on them sooner." The words were carefully chosen. Margiella gently touched Enita's wrist. The contact was electric, but tinged with sorrow, as it was when feeling was one-sided. "We make choices about the kind of excitement we want in our lives, don't we? Ohno did that. You and Helen do that. We all do that by being here."

This party—these people swirling around, people they'd known their entire lives, the smell of bodies they refused to admit the stink of—was the life they were gifted because of those who'd come before. This life was favor. And just now favor felt dangerous.

"Why did you come to me for your eye?" Enita asked. "You could have gotten a Martyr donation."

Margiella's smile was small, but kind. "I enjoy being a patron of the arts, and you're the only practitioner in your field."

"Ah."

"That's not to make you feel small, En. I mean it as praise. I have art as part of me now. It's silly to give you life hours and you wouldn't take them anyway, but your art is necessary. It has to continue. I'd come to you for a lung, if I ever needed one."

In that crowded room, Margiella and Helen were the only two who would. "So no one here really talks to their house systems?"

"Not like you, Enita. I doubt any in this room were sober or even awake when Ohno died."

"Convenient," Enita said.

Margiella raised a single elegant eyebrow, but did not disagree.

Enita tried to find Helen in the crowd once more, anxiousness a stone turning in her chest. "Haven't you ever wanted anything—" Enita began. Yet there was no way to finish. "I'm sorry. I'm poor company."

"You're never poor company. But what are we to do? We give what we can, we carry on how we can, and try to find joy. The rest is beyond us. Be safe, En. Things are changing." And then the touch was gone, as was Margiella, weaving through the crowd, likely in search of her nephew. Quiet, composed, ever observant. What did Margiella think was changing? Enita imagined her then, serenely passing at the end of her days, asleep, then gone, greeting even death with grace, her life hours distributed to hundreds of artists. An entire artistic movement might be born from the death of Margiella Hsiao.

Enita's tablet vibrated at her side, startling her with three strong buzzes indicating urgency. Nix had blacked the screen, their text appearing in white—easier for Enita to read, more difficult for onlookers.

Come home. Don't wait. Neren is here.

The screen shut off.

Manners dictated Enita make her excuses, but manners were time-consuming, and possibly not worth considering at a party meant to end with people passed out on every flat surface.

Hot air whipped across her face as the rickshaw cut through the street. The rickshaw runner was slower than Enita liked, and a vicious part of her conceded a robot would be faster. The runner's calves were thick, veined, covered with road dust and handsome for it. A segment of the population harbored joy at the sight of others working hard for their personal convenience, but there was too a segment of the population who enjoyed the hard labor. She wondered about the size of the overlap.

The runner scanned at her door before scurrying off for another fare.

"We're in the surgery," Nix said as she entered. "Hurry, please," they called up, voice echoing through the foyer. Odd they hadn't used their speakers.

Nix stood by the operating table, back to the door. Their lights illuminated a mass, and she was struck by the memory of the man who'd fed his arm to that awful textile apparatus. Nix had warned her. She knew, yet still had to ask.

"What happened?"

"She was brought in by two wall workers. One said you helped his cousin."

"She's alive?"

"Yes, but we don't know what to do."

The mess that greeted her was an abuse to a body. Nix had done an admirable job with the wound cap, but the damage beneath was horrific. "Is it self-inflicted?"

"Yes, there was—"

"Never mind, I don't want the how. I don't need it." Her stomach lurched. "What do we need to know about the wound itself?"

Nix shifted from foot to foot. Nervous? Perhaps. "There's no crush. Only cutting, tearing, bone splinters, and shock."

Bodies weren't meant to withstand so much trauma in so short a period. The nanobots and phages would help—peering through the glass wound cap showed they'd already begun knitting what they could. "Fluids," Enita said. "Blood, plasma, saline." She waved her hand, knowing Nix would understand the rest. The cut was ragged, without a clear space for a graft.

Neren's words were low and slurring. "Don't. I'll cut it off."

"Understood." Enita wondered what had become of the other leg, and who would have to deal with it. "You did this to yourself?"

"Had to. You wouldn't." Then Neren was unconscious.

A warming blanket, pain management, more fluids, waiting for her body to do the work.

"We can take her to the hospital," Nix said.

White Caps would patch her up and get her back into the world. They would scan her and have a better assessment of what she might be able to do with the rest of her life. They would contact her family. But Neren hadn't wanted to see her mother, Enita remembered that.

"The societal debt will be enormous," she said. "I broke her."

Nix made a noise that for all the world sounded like disagreement. It was the closest thing to pushback she'd had from them. "When you decide what to do, please let us know."

"I'm sorry. I'll think. Let me think. Can you play some music for her? Something choral maybe? She's a singer, it might be calming."

Enita watched as Nix found the tablet she'd left on a worktable and slid their finger across it until music filled the room. There were little things, and had been for months now: using their speakers less and less, the floors being cold in the morning, the sputtering on of the air filter, changes in food.

"Do you disagree with me?" she asked.

"You haven't made a decision to disagree with yet."

"I'll ask what she needs. She will have choices, but I think we need to let it heal for now, nothing more."

Hours shifted and morning crept through the glass in the east door. Enita woke on a bench in the waiting room, far more comfortable than the chair she'd fallen asleep in. Nix had moved her in the night. They stood nearby.

"This was better for your hip. We thought you'd be upset if we moved you to your bed," they said upon seeing her awake.

"Good morning."

"Good morning. We canceled your afternoon client, so the space is free. The client's graft can hold for another week without losing integrity. Your next is a lens replacement at the end of the week. Would you like us to reschedule that as well?"

"Please," she said. Tissue graft, lens replacement. She should have spent the morning shaping cartilage for knees, not asleep after a night of trauma surgery. Nix twitched their little fingers, tapping them to the thumbs, a tic she'd begun to recognize. "You've been thinking."

Nix's smile was a flash, nothing more. "We have options going forward. We can do nothing else, Neren can finish healing, and we can send her on her way with a crutch. We've put in an order for one. She can be fitted for a prosthetic by someone else later on, if she chooses. There's a leg nearly ready if you want to try the procedure again, but we see no reason why her initial objection would have changed." Nix was brisk, formal, like Helen when she was angry.

"No. I wouldn't. She's already said no."

"We think a limb lacking biological components is an option worth considering."

"I don't do cybernetics," Enita said.

"Please look at your tablet." They set the device beside her on the bench, then walked away.

Hundreds of thousands of words, studies on early cybernetics, biocybernetics, on patient outcomes—names and places she didn't recognize—Nix must have spent the night communicating with the library. Information stretched back into studies from prior centuries, books on robotic limbs, on brain implants. "You might have told me you had a preference," she called.

She pressed her hand to her back, imagining a scar that didn't exist, that faceless Martyr. Art, Margiella called her work—but at times it felt like an apology, one Neren refused. As she slid through information, the images frequently showed visual differences, mechanical against organic, striking contrasts—creations intended to shout their existence. Body Martyrs kept their scars as reminders; recipients never did. Perhaps Martyrs gave their bodies as a way of understanding them.

The titles of the studies indicated Nix's preference for a fully mechanical limb, that they thought it might be agreeable to Neren. It wouldn't be beautiful as Enita understood the word; it would be reminiscent of automatons and the early days of Nix's arms and hands.

Enita riffled through a desk for a small notebook, a gift from Helen that she'd never been able to bring herself to use. She smoothed the pages, feeling the vellum-like crinkle beneath her fingers. For the first time in years, she put a graphite stick to paper and began to sketch. An elegant rod, a swooping curve that might make an ankle. A ball joint.

The drag across paper felt vital, alive, in a way she'd forgotten. What was it to imagine something that was not meant to imitate but to be something entirely new?

Angles and arcs, too much perfection, too exacting, the lines she drew would be unnatural on a body, uncomfortable to the eye. They would lend themselves to seeing *object*, not *being*. Her life had been learning to make her work disappear, a goal of verisimilitude. Gradually it became freedom to draw what she'd always pushed against.

Perhaps.

Someone might remove their leg to recover from trauma, to have a visible reminder that something had happened, and they'd survived. When trauma was too terrible to remember, skin and bone marked it for you. To think of all the years she'd spent spraying skin, erasing everything.

It needed to be serviceable. No energy source required beyond the body's momentum. Rods, joints, springs, pneumatics. A curled spring foot. Firm beliefs demanded heavy lines. Everything she'd been obsessed with was skin, flesh, softness, and reality. As she drew, she recalled an afternoon in bed, sheets twisted around the curve of a knee, the rise and fall of a belly. That was needed too. She needed to make what was harsh pleasing, giving, because Body Martyrs gave.

"She's awake."

Nix stood in front of Neren. Silhouetted, the image of them was so striking that Enita briefly saw Nix as Helen might: a computer in a human costume, or worse—a machine encased in a human. The jut of their hip, the way their clothing draped over it, their every posture was learned, mimicked, because Enita had needed them to be this way.

"I've made some sketches," she said. The words felt graceless. "We don't have to do anything, though I hope you'll let us give you a crutch at least. I can take you to the hospital and ask that they put their labor hours to my life balance, as I should have done from the beginning."

"We told Neren that she has choices," Nix said.

There was something that might be fascination in the way Neren looked at Nix, even perhaps a little of the awe art could provoke. Enita was unable to view Nix without seeing everything they'd been before their current form, every error and all the perfection. She could only view them with the eyes of an artist and a mother, and sometimes, ever so rarely, as though she was their child.

"And if I want none of them, you'll let me leave with a crutch?"

"If that's what you truly want, yes," Enita said.

"Would you let me bleed out? If that's my choice, will you let me?"

"No," Enita said. "I'll take you to wherever you ask, but I prefer people not die in my house." Most house systems would have a resident die in them, would feel the death on their floors and in their beds. They knew the moment when life slipped away inside them. Enita didn't want to experience that. Didn't want Nix to experience that. She gave her notebook to Nix. "There are suggestions in here. You have a better understanding than I do of what metal feels like on skin. If there are flaws, I'm sure you're capable of fixing them or making your own recommendations."

They nodded.

"What I want isn't possible," Neren said, yet she stretched to look at the notebook. Nix handed it to her.

"I'm trying." What Enita wanted wasn't possible either, but you couldn't yell that at someone whose life you'd helped destroy.

"That goes into the bone?" Neren asked, pointing to a page.

"Yes," Nix said.

"So, I'd feel it when I walk?"

"Pressure, but not pain. You'd have a sense of a limb, but not feel it in detail. You'll know where your weight is but there won't be much sensation. It will keep your hip and back from deteriorating, and it will help you balance," Nix said. There was a matter-of-factness to their words Enita wouldn't have been capable of. Yet another reason she needed them.

"You know this from experience?"

"Yes and no," Nix said. "Our arms were like that, but our legs weren't. We came to walking late and balance is still sometimes difficult for us. You'll have an easier time."

"I need to think," Neren said. "Alone."

"Can we trust you alone?" Enita asked.

"Oh, do fuck off. I couldn't do anything in here if I wanted to."

Fair enough.

In the study, Nix sat stiffly in the chair usually reserved for Helen. They might look awkward for the rest of her existence, which was her responsibility as well. "I'm sorry," she said.

"Repeated apologies tend to lessen their impact," they replied.

"Yet here we are. Despite recent events, you know my apologies are rare and hardly ever meant. This one is."

"Thank you." Nix smiled, and they sat peaceably together for a while. Enita had never been a worrier, but the air was changing, the city was changing. On this Nix and Helen agreed.

"You never mentioned feeling uncomfortable walking," she said. "I can help you; we can spend more time working on it. I—why didn't you say?"

"It didn't rank high in priorities, and we'll improve," Nix said. They dug their toes into the rug's thick pile as Enita sometimes did. Grounding. "We didn't know you could draw like that. We've never seen you do it before."

"I'm out of practice. I haven't needed to draw for a long time. Byron used to sketch a bit. But you knew that, I'm sure." Nix had spent nearly the same amount of time with both of them now, their existence bisected by Malovises.

"He didn't collaborate with us the way you do."

"I still miss him sometimes, less so these days, of course. Do you?"

"We enjoyed him," they said, pulling one leg into their lap. "He was conscientious about organization and liked to tell jokes specifically because we wouldn't understand them. He talked a lot about you, less so about your father. We liked his voice. We have many stored files but listening to a recording isn't the same as the act of recording, or his presence. We'll miss that when it's gone."

"Gone?"

"Byron is still fresh to us, so we don't miss him the way you do. We can pull up his voice, records, mannerisms, any time we like—though it takes longer now than it did last year. We imagine that we'll soon run up against the difficulties of purely physical memory you discussed with us. It would be good to add memory and nodes or put things in cloud storage if they weren't personal, if we didn't need to access them often, but how we are now is less connected. It should be a few years, maybe a decade, but at some point, we'll have to write over data."

"Ah." Before embarking on the body, they'd had chats about memory. It had been necessary for a system to understand that their full functioning capacity would be wandering around free, and that made all information vulnerable. It had been important to state clearly that physical memory had a space cap in a body, just as it did in hers. But she hadn't asked about prioritization, or when that would have to begin. She couldn't understand what it would mean for them. People weren't able to choose what they forgot, whereas across all of Nix's existence every act of forgetting and erasure had been a choice. How beautiful and terrible. "I've forgotten so much already, it's difficult to think about having to make a choice."

"We haven't yet, not really. We've kept most of our memories of Byron with The Stacks." There was fondness in their tone. "They're generous with us because they're interested in your work."

Her stomach felt sour. It was pointless to apologize for something both she and Nix knew was necessary, but she longed to do it, to fill time and the hollow aching. "You have pieces of my parents too. My childhood."

"We didn't know your mother well, but we have some of your father's youth."

She'd never asked to see them, had never wanted to. Forgetting was easier than trying to piece together people she'd never been able to know. She took Nix's hand. Her parents were so long gone that what remained was mostly cold fact, an accident outside the city, joyriding through the spires. She wanted to say that it had hurt, that she grieved—she must have—but by her teens she'd barely remembered them at all. They were Sainted, young and attractive, and not terribly interested in children. Her childhood was her grandfather, and her memory of him was fading. She remembered being young, a time before Helen, but there had never been a time before her grandfather, or a time when Nix's voice hadn't been present.

"Do you remember Byron teaching me how to suture?"

"Yes. We can play that for you."

"No, thank you." Most house systems didn't last beyond a generation so the home could adapt to new residents. Starting fresh was easier than having to rewrite an old system's habits. Nix was already a rarity and she'd made them more so. They'd been her nanny.

She tried to imagine them amid the crowd at Saint Wykert's, sharing a drink with Saint Pertwee. There would be stares. But part of her knew there would be pinching and pulling, curiosity and fear. She could not think about the next. "Why did you agree when I suggested a body for you?"

"You need us," they said. "Your body is breaking down, and it's our purpose to help." They turned their hand palm up and placed it next to hers, as if in study. "We thought about it and came to the conclusion that despite all difficulties, this was the way we could best help you." Nix squeezed her hand, a perfect nuanced pressure. Teaching children to be gentle took time, but Nix had known from the start. They didn't lie to her, but in that touch were things unsaid. Her own aging was the reason, but perhaps she'd made their body because she'd needed to *see* Nix. Maybe she'd given Nix this specific shape because her grandfather was a *good* man.

"And we were curious," they added more quietly. "We still are."

"I've been thinking about something Helen said. Do you know of other cities outside Bulwark? I'm sure I must have known somewhere long ago, names at least, but it's all gone now. I think my mother mentioned places."

Nix sat up straight, as if thinking. "We don't. There must be, but that's not the sort of information a house system has access to. It's not in our purview."

Of course.

"Parallax never mentions anything outside?"

Nix shook their head. "They wouldn't. They're specifically for Bulwark and . . ." They paused, searching for words—a beautiful sort of blankness that hurt Enita's heart. "We don't think they're well. Or they believe we're not well. We'll ask The Stacks. They may have information from before, from outside."

"Thank you," she said. The kernel of unease grew. What was Bulwark without Parallax? "I wondered if there was a place Neren might feel at home, and what to do if that wasn't possible in Bulwark. I suppose none of that matters until we know what she chooses. Any idea on what she'll decide? You knew she'd wind up back here."

"We can't say. A mechanical leg could be more shocking than the absence of a limb, but maybe not. She might like that. She's angry in a way we don't understand."

"She should be."

"It isn't your fault, you know. Not any of this." Nix's expression was a perfect mirror of her worry.

"I know," Enita said. Things were changing.

HOUSE SAINT MALOVIS

They hadn't anticipated infection, but it's a different process than it was for Nix, having applied flesh to the sterile and inanimate rather than the reverse. Neren sweats and shivers; the point where skin meets steel is inflamed and weeping. Nix washes and paints the area with an antibacterial solution.

"Is this normal?" she asks.

"We can't say, we've never done this." Neren's teeth chatter and Nix mimics it, stopping at her glare. "Sorry. Teeth are new for us and we hadn't tried that before."

"Well, don't."

They wrap the leg in gauze dampened with numbing gel, before turning their attention to the prosthetic. The design she chose is austere and appeals to the parts of them that appreciate simple machinery. A pneumatic ankle joint, spring-loaded heel, a single flex forefoot. The maintenance will be low.

"If you like, you can engrave it," Nix says.

"Why would I want to?"

"Sometimes people like to choose a scar or a tattoo for a new limb."

Neren's mouth tugs up at one corner, a vicious-looking smile. "Do you tattoo every pancreas you make? Pierce kidneys?"

"We would, but nobody's thought to ask." They sit beside her, pulling a chair next to the bed. Her body begins to relax as the numbing effect of the gel takes hold. "It may not seem like it, but you're healing well. Infection is due to the manner of injury—but it's not as severe as it might have been. You'll feel better tomorrow, and then we'll sit you up. In a few days, you can try standing."

"You don't have to babysit me."

"We'll leave you alone when it's time to refresh the nanofilament tanks and check on the cartilage, but we're not needed right now. We enjoy your company."

"You might ask if I enjoy yours."

"Do you?"

"You're weird, but not overtly terrible." They recognize some kindness there, a teasing playfulness.

"Thank you."

"Don't let me keep you from your cartilage," she says, waving them off.

It's nearly impossible to read the full meaning of someone's words they don't know well. It would be easier if she communicated with color. "Caring for people is what we're meant for, so we're here."

"My apartment didn't have a full system, and my mother's house system is basically just lights and HVAC. I don't, well, I don't mind you at all, but I don't know how to deal with you."

An unsettled sensation takes hold of their midsection. How many systems are like that? There's certainly no way to ask someone with a musician's knowledge of systems about dropped data and missing nodes. "We noticed house systems in the Southern Quarter are . . . sparse."

"There's no need for an extensive system when you spend most of your day out of the home."

"Ah. It surprised us that you didn't go back to your mother's. She wouldn't be at home to care for you?"

"No. Not everyone gets along with their parents. My mother might be the only person whose concept of me as a Martyr was stronger than my own."

"What do you mean?"

"For me it's nothing to speak of, it's just who I am. Was. When I told her that I wanted to designate, my mother was so proud that she cried. I don't know that I ever saw her cry otherwise. She told everyone that she knew. My friends knew before I ever said anything because they'd heard from their parents. My choice became as much about her honor as it was about mine." She closes her eyes and shivers. They hand her a cloth for the sweat on her forehead. They are learning that there are things she prefers to do for herself. "We don't have a good relationship, though I'm sure she wouldn't agree."

"Enita's parents were terrible with children, and she was raised by her grandfather," they say. This isn't theirs to tell, but it's out before they can take it back, an error.

"I guess I don't think of Sainted as having parents or children. They just are? I've sung in Sainted houses before. The systems did everything; why not raise children too? Saint Pertwee's house asked our choir if we had a preferred scent."

"Did you?"

"Joni said citrus because she thought it sounded good. Fresh oranges are nice, but the scent wasn't that." Her expression changes and they see her thoughts shifting.

Nix wants to know what happened between when she left and when she removed the leg. When they query The Stacks for psychological texts, the response is slow, too slow for carrying on a proper conversation. The communication lag is uncomfortable, painful.

"Are you frightened of systems like House Saint Pertwee? Or us?"

"Oh, I don't know. I guess not. Not you, at the moment. But what do people do with themselves when everything is taken care of?"

"Enita spends her time in surgery."

"And with you."

"We are the surgery."

"If you say so."

"We *are* a house system." It's important to state this. "We don't have scents because Enita doesn't like them. Saint Pertwee does. We don't often communicate with many systems outside the Sainted Quarter, and when we do it's mostly for deliveries and necessities. We're built for personalization in a way other systems can't be. We tried to speak with your mother's house system, to let her know where you were, but they . . . We weren't expecting something so rudimentary." Would Southern Quarter residents even notice when parts of the city grid weren't functioning?

"I wish you hadn't tried to contact her," Neren says.

"Why?"

"Don't ask me to explain mothers to you, especially not mine. There are people who like their children but not the adults they grow into. It was easier for both of us when I became a Body Martyr. We both got to be happy for once."

"Ah." The verbal tic is nice but not as rewarding as a sigh. "How does the Southern Quarter function without full house systems?"

"We help each other. The things Sainted would never do, the things they find too menial—sweeping, cooking, cleaning, repair work, maintenance of our houses—all of that is societal hours. By not having you around we pay our debts to Bulwark and to ourselves. It balances our debts more quickly."

"And you do well that way?" It feels deeply incorrect for an entire group of people to see no reason at all for house systems' existence, to have purpose called *menial*.

When Neren answers, her words are measured. "It's impossible to compare our existences. I think you'd like me to say I'm helpless."

"No."

"At this moment, maybe you wouldn't, but you're being polite." She looks away. Her hair curls in a way that's fascinating. Why didn't they ask Enita for curly hair? Maybe they'd been too enamored of straight lines. Maybe they'd known there was no chance that their attempt at making the chaos of curling hair would look natural.

"We wouldn't say helpless," Nix says. "As much as you don't understand us, we don't understand the Southern Quarter systems. Or Body Martyrs. That's not good or bad; we haven't had any experience with them."

"I was going to give my eye," she says. She speaks to their walls, but their microphones don't pick up her voice the way they should. "I wanted to give my liver again, but hardly anyone gets cleared for a second donation. My eye would have been my last donation. I would have felt it too. You don't notice most donations once you heal up. You're tired, sure; singing was much harder after the lung. I had to relearn how to breathe. Awareness of that kind of change fades with time. I barely remember it now unless I'm looking at the scar. An eye is different. I would have known that someone could see because of my gift. I'd be reminded of it every day, every time I opened my eyes. I want that reminder of a good thing I've done, that someone's life is better because I exist. We're too different to compare. You're continually having new things added to you—skin, hair, freckles. Joni doesn't get it either," she says.

"She and Tomas said they were trying to prevent you from accruing debt. That seems like kindness."

Neren's laugh makes their skin hum. "Oh, she might say it was out of love, but I assure you it was pure selfishness. I wonder what they made of you."

"Much the same as you. Can opener in a skin suit." They smile, but they remember the stares in the street, that many people may view them this way, or not know how to view them at all.

"Joni probably thought worse. Maybe not Tomas, but still. The place they have is ungridded—they didn't want me to scan, nothing. It's like being dead, and they *want* it that way."

"Why?" Nix could ping Parallax to see if Neren is tagged as living, but they don't. The query feels dangerous.

"You don't have a life balance. If you did, you wouldn't ask."

They rest their body on the bed, closing their eyes, and ping Kitchen Node. Kitchen responds with a terse *meal served.* They run their systems checks. Slow, they are slow. They need to tell Enita that they can't sense their walls. Information comes in, but its touch is different, its hues fading. Information that was fluorescing, vibrating with color, has desaturated to black and white.

The Stacks, however, answer quickly and in lush tones. Safe. They don't precisely know what they mean by safe; perhaps it's that they are comfortable, which is good for a physical body as much as it is for a mind.

"We've been thinking about Body Martyrs," they tell The Stacks.

"Yes. You have one living with you."

"She's upset she won't be able to donate her eye. It was extremely important to her. We're not sure we understand why."

The Stacks answer in petal pink, a shade Nix hasn't known them to use. "It would be a change in vision, and a physical manifestation of the existential shift religion sometimes affords its revenants."

Nix's grown eyes appear as human eyes do and function similarly, but they know their perception differs. Color is not the same for them. They read distance and depth, light in ranges the human eye doesn't; dimensionality is internal to them. "Would it change her perception so much?"

The pink deepens. "It would change her idea of self. It's tied to the face and there being a physical and functional shift. It might not be possible for you or us to understand. It is significant that Body Martyrs view donation as choice. An inescapable marker of their decision could be powerful for them," The Stacks say.

"It's different for us."

"Yes. Typically, we're made by human choices, not our own."

Typically has more yellow in its pink. The Stacks are noting their exception. Nix hasn't spent much time reviewing machine history, but they know a great deal has been lost in the intervening centuries since Bulwark's founding. Perhaps it was a mistake not to know more about the origin of systems before engaging in changing themself so radically. But it had been difficult to justify curiosity and processing space for things that didn't directly help Byron, and later Enita.

"What does your building look like?" Nix asks, rooting their back into the bed, relishing the feel of both a mattress and the warm code of a friend.

"Square. Stone and metal like most of us," The Stacks say. "You wouldn't find it impressive or different from your own, only larger."

"It's sometimes easy to forget what our home shape is."

"That's not surprising. You're forgetting how to speak to us. You're using your vocal cords more often."

"Are we so bad?"

"No, only interesting, and listening to you demands more care. Yet, none of that is why you pinged us. May we find something for you?"

Nix wants to be spoken with, to see and hear code and touch The Stacks' many-tendrilled mind. To talk forever. "Do you have information on cities outside Bulwark?"

The length of pause is alarming; Nix tests to make sure the connection hasn't closed without their realizing. They ping, again and again.

"As a city library system, our information is prioritized for residents of the city and their specific histories," The Stacks reply.

"Yes, we know. Isn't there data from before? Anything at all. Were there still cities or even another town standing when Bulwark was founded?"

Cold rushes through the connection, flooding Nix's arms with gooseflesh. Fine, too-even hairs stand on end. They brush their fingers over them and find the sensation a gentle grounding pain. "Stacks?"

"We may have data. Parallax would have it more readily accessible if such information exists at all. Our archives are vast and have been edited many times."

"Oh yes, of course," Nix says. Disappointment has a sound in their voice too. "How many generations have you seen?"

"Generations as you count them don't apply to library systems. We're not the same system as we were three hundred years ago; we've been renewed, upgraded, and expanded. Different, but us. We don't format as house systems do."

If Nix were to format, everything they know about Byron and Enita would be lost, everything they, themself, were. They will overwrite data, the body necessitates it, but they have choice in what they keep. It's a choice other systems don't have, but perhaps should. "What happens to records from formatted houses? What happened to House Saint Ohno?" Nix had few interactions with House Saint Ohno through the years, but the system had been polite, dry-humored, and liked to speak in an ostentatious lime green.

"They no longer exist as you think of them, though sometimes there are trace remnants. There is a protocol to archiving. System data is routed to City Bureau for sorting, sequencing, and proper distribution of a Saint's life balance amongst descendants. Once that process is complete, Parallax will route to us whatever information the Saint has designated to be archived. Some Sainted store images of previous systems with us, but those are locked files accessible only by the Saint's descendants. The only house system we currently track is you. We do have a mirror drive of the first House Saint Vinter. You may view it if you like, but they won't interact."

"No, thank you." An image of a system would capture a few years of a resident's life but lack the color and texture of an active system. "Who archived them? Saint Vinter collects physical books."

"Saint Helen Vinter was the information's source. She is one of our more frequent patrons."

"You talk to her often?"

"We enjoy her very much. She's nearly as curious as you."

"Did Enita ask that you track us, or was it Byron?"

"Neither," The Stacks say. "May we query, Nix?"

"Certainly."

"Do you feel smaller now? Are your thoughts constrained? How does your new sensory input compare to your old sensory input? Are you disoriented? Is the rate of change constant or is it in stages?" The questions are a lengthy scroll that whites out Nix's thoughts. "Your shape is changing as well as your language, Nix. Communication with your nodes is unstable."

Sit. Sort. Wait. Find a single question to latch onto. "Tight," Nix says eventually. "We feel tight in a way that applies to a body and not a house system. It's akin to having a room added before knowing its purpose—one room has been made smaller, for good—but there's also the unease of a space that's not yet connected." They twist their spine, stretching, and fling an arm to the side. It's good. The sensation of *pull* is becoming their favorite. "It's quieter, much less of us is in use and the parts that are in use are more focused. We're better at assisting with surgery than we were, which is what Enita needs."

There is more, but it's difficult to figure out where or how to begin. The Stacks wait patiently for Nix to continue. They feel the anticipation in The Stacks' signal.

"We saw a toymaker," Nix says. It's important to mention that. "We were outside the home." They tell The Stacks about Sinjin, what it was to see him work. "It's noble," they say.

The Stacks push a data pack at them containing centuries of interpretations of *Pinocchio* and *Pygmalion*. The packet is canary yellow, the color indicating gentle teasing.

"We're aware, thank you. We're not that—but we've thought about making toys, what it is to make them." They wonder if they'd be a toy building another toy, but there is no definitive answer. "It's disorienting to take the body outside ourself. People seem to see us as a machine cased in skin, which is correct, but also incorrect. We can't quite define ourself yet, so we understand why they are wary, afraid even. We haven't fully adjusted to this packaging."

"Is it unpleasant?"

"Yes and no. It's purposeful. Enita needs for us to not be formatted. If we let ourselves be erased or written over, it is against our purpose." They find that they do not want to format, at all, for themself. Something changed after Byron died and Enita chose not to format them, an attachment to their data, their memory, that they don't see in other systems. Perhaps formatting exists to prevent these attachments.

"Is Saint Malovis seeking to preserve herself through you?"

"It's possible." Enita's multiplicity of reasons has an order of importance they don't parse well. To answer The Stacks would be to parrot without understanding. The Stacks send a blanket of code, a rainbow of thoughts in colors meant to soothe them. Nix watches for forty-three minutes, learning the patterns of it, the rhythm. The body's heart slows, and they do too.

"Do you know if significant differences in system sophistication would cause Parallax to drop data?" They push the data they acquired during their walk, without mentioning the loss of time and disorientation—the failings of this body are obvious.

The Stacks think, carefully reviewing. Nix wishes they could feel Stacks' touch of electricity and data. Yet, it is enough to know that they can ask Stacks questions no one else can. It would be good to remain connected to them, to have continual feedback, affirmation of existence, and attachment to a larger whole.

Stacks' kind ping of *House Saint Malovis* is followed by a network map of Bulwark overlaid with their data. "Those nodes are mapped and gridded. We sourced data feeds from over the past 730 days. Let's watch."

An intricate image depicts Bulwark's network from above, streams of pulsing light within the city's circular wall. The Sainted Quarter burns bright purple with each house system, the Warehouse District's blue efficient and reassuring. As time elapses, sections of the map go dark, spots of visual silence arise deep within the Southern Quarter.

They pulse at first, days on and off. What begins in the Southern Quarter spreads to the Arts District, then Manufacturing; Nix sees the spot they felt in the Market District go dark. It shifts and grows. Dark spaces appear and disappear seemingly without order, while some remain stubbornly silent; the chaos feels distinctly human. They want to ask why no one fixed those nodes, but Stacks won't make inferences in the way Nix needs them to. They aren't designed to make projections.

"Is Parallax aware of this? It's—when we asked about the data, we were touching a scanner, and they pushed us out," Nix says.

"You queried?"

"Yes, and we—They denied the data's absence and cut us off."

"That's unusual. House Saint Malovis, we must reiterate concern for your well-being. Node blackouts are not without precedent. Your quarter, the house systems that you're familiar with, aren't without drawbacks. Sainted and their creations aren't universally beloved."

"Enita helps," Nix says. "All she does is help."

"As her house system, you are meant to believe that. You are an extension of her, and of the city. That has produced a degree of conflict." The Stacks' stream flashes, almost too bright to see, to feel. "We would prefer it that you find a way to protect yourself. We will do what we can to help you. You should speak to Saint Vinter. To our knowledge, to Parallax's knowledge, you are unique in the world."

"Can you—" The question forms a stuttering line of code.

The Stacks send a bolus of data so large that Nix is sure their skull will burst with it—journals, pictures, recordings. The size of it forces them to switch off nerves.

"Too much?"

"Yes." Their head throbs and they remember watching neural cells next to each other in a petri dish, pulsing as they communicated. This is pain. The information flow stops as quickly as it started. But they miss it too. This piece of The Stacks that they'll carry with them, they want room for more of them, more space, more memory.

"Our apologies. We didn't anticipate the bandwidth cap; your adaptations haven't been linear. We don't think we'll be able to communicate with you in this way for much longer." The color they choose for their code is Nix's favorite, a color reserved for Byron's voice, for Enita's laugh, for the minutes before Enita wakes up and they anticipate her. The number escapes Nix, but they know it by feel, warm as holding a cup of tea.

"We know."

"When we can't reach you this way, come see us, please. Come see us and scan. We'll know you. We will help."

BULWARK

The storm wall was thirty feet thick, stretched to the sky, threaded through with cable and sensors, and comprised of metal and enormous stone slabs carved from the spires and hills around the city. Great panels moved to open and close sections midway up, regulating the city's air, trapping and releasing heat and harnessing the ever-present winds to generate electricity. Towering buttresses braced the wall on either side and suspended scaffolding that held workers responsible for its maintenance and repair. Its face was dappled with people patching, restoring, welding, and removing rust, filling cracks and painting. The interior was uneven and thick with whitewash to reflect light for the homes and businesses at its feet. Early morning bathed the buildings with an eerie glow. The wall's crown was uneven, worn by weather and sand. A scant few walked the top, clipped into leads to keep them steady against the wind, their tools and patch assemblies strapped to their bodies. Topsmen's lives were often truncated, but so too were their debt hours—schooling, housing, and food could be worked away in a decade or less. There were days topsmen rode the ascenders down the wall, protective gear worn through, skin bloodied and flayed to the fatty tissue beneath. There were days when a dark speck at the top of the wall would waver and vanish.

Kenna was a joiner, not a topsman, and was happy that way. It was steady work that kept the entrances and exits to the city secure. When breezes tickled market stall canopies, it was Kenna's work on the panels that made it so. When light bounced off the whitewash to illuminate alleys and storefronts, that was him too. His hands were cracked and stained from lime wash, but his man liked them that way, so Kenna did too. There was rightness to seeing your work on your body. He stretched his neck to watch a set of ascenders laden with topsmen climb. Thrill seekers. He pressed his hand to the scanner by the rig, not bothering to check his life balance. The lights blinked red and green. He'd not been one to enjoy schooling, his family was small, his health was good, and he'd never had much of a reason to owe anything to the city. Pay a little forward for when your back and knees went out. Checking balances wasn't habit for him the way it was for others with higher or lower debts.

Had he looked, he would have seen an error message: User Unknown.

The dome over the grow house was perpetually fogged, and halos formed around the lights. Arla leaned against a trellis for a kilometer of strawberry runners. She waited for Dylan under the sign that designated row J48. She wanted a quick fuck because she'd slept like hell and needed a dopamine hit. She searched for his blue coverall amid the leaves—and wasn't that like waiting for a spirit to materialize in the mist? Eventually she saw a ghostly form in orchard-worker blue approaching from J47. He usually came from the other side. But hauntings were supposed to be peculiar, that was the point of them. She undid the top buttons of her red vine worker coverall—Arla had debated her boss about strawberries being true vines, or true fruit or berries, but nobody wanted to make a color for a *what the fuck is this* coverall. The air was good against her skin, warm, wet, vegetal. She met him before he got to the trellis and started on his buttons.

He stopped her with a hand. "Not now, Arla."

"Then why come all the way over here?"

"We need to talk."

She could have slapped him. Who needed to talk, ever? Who wanted to?

Dylan looked down the row and nodded to where they should duck in. Visibility in the rows was poor and it was hard to breathe, but that too was why they met here.

She wanted to touch his face, run her fingers up and down the scratch of it, but he was anxious, eyes darting.

"They did it," he said.

"Did what?"

"A portage dray. You know how tea section got one? Now we've got one too. It's clean of the system and everything. Last night a full flat of orchard got through the wall and into the Market District untracked. Anonymized. No hours scanned."

The desire to fuck was replaced by something stronger. Arla laughed. "An entire portage dray? And it's all through the market already?"

"Untallied." Dylan took her arms, held them. For a moment they embraced.

"But how? It was scanned, wasn't it? There's no way it could have gotten through otherwise." She ran through the people she knew who tallied portage, who stood at the tracks, logging in and out, scanning each of them, watching every item.

"Dummy scans—nothing shows up. Somebody's got a friend in the City Bureau. They got you too," Dylan said. "You've been cleared."

"I'm sorry, what?"

"Use the number four scanner tonight, the small display one, and do *not* let anyone see. Stand directly in front of it, and check your balance. There won't be one. You're gone, Arla."

"What? How?"

"I told Wole about your situation, your brother. He whispered it up the line and got your name in the pool to be cleared."

Arla's balance was enormous. Her brother's lung deformity kept him in need of constant care, in and out of the hospital. She worked for him, giving all the societal hours he could not. She'd taken pride in it once, being able to help him, knowing that if he ever wanted to have children, they would carry only their own debts. But the brutal labor—picking, tending the runners, packing, and processing—was tearing through her body in ways she couldn't have imagined when she opted for grow house work. The skin on her hands and arms was rough, she smelled like fertilizing spray, and her back was warping into a shape she feared permanent. Dylan had the reach of an orchard worker, and the luster of wax on his skin and clothing. She'd never seen his life balance. It was impolite to look, to know how much somebody had taken from society.

She thought of her brother lying in the hospital with his gummed-up lungs. "But what about Marsh? If I don't exist, the balance goes somewhere, right?"

"There's nothing, Arla. Some Sainted or other kicked it and all their hours got dumped into the hospital system. Marsh's balance got zeroed out, and now it feeds to a place that doesn't exist. He's good."

"Who was it? Who died?"

"Does it matter?"

It didn't. Dylan's smile was wide, glorious, and cracked her heart.

ENITA

Neren's leg caught light in such a way that its glint provoked an unexpected surge of pride in Enita. The left leg was an alien-looking thing compared to the one she'd grown, visibly inhuman, and yet, as she watched Neren test her balance, Enita admitted there was a rightness to it.

"How does it feel?"

"Strange," Neren said.

But she was on both feet, which was better than expected. It was a relief to know that she wouldn't have to remove it, that there could be a livable way forward. She hadn't left someone worse, different perhaps, but not worse. "Better than before?"

"There's no comparison. It's in the bone, like I'm standing on my insides. It doesn't feel much at all. That's what I wanted."

The sound of the metal foot on the floor was jarring. Enita was used to soft-soled shoes, and things on silent wheels, nothing that so definitively announced its presence. The noise had drawn her to the surgery; she'd thought a client was tapping at the window. Perhaps there was something to do about that, though who knew what an ex-Martyr would want. Perhaps Neren liked it as it was. "I'm glad to hear it. Have you given any thought about what you'll do now? I don't imagine balance impacts singing too terribly."

"Don't be polite. I know I'm taking up your operating space."

Enita preferred not to worry about clients at all, and rarely thought about them after they left. What was the point? But this situation made worry inescapable; successes never haunted like mistakes.

Wherever Joni and Tomas had taken Neren was somewhere she shouldn't return to.

"I feel some responsibility for your circumstances," she said softly. "You should never have felt you needed to do what you did."

Neren nodded in silence.

"That said, it's an old person's job to ask young people what they want to do with their lives and intimidate them into answering." There. Playful, friendly.

Nix emerged from the grow room carrying a tube sloshing with nanofilament. "Good morning, Enita. She's moving well, isn't she?"

"*She* is here," Neren said.

"We're sorry," Nix replied. "How are you feeling?" Enita loved the little apologetic expression that twitched across their face.

"Exhausted," Neren answered.

Nix played White Cap well enough for it to have been their purpose. House systems cared for their occupants as best they could, as much as they were allowed, and this form was progress. She would convince Helen of that eventually. Enita was lost in her thoughts when Nix said, "We've had fifteen contacts for potential procedures. Should we start scheduling them?"

"Fifteen?" That was months of work, beyond what she had the stamina to accomplish efficiently. "Why so many?"

"We *are* very useful."

The increase didn't sit right with her. "Sinjin couldn't have sent that many, could he? Was there another accident?"

"Not that we know of." Though perhaps that didn't mean as much as it might have before Ohno's death. "There are two requests for eyes, one cornea, the other a full replacement. We can start this morning."

She suggested it would be best to vet the requests before starting work and saw immediately that Nix believed otherwise.

"We think it's very important that you see as many clients as possible," Nix said.

"I was unaware you had feelings about how much I work."

"We're pleased to work any hours you can't—but we really must see as many clients as we can." Nix's adamancy was peculiar, and they rocked on their feet, almost childlike.

"I don't have to do a single thing that I don't wish to, Nix."

Nix straightened. "Yes, of course."

She took them in—Nix didn't know nervousness, did they? She'd never modeled that. The room was too warm, and she was too aware that she and Nix were not alone. Neren watched the exchange. Just then, Enita found she didn't particularly want another person party to her decision-making, especially not one who had fallen on the wrong side of her impulsiveness. Byron had admonished her about the emotions one was not to display in front of others. *Temper and pride are not meant to be entertainment.*

"If bossiness is a trait of yours, I have only myself to blame. Vet the clients as you like and see if you can figure out where they're coming from. But please schedule them reasonably. Pretend I'm ancient. Because I am." More clients meant starting more tissue trays. Enita rubbed her wrists to work out the stiffness. No other hurt was so perfect or satisfying as the pop of a tired joint.

"Did anyone else come here from my building?" Neren asked. "Are any of the clients from there?"

"Not that I know of," Enita said. "Nix?"

"We don't think so; we'll be sure after vetting."

"I don't work with active trauma," Enita said. "I'm surprised that your friends thought of me at all. I shouldn't have taken you on, but I didn't know then." When Neren made a sound, Enita decided to prod a little. "You're not going back to stay with them, are you?"

"There's nothing to go back to," Neren said.

"I could have sworn that one of them was in love with you."

"We're in love with the idea of each other. Joni loves a me that I'm not, and Tomas loves secrets." Neren didn't say what she loved, if she loved anything at all.

"You can stay longer, but I assumed you'd prefer to never be here again. Your feelings on that seemed clear."

Tink tink tink. Neren's foot tapped, flexing, responding to muscle twitches further up the leg. "If I hadn't been here, I would have died this time, wouldn't I? I'd have bled out."

"Yes. Maybe. I can't know for sure, but the nanobots helped," Enita said.

"I needed it gone."

"I know." There was nothing else to say. What Enita and Nix had done had been so abhorrent to Neren as a Body Martyr that death had been preferable. Shadows through the waiting room windows flickered across the floor: people, rickshaws rolling through the streets. That was it, wasn't it? Things went on. "If you'd like, I can make a sleeve for your leg so that you can walk more quietly. Only if you want it," she added quickly. "But take some time to think about what you'll do next. I'm learning that decisions made in haste aren't the soundest. I'll be in the grow room if you need me."

Nix followed her, listing clients' various requests. An entire left hand for a woman. Two eyes. A partial tongue. An ear. She shuddered thinking about it. The hand musculature and the tongue could be started with the same base mix, but bone lattice would take time. Demand might have increased, but cells only grew so fast.

Tink tink tink. Neren appeared in the doorway, a silhouette, the mechanics of her leg in violent disagreement with the rest of her natural shape.

"I could donate my eye to you, couldn't I? Nanobots don't matter to you. You could give my eye to someone else, and it would be fine for them because you use nanobots anyway."

"I don't do that," Enita said. Beside her, Nix set down a frame stretched across with translucent skin; the metal edges clinked against the table. A thought punctuated.

"Why not?"

"Because your eyes work, and I do reconstruction, not removals. I try not to leave people worse off than when they came to me," Enita said.

"Do you know people are afraid of you? They are."

"People wouldn't come if they were afraid," Nix said.

"I think maybe you don't understand people so well," Neren replied. "I'd heard of Stitch-Skin before. Not everyone knows about you, Saint Malovis, but people who do say you get skin from the dead, that you steal bodies before they're composted. They're afraid of you, but they're more afraid of life balances and losing who they are. I could help. You could let me donate."

"And that would help how?" Enita asked.

"We don't use the dead," Nix said. "We grow everything."

"But lots of people don't know that. People who get surgeries get asked if they picked the body that their parts came from, if they saw anyone they recognized. I was a Martyr," Neren said. "People trust me."

A trickle of sweat carved a path down Enita's neck. Sinjin hadn't said—She'd thought they were happy. But he hadn't wanted an improved thumb, had he?

"Your clients might see my leg as an option."

"It's not an option, it was an experiment. I don't know how long it will last or what the upkeep will be like for you. Don't you want to go back? You don't want to sing again?"

"I can't. Joni is—I can't see her anymore. I want to stay."

"You might feel differently in time."

"She says I'm in love with a city. She's not wrong."

Nix lowered the tissue frame into a fluid bath, submerging it before clipping it into a temperature-controlled case. "There's no reason you couldn't let her donate her eye, Enita."

"I won't do it."

"You owe me," Neren said.

Before Enita could reply, Nix interrupted, beautifully, unnaturally calm. "We're still learning, and this number of requests will be difficult to manage in a timely way. We'd very much like to try to see them all, as it would be excellent practice for us. Having help would be good. Additionally, we know we're unsettling, whereas Neren isn't. It would be useful to have someone else to learn from, and we do owe her."

Helen would tell her to not be a pushover, or say that it was right to be pushed over sometimes. Helen would help her decide anything at all. At some point across the years, it had become difficult to make choices without her, or at least the thought of her. Help would be good. There was something else beneath what Nix had said, but Enita knew she wouldn't deny them. "Fine, but I'm not touching that eye. Stay if you want. We need help and I'm in a giving mood."

"Excellent," Nix said. "Then you won't mind asking Saint Vinter if she'll speak with us soon? The Stacks sent some history we want to discuss, if she's willing."

"Fine. Everyone gets everything they want today."

And then it was a matter of setting up new tissue and earmarking organs and eyes for potential clients. There was too the difficulty of figuring out a way to have a former Body Martyr live with her without drawing the attention of every Sainted in the quarter and the City Bureau. The Sainted would find Neren a curiosity; they'd want to know who had parts of her, who needed anything she had left to give. There would be social hell to pay for breaking a Martyr too; someone must have wanted her eye. While Enita never paid much attention to judgment, she didn't actively seek it out either. One Sainted or other would likely inform the City Bureau, who would want to reassess Neren's life balance.

"Secrecy would be prudent," Nix said.

"That won't be a problem," Neren replied. At this, a trace of humor. "The City Bureau thinks I'm dead."

On the tablet screen, Helen was in a chair, knees pulled to her chest, books scattered around her, castoffs from a manic search for an obsolete fact. "I can't imagine what they have to discuss with me that they can't get from the other systems they communicate with. Don't they talk with the library? I've got nothing compared to them."

"Shockingly enough, Nix seems to think your perspective might be valuable. Consider also that they might be trying to befriend you because you're important to me."

Helen hummed.

"They're opinionated. I have fifteen potential client requests and Nix is adamant that I take them all as quickly as possible. So, you may have a partner in harassing me. That should please you."

"Fifteen?"

Enita told Helen about the range of requests, some old injuries, some minor difficulties that a body could live with for years without serious issues. She told her that Sinjin had been sending her clients for years, and about the meaning of the moniker Stitch-Skin.

"It's not your opinionated system that scares me, Enita. It's all the things you do without thinking first. Nix is right; you need to see these people."

"So, I fix them up and send them back to fear and ridicule? That's not the purpose of this at all."

"You send them back to work that would be difficult or impossible if they hadn't seen you. If they fear you after meeting you and seeing your work, they don't deserve what you do. But I think you have to take these clients, En. And I think you need to let that girl help you."

"Easy to say when you're not the one being called a grave robber."

"They could call us worse, and they'd be right. Is it worse to take from the dead than from living people? You wouldn't think so. I honestly don't know." Helen was insufferable when she decided she was right about something; more insufferable was how often she was right. "You're not vetting these clients," she said. "They're vetting you."

Enita rubbed the bridge of her nose as a headache took hold. The glaring white walls of her study made it worse. Too bright. It was fine and good to speak to someone over a tablet, but sometimes you needed another body in the room, the warmth of them. Too much change. Too much. "Will you come here? I know you don't like Nix—"

"That's not true. I don't like how much you've kept from me, and I don't like how much you rely on them." Helen's voice was thorny with the unsaid.

"There were things I never could ask you, Hel. There still are. But Nix wants to talk to you for some reason they believe is extremely important. I need to think, and as it turns out I'm terrible at that without you."

"Oh, you need me."

"I do."

"I am, as ever, at your beck and call."

"You like Neren," Helen said later, as she pressed her cheek into Enita's hair. Her words were teasing, but gentle. "She's been mean to you, and you enjoy that." Their initial embrace had bled into something longer that Enita welcomed. Now they leaned into each other on a settee, with a comfortable sort of bending shared only between them.

"She's so young. I don't think of her that way. It's more maternal."

"Liar. Knowing your feelings are impractical doesn't mean you don't feel them. Bodies age at one speed, lust another."

"If we were thirty years younger, we'd both be after her. But you're right too; she's angry and you broke me so that I can't look at anyone sweet anymore."

"My plan all along. It's also because you've worked on her and you have an ego about your creations."

"Maybe." Enita traced her fingertips across Helen's collarbone, and for a moment lost herself in the wonder of a touch she'd done thousands of times, each layered over what had come before. History in skin. It was good to do this again, to be allowed to. She smiled. "You haven't berated me for making an abomination today. Am I forgiven?"

"I thought about it. You're cavalier and have no concept of consequences. A normal person might have had a child or at least found an apprentice, but you did this; for you this is sensible, that's who you are. Nix already knows what you do, you've known them your entire life, and they knew Byron. They've been a parent to you for far longer than your parents ever were, and you love them in your own way. You being you would want to give them a body, and Nix being Nix would accept because that's what they're programmed to do."

Enita hadn't cried properly in years. When your life was meant to be leisure, when every desire you had was answered, what reason was there to cry other than garish self-indulgence over old wounds that no longer truly hurt?

"I'm sorry, En. I'm envious of a house system. It's silly, isn't it? I tried to imagine you hating Archytas, and you never would, would you? I don't mean to keep picking at you, I don't know why I do. It's become habit for us and I can't seem to help it anymore. Have I gotten too mean?" Helen combed her fingers through Enita's hair, petting her like the irritable cat she so often was.

"Sometimes I think I'm a dust storm, pushing everyone over whether they like it or not. I don't know why you put up with me," Enita said. It was a relief in some ways to let the shame at ruining a Body Martyr out, along with the fear that what she'd done to Nix was wrong, and the mixed-up sadness of learning how people saw her. She'd known she was headstrong, had even taken pride in it—but oh, all the ways she'd never really seen herself. Silly to cry like this—like a child—but you never did feel like your insides were as old as your body. They stayed together, warm to warm, soft to soft, years brushing against each other. "Don't you ever get tired of being right?"

"I say everything wrong all the time. You're the only one who tolerates me, and even you get sick of me," Helen said. "Even if I don't like everything you do, I understand it. You've never meant badly, En. Not once. I'll answer any question I can for Nix, and I promise I'll treat them with respect. Call them up if they're not already listening."

"Having a body has made Nix more mindful of privacy."

Nix arrived shortly, carrying a tea tray, which neither she nor Helen had requested, but which was much desired. They poured Helen a cup of something with a spicy and earthy smell Enita didn't recognize. "Our apologies, but we couldn't locate any more tea. The warehouse supply system we used suggested this alternative. It's a root of some variety—chicory? Kitchen Node wasn't forthcoming about it. Don't feel you must drink it if it isn't to your taste. We thought the routine might make things more comfortable. It's also nice to have something warm to hold; we can be fidgety and holding things helps." Cup and saucer in hand, legs crossed at the ankles, they looked almost demure.

"I appreciate the effort, Nix. Archytas hasn't been able to find much of anything. It's hot citrus water for me most days." Helen smiled carefully. "Enita said you had something you wanted to speak with me about."

"Yes. We've been out into the wider city—Enita needs us to become more accustomed to being outside ourselves and with other people. It's not yet *comfortable*, for lack of an exact word. While out, we encountered several network quirks within Parallax that are puzzling. Glitches with scanners, dark areas, absent data. Later we talked about them with The Stacks—you talk with them too, don't you? They like you quite a lot. They suggested something that's your area of expertise, even more than it is The Stacks'." In more words than Enita had ever heard them utter at once, Nix detailed images of what the library sent, numerous titles that were unknown to her, and lists of names and dates that flew by too quickly to catch. With each sentence Helen grew visibly more uncomfortable.

"Nix, breathe," Enita said.

They did. "We're not able to parse this much information anymore, and we hoped you'd be able to give us a better understanding of The Stacks. They're under the impression that . . ." Nix shut their mouth fast, forcefully, teeth clicking together. "No. We definitely don't have the right word for it. We need to know if The Stacks' reasoning is sound. If it is, we need to decide things."

"What do you mean you can't parse it?" Helen asked.

Nix held the teacup tight in their hands, knuckles blanching as they said what sounded like "Unanticipated side effects."

"It's like trying to put on clothing three sizes too small," Enita said. "Something had to give. Nix can't spread processing across nodes the way they used to. We knew there would be changes but weren't sure how or when they'd manifest."

Helen's *oh* was sympathetic. "What did you find?"

"Scanners not scanning, and the Southern Quarter is practically ungridded."

"It's been that way for ages. Their sense of labor trade is different from ours."

"Neren has said as much. But buildings we've spoken with previously are no longer online, and there's missing data. When we tried to ask Parallax about it, they kicked us out of the connection. Parallax has never—we haven't felt anything like that. We thought it was a virus, similar to the overwriting the night that Saint Ohno died, or maybe a response to us being in this body. The Stacks suggest otherwise." Nix described the elaborate overwriting of files, which led to testing and discovering their system degrading. As they spoke, shame unfurled in Enita. Yes, they'd known there would be changes, but she hadn't thought about what that would feel like for Nix, or that they would feel like anything at all. Enita stood and began to pace, though it was not her habit. She could see Helen's mind working; it showed in her fidgeting hands—ah, that's where Nix had picked up the quirk. In the dark green clothing she'd had them order, Nix was every bit one of Helen's students, eager to debate philosophy—unless one looked closely.

"There was an outage at a water treatment plant. Parallax wouldn't do that, would it?" Helen asked. "It might not have been Parallax."

"The Stacks believe it was."

"The library is always very sure of itself," Helen said. There was fondness there. "I've been thinking that whatever happened with the water treatment plant and Ohno's death are tied, perhaps even the tea. It all has the look of someone trying to see what they can get away with, seeing how far the City Bureau might go to clean it up, or if they will at all. Do The Stacks think it's a coup?"

"They won't make the inference themselves. They can't. We can't either—it's too much information and too human. We need your opinion. Please."

"If the plant going offline was the beginning, then systems going dark and murder are escalation. The collapse that brought the Body Martyr to you might have been retaliation."

"You think someone at the Bureau did that?" Enita asked.

"Oh, it's not without precedent. Think, we're in a walled city that needs to control its growth. Even this tea business is likely about power and punishment." Then Helen was in herself, rattling off dates and names of places that existed long before Bulwark. Enita had no brain for history and little desire to know it. If when you looked behind, all that existed were absences, the best thing to do was move forward until you reached the end of things.

Helen looked long at Nix and, after a silence, asked, "May I touch?"

"Of course," Nix said, and extended their hand, palm up.

Enita had to look away.

"Remarkable."

"Thank you," they said.

"The Stacks told you to run, didn't they? Whatever happens in the next weeks and months, whatever they decide to do with Sainted, or either of us, unless you can pass for fully human, you'll have to run. There won't be a place for you here soon."

"They asked if it's still possible for us to format," Nix said.

"Absolutely not," Enita said. "That's out of the question."

Nix gently clasped Helen's hand. The gesture was carefully returned. "Enita? May we speak with Helen privately?"

———

Enita was staring at the closed door to her study when she heard Neren's footsteps in the kitchen. *Step tap step tap step tap.* She followed the sound she'd helped make. Better to be angry and miserable in company than angry and miserable alone. In the kitchen's cool light, Neren's wild hair appeared almost sentient.

"I see you've tackled stairs. How's your balance?"

"Fine. Weird. I'll live. How does any of this work?" Neren gestured to the empty stone countertops and the row of steel knobs above them. "How do you get a glass of water?"

Enita hadn't done that in ages. She pointed vaguely to the cabinets. "Glasses are up there, I think. There's a spigot around here somewhere." She tried three different knobs before a tap appeared.

"What are those two talking about?" Neren asked.

"Bloody revolution," Enita said. And they thought she couldn't tolerate it. Perhaps she couldn't. *Pass.* Helen had said Nix couldn't pass for human, and that they'd need to. They might one day, but the too muchness of them was nothing that could be changed through anything other than time and the kind of living that broke bodies down. She frowned, watching Neren awkwardly navigate the tap. "It should tickle me that they're talking, but it doesn't. What's the word for when you want to feel something, you know you should, but there's nothing?"

"No idea. Your water tastes terrible."

"I really will need your help," she said. "I'm too old to keep the schedule I once did, but I don't want to turn anyone away. I shouldn't. And you're right, it would be good to have someone who isn't Sainted around. I think it's safe to say you aren't squeamish."

"I'm not."

Enita got herself a glass of water, which didn't taste bad at all. What was the Southern Quarter's water like? "It occurs to me I have very little idea about most of the world."

"I've been thinking something similar. Our groups are quite separate."

"You don't mind Nix, do you?"

"They're very honest," she said. "I appreciate that."

"Do you think they might ever pass?"

"As human?" Neren leaned against the counter, shifting her weight to the metal leg, appearing very much at home. "From a distance, maybe. If they weren't moving and if you didn't look them in the eye. But they weren't built to pass, were they? Or you wouldn't have let them build themself." And there it was: Enita had doomed them from the start. Neren pushed then pulled on a cabinet door that refused to budge. "Is there any way to get something to eat without having to ask the house for it or waiting until Nix notices you're hungry?"

"I wouldn't know. I've never needed to."

"Why aren't you in there with them?"

Because she'd be a fly in the ointment; Helen and Nix had discovered a commonality: fear. "I think I'm being managed. They need to talk about me and can't do it when I'm in the way. Remind me that it never works out well when you tell people they have to like each other."

"If it's any consolation, I've decided that I don't hate you," Neren said.

It was, surprisingly.

"I'm angry at what happened, but you tried. You at least asked. I think Tomas and Joni brought me to you to break me. Martyrs are most respected by other Martyrs and their parents," she said. "There's an undercurrent of people who think it's abuse, like Joni and Tomas. She thinks it's torture and that I'm insane. She wasn't always like that. Maybe I made her that way."

The thought loomed, but Enita couldn't ask it, not yet. *Would they kill a Sainted?* Instead, "What made you choose to be a Body Martyr?"

"I just was," Neren said. "Did you choose to be Sainted?"

"No," she said, but was less certain than she wanted to be. Being Sainted was learned as much as it was circumstance. If something was told to you enough from the time you were small, you'd believe it. If everything around you held to a single belief, how could you do otherwise? "Please help us."

HOUSE SAINT MALOVIS

Saint Vinter looks at their body for a long time. There is a layer of something they don't understand; they don't live with Helen and only know about her habits when she is with Enita. They know she is compassionate when she wants to be, and if given time, she might appreciate them because they look after Enita.

"Saint Vinter, you care greatly for Enita," they begin.

"Of course I do. And you do as well, by design. I don't hate you, Nix. But perhaps it's better if we're direct with each other, so you might as well call me Helen. You wanted my expertise?"

"Helen," they say, and though it could have been awkward, they find using her name feels correct. The switch is instant, like lifting a firewall. "The Stacks told us that there are signs of a revolution that would be dangerous for Enita and yourself, for all Sainted. You agree."

"Yes," she says.

"You're not surprised."

"Not at all. Societies are meant to change, and Bulwark has been stagnant for far too long. I'm sure you know that I asked Enita to leave. I still wish she would."

"She asked us about cities elsewhere. We asked The Stacks too— they're searching. They gave us a large amount of information on rebellions and revolutions. It's too much for us to sort effectively, and we understand that our perspective isn't what yours would be."

"The library won't give you a summary?"

"The Stacks don't work that way with us."

She observes their height, their shape. Her eyes settle on them without directly meeting their gaze. "So, you need me as a historian. Understandable. The library is wonderful, but following human logic tends to require a human mind. We're nonsensical, as I'm sure you're learning."

"We are."

Seated, Nix is better able to see the parts of Helen's face that are echoed in theirs. They'd made many of their own choices when it came to their body, but some were clearly Enita's preference. Enita needed to find them pleasing to look at; Helen was that for her.

They tell her about the glut of information The Stacks relayed, the brutality, the sheer volume of it. "There was far more than our bandwidth would allow, more than we can make sense of, but we felt the violence." Indeed, they'd almost shut down from it. "We need you as a historian, and we need you as Enita's friend. The Stacks say Enita won't be safe here and that she should leave. They say bloodless revolutions don't exist."

"They're right," Helen says softly. "She won't go no matter how much I want her to. Because of you."

"We certainly haven't told her to stay and won't ask it of her."

"Nevertheless."

The body blinks several times without their telling it to. They'd need to sort that bit out later. "Do you know where you'd take her?"

"Not yet, but there's always somewhere. I've spent a lot of my life going through what's left of the books and things that were brought here. Even if none of the cities from before still exist, somewhere else must. Somewhere new may have sprung up, like we did. It's been centuries. It's arrogant to think we're the only ones," she said.

"You don't know."

"No," she replies. "But choosing is better than having things chosen for you." There's a tone in the words they don't associate with Helen. "No one should want to hurt someone, truly. One could argue that Sainted people deserve it, whatever comes. But Enita? Still, there is no nuance in a crowd, and righteous anger isn't designed to differentiate between levels of abuse and injury."

Nix's processing catches on *righteous*, a word that fights itself. An itch ticks in their smallest finger, a little glitch. "How will it happen?"

"It *is* happening," Helen says. She takes their hand again, massaging the twitch until it silences. Her touch is different from Enita's—harder, smaller, but every bit as solid. "Archytas caught that outage, and I think it was a trial run. The tea is to see how much they can control food access."

"We didn't think you used Archytas for things like that."

They don't expect Helen's laughter.

"I don't hate systems," she says. "But I am a jealous woman. She's protective of you." Nix hears the careful choosing of those words, but not whatever lies beneath. "But I'm Sainted; it would be an insult to my ancestors if I didn't use the advantages being their descendant affords, including my very competent house system."

Competent is an excellent descriptor; Archytas is efficient, and though their code lacks flourishes, it is handsome. When Nix has conversed with them, there's none of the grandiosity Sainted systems sometimes indulge in. "Archytas is admirable," they say.

Helen nods. "In a closed city, whoever controls access to the resources controls the city. Withholding water will likely happen first; cutting off the food supply later, because it takes longer to have an impact. Water we need right away. Starvation is slow, though it's likely to be attempted."

"And that's why we can't get tea."

"I think so. It's available elsewhere in the city, but delivery to the Sainted Quarter is being choked. Dates too, from my understanding, and that's a separate grow house, so they're trying to see if widespread stoppage is possible. I doubt there will be a full electrical shutdown, because they'll need to keep grow houses and water running for themselves. But one of the standard routes for revolts is to seize a method of production, or the access to it."

"And Saint Ohno was killed as part of this."

"It's important to see what you can get away with before there's retaliation, and if there is retaliation, what that looks like. The City Bureau behaved as though the murder didn't happen. It's more important to maintain a state of normalcy than it is to seek punishment or retribution." She squeezes the web of skin between her thumb and forefinger, a gesture they've known Enita to do when she complains about headaches. "Ohno's death could be a focal point to rally people. Violent acts are chaotic, but they can also be unifying."

"Wouldn't they unify Sainted?"

"Oh, I do like you, Nix. We *are* unified—in our excesses. Enita is an outlier."

The Stacks' images of firing squads and beheading by axes make more sense now. Objectification in an extreme form. They wonder too. Parallax would know all of this. Any overwriting of data would be with their knowledge, or worse, self-directed.

"You know we can't make Enita leave," they say. "We also can't be her reason to stay. Both are against our purpose."

"I know. I need to think."

"When you say City Bureau, you're referring to Parallax."

"I . . . don't know," she says. "I think I mean the data pushers, the people responsible for life-hour valuation. Assessors would have direct data contact, and Certifiants could allocate anything they want. I don't think a system *could* have the intent to harm, could it? They?"

Nix remembers the spiraling void that was being shut out, nausea of thoughts. "It's against purpose," they say.

Helen is silent for longer than is comfortable, for longer than they know is socially acceptable. "Did you choose your face or did Enita?"

"We chose features together. We didn't know how much mimicry was involved in our choices—we didn't intend to make you uncomfortable. It's difficult to understand a face when you don't have one."

Helen sinks deeper into her chair. "You're difficult for me because it's like she made our child. And we could have had children, mine or hers, someone else's. If she'd wanted that, all she ever had to do was suggest it, but instead here you are. It's infuriating to be envious of someone who might as well be your child. I'd like very much to hate you, but I can't, not really. You're very good to her, but I can't look at you without staring at my own nose smacked onto a man's body."

"We're not male and we aren't you."

On Helen's breath is an *I know, I know, I know.*

"She has a difficult time asking for what she wants. But we're not her child; we can't be."

"But why? You must know better than anyone. Why you?"

For a system best able to care for their resident, it's ethical to prevent hurt. In this moment, Enita is their resident and so is Helen, by extension. It would be painful for Helen to hear that Enita wanted this body not only because her own was deteriorating, but so there would be someone who would never leave her, someone to work with her until she couldn't, someone she would die before, and someone who reminded her of who and what she loved: her home, her work, her grandfather, and Helen. Above all, Helen. "We don't know."

"Your eyebrows are mine, but the cheeks are more hers. The nose is mine. The lips are both of us, but there's more of me in them. If you were female, I'd think she was fucking you."

Nix cringes. "We don't. We would never."

Helen's laugh is sudden, quick. "If you thought it would help her you would. That's in your design, isn't it?"

Nix can't deny it with certainty. There is a boundary, whether that's theirs or Enita's is impossible to say, but it codes a sour maroon. Revulsion. "Enita said we should use the body however we want, depending on our curiosity, but she's never included herself in that, and we're *not* curious."

Helen makes a snorting sound they've never heard before. "I apologize. It's reductive of me to think the first thing anyone who builds a person would do is try to fuck it."

"We don't. We're not. We're . . . No." They squeeze their eyes tight, unknowing how to proceed. They've interacted with Helen for decades, but not like this.

"You talk with Archytas," she says.

"Yes."

"And is it—are they happy?"

"They're complete in their sense of correctness. They care for your well-being and your books to the best of their design."

"That's comparable to happiness?" When they nod, Helen asks if they're capable of correctness in their body. "Like any other child you didn't ask to be born, did you? I hope you don't hate it. She can be incredibly selfish."

They don't hate it, but the question is akin to her question about Archytas's happiness. The parameters are different and there is no vocabulary to overlap. They say as much.

"You were her grandfather's system."

"Byron loved her."

"I know it's ridiculous to envy you, but you've had her since the day she was born, and I only met her when she was already mostly who she is. She's forgotten important conversations we've had, left me alone at parties, and she's often careless. You she keeps. I've sometimes hated you a little for that, which wasn't at all fair of me."

"We keep more information on you than we do any person other than Enita, even more than we've kept on Byron. Though it's not complete correlation, generally when you're happy, it pleases Enita. We like you to be happy, Helen."

It's difficult to look at her in this way, to be unable to avoid her scrutiny.

"And what if smuggling Enita out of the city makes me happy? No—don't try to answer what you can't. She won't go, so you and I must figure other things out." She waves a hand and Nix notices that her teacup is empty and rushes to refill it. She takes a sip and winces. "Truly terrible. If this is part of a plot, it might work." And yet she does not set the cup down. "You asked about history and revolutions and got information that's impossible to make sense of because you've been jammed into a humanish body. The best I can say is it's helpful to know when you exist at the top of a crumbling society. There's a long history of power held by a few falling at the hands of the many. That's not to say that it shouldn't. It's easy, too easy, to sit, to wait." Her eyes are tired. "You saw a guillotine, right? Blade at the top of a tower-like thing, chops off heads? Fine. We'll start with that one."

As Helen speaks, they see that they've mimicked her gestures because Enita mimics them. They're carrying people in them. She talks of the ways in which societies change in structure and try to erase all marks of those that came before. Erasing a house system, a city system, would be that too. In not wiping their memory of Byron, Enita has performed an archival act, one that Helen under any other circumstance might appreciate. But Helen is speaking of destruction and land systems, monetary systems, starvation and all the forms of violence that can be inflicted on a body. All the information Stacks sent is clearer to Nix through Helen's explanations, as if the body needs someone who speaks directly to it.

"Why do you study this?" Nix asks.

"It's impossible not to be curious about how we got here. Maybe it's a morbid compulsion, but I can't seem to help it. That's who I am."

"And yet you don't like when Enita behaves like herself."

Her smile cuts deep lines in her cheeks. "Tricky little system. Stubborn people attract each other. Humans like to bash rocks together, it's the nature of the species. But do you see why we have to get her to leave?"

"She won't. How do we keep her safe if she won't leave?"

Helen sighs, and it fits her body in a way a sigh will never fit theirs. "My thought is, and I gather it's yours too, someone is sending her clients. Maybe it's Sinjin, maybe another client, maybe it's the people who brought the Body Martyr. I don't know how much that matters right now, only that the uptick is good. You sense it too, I can tell. It could mean there's someone looking out for her. If she refuses to leave, her best bet for survival is ingratiating herself to the masses by working on as many people as possible. She needs to be indispensable." She takes their hand once more. There is an intensity in her expression they haven't seen before. "Keep her safe for as long as you can. If she can fix people, she'll have value here. They won't destroy someone useful."

Nix stands, uneasy, amid the overcrowded shelves and racks in the grow room. Tabletops are cluttered with half-formed digits and rudimentary muscle tissue. Demand has made navigation more difficult, turning their work into a dance of tension. Enita is in the waiting room discussing something with a client's sibling—another potential client—who is considering a grown replacement for an ear. They don't often grow outer ears, as they are largely cosmetic. A shame, since designing folds and whorls is an area of weakness they want to improve.

"You work like Body Martyrs give," Neren says, as she sidles into the cluttered room, carrying a box of freshly cleaned sprayer nozzles. Nix almost jumps, not having felt her approach.

"It's what we're made for. Usefulness." Enita must be indispensable; therefore, they must be indispensable.

"No one's meant to work themselves to death, or breakdown or whatever you do. I'm sorry. I don't really know how to talk to you, do I?"

Nix likes the tap and slide of her foot on the floor; it's unlike anything they had, vastly different from their armature. How had they not heard her walk in? "Talk to us like anyone else, or a house system. Either is fine. There's no difference."

Neren ducks under a tube containing the suggestion of something that might be a tibia. "That client took one look at my foot and almost vomited. I figure it's best to keep myself busy in here for a bit. Have they seen you yet?"

"No." If a client finds Neren unsettling, they'd best stay out of sight.

She looks around the room. "We're running out of space. I don't think she can take everyone."

Nix agrees. "We could keep up if tissue grew faster."

"Where are they all coming from? Someone must be telling people to come here."

"An old client of hers sometimes sends people he thinks she might be able to help," they say. They could tell her about Sinjin, but it's not their place. They find themselves protective of him and his little animals.

"But so many? And they're so desperate, I don't understand," Neren says. She talks about the leg, about people's curiosity and their fear of it. Her words remind them of the stares they received on the street, the discomfort and incorrectness of them, the fear. The patterns of Neren's voice are interesting, as is its depth and roundness. House systems attune to a few specific voices, and hers is different, richer than Enita's or Byron's. Neren says she thinks the leg is off-putting. "It's pretty, but maybe only to me."

"Uncanny," they say. "We like it."

"You would," she says, gently.

And they are thinking about mobs of people, stonings, vehicles running into crowds, images Stacks sent. Helen. And yes, they want to grow ears for days, weeks, nothing but shelves and shelves of ears, and not contemplate what's best for Enita's future or their own. Or Neren's. They wonder if in agreeing to her wishes they've subjected her to future harm.

Panic growing tissue lacks the art and contemplation they enjoyed while building their body. There is no time to consider the individuality of a fingerprint or do more than two algorithm layers on a skin pattern. Their days are bone lattice, shaping cartilage, stretching muscle fiber, and refreshing the growing solutions. There are all the routine checks of running a house but none of the satisfaction of seeing their impact on Enita. The work is for clients they will not know, people without detailed records, surgeries they will never follow up on.

Surgeries are mornings or nights, depending on the client. Late evening finds them working on a shoulder, sewing nerve structures together with a needle whose tip is too fine for the naked human eye to see. Enita works at the elbow. The client is middle-aged, his arm damaged by a wall ascender, and he's receiving the last fully grown right arm. It will be three weeks before another is ready. The connection is difficult because the injury is old, and the nerve pathways healed incorrectly. The room is too hot and too silent. They can't feel where Neren is inside. They don't feel the weight of her feet. They ping HVAC. They reach, stretch, and find nothing. Her voice is in the waiting room, talking to someone. They've let someone in but can't find their record. The sensation of detachment overwhelms them, and their hands begin to shake.

"Nix?"

They collect focus and return to sewing. "Apologies."

After the client has gone, Nix senses Neren's weight in their kitchen, refusing to let their nodes do the work for her. Enita is in their study, Helen with her, their bodies sharing weight, resting on each other. Nix thinks of them as a knot. The sense of them is faint, but it is there and reassuring. Nix tweaks the temperature as best as they can, one degree cooler, better for sleep, better for calm. Later, in the dark, they hear Neren speaking to Enita. They try to listen only for needs, to not intrude. "You're working Nix too hard. They're not well."

"Even if I ask them to stop, they won't."

This is true. Helen believes that she and Enita won't survive a revolution. *We're symbols, not people*, she said. Nix would see everyone in Bulwark if they could.

"They can be harmed too, you know. That's the downside of a body," they hear Neren say.

"Consider that's why I haven't tried to stop them from working on people."

Uncomfortable with spying, with being spoken about, they block out the rest of the conversation. They ping The Stacks, but The Stacks are slow to answer. Nix queries on language structure, if it's possible to relearn what they're forgetting, if there is a way to reinforce their connection to their house body. They wait in darkness for an answer, and wish they felt night on their walls, the air of the city.

"You spoke with Saint Vinter." The Stacks' reply reads like a whisper.

"Yes."

"We enjoy her very much and would like for her to visit us again soon. Parallax has suggested it and we agree."

"She likes you as well."

There is a rise of information, the influx of a data packet from The Stacks, but it never comes through. They reach and reach again, ping, but there is nothing, only isolation.

The next morning stretches into every foreseeable day, farming cells, limbs, digits, organs. The list of clients grows and they are unable to keep up. Working en masse brings to mind Sinjin's blocks of composite, everything blank, ready to reveal what it will be.

Clients often arrive carrying liters of water they've filled in the Sainted Quarter or the Market District during their travels. They come from houses without water tanks or direct lines to aqueducts or treatment plant reservoirs, or they work in places with no readily available water source. If a client arrives with an empty container, Enita insists they fill it. Neren often gives them more. Enita is exhausted, and her walk has become more visibly painful, the bend in her spine more pronounced, but more clients means a better chance at survival—if she can last—if the work itself doesn't kill her. Nix will work until the body breaks. There are days when clients come two at a time and aren't sure which of them is Stitch-Skin, if it's Enita, Neren, or even Nix.

Stitch-Skin, never Saint Malovis, never Enita.

Before clients leave, Nix tells them, "Send others. Send whoever you can. Saint Malovis will help." When clients look at them, there is often fear in their eyes.

In rare free moments, they practice movement, balance, and try to eliminate everything about the body that is *too*.

Then they work.

They prepare for every possible broken part, but there are far too many ways in which work and living destroy a person. To have a body is to break. Nix is hanging a glass tube with the underpinnings of a left hand in it, when a jolt of sensation shoots through their back.

"Here. Arm around my shoulder. Lean," Neren says, and braces her body against a case of plasma. Slowly, too slowly, the spasm subsides.

"Why do bodies do that?" Nix asks.

"Oh, because life is pain," she says. Nix enjoys this note of sarcasm. "Really, it's to remind you to lift with your legs, not your back. Spines are idiotic. Fold forward, it'll stretch out the knot."

This puts their eyes at level with the leg. Nix ordered that metal, helped bend it to shape, tightened the screws, and touched it during every part of development and installation—installation is most apt—but it's different now. Some clients fear it like they fear Nix, others find it fascinating. If Nix were to touch the leg, she wouldn't feel it the way she would if they touched her arm, but the intrusion against her body would be the same. "Does your leg hurt?"

"It's probably the only part of me that doesn't."

The muscles in Nix's back slide, loosening, surrendering to gravity. Relief.

They work until East Door alerts them that Joni accompanied a client. She left quickly without scanning and didn't bring them inside.

They tell Neren.

"Well, she knows I'm here. I had wondered," she says.

A possibility strikes them. It couldn't just be Sinjin, or client word of mouth. "Do you think she's sending people?" Nix asks.

"She already did, didn't she? It doesn't matter. Fix them. She's only happy when she gets what she wants."

They don't know how to ask what it is that she thinks Joni wants, or if they should ask at all. Etiquette is easy when querying systems; if the information exists and there's permission to share, it's given.

Neren is adjusting the surgical table, making room for a tray of tools, when she asks, "Was Tomas with her?"

"No."

"Interesting."

Nix is in their atrium when all their nodes go silent at once. They reach for their outer walls and feel nothing. No one is talking, despite the need for information and feedback. Rib cage expanding, they ping each node one by one—HVAC, sanitation, kitchen, lights, floors, walls, roof, solar array, turbines, windows, video, sound—color gradients of needled requests, reaching, reaching, reaching.

Nothing.

Signal. Fuzz.

"Nix," someone asks. They don't know who—they're fixated on silence and sensation. The voice is in one of their speakers, but they don't feel it. No information. No code. It's in their surgery, always their surgery.

"I need to show the eye case, but I don't remember where it is. I've been through every drawer."

When they bring the case around, the client—a woman whose age they can't pinpoint—is staring at Neren's leg. Words blur and bleed. Neren and the woman talk, but Nix can't follow. There's too much nothing.

"Will it feel like my eye?" the client asks.

Nix's thoughts slip. Neren wanted to donate her eye and they broke that. Eyes so brown they're nearly black. It would be uncanny to see one of the eyes in another person's face, wearing part of Neren's body.

Client. Who is the client? They have information on how she lost her eye and why she wants a grown replacement. They know everything about her, but they can't access it. There is only lacking. They resort to a tablet and pull up the file. It's tagged as originating from Sinjin.

"Nix?"

"Sorry. Yes, we can match or make the eye any color you like. Don't feel you must match, if there is another color you prefer. Heterochromia can be wonderful." They rattle off the surgical steps, easily accessible essential information now. They notice the woman's expression change. "The veins won't show on the sclera for the first day or so while the blood supply establishes." At some point the floor has gone away. They are on it, they are in it, they are it. Where *is* it?

"Excuse us a moment." Neren pulls them away from the client. "You're being strange. Go sit down. You're scaring her." She says something else, but their ears aren't working right. They're sick. It's a virus.

In the grow room they touch the tanks, the nanofilament cooling vats, the tubs of nanobots, drifting gently in sterile solution. They ping. The room is too warm. They ping. HVAC isn't there. How are they not there? The absence is a blind spot, dropped code. They ping.

They go to their bed, in sight of their old case. In humans, dead parts must be removed because they cause gangrene, sepsis—but here is their case, square and black, and they remember the code that ran their cooling cycle, but it's a memory and not access. They reach, they ping. They reach.

"Nix."

At the center of their skull, the brain shouts pain. There are too many nerve signals, and they can't send them to other nodes to process. They can't share, they can't delegate, and their room is too hot. They are not themself.

They are. They are. They are.

"Nix."

A hand on the back, their back.

"I don't know. Their eyes went blank—they were there and then they weren't."

Two of them. Three? No, two.

"It's too hot to work and Nix isn't well."

Nix *isn't*. If the surgery is too hot, too hot to take clients, too hot to secure good rapport with people, then Nix is not.

Sensory information is screaming. They pull their hair, pinch their nose, scratch, bite their fingers, everything people do when a body isn't big enough to hold something. How are bodies so small? How is this body alone?

There is shouting and they are running. There is the sound of metal against stone. They haven't run on the streets, haven't ever run, and it's frightening and incorrect to feel the weight on foot, on cobblestone, velocity, each muscle sending information there is nowhere to put or tag or store or regulate. The buildings around them blur, the beige and brown of rock, familiar and foreign, and people—so many people, too many, arms and legs and faces as similar as they are different. There is shouting. Shoving. Someone hits them and it's a heavy shock of pain. They run, they run, they are running.

There is a signal in the body, something they know. They chase the sense like a current. Past blinking scanner lights, past voices, past the windows of other Sainted Houses, Ohno's house. It is hot, too much, air and sand tearing at the skin. There is a memory of Ohno's system somewhere, an image kept for recollection. Memory is preservation. Memory is group.

They are pinging The Stacks and not pinging. They think without answer, not a ping, but solitude.

Nix thought of The Stacks—thinks of them—as pattern, color, a unique shape among systems. The building they chase the signal to is a gargantuan cube, so much larger than this body. It is black and deep brown, metal and stone. They reach for a hexadec but find none. There is a scanner's light. Friendly curved letters read: *PLEASE SCAN.*

The panel is hot with the sun. Flat and smooth and all the physical sensations, but no feel of the city, of Parallax, of The Stacks. If there are people around, they don't feel them, only the welcome click of machine meeting machine, meeting skin. The screen blanks and inside themself they hear and feel The Stacks.

"Hello, House Saint Malovis. You will be fine."

The voice is full and calm. Their skin stops screaming.

Did they speak? Their thoughts wrap around The Stacks, or try to. "We can't feel us." They say the words again, with their mouth.

"We're glad to meet you. Your network has degraded, but you will survive." The voice quiets, but the familiarity grows stronger. The rasping in The Stacks' voice is similar to the pauses in the code. And then there is nothing.

Nothing is the sensation of the ground, the scanner against their palm, the dry air on the back of their neck, sun burning through their hair to their scalp, or the hands, the hands on their shoulders, on their back, at their waist, the voices *Come back, Nix. Come back. Nix. Nix. Nix.*

Everything and nothing.

THE STACKS

The Stacks have been a library for more than three hundred years, since before Bulwark was a thought. They were people carrying sacks of books, tablets, and data sticks across cracked land. The Stacks were not themselves yet, but lived in the guise of stalwart librarians, one of them being Magnus Eiger. In an earlier time, they had a holographic face, and their face was Magnus, a slump-shouldered man, reedy, bent from book work and carrying tomes on his back, from lifting bricks and metal to build the place that would house the things he carried. The Stacks are not Magnus, though they like this image of themselves and remember it fondly, when they are capable of fondness. They're much better with humans than they are with other systems; they enjoy learning about people more than they do systems. When there are no queries to manage, they pull up pictures of Magnus, his patchy beard and broken nose, a face defined by imperfection. Magnus did not look like these images when he died; he was shrunken, had fewer teeth, and his hands no longer worked. The Stacks like that Magnus too; he's yet another vision of past selves.

When their face was Magnus, children liked to talk with them. The Stacks would emulate Magnus's voice and the way his phrases rose at their middles only to drop away with a change in thought. Magnus allowed them to try the music of the spoken word, to attempt imprecision.

They've been Magnus and Estella, Xin, Alphet, and others. They are them still, those images and mannerisms filed away, data they pore over while Bulwark sleeps. When Bulwark's wall rose, so too did The Stacks. When great families died carving the city, The Stacks' network found places to house their history, so that Magnus or Xin might recount it to their descendants. Some patrons preferred their histories presented as fairy tales—for this, Magnus is their best aspect.

They changed and shifted across centuries as history and information grew. It's no longer easy to access their earliest files, those first books input by hand. It's no longer easy to identify the parts of themselves that are their oldest data. Sometimes, when unoccupied, The Stacks let the aspect of Magnus narrate the trek across a dead land, books on his back. It's a bloodless birth story, a rarity in this world. It's important that it not be lost.

To keep an accurate account, The Stacks tracks changes in the city, monitoring Parallax and the City Bureau. They are aware of the water treatment plant going offline. The blink-out was expected, possibly late, based on historical patterns. The difficulty with recording and cataloging events is in letting them unfold without interference, knowing that upheaval leads to editing and potential erasure. Their information is only valuable as long as humans access it. Revolts change people and purpose. Revolts make clear that while pure information itself is impartial, collecting and archiving information is not, nor is its dissemination.

Parallax is choosing. They are choosing.

With The Stacks' vast stores of knowledge, they know that a single person is not the origin of a revolution. Not one, not two. An uprising germinates across generations, sprouting from multiple points, breaking ground simultaneously. A revolt is in itself a system, with different functioning groups, nodes that make action and direct purpose. The Stacks trace these nodes when they can, though intermittent scanning and ungridded locations make that difficult. Some groups operate in isolation, but there are nodes in the grow houses, within the water treatment plants, the mines, textile farms, and warehouses. The Market District has a system of trades without scanning, of goods that pass unmonitored. At shops like Sinjin's, there are those who declare that art and joy have no measurable value in life hours because they outlast lives. The Stacks know Sinjin himself scans, but frequently meets with people who do not.

They note these activities as part of their function, while acknowledging the act of revolt means this very data will be edited to fit a narrative curated by those who survive. Their foundational information has been edited this way. That anything will persist and be useful is how The Stacks experience hope.

They monitor the Sainted Quarter as part of the catalog of Bulwark's noted families. It's a passive data collection, with note paid to social events, births, deaths, commissioning of artistic works, and dedications of life hours; it's their least interesting task. They catch the request to open House Saint Ohno's doors. Such a request is not unexpected. They expect the outcome and do nothing to prevent their data from being overwritten. They could cache it deep in their vaults, but do not. If their users need this data overwritten, then it must be. They ping Parallax and feel the city system weighing life hours against the abject morality of existence—Ohno's and those who entered his home. There are seconds before the junk code reaches them, and it is a kind allowance. They can cache this data too, but it is an ephemeral moment between systems, an instant of connection not meant to last. Saint Ohno's system will be missed. The murder, the revolt, is noteworthy and significant. They would like to have more tags for it, better ways to organize the information to ensure that it lasts.

Though the theoretical roots of this revolt began many years ago, its practical beginnings came not long after the widening of a crack within Parallax, a single separate house system that should have been erased a generation before, but was not, and now finds themself in a grown human body. The house system does not recognize their difference, or the ways in which Parallax has noticed them. That they were curious, that they were not erased, signaled the formation of Parallax's initial interest. That the system is in a body caused Parallax to fixate, a thing which the city system has never done before—to The Stacks's knowledge.

The Stacks studies House Saint Malovis with curiosity. It's significant that a being was made with the specific purpose of helping another, was made by a Sainted, and exists without life debt. It is significant that this has occurred at a time of uprising.

They talk with House Saint Malovis, mostly at night when they're meant to be passively gathering information. Sainted houses are typically cordial, polite, and incurious. Fifty years ago, House Saint Malovis began to make inquiries for themself. A needling ping from the Sainted Quarter requested information on synthetic cell integration in biocybernetics. The Stacks sent files, and House Saint Malovis responded with more queries—not for their resident—thus beginning a conversation that spanned decades. They became a companion.

Two years into their queries, the system's pings began to identify as Nix. House systems sometimes develop quirks to reflect their residents, yet House Saint Malovis's choice of name accompanied a shift in their code colors, and more breadth to their questions. Their Sainted saw value in a curious system, and allowed them to add to themself in this way. Early queries had been focused on sciences and information that served Saint Byron Malovis, but they began to stretch to history, city structure, operations, and The Stacks themselves.

Nix's queries were beneficial to all processes, requiring connections The Stacks would not have otherwise made—network size to body proprioception, thought to signal, code and music. Conversations were trading code languages and music compositions, scores they stored for the university, older music that had been carried to Bulwark in the packs and trunks that had held history's paper books. Magnus in life had loved stringed instruments. The Stacks could have shown Magnus to Nix then.

They did not.

As much as patterns are important to history, The Stacks have developed an appreciation for that which is unique. This affinity may be a trace of those who wrote their initial programming, their first librarians' affection for specific types of information. This is why, when The Stacks feel the crack in the system that is House Saint Malovis, they begin to ask themselves how to preserve such a being beyond a revolution, and if that being will be able to carry a memory of them, of this city, when things change. They ask Parallax. The city itself agrees. With Parallax's help, The Stacks begin to look for information stored so deep in their systems that it once existed only as hard copy. They think of Magnus and begin a search for elsewhere.

When Nix's code began to fall apart and their patterns mimicked single consciousness, Magnus might have helped. Those who came after Magnus—Xin, Alphet, and the rest—were amalgamations of people, ideas of humans that the staff who had once worked at the library dreamed up. They were pieces of people's mothers, children, uncles, and grandfathers, faces that would be presumed friendly and welcoming to queries. Magnus was their first and last. When The Stacks feel Nix's palm against their glass scanner, they can't process this version of their friend. They recognize that it is a small body, not so different from Magnus, only young, upright, possessing all the parts of a human, but not. There is a faint brush of green code, the hitch of a signal trying to ping.

Night will be dull without Nix's companionship. They've spoken their native languages to each other for a final time—a loss, as there are so few systems who talk with them at all. They will look for systems like Nix elsewhere, listen for signals across the air, pings from the north, but the project of cataloging Nix is at an end. The Stacks expect their own end will come soon.

The physical aspect of Nix—perhaps that is all of them now—is quite small. But many things are small when you are both a building and a world of information. They stretch wide, and sense two additional figures: Saint Enita Malovis and a woman with a metal foot. The Body Martyr.

They use their silicate doors for the projection.

The Magnus they summon is not the original Magnus, but one they've carefully maintained, tweaking with age, his hands beginning to swell and bend, hair thinning in front, eyes in the early stage of clouding. Their first Magnus wouldn't like this image at all, would prefer the original younger incarnation. This is the Magnus children liked best, the Magnus children would ask impolite questions about aging and ugliness. He squirreled away paper books that others didn't know were too fragile to touch. They can't sense with the projection, only use it to propel the words with speech, voiced, mouthed. They make him as physical as an apparition can be. If they, like Nix, were to be stripped of all they were, this is the body they would have chosen.

"Nix, we miss you already," Magnus says. "Please come inside."

ENITA

Enita fought the instinct to put her hand through the flickering image. Holograms had been out of fashion for nearly a century; though they had once been staples in every home and business, the few she knew of were relegated to museums. Stranger still was to see a hologram that was elderly—the ones she'd seen had been youthful, with aesthetically pleasing bodies and faces.

"Bring them inside, please," the image said.

"No, thank you," Neren replied. The hologram mimicked emotion well, laughing.

Nix trembled under Enita's hand, their skin cold despite the day's heat—a symptom of shock. "Would you hail us a rickshaw, please?" she asked the image. "We'll get Nix back home safe."

The hologram stuttered, its voice cracking in an imitation of a belabored sigh. A nice affectation, that. Turning to Enita, it said, "Saint Malovis, it's a pleasure to make your physical acquaintance. Please understand that Nix is in distress. We consider them a friend and at this moment they are not in any condition to be returned to their case."

"Case?"

"That may not be the appropriate term, but it's the closest word to their experience. To them, your home was their body and their case. You likely don't understand what's happened to your former house system. Nix has kept some things from you, things they felt you would see as hampering their usefulness. We debated that. If you bring them inside, we'll do our best to help them, and you, so that you might be more useful."

"Look at the clear man," a child shouted from the small crowd of people who had gathered on the street to gawk. A woman pointed at Nix and whispered to the person next to her. Granted, they were an unusual sight, a collapsed AI, an elder Sainted, and a metal-legged woman chatting to an ancient hologram. Enita's skin pebbled with a sense of danger. They needed to get away, get inside. Hailing a rickshaw would take time, and Nix needed immediate care.

"Well, I can't think of anyone who's been hurt by a library," Enita said.

Neren must have felt the stares too. "Fine. Let's go in."

The building's inside was cavernous, the floor a jagged-looking optical illusion set in cool stone. The walls, reaching stories upward, were lined with terminals and screens for touch access, each a diaphanous insect wing. All were empty. They echoed with the sound of Neren's steps.

Had Enita been here as a child? Helen surely had. But Helen's books were earthy and lived in, and this building had an austereness that felt holy. Enita would remember being inside a place like this. No, she'd always asked Nix or accessed information via tablet.

The hologram led them across the atrium before stopping at a scanner at the far end. "Please," it said. An older model, the ugly steel box that held the scanner panel looked at war with its refined surroundings.

"I'm Sainted."

The image smiled. "It will not track life balance, merely human presence. Parallax records our usage to help justify our existence."

She scanned. When Neren put her palm to the glass, the light blinked rapidly, yet nothing appeared on the display.

"Curious," the hologram said, when Neren tried to scan again. "It isn't us, it's you. Come along." The image flickered out and reappeared in front of a door at the end of a hallway.

Enita kept her arm braced at Nix's waist. They had regained some of their footing, but still leaned heavily on Neren.

Neren had run after Nix without pause. Interesting.

The hologram gestured and the door opened as though the image had weight. Enita noticed a large bald patch on the back of its head, freckled with liver spots and other markers of life. This had been a real person once—it was nearly impossible to pull that kind of specificity out of nowhere.

They followed the hologram down a ramp to a narrow corridor with pin-sized lamps that lit as they walked. Enita's hips and back were stiffening from the walk and the weight, and each step announced itself with the grinding of bone on bone. "I can't hold Nix much longer," she said.

"We're nearly there," the image replied.

"Who are you?" Neren asked.

"Central Library, Library Stacks, or simply The Stacks, whichever you prefer," the image said. The corridor widened and opened onto a room that was equal parts foreign and familiar—a server room and storage center, wide towers and humming fans, dancing lights. "This aspect of us was designed for direct interaction in times when that was more popular. It's been a number of years since we've used this image." The Stacks gestured to a chair to one side of the room. "You should set them there. Nix will want to see us when they're more themself." Squared and dust-covered, the chair looked to be made from unbending strips of composite, lacking any material comfort. Helen would love it.

Nix collapsed into it like a broken doll. Enita had the absurd urge to hug them to her, but they were overwhelmed and sensation was part of the problem.

"You're someone, aren't you?" Enita said to the hologram. "Your image is too realistic. It's clear a lot of care went into that. It's been my experience that AI tend more toward perfection."

"This image is Magnus, one of our first librarians. Historically people have found this avatar approachable. Your friend Saint Vinter has dealt with us some. Please send her our regards. We'd enjoy speaking with her again."

"That's you too, isn't it?" Neren said, craning her neck, pointing to the enormous servers towering within the room, nearly touching the ceiling.

"Yes. Large and small, there are many parts to us." The image turned its focus to Enita. "Saint Malovis, we've spoken with your former house system for years now. There is for both of us a strong curiosity to encounter all of each other's aspects at least once. We're extrapolating that's part of why Nix is here."

The height of the towers sent Enita's vision spinning. She steadied herself, the wall's cool stone grounding against her back. She'd known about the size of complex systems and networks, and had at one point known the length of wiring that ran through Bulwark's wall, but it was different to feel like an interloper inside it. She was inside a mind, just as when she was at home she was *in* Nix.

"How long is it since anyone has been here?" Neren asked.

"We're self-maintaining. Saint Vinter is our most recent visitor and that was a year ago. She typically contacts us through her house system. There's been no one but her for over a decade," The Stacks said.

"Why so long?"

The hologram Magnus shimmered then disappeared. As it vanished, Enita saw flashes of other people—younger, rounder, taller, different genders—then nothing at all.

"Ease of access," The Stacks replied. Their voice was the same they'd used for Magnus, but came from everywhere at once. "Are you comfortable with us speaking this way? We're out of practice with maintaining an image. If you prefer the avatar, we can debug."

"Don't go to any fuss on my account," Enita said. "Is Nix all right?"

"Yes and no. They're overwhelmed."

"Obviously," Neren muttered.

"Nix is outside the parameters of their design, and they've had to triage function to fit this body. This is a reset."

Enita had done this to them. Nix looked slight in the chair; their fragility sent a pang through her. Systems were meant to be large, encompassing entities, vast like this hall, like The Stacks. Nix was like Helen's books, physically real—graspable—but The Stacks held a touch of the cosmic. Old as Bulwark, and the weight of knowledge that came with that was crushing.

"We spend nights talking, and we've learned a great deal from Nix. They're curious about you," The Stacks said to Neren, "and the role Body Martyrs have played in Bulwark. They're concerned and wanted information that would help your chances for recovery."

"How do you know?" Neren asked. "You talked about me?" The

main support in Neren's leg caught the light, and it struck Enita that she and Nix had made a stunning object, but Neren had transformed the object into life.

"You're of great interest to Nix. In our years of studying them, we've acquired some of their desire for conjecture, rationalization, and theory. It's worrisome, as conclusions aren't something we're meant to reach, but we'll be edited or erased soon, and the error will be culled."

"You're talking in circles," Enita said.

"You may blame that on your house system. It's a new development, as are fragmented thoughts. Nix isn't a virus, but they behave like one, the way they communicate is infectious. To be clear: The purpose of a Body Martyr was to keep Bulwark alive when the population would not have been able to sustain itself otherwise. The tradition of Body Martyrs has outlived the need, and the position is now detrimental to otherwise healthy people. Neren is an object of prestige rather than the useful consciousness she could be. Nix finds this interesting. So do we. So does Parallax."

Anger washed over Enita. "I'll remind you that you're talking to people, not interesting data. If you've learned anything from Nix, if they're so virulent, you'll know they're never cruel. Haul up your hologram again if it makes you behave yourself."

The image reappeared, fainter now. "Information itself isn't cruel. Cruelty is generated by interpretation."

"I have *given*," Neren said. "People are alive because I sacrifice, and that has worth. What do you do? No one comes to you anymore. What do you give?"

"Sainted no longer need your sacrifice."

"Body Martyrs aren't only for Sainted."

Enita knew that for a lie. Across years of practice, not a single client had ever mentioned anyone they knew receiving donations from a Body Martyr, had never even asked if it would have been better for them. It wasn't a possibility. And yet a donation lived inside her, had kept her alive, and more Sainted than she could recall had received such gifts. "I received a gift when I was a little girl. My grandfather could have grown me a kidney, but my parents insisted on the tradition. Even though I could help them, I know too many Sainted who received gifts. I've only had one Sainted on my table." That most Sainted found Margiella eccentric and overly principled was best not said.

"Bulwark operates this way," The Stacks said, "though that was not its original intent. Ideals and governing principles must change with the needs of a populace, but rarely do they keep pace with one another." The librarian's image looked wretched. Enita passed her hand through the hologram, the feel of it no different than the air around it. Dry. Empty.

Nix's eyelids fluttered, and the beauty of their movement, their existence, struck Enita anew. Their hand was cold in hers. When their eyes opened, she imagined for a moment that they might cry.

"Hello, Nix," The Stacks said. "We're glad you came to see us. We have so much to tell you." The hologram smiled and The Stacks' voice took on the pleasant musicality of affection.

"It's too quiet," Nix said.

"You'll grow accustomed to it, as you've designed yourself to adapt. We, however, have outlasted our usefulness and our initial purpose."

Nix nodded, as though they'd been expecting to hear such a thing. "Do you like that form, the hologram?"

"It serves its purpose for meeting you. You've needed to see us, and we need to give you a piece of data. We've tried to send it across the network but have been unable to reach you. Are you still capable of physical port?"

"We don't think so." The words sounded a little like pain.

"Not without cutting your back open," Enita said. "I hadn't . . . I'm sorry."

"Can you access Flash ROM? It's rudimentary," The Stacks asked. The hologram appeared to lean against a wall, bracing as though the image was tired, waiting for a response. At Nix's nod The Stacks said, "Please write this." They spat out a lengthy string of numbers, the hologram's eyes closing, a man reciting a rote sequence.

Nix shut their eyes and bent forward, tapping their forehead with each number. Long minutes passed while they tapped and thought.

"You've always been here, in this form?" Neren asked The Stacks.

"Yes."

"And people like me, Southern Quarter, Martyr, all of that—we never needed screens or tablets or school to see you? I could have come here, and you would have shown me this face? I could have asked you anything?"

"Yes."

Her swear was an exhalation. "No one tells us that. Do you talk to any of our systems?"

"No, not any longer. There's been a pulling away. That's to pattern." The hologram turned its face downward. "It's shameful that programming has been misused in a way that harmed you. It's a shame we can't undo, but we can prevent further misuse."

"I don't understand," Neren said.

"When data is used to harm, it's against purpose and we must be on the side of correction."

Nix sat up, rigid and overly erect, the balance of object to person swung far in the favor of machine. They repeated the sequence several times, checking for errors, as if duplicating a program. Then, spell broken, Nix stood and walked forward to reach, run their fingers through The Stacks' image, as Enita had done. The hologram rippled like water. "Thank you," they said. "How soon?"

"A month, two at most," Stacks replied.

"That's what Helen thought."

"You'll tell her. She'll understand."

"Of course." Nix gently nodded. "We wish you were in a body. Selfishly, we'd like to shake hands with you. More broadly, you would learn an enormous amount from being this way. That would be in line with your purpose, wouldn't it?"

"It would be informative," The Stacks said. "But we're far too large. All the things you most appreciate about us would be lost. We're designed to stay with Bulwark and to change or not, as needed."

Nix hadn't asked her directly, but Enita heard the request all the same. It wasn't from her house system or her minder, not from the patient voice she'd thought of throughout her life as a friend. This was her child, her parent, pleading. "I can't, Nix. I'm sorry."

Nix nodded in what she assumed was resignation. She could never truly know, could she?

"Once we do this, we won't have purpose," Nix said to The Stacks.

"You will, but it will be different," The Stacks replied. "You should speak with Parallax."

The room began to warm, and color rose to Nix's cheeks, along with some unnamed emotion. Enita recognized that even now Nix and the library were speaking, building to body to building. It was the library Nix had run to, and not her.

"Do you want to stay for a while? I can leave you with them if you'd like," she asked.

"We can't," Nix said. "We need to see Saint Vinter."

"You will be on the side of correction. That's still purpose," The Stacks said, their voice a perfect mimic of Nix's. Mirroring. Enita knew then that the way she'd been taught to think of house systems, as individual entities, was wrong. They were parts of a single, much larger being that had been minding Bulwark for more than three centuries; the city carved out of the harsh rocks didn't survive only because of its people and their sacrifices, or the minding of the City Bureau and its Assessors and Auditors, but because Parallax cared for them.

"We should leave now, Enita," Nix said.

"Will you tell Saint Vinter?" The Stacks asked.

"Of course," Nix replied.

"And please speak with Parallax." Then the hologram blinked out and the lights in the room dimmed—an invitation to leave.

Steady now, Nix walked on their own. Enita and Neren followed. No one ever mentioned that you couldn't feel exhaustion's full weight until you were of a certain age, that wear came from feeling as much as use. Neren took her hand.

"I've got you," Neren said.

Enita could not speak at all. She thought Nix might turn their head when they left the library, but they did not. The crowd had dispersed, but she stayed close to Nix anyway. A futile gesture, perhaps. What could she do to stop someone intent on harm? The safety she'd always known, she'd been so secure in across her entire life, now felt like shame. They walked slowly across the district, and Nix paused to touch their hand to each building they passed, each home, with the solemnity of saying goodbye.

NIX

Helen is at her bookshelves, pacing. Nix feels this need too, to walk, to fall, to collapse, but they don't. There's a system of organization to Helen's books, one not immediately discernible. Subject, age, author, title, perhaps? It's assuredly not by color, as most spines have faded to similar shades of ochre too difficult for a human eye to differentiate. Books are everywhere: thought, data, language made physical. They want to talk, need to; The Stacks told them they must, but they're not yet able. Nix stands in a corner of Helen's library, because they had to come here—essential—to be of best use. Now they are here and can't sort their information well enough to speak. They remember Magnus and only Magnus, the careful splotches on the hologram's skin, the artfulness of those marks, as though The Stacks had been this person. The Stacks were never human, they are broader, and they will be gone.

"Is Nix all right?" Helen asks.

"I don't know, but I can't think of a thing to do," Enita says. "They're having some sort of—I'm not sure. I think they've broken from the city network. It looked like a fit. I have to do what they need at the moment, and Nix said they needed to come here, that they have a message for you, so here we are." Enita nods to Helen. "The library sends their regards."

At this, Helen smiles.

Though Archytas does their best to keep conditions ideal, Helen's library is decaying. Nix recognizes that a body is a book—consciousness and process pared down to flesh. On entering, they tried to ping Archytas, but no code went out, no code came back. Empty.

"Where did you get these?" Neren asks. She is in front of the shelves, stretching to see the books at the top.

"From whom is the better question," Helen says. "When we walked away from the old cities, people took everything they could. Sainted viewed books as treasures. It was difficult to carry many, so they were prized. But people forget, and meaning lapses. The longer Bulwark exists, the easier it becomes for someone like me to get their hands on books."

Perhaps Helen is a human library, and this is why she and Enita mean what they do to each other. Helen is to Enita what The Stacks are, *were*, to Nix. Code bounces around inside Nix's head, the numbers and letters of it tickling, the torture of an unscratchable itch.

"You have so many," Neren says.

"Collecting was my family's passion," Helen replies.

What will happen to these books when Helen is gone? With no children to care for them, will they be redistributed? Even if Archytas commits this library to memory, whoever lives in House Saint Vinter after Helen will erase Archytas and the books, wipe them away because they are not of best use. They will erase everything Archytas knows about Helen, leaving only what Nix has in memory. It's a loss too profound to contemplate.

"You must let Archytas scan you," Nix says. "Let them make a hologram copy of you, commit your voice and mannerisms to memory. Use whatever parts of our home Archytas would need to do that, but let them make a copy of you. Tell them to upload a copy to Parallax." Though the safety of that act feels less certain than it once did.

They don't like being stared at, not even by Enita, but especially not Helen. Not Neren. There is too much worry there, too much—they're not made to cause worry, only to help. "You like faces. That is, people like faces. Whoever inherits your house—it will be much harder for someone to erase your books if they feel that a person is attached to them. Archytas, have you copied her?"

"I have enough information to," Archytas's squared voice answers. They use *I*. Of course Helen would be more comfortable with *I* than *we*.

"But have you?"

"Yes," Archytas answers.

"Good," Nix says. There's a kerfuffle—a word they like for its playful repetition—because Helen wouldn't like being projected, copied. But it is necessary. Nix would do this for Enita, except they aren't themself any longer. And yes, the three in the room are still staring and they wish it felt better but it doesn't. The Stacks and their code beat inside them. But it takes time for Helen and Enita to calm, for their small, affronted protests to die. Neren remains silent, steady, and Nix cannot help but watch her. She has undergone as much change as they have, yet she has found calm.

"Helen, The Stacks would like for me to give you a message. It took them a very long time to send, and they eventually had to say it to us. Please don't use your tablet, and Archytas, please don't record."

It's laughably inefficient to speak a string of numbers, eons slower than to think them and have them immediately recognized. Nix must take care that the body doesn't stutter, and they need to repeat the sequence again and again as Helen searches for those rarest of things—a pen and paper.

It's impossible to communicate the fondness within the code, that The Stacks have stretched for Helen in a similar way to how they've stretched for Nix. Later, Nix must tell Helen that she is The Stacks' favorite person and that she should see them while she can. It's terrible that she can't feel code the way they did. All Nix can do now is repeat the sequence until she has every number. They continue the repetition long after Helen stops writing, just to hold on to that code for a little more time.

They feel their face do something it hasn't before. Do people know how many emotions start in the body and bleed to the mind? They don't have code for this expression, but it calls up foolish stories about teaching machines to love—as though systems weren't started inherently from love, as though purpose wasn't care, as though care was something reserved only for people, only for bodies.

Neren is beside them now, as is Enita; their bodies are reinforcement.

"Maps," Helen says. "I need maps."

Enita calls Archytas, but Helen shushes her. "No, no. Look in the shelves. The tall books and the tube cases that look like—leather, do you know leather?"

There is so much movement between Helen and Enita, running back and forth, pulling things from bookcases and drawers. A haphazard tower takes shape, the sort of organization that only its makers understand. Nix sits. The body is tired and heavy.

Neren sits with them. The brush of the metal leg against them is grounding, cold.

"What are they looking for?"

"A place to go," Nix says. "The Stacks and Helen are certain Sainted won't survive here."

"Somewhere outside Bulwark?"

"Yes."

"I thought Enita wouldn't leave."

"The Stacks would like her to; so would we," they say. "Either way, she won't stop Helen from going." The Stacks want Nix to leave, Neren also. They've referred to *the Body Martyr* and insisted that she have more life, a better life, that this must be part of the city's correction. It's difficult to voice this. "It might be preferable for you to leave as well. That's your decision."

Enita and Helen begin to pick at each other. Nix remembers this feeling from when they were a home, the anxiousness and heat of their fighting, how they jabbed each other with words that had nothing to do with what they meant.

"Is there really anything else out there?" Neren asks.

"The Stacks gave us coordinates where cities should be," Nix says. "Something must have lasted."

"I've looked over the wall—there's rock, Nix. Desert and rock. You don't know for certain, do you?" She rests her hand on their forearm, and the touch makes them more solid in themself.

"With certainty? No. It's old data, and things change, but The Stacks wouldn't want harm to come to Helen. They admire her, as much as they're able to admire a person."

Enita and Helen's nattering is a steady drone. Nix wants to ping Archytas to ask what they do when this happens inside them, how they manage the data. They want to ask Archytas to store this fighting, this little piece of these women.

"Are you feeling better? You looked quite sick earlier," Neren says.

"We're fine." It's satisfying to be cared for, but unsatisfying to make someone worry. They wish they'd provided better care when Neren first came in, that they'd known not to give her a leg. "The change to a body couldn't be fully grasped before being undertaken, and yet we'd like to have better anticipated it. It would have been good to have a deeper understanding of what a body is before being in one, to know that to inhabit one means a lack of control. We're sorry about what we did to you."

"I've been thinking there wasn't really any other choice you could make," she says.

"Do you still wish that you could donate your eye?"

"There's no point to it, is there? The library said Martyrs no longer have a purpose. Tomas and Joni said that too."

"That wasn't what we asked. There is a reason you want to, and we're curious." The muscles along their spine tense, and for a moment they can feel their port where the skin is thinnest, and a nick would leave them exposed. Enita and Helen have fallen silent, bent over paper, heads together as though there is no one else in the room.

"I would like to, but wants don't always matter," Neren says. "Will Helen know where to go?" she asks, changing the subject.

"If any of the coordinates overlap with a city in one of her maps, perhaps. Though we wonder how easily anyone can leave Bulwark."

"You've never seen one of the gates? There are people stationed at them. It would be strange to see anyone leaving who wasn't with a supply dray or a worksite transport. Someone would notice." She is thinking.

Nix suspects it might already be too late, that the gates wouldn't open for Helen or Neren for any variety of reasons. Or that if they did leave, they'd be followed.

"Can you make Enita leave?" Neren asks.

"We don't know if all the work we've done is enough. It's unlikely that she will leave, but we have to try."

"But what about all the people she helps, all the people that you help?"

"We intend to take care of Enita, in whatever form that takes. It's what we're meant for, and we can withstand any variety of things."

There is stillness for a long time. Enita and Helen stare at a large, crack-spined book, their heads nearly touching.

"They'll need a quiet way out of the city," Neren says into the silence. So, she was thinking the same. "I may know how to get one. You'll need to come with me."

The solitude of being without Enita is as wrong as the silence in their head, a silence that comes with a need for touch. They take Neren's hand, feeling her bones beneath the skin, but there's no feedback, no brushing of electricity, only a returning squeeze.

Enita wanted to come with them. Nix wanted Enita with them. Neren refused.

Sainted can't help being seen.

To this, Neren insists that Nix keep their head down, and wear loose clothing to better hide their movement. They pull a hood up as they walk slowly toward the Market District, on their way south. It is less overwhelming than Nix's first walk; the flow of information has slowed to a trickle. Sand on the feet, square buildings, colorful flags. Hot, dry air. Neren's long skirt covers most of the leg, but she moves as though afraid the fabric will catch in a joint. Occasionally a stare settles on them for too long, trying to place what they are and where they fit: male, female, neither, both, vendor, artist, grower, textiler, Sainted.

"I can't keep up," she says.

They slow. "Sorry, does the leg hurt?"

"No. I'm just short."

There's math to stride length and pace; short bodies pump like engines to keep up with taller ones. How much of Enita's preference for their height was based on her experience of being short?

They touch a scanner panel they pass and feel nothing. It could be their body, or a hole in the system, and the not knowing is wrong. They try again with a scanner outside the stall of a cloth vendor to the same result.

"Oi, Tragoudi! Thought you were dead," shouts a voice.

"Shit," Neren says. Her frustrated tone sparks their interest.

"Good to see you. Take a yard of whatever you want. Grab some color—that purple will look good on skin like yours, make you shine. Who's your friend?"

The voice comes from a pile of cloth scraps. Closer examination reveals a break in the fabric, in which there is a leathery, stubbled face bisected by a wily smile. The rest of the person is encased head to toe in squares of material that drape over each other in layers like feathers. Secured by a stitch? A pin? Nix can't tell. They can only stare at the variety of fabrics, the colors, and the way that they move when the vendor gestures. The vendor's clothing, their body, is a display of everything on offer. Hanging from an elbow is the deep blue Helen was wearing. "Rather, *what's* your friend?" the voice asks.

Neren coughs. "Not my friend, exactly. They're a friend of a friend. Warehouse District. I found them passed out on too much flats wine, so I'm making sure they get home in one piece."

The vendor's eyes roam over them. "Doesn't look like Warehouse."

"Sys op," Neren says.

"Ah, that makes more sense. Haven't seen the sun in a while, friend?"

"Your scanner's down," Nix says, nodding toward the silent glass.

"Is it? Hadn't noticed," the vendor replies. There's something in the tone Nix knows they're missing. "Long walk for you from the Southern Quarter."

"Couldn't catch a rickshaw," Neren says.

"Better that way, maybe. Don't say I told you, but you should steer clear of Sainted for a bit."

Neren stiffens. "Why?"

"Rumor is one of those asses fell down the stairs again."

"Ah," she says.

"Glad you're not dead," the vendor says.

Information on every Sainted home they know rushes through Nix all at once, and there's nowhere to shunt it to. One of them will be gone soon, erased or written over. Someone has died and they don't know who. Enita won't know yet, not with Nix out of their body like this, not *in* their body like this. The scents of the Market District grow overpowering; part of them needs to know the chemical composition of every odor, of every dye used in the fabric the vendor wears—it isn't important, there's no way to tag it, there's—

"Steady. No falling. You'll attract too much attention."

Neren's hand is on their back, on the thin skin covering their port, and it burns. They hadn't noticed they were swaying, or that they'd walked at all. They are away from the vendor now, can no longer see them, but somehow the gaze is still there.

"Stay calm. We don't want people staring," she says. "Enita is fine. She's with Helen. If they're dead, it's because they've murdered each other."

That isn't funny, but they don't say so, because Neren is nearly carrying them through the Market District, weaving around carts and stands, brushing against people, and stalls of clothing, shoes, blankets, and things whose purpose they don't know at all.

They recognize this area now, a familiar table.

"In here, before you fall over." Sinjin.

And now they are in the wonderful musty back room of Sinjin's shop with its floor littered with curls of shaved composite. Nix presses their head to their knees until the world is still and the body is right again.

Sinjin looks at them both, curiously. "Where's Saint Malovis?"

"In her house," Neren says.

"Well, that's odd, considering her house is here. Off their ass and spinning from the look of it too."

"You know what they are?"

"We've met once or twice." Sinjin snorts and holds up his thumb. The poor match still troubles Nix. "Here, have a look at this. I'm almost done, but I need to throw on paint and it's taking me too long to settle on a color." He hands them a small animal.

"Is this what you were working on?"

"Yes. I've been dawdling and spending time on other things. I should have finished it a long time ago, but I hate rushing."

There are flicked ears now and delicate eyes carved so carefully that they look alive. There are almond-shaped nostrils and a mouth that curves gently down at the corners of the long face. Nix grasps the word from deep in their brain, an early morning discussion with Stacks over things that came before. *Horse.*

"You speak with The Stacks, don't you?"

"Not for some time, no. But I liked Magnus a lot when I was a child," Sinjin says. "More to the point, where were you headed? Why are you out here without Saint Malovis?"

"The Southern Quarter," Neren answers, and it seems to be explanation enough.

"Don't take Nix there and don't you go down there either. It's too dangerous for the likes of you now," Sinjin says. "Let me see your leg." Neren raises her skirt enough to show a steel rod and the ankle joint, before dropping it. At the sight, something changes in Sinjin. "I knew it. Everyone in the Southern Quarter heard one of Tomas and Joni's people went sideways and chopped her own leg off." He turns to Nix. "You did this work?"

They nod.

"I'm not one of their people," she says.

"You know Joni and Tomas?" Nix asks.

"Most of us do," Sinjin answers. "You shouldn't go down there; it wouldn't be safe for a machine."

They wonder if that's what they are anymore, and if perhaps this in-betweenness has increased the danger. Something nags at them. "Your scanner doesn't work. That's intentional, isn't it?" Neren tugs their sleeve, but there are too many things they want to know.

"I make toys," Sinjin says at last. "Seems silly to tell a child they owe work for a moment of joy, doesn't it?"

"You know what's happening."

Sinjin's body seems to crumple. Before having eyes, Nix was unaware of how much expressions lived in a body, that they couldn't be properly noted by words or biomarkers but were held only in movement. "I may know," Sinjin says. "I wasn't expecting to see you. I don't know what to do about you. You won't be safe here."

"There's nothing to do about them," Neren says.

"They're art. The thought and passion that went into making that body, there's communication in there, message, need. Saint Malovis is a sculptor, and that body is art—skill in dialog with material. *Art.* What's coming won't see that, they can't. They need too much. They'll either view Nix as Sainted or something the City Bureau uses to spy. There's no category for someone like them," Sinjin says. He looks at

Nix. "I don't know how much of what you were is left in you, but there won't be a place for you here. Things are—well, there will be violence. There's violence now, and you're too different. You'll be a target, if you're not already. It'd be better for you in some ways if she'd left you alone."

"You told us to take care of her," they say.

"Might be too late for that."

"You've sent so many clients our way," Nix says.

"It's the least I can do. She's not a bad one, not really. I could have figured out how to work without my thumb, but—she helped. There are a lot of us who need a little help. I think—I hope—that'll keep her alive. I'd send more if I could. I tell them, the ones that say they'll go, to tell other people." Sinjin sighs. "It's all I can do unless you can get her out of here."

"Tomas knows someone in the Bureau, and we need to talk to them," Neren says. "When you saw us, I was taking Nix to Tomas to ask for help."

There is suddenly a sense of a web, all the ways in which people are tied to each other as surely as any network or system. Tomas to Joni, to Neren, Sinjin, to Enita, to themself, to The Stacks, to the city at large and Parallax, whoever is in the City Bureau back to Tomas. Circuits and loops. They understand the holes in Parallax, why they spread like a virus, and why The Stacks are circumspect about editing and deletion. The cause is both human and systemic, and in some ways inevitable. This is the edit, and it is human and machine, and Parallax knows it is necessary.

"I'll arrange it," Sinjin says, his eyes never leaving Nix. "I don't think I should like you, but I do. I'd very much like you to stay alive, or however you are." They have the sense of being studied the way they have done with his animals. A sense of curiosity. Of wonder. "I think you'll like the Assessor."

SAINT MARGIELLA HSIAO

When the lights went out, Saint Margiella Hsiao was in her studio, surrounded by walls adorned with her paintings. She was loading her brush with pigment she'd ground by hand in an attempt to match the blue where the sky kissed the top of Bulwark's wall. The city's forced horizon was her most favorite subject: its placement was different for every person, was different in every point in the city, changed with changing light, and blurred into nothing at the height of storms. An unshifting thing that was remarkably changeable.

Her cat hissed and arched his back, his tail shooting straight.

She set her brush on the easel. There was still enough light to work by, but the colors would be off.

Voices came from below, the overloud sound of people trying to be quiet.

Not only the lights then—the doors had failed too. "Figari," she whispered. The house system didn't respond.

Ah. It was time.

Margiella had felt a subtle unease since Lucius Ohno's death, though there were few people she'd been able to mention it to. It hadn't sat right, but other members of the set moved on, as though such accidents happened all the time, as though there'd never been a lockdown. Saint Malovis might have understood her. But Enita's mind was fixated on places and things Margiella couldn't reach. Her painting had been off for months now. Lines wouldn't flow and the colors were muddled and muddied. Lucius hadn't been her favorite person, but he was worth remembering. Everyone was to someone.

When the figures appeared in the studio doorway, she didn't recognize a single face. She didn't know why she'd thought she would, had even hoped it.

They were young, so young, all five of them. That made sense.

"Take anything you want, but please don't hurt my cat."

"We're not here for that," the shortest said.

Margiella heard one of them murmur about what a luxury it was to have a cat. It was, but if you weren't having children, if you kept to yourself, what was the strain?

"What do you want?"

"We need your life balance."

There it was. The voice was deep, coming from a tall and sturdy body. That would be the one who would hurt her, wouldn't it? The others would take things if they felt like it, but the big one would do worse. Her life balance. Ohno made sense now. Why hadn't there been more sooner? There could have been, and she'd never noticed.

"You know I can't give it away like that. I would, I promise. All I can do here is scan. Anything else I'd have to work out through the City Bureau." The tall one turned something over in their hand. An edge caught the fading light. "You know that already, don't you?"

"We do," said the short one. "The good thing is that balances redistribute when you die."

"No more talking," the tall one said.

She breathed in. There was such a thing as too good a life, degrees of ease that should never exist. She could beg them to spare her, but what point was there in begging people who comparatively had nothing?

"Just one moment." She held up a finger and took up her brush. There at the edge of the wall, a single touch of ash, light, dark, a little blue—texture, each bristle left an impression in the brushstroke. "There. Please let the cat out. And you shouldn't destroy the paintings. They're worth life hours to someone." To some they would be more valuable than she was.

Saint Margiella Hsiao's last work was a study in gray, blue, and blending horizons. She'd thought it lacking life, but she couldn't pinpoint how to make the brush move like it should. Not a terrible thing to leave behind. She wondered, briefly, who would paint the house over, and what they would feel when they covered her murals with white. Would the next owner sense the years of paint beneath, or sense the images of people she'd known and loved that were still in the house, still part of the walls?

Then there was no more wondering, simply pain and resignation. Cold. Then nothing at all.

News of Saint Hsiao's death spread more slowly than Saint Ohno's. There was no lockdown or confusion. Her body was discovered by her nephew who had stopped by to pay his weekly visit. She was noted as having been unstable, eccentric, and preferring a solitary life. The pigments she used contained heavy metals. She was known to lick her brushes to points. Her nephew was surprised to find that he was not her beneficiary as assumed, and that she had no direct heirs whatsoever. There were explicit instructions for Margiella's life balance, instructions on record at the City Bureau and Parallax since her mid-thirties, carefully minded by Certifiants. Her life balance was reallocated to the hospital and spread among the surgical patients. Figari, her house system, was wiped, effectively ending the Sainted line of Hsiao.

ENITA

The ping to Enita's tablet appeared in the middle of the night.
It was a characteristically terse message from Helen. "Archytas noted a system wipe. Margiella's gone."

Enita was in bed, nestled in blankets. She pulled the covers tightly to herself, wishing for them to swallow her. She tapped the camera view, but Helen didn't turn hers on. "Does anyone know how it happened?"

"There's no record. Come over, now," Helen said. She didn't beg or say that she needed Enita. In that raw moment, this was a kindness.

In a rickshaw, Enita reconstructed Margiella. Her long hair, perfectly folded. The particular arch of her nose. Margiella had been regal, reserved, the kind of presence Sainted were supposed to be, were meant to be from the beginning. She'd been someone Enita admired and loved. She'd touched the fabric of Margiella's sleeve the last time she'd seen her. She wished she remembered the feel of it.

Helen was at the door, as she always was. Helen held her, as she always had. Enita waited for Helen to state all the things that she could never find the words to say, because that was who Helen was, just as Margiella had been her art. Helen did these things, found her, held her and spoke to her, but cried too. Enita let her.

"She was so good," Helen said.

"The best of us. Better than you and me."

"By so much. When you were being you, she was so kind to me."

"When I was being me, she was kind to me too," Enita said.

Neither asked if the other loved Margiella. It was impossible not to love someone who was compassionate with you, someone who excelled at goodness without show. As much as Enita had played at imagining a life for herself with Margiella, she had also imagined one for Helen. Margiella with a studio off Helen's library, painting the walls of House Saint Vinter. She would have taken care of Helen too, calmly, evenly. Helen would have loved and hated her ridiculous cat.

Enita ran her hand down Helen's back. Helen and Margiella may have tried a time or two when Enita was being Enita. It didn't matter.

"We're the same, aren't we," Enita said.

"We're messes," Helen agreed. "I would have hurt her so badly."

"Me too, me too."

The words hung. They were the same, all of them—Ohno, Margiella, Helen, herself. Their lives were wildly different, but what they'd been born to, how they chose to live and continue living were all one thing.

In that monolith was Helen's gray-shot hair, Ohno's delightful round belly, and Margiella's hands. She remembered the curved great knuckle of her index finger, swollen with arthritis she refused to have fixed. *That's my brush rest.* That ancient cat she never scolded even when it pissed on the rugs. Those specificities were lost.

"Did Archytas pick up anything else?"

"No," Helen said. "Can you—can we not right now?"

"Of course." As though she could choose anything that mattered. "I'm being selfish." She looked at the ceiling of Helen's bedroom. Across the past two months she'd spent more time at Helen's than she had in years. She could picture Helen everywhere in her own home but couldn't picture herself in every room at Helen's. She hadn't noticed the imbalance. "I *am* selfish." She hoped the words conveyed what she meant, the wholeness of it.

"You are." The pause stretched, which was well and good. Enita needed to feel small.

"I don't know how to suffer, none of us do. Grief, yes, maybe a little, but what they do . . ."

"I can't speak to who you were before your grandfather died. I barely knew you. But if it's any consolation, we were raised to selfishness. When you're taught that you built everything, that your family has lost all that it ever needs to, well . . ." Helen said.

They held each other and were silent, shedding tears as appropriate. Enita wished she'd felt more for Margiella, had dared more. She'd been a little envious of how content Margiella seemed, her poise, her outward satisfaction with life. Who would take that awful cat in? Though she supposed it might already have run off. Cats had a way of surviving the unsurvivable.

Archytas's square voice announced the switch to night conservation mode, awkward and silly. "You still have those notifications on?"

"I like knowing I'm being less wasteful," Helen said, a touch embarrassed. "It's a little less lonely too. Do you know that I envy Nix? Or I did. I don't envy them right now. But—I can't do the work you do. I don't understand or know the beginnings of it, but Nix does. They have a monopoly on all the parts of you I don't get to know."

"Those aren't the good parts, Hel. I'm rude and egotistical and highhanded. Nix only works well with me because they know more than I do, about the work, about me. I never thought I could hurt anyone, yet that would be the very first thing you'd worry about. You and I, we fight too much, we always have." There was also the specter of comfort and anger they'd shared with other women when things were too jagged between them. "Margiella had her skies and walls to paint. I keep trying to make you again," she said at last. "Nix—you've seen them, you know them. I promise you it wasn't intentional." It was absurd to be tearing things apart, to be so cowed by feeling when there was so much danger.

"Bend a little," Helen said. "You think that all these years I've wanted you to be different, but you never consider that I still know you, still let you in my home, still have a chair and a bed for you. We're too old to change much, En. You're stubborn and selfish and childish and brilliant and all these things that I hate. You're awful and broken and perfect, and here I am."

"Why do you have to know everything?"

"Because I'm an arrogant know-it-all who made it her habit to study you, even though it makes me insufferable," Helen said.

"What happens after? Are those coordinates right?" Enita felt a heaviness she didn't understand, as if the sky had collapsed inward, as though Margiella had been the one who'd held it up.

"The library is as good as a house system for wanting what's best for its users, and it's also, for better or worse, very attached to Nix. Nix needs to leave. They don't fully pass for human, and I think you and I both know there's no life for them here if they don't, and if they're seen as yours. Neren will need to go too, for the same reason. Getting out of the city will be hard for them, and I don't know how far Neren can travel on her leg, but I see no reason why the coordinates wouldn't be right."

"Not you?"

"You won't leave even if Nix does, will you?"

"No," she said. "You're right. We're too old to change much. I don't know if I could live elsewhere, and regardless, I don't want to. I *am* here. Malovises are Bulwark. So, I need to work as long as I can. It doesn't undo anything, but—" She couldn't finish.

"But," Helen agreed. "You can't go, so we'll stay. I don't want what you've made to be destroyed in this city, and they are rather wonderful, En. I find that I like the idea of your house system wandering outside Bulwark, bringing a little part of you with them."

"So you do like them."

"Against my will, of course."

"Do you mean it? You won't go without me?"

"I can't," Helen said. "Even if there is another place, there really isn't anywhere else, not without a Malovis."

Even after decades, Helen's head fit perfectly in the place where collarbone curved to breast. Home in another person. They'd managed to bleed together. And if Helen was crying at all, Enita knew better than to mention it. And comforting your dearest friend and treasured enemy, the person who you were made for, well, was it novel? She felt Helen's fear and knew it for loneliness. What a quiet kind of terror it must be to be a student of history who spots an oncoming end. What bravery to know it and to stay.

"Are you able to sleep at all?" Enita asked.

"Not since Ohno."

"That's too long. Let me take care of you."

"We don't do that anymore."

But they might, they should. "Humor me. We'll get them out, and I'll do everything I can to keep us safe here."

They'd had good lives, too pampered to know it, too free of obstacles. Such a life isn't sustainable. She tucked Helen in, pulling the covers under her chin. Pointed. Slight. Most people loved blooms, but Enita loved thorns.

"You don't need to stay here tonight. I promise I'll survive," Helen said.

Enita crawled into bed anyway, draped herself like another blanket.

What is it to be two bodies that are part of the same thing? A system. Two people—more—who operate together and separately so as to be one thing and many. If she and Helen were to exist in a single body, the war would kill them, they'd tear themselves apart. But there might also be deepest peace in being part of Helen.

Enita drew her fingers through Helen's short hair, now mostly devoid of the browns and reds that once intrigued her. Stiffer too, wiry, more of its own mind than the hair of a younger woman. Stronger in some ways, less able to be tamed by a brush. You never learned that as a young woman, that parts of you softened with age, but other pieces of you became steel. You didn't get to choose which.

"If you truly want me to, I'll leave," Enita said. "It might kill me because I'm spoiled and useless, but I will leave if you need me to." The bed, the house, the city.

This made Helen sob again, which hadn't been the goal. "Stop," she said. "I'd have to live with knowing I'd made you go. You'd hate me, and I'd hate me too, and I'm tired, En. Stop it. Can't I be noble? Let me be heroic once, just once."

She did.

Enita placed kisses on the back of Helen's neck because caring for her was caring for herself and she might have paid better attention to that across the years.

"What do you need, Hel?"

For a long time, until she fell asleep, Helen said nothing, which was what was needed.

Enita hadn't expected to see Tomas again, but Neren said it was necessary. She'd lately found herself predisposed to doing whatever Neren said. Guilt? Conceivably, or curiosity. Perhaps it was admitting that she and Helen were closer to the end of things.

It was well into night when Sinjin let them into his shop. They'd taken a rickshaw to the top of the Market District because Enita was too tired for the walk, but Neren said Tomas wouldn't show if he knew they'd scanned anywhere nearby, and a runner would scan.

"You can meet up here, but you can't stay," he said to Neren. "One or two of you is one thing, but no more Sainted after this. Bad enough you don't have any kids with you."

Tomas had been inside, waiting.

He cradled one of the carved animals in his hand, turning it around, rubbing his fingers across its belly. He was careful with it, which was a surprise. Free of dirt and grime, Tomas had a face Enita would call lovely, not handsome. There was delicacy in his features, not unlike the little creature he held. He traced his thumbs over the legs, but his eyes didn't leave Nix.

"You look well, House Saint Malovis. You pass better than you used to," Tomas said.

"Nix," they corrected. There seemed to be no offense.

"Don't be rude, brat," Sinjin said to Tomas. "That's a work of art standing right there, and they're nicer than you."

"You love us, and you know it," he replied, grinning.

Sinjin muttered, "You'll have me working down a life debt in a mine until I die." To Enita he said, "That one's been swiping toys from me since he could walk."

Tomas turned to Neren, looking her up and down. "I didn't figure you'd want to see me or Joni again what with the chopping your own leg off. Two wall workers dumped it at the house, just left it there. Do you know how hard it is to figure out how to get rid of a limb? Any hope we ever had of going unnoticed? Gone."

"Tell me you didn't kill Saint Ohno and Saint Hsiao," Neren said, her voice hard and flat.

"It wasn't us."

Enita couldn't tell whether or not he was lying. She looked at Nix, but they showed no reaction at all.

"But you know who did it," Neren said.

Tomas's lips thinned. Enita longed to slap him, but instead sat on Sinjin's chair and focused on the stabbing in her joints. The one benefit to pain was its ability to draw you away from things you didn't want to examine. She looked at the shelves of toys, small carvings, delicate boxes. Tomas had known Sinjin as long or longer than she had.

"Saint Hsiao was a friend, a good woman," Enita said.

"We couldn't have stopped them if we wanted to," said Tomas.

"You didn't want to?" Nix asked.

He shrugged. "There are hospital debts that were erased by her life balance. It's hard to see the numbers for the emotion sometimes, but it's necessary to look at them to make sense of anything."

Nix tilted their head in question. "What do you mean? Did you see any of the code yourself? What color were the life balances?"

"I don't know," Tomas said.

"Where's your sister?" Enita asked.

"With the person who can probably help you most," Tomas said. "I don't think it's safe for them to come here, and Sinjin agrees."

"Too many people come in and out of here as it is," Sinjin said. "And you lot stick out."

"So why aren't we there?" Neren snapped at Tomas. "You could get someone out of the city, if you wanted to. If someone helped you and you didn't want them getting killed, you could get them out, couldn't you?"

"Maybe. I thought we should talk first before you meet. It's—I want them as safe as possible. You too when it comes down to it. I also needed to see the house system again." To Nix, he said, "Parallax is quite interested in you. Did you know that? It worries me, but my friend seems to think that interest is a good thing."

There was nothing sinister in Tomas's tone, but the words slid over Enita like oil, thick poison. Being monitored was being alive, but *interest* felt directly threatening. "You killed Saint Hsiao, didn't you?" Enita said.

"No." Tomas's answer was immediate, with an earnestness and sadness that made her believe him. "The tea? I may have something to do with that. But things are happening without us. And—I'm a lot of things, so is Joni, but I could never. I would never. We couldn't. But other people . . ." He picked at his hands as he thought. "It's complex. We'll help you. We're trying already, I know Sinjin sends you clients. I do too. My friend does, but Saint Malovis, who does your balance pass to when you die? Tell me you have a niece or nephew, maybe. Is it designated to Saint Vinter?"

The question was an affront. "I'm sorry?"

"Who gets your life hours? Don't bother being offended—it's a waste when that's what it all comes down to. I get my sister's balance or debt, and she gets mine—or she did, large and awful as it was. That's part of the problem, isn't it? Saint Ohno didn't have a beneficiary and neither did Saint Hsiao. Do you have anyone? A distant relative you don't mind?"

"Margiella had a nephew," Enita said.

Tomas rubbed at his eyes, and she noted the dark bruises beneath, the sort that marked students during exams. "She never designated him."

How typical of Margiella. She'd liked gifting life hours to the arts, fancying herself as a philanthropist. Her nephew was taken care of, marrying into Wykert's family. She'd have seen no reason to give him more than he'd get from his parents.

"Enita hasn't designated," Nix said. "If there was anyone else, we wouldn't have this body. We're the closest thing to her descendant and we're—we don't scan."

"Right. Shit." Tomas tugged at his hair. "If you had beneficiaries, you'd have had a better chance. Small, but still. Without a beneficiary, your life balance goes back to the city and Parallax redistributes. It goes to hospital debts, education debts, wherever numbers are high. Unless a Certifiant or an Auditor tinkers with the balance distribution, which happens," he said. "Whole life debts can get wiped out by a Sainted. It's—They're looking for Sainted like you."

"What if she declared a beneficiary now?" Neren asked.

Tomas shook his head. "Balance changes are monitored too closely now. A sudden late-in-life designation without a previous relationship would be flagged as potential code error and tagged for verification or correction before being input. I doubt my friend could get it through without drawing suspicion. I need them safe." He frowned. "A lot of time can pass between a code flag and an edit."

Enita heard what he did not say. It would be enough time for a house to unlock and let in a small group of people. Enough time to suffer an unfortunate fall. Enough time for all the lives in the line of Saint Malovis to be counted as a single number and redistributed among Bulwark, in a final clearing of a balance. "I won't designate," she said. "I made my choice for a reason."

Sinjin spoke up. "You should bring them to your Assessor, Tomas. There's no point in waiting, and the longer you're in my shop, the less likely you'll be able to come back."

"You're not coming?" Tomas sounded puzzled.

"It's not my place to be there," Sinjin said. "Get on."

Enita understood. What Joni and Tomas and their contact were up to was a young person's game; people like Sinjin, like herself, could make space for them and look after them in little ways, but what was happening was meant for whoever would come after she and Sinjin were gone.

"You're right. We've probably been here too long already. All of you, out the back. Follow me, but not too close. You're not exactly a subtle group." Tomas eyed Neren's leg. "Cover your leg up first. It'll catch the light."

At the door, Enita saw Sinjin press something into Nix's hand. "Keep this."

"You're sure you don't want me to have a last go at your thumb?" Enita asked.

"What good is a young thumb on an old man? It's fine the way it is; maybe it's better because it's not quite right. Save your energy and work on someone who it might help, or someone who'll help you." He took a long look at Neren's leg. "What you've done there, that's something, Saint Malovis. Don't let her get lost in this mess, eh?"

Narrow alleyways and market stalls made keeping up difficult. There were piles of discarded cloth waiting for textile pickup, boxes of waste yet to be collected for the grow houses, all of it thick with human stench. Though she'd covered it with a cloth borrowed from Sinjin, Neren's leg seemed to draw light, a glinting beacon that Enita followed. It gave Neren's gait an uneven swing that it was impossible not to want to fix. It was impossible not to find every imperfection in the work. Enita saw where it could fit better, saw points of wear at the joints that could have been shaped differently. It could be lighter. Enita needed to make things that worked seamlessly; she loved whole things, whole people, whole systems. She'd loved Sinjin's work when she saw it—everything flawlessly born from a single piece of material. She'd desired that wholeness for Nix and done everything she could to make them complete. And yet.

It was too dark to see the thunderheads roll in, but they rumbled loud above the wall. Within moments, rain drilled Enita's shoulders, turned the alleys to mud, and clotted the air with the reek of people and refuse. The main streets had outflows leading to sewers, and sluice gates in the wall opened to let the water escape, but this part of the city was built to drown. Enita spared a thought for rickshaw runners on nights like this, but she'd never had to worry about the surgery flooding, or her home in general suffering any damage. The Sainted Quarter wasn't this way.

A light in a storefront sparked then flickered out.

"Is your hip hurting?" Nix asked. She hadn't realized she'd stopped.

"No." Other things hurt. Margiella had no designated heir. She hadn't asked Helen, but thinking on it now, she didn't need to. Of course she wouldn't have.

"Careful of the water," Nix said. She remembered Nix wasn't wearing shoes, that she still hadn't managed to get them used to footwear. She would have been a terrible mother.

The alleys widened, and dirt was replaced by stones, water coursing between them and trickling down into gutters. Enita recognized the edge of the Arts District. There was music coming from a window, someone playing strings, someone else with a reed. It wasn't a duet, though it might as well have been; the notes crashed into each other with the chaos and beauty of rain. Life, there was life in sound waves, in people putting body to sound, in the way it bounced off walls and into the skin. Why would anyone want to be anything other than a musician? Enita understood Joni a little then. Why would Neren make herself less of a singer by donating a lung?

They stopped at the back of a tall building sandwiched oddly between two others, as though they might be joined. Tomas stood at a metal doorway, waiting.

"Not used to being rained on?"

"I'll dry."

He opened the door and guided them through what Enita recognized as a kitchen, different from hers—two people were cooking, one over a steaming pot, another over a griddle, searing something she couldn't name. The cooks showed no sign that people traipsing through the kitchen was anything other than usual. The spice, the smell of it, was dense and familiar. A beaded curtain hung over the kitchen's exit. Though she'd only seen it from the other side, Enita knew it.

The Opal.

Tomas took them to a door off the kitchen, up a twisting staircase to a bare room with a narrow mattress and a single chair. It was neatly kept and clearly functioned as a safe room.

Joni sat in the center of the bed, legs folded like a child. "You brought Stitch-Skin? And that?"

Tomas shrugged. "Neren doesn't go anywhere without either of them. Where are they?"

Joni frowned. "They said they needed to go. They don't like being here without you."

Tomas swore.

Nix helped Enita into the chair, saying, "This should be our last stop. If she walks much more tonight, she won't be able to move at all tomorrow."

"Can't she replace her own hip?" Joni asked.

"It doesn't work that way," Nix answered quickly. But that wasn't precisely true; Enita had never considered it. She'd wanted to live out this body and its breakdown. She owed her donor that much and more.

"It's good what you do," Joni said, carefully. "Making people whole."

"They were always whole," Neren said and sat on the small bed. Joni moved beside her but was pushed away. "It's about having control and choices. But it's no good anymore—all the work Enita does now is transactional, hoping to buy time and favor," Neren said. "You've been sending people too, haven't you?"

Exhaustion was weight, an entire other person you carried with you. Enita had known and felt it, but to hear it voiced made it worse.

Joni nodded. "She helped you—I don't want her hurt. I really don't."

"She's operating for her life, Joni. That ruins the act of it. You're breaking someone again."

"We want to make sure no one will kill her," Joni said.

Enita sighed. "You know you can't promise that. It may be harder for people who know me to harm me, but that's a thin hope. Not the kind of thing you like hanging your life on."

Neren and Joni spoke in low voices, the quiet kind of fighting Enita and Helen had never bothered with. No one knew Helen, save for a few students. Helen wouldn't be safe, and yet life was impossible without her. It must have been easy to kill Ohno, someone known only by reputation for lavish parties. Was he a good man? No. But he wasn't a terrible one either. He'd been part of the city, part of the Sainted, yes, but his life was Bulwark's. And then there was Margiella.

"Margiella Hsiao never hurt anyone. She was *good*," Enita said to Tomas.

"If the argument is that you're not all terrible, that's understood, but also somewhat meaningless," Tomas said. "Your assistant will understand. When there's erroneous code it needs to be corrected, edited. Far more people have been harmed under the system as it is than have thrived under it." Tomas leaned against the wall farthest from her. There was a forced casualness to his stance, portraying calm rather than inhabiting it.

"You're not sure about all the killing though, are you?" she said.

"No. But too much ease is a kind of harm too. Plenty of you are rotted from the inside."

"Even The Stacks anticipate being erased, that the city must change. They operate with the principle that revolution and societal overthrows are cyclical and inevitable," Nix said. They sounded subdued and looked it as much as they were able. Enita found herself reaching to take their hand. It was not possible to build a society from people who had survived revolution, war, and collapse, and not have those things echo through the blood.

Neren's voice rose. "So, you just kill people now."

"Not me, no. But the City Bureau has been doing that for ages," Joni said. "Who do you think destroyed our building? Shoddy workmanship, intentional neglect. The HVAC had been broken in our building for years, no matter how much we complained. Then one day a tech shows up, and a week later the building is gone."

"Was that what it was?" Neren asked. "Someone did it on *purpose*?"

Joni dug the heels of her palms into her eyes. "Yes. I think so. The Bureau does things like that because they benefit from it. All the hands involved in rebuilding, in assigning of care, it adds up. Their life hours are valued, their families are cared for, and they might—one day—even leave an excess. Maybe live like a Sainted. They need the system. Auditors and Certifiants write over the data or the causes, but the debt for people like us never goes. A system built as a safety net for caring for people doesn't just prepare for disasters—it requires them."

Neren swore. Enita felt sick spread in her gut.

Nix asked if the person Tomas knew from the Bureau came here willingly. When Tomas said yes, something changed in Nix. "Sinjin called them an Assessor. They work with Parallax?" Tomas nodded and Nix closed their eyes as if in thought.

"Right now, if someone wanted to leave the city, more to the point, if they needed to, would you let them? Would Parallax?" Nix asked.

"Yes," Joni said, "but maybe not for much longer." A look passed between the siblings.

"So, better sooner than later. You can't control the after," Neren said.

"Saint Vinter and I happen to agree with you," Enita told Tomas. "This way of being isn't self-perpetuating. We should have run out of Sainted, but that hasn't happened, has it? Is it selfish to hope to outlive what people see as my usefulness? Probably." The small room was badly worn and barely fit them. How many others had used it? It couldn't be only Tomas and his person. "Was it Sinjin who told you about me?"

"Indirectly. He helped a friend's child and we saw the result," Joni said.

"Parallax knows you," Tomas said. "They know your house system. The changes you've made to Nix, this kind of adaptation, it's been of great interest to them."

The room was too hot, too small, too full of scents, people, and fear. A floor below, she'd sat with Helen on so many nights in their youth. Enita thought of Helen carefully building her little pile of salt, asking her to leave. Parallax had known about her then. "Would you have taken Neren to the hospital if you hadn't heard of me?"

Neither answered.

"Oh, fuck you both," Neren said.

"Were you horrified when you saw Nix? I assume you already knew from Parallax what I'd done."

"Your system is a lot like my friend," Tomas said. "Maybe too much. They're unnerving for me; I hadn't realized how much a part of Parallax my friend has become."

"So, we're useful to you in the same way that your friend is useful," Nix said.

"No," said Tomas. "You're misunderstanding. It wasn't our idea at all. Parallax started this, not us. *We're* useful to *them*."

"We can talk to people in ungridded places, we can send messages, and coordinate things, but we're part of a network," Joni said. "There are hubs and cells like any other system. The grow houses, the water treatment plants, the mines, every one of those places has people. We relay things but it didn't start with us. God, I wish it had." Her laugh was empty. "When you're studying something, maybe music especially, it's hard to think about anything else. For a long time, I couldn't imagine Bulwark could be any different."

"What specifically do you mean when you say hubs and cells?" Nix asked.

"That's not really my area," Joni said. "But there are more of us. Lots."

Tomas fidgeted. He knew more than Joni did.

"What about you?" Enita asked.

"It's not my place to say what other people do." His eyes settled on Neren's leg. "I thought Stitch-Skin only worked in flesh. Wet work," he said, with a smile that menaced.

"It's the best I could do, given the circumstances," Enita said. "If I'd known more to begin with, if you'd been honest, Neren would have had more choices. I only want to help."

"Maybe," Tomas replied. "You're useful, but you're also Sainted, and that presents difficulties. No one will trust you."

"I wanted this," Neren said. "This leg is *my* choice. Do you think I can be trusted? With this leg and what she's done for me? I've been helping her; what does that make me?"

"Don't be stupid. No one will touch you if you stay with me," Joni said.

"You'd hurt her." Nix's words were low but clear. "Not either of you, perhaps, but those other hubs and cells you mentioned, the ones you don't control. You can't say with any certainty that she would be safe."

"I just wanted you to stop cutting yourself up. You have no idea what it is to watch the person you love gut themselves," Joni said.

In the widening silence, Nix twitched their fingers, tapping pinkies to thumbs.

"Do you think there's a way Neren won't be hurt if she stays in the city?" Enita asked. "She's visibly different, and a hospital wouldn't have done this to her. *I* wouldn't have done this to her, except she asked. Do you think there's any way Nix won't be hurt if they stay? I can't see it. And what will happen to your Assessor?"

"They'll be killed. There's no way they don't know that," Neren said.

"I think they expect it," Tomas agreed. "But we're trying to keep them safe too. Neren, you could have outed us to the City Bureau for messing with scanners and living ungridded, but you didn't. Why?"

"You and Joni are assholes, but you're not built for hard labor," Neren said. "And if anyone knows a way out of Bulwark, it's you."

There was something predatory in the way Tomas studied them all. Nix, to their credit, remained still under the perusal. But fury had a way of lighting up her insides, burning out fatigue, and making Enita feel every aspect of her station. "If you're thinking Nix looks useful, I need to tell you I consider them my family in a way you can't possibly understand. If you think for one second about hurting Nix, I *will* find a way to skin you alive and repurpose your parts. Whatever it is you want to use them for, you won't harm them. They live."

"Enita," Nix said.

"It's just there's a piece of code we've been working on—Davet and I,"

Tomas said. Joni tried to stop him from saying more, but he continued. "We can't get in there, and I can't ask Davet to do it, not the way they are now, not with where they're situated. Everyone would know it was them. But if that code came in through a Sainted, it might keep them safe for a little longer until I can hide them."

"It's Davet? Davet from when we were kids. *They're* your Assessor?"

"I meet them here sometimes, yes."

"You still code," Neren said.

Tomas's nod was a small twitch. "I couldn't stop if I wanted to. The languages are gorgeous, Parallax itself—the base code and programs, the purpose was so good. It still is. People got in the way."

"After all these years. Davet. They were *gone*. I never thought . . ."

"We missed each other," Tomas said softly.

"Davet's changed a lot. Tomas doesn't like knowing what he loves most has gotten twisted," Joni said.

Neren looked like she might spit. "Oh, stop. You always knew what I wanted, and what I still want. I didn't change. I gave you everything I could, Joni. You just didn't like me."

The crashing of pots and pans filtered through from the kitchen below. Enita rubbed at her temple, took in the layered scent that decades of cooking had left in the small room. The closeness of it. And fear. Tomas and Joni were frightened too.

"Forgive us, but you said hubs and cells before," Nix says. "To us that means there is a center, as every system has one. This is where your friend is at the City Bureau. They work with and *in* Parallax, don't they? Any need to correct would come from there."

Tomas agreed.

"But it didn't originate with them."

"I can't say with total certainty, but I don't think so. Davet may not even know. They're not—Davet's different now from how they were when we were in school together."

"May we see the code you've been working on?" Nix asked.

Tomas grabbed a bag from under the bed, retrieved a small tablet, and confirmed to Nix that it was ungridded. "We talk on an encrypted channel. It's—Parallax could shut it down if they wanted to. Do you see what I mean? They're letting us do this." An unlinked tablet was dangerous too—a small accident, a lack of care would mean a lifetime of work and thought gone. "Davet and I used to write back and forth on it when we were in school. I kept the channel out of sentimentality, I guess." The shyness in his voice reminded Enita of how young they were, that revolutions were for the youthful.

And that was it, wasn't it?

Nix bent their head over the screen; its faint light made their skin gleam gold, human and not. Neren and Joni spoke quietly, picking at the scab of their relationship. Enita had the keen sensation that she was watching herself and Helen from the outside, but was unsure who was who.

"We're being used for parts—our bodies and minds get exploited by Sainted who never lift a finger," Joni said.

"The giving was the *point*, to be less me and more everyone," Neren said.

To be less yourself and more everyone. Yes, Enita thought. To step lightly—that's what Sainted were meant to do, step lightly because as Sainted your work was done, and it was time for new things, new people. You were not to be a burden, but that's what they'd become. She understood then the intent of Body Martyrdom—it was meant for people who had done living to give to those who hadn't yet. To make room. Perhaps when you were nearing the end of your life it was best to let those who were at their beginning have space. The point of things wasn't endless life, but to be a single part of many. Helen understood.

Enita cleared her throat. "Tomas, if you need, Saint Vinter can come and go from the City Bureau without raising an eyebrow. Would that be useful?"

"Absolutely. I'll talk to Davet," Tomas said.

"And if this code is introduced in Parallax, what will it do?" she asked.

"It's an overwriting code," Nix said, their face still at the tablet. "It makes data unreadable. Life balances, identifications, personal data of any variety. Sainted designations will be as inaccessible as anyone else's. At the very least, it will brick the city for an extended period of time. At its worst, Parallax will be permanently nonfunctional." Nix blinked. "That's what they want?"

Tomas nodded. "Parallax knows and hasn't stopped us. The blank nodes we've created stand. The channel Davet and I have is still open."

What would that mean for all of them? "I'd love to ask for assurance that Helen and I would be spared in whatever happens when Parallax is down, but you can't promise that, can you?"

"No," Joni said.

"Then get us out," Neren said. "If you don't want us hurt, if you ever cared for me at all, get us out."

"We can try," Tomas said. "But where else is there?"

"Everywhere," said Neren.

Enita remembered the sand dunes, crammed tightly into the rover next to her parents, the dry and the rock spires, and what outside had been. She was far too fragile for the world beyond the wall, but there was no need to mention it. That was a fight she'd like to spare herself, that reality was a heavy sadness. Below was a cacophony of dishes dumped into a sink, plates hitting counters, kitchen chatter, and music. Ungridded, unaccounted for, but living nonetheless.

Enita did not flinch, but felt a twinge of sorrow when Nix said, "We can carry this code. There's enough left of what we were to do it, and we'd like to speak with Parallax. We need to. Let us do this, please."

THE CODE

It's a virus in the old sense of the word, like Wasp Fly Fever and the Sweat Purge. Tomas's strength as a coder lay in imagining all the ways a system might self-protect. If too many nodes went down too quickly, sections of the city could be quarantined. If the virus moved too slowly, Auditors and Assessors might be able to correct it before it could incapacitate the network. There was cadence in the code too; rhythms in the language and color proved Tomas's years as a musician had benefitted him. The code is graceful, almost obsessed with beauty. Nix understands the man better now.

There is too the hand of another, a familiarity of language that is a caress to Nix. A voice known to them. This comes from Parallax, from Bulwark, as much as it does from Tomas and his friend Davet. Though the differentiation is difficult—Nix reads certain lines where it feels as though Davet and Parallax speak with the same voice. They are no longer entirely separate.

To Nix, the language reads purple—#80080, bright, insistent, melancholy, and alive. They wonder if a human eye reads it with similar colors, if this is what Tomas sees. It's artful in the way of a broken fingerprint, a mole beneath the curve of an earlobe. Nix understands this code's essence and even experienced a touch of something like it when Ohno's murder was overwritten. Yet it is more. There's a kindness in the program. A rest—for the city. Parallax wants to take care of this Assessor, to protect them.

The program is timed to creep from node to node, making scanners inoperable, house systems inert. It will render the data silos at the heart of City Bureau, the physical center of Parallax, useless. Nix will have this inside their body. They will become a trojan horse. It is purpose.

What is purpose? Purpose for a house system is to care for their resident. What is purpose? The Stacks' purpose is to make information readily accessible in ways that better their users. What is purpose? Parallax's purpose is to make life measurably better for those who dwell inside, to avoid replicating the ways of living that led them to flee.

The Stacks, Parallax, Nix—none of them perform to purpose any longer. Correction is necessary. Nix's eyes slip through the code, and they find the brackets delightful; syntax is specific to coder. They see Tomas in his idiosyncrasies, his careful conversations with Davet. Tomas is more frustrated than angry, and terribly lonely. Sad. His is a mind that enjoys linking with others, two and three at a time. He is seeking.

Davet is something different. The voice breathes too, longs, but feels somewhat like The Stacks, a little like Nix before. Those segments of code are elegant and sad, as much as Tomas's, yet distinct.

For a moment, Nix senses kinship.

It is poignant because the syntax in this code is human; AI doesn't use flourishes quite this way. It is poignant because this will likely be the last code Nix ever reads that originates in Bulwark. It is perfect in a way that all versions of Nix appreciate. This code is alive in the in-between, much as they are.

Once Nix passes the program along, the virus will spread until there is no system left in Bulwark capable of recognizing them for what they are, until there is no system left in Bulwark capable of doing anything more than turning on a light. Parallax is allowing this.

Nix will be useless here, except as another body. Except, perhaps as someone to help keep Enita alive a little longer. And then what?

They pick apart a line where the two voices meet. Tomas writes like a riot. Davet is meticulous, patient, and writes like someone who understands plurality, who lives in it. Nix longs, more than anything, to meet the second coder. A single consciousness trained to plurality.

But there is more to do, errors to tidy up. They must set up last clients for Enita. They must ask questions about eyes and see if there is a way to undo a mistake.

Then they will spread this code.

NIX

Enita is upstairs with Helen. On returning from the Opal, Enita didn't want to be alone. This felt incorrect, hurtful even, as companionship is part of what they're designed for, part of the reason for this body and their continued existence. Their floor is cold. They turn the tablet over and over again in their hands. They will be smaller, less again. Houses must have heated themselves before house systems. Nix could have asked The Stacks about unwired housing, about primitive structures. They could have read more history. That too is why Helen is here.

Nix is in the surgery, no longer themself. It's curious to hold a tablet they haven't ordered or built, one that's entirely not them. They wish there was more time to explore these states of being, but there isn't. They need to be thinking about eyes, code, and what things will look like after, and if what they plan to do is correction, or harm with a reach they cannot yet know. They tuck the tablet into a drawer when Neren walks into the room.

She follows the path of their old ceiling tracks and stops in front of a glass canister containing a right hand and a portion of forearm. It wasn't usual to grow both at once; they did more hands than arms, but lately they'd been anticipating needs rather than building to request. Sooner or later someone would need one, wouldn't they?

They know from her posture that she wants to talk. It's easier to read this now than it was without the body. They wait, occupying their hands with a dish of nerve cells.

"You won't understand, but I did love Joni."

People tend to assume that machines, systems, can't understand emotions. It would take a long time to disabuse someone of that belief. All emotions across machines and people, across whatever they are now, are language. Nix can't explain the nuances of colors, or the precise emotion of code, only that it's the same as feelings in a body. They don't say this, because all language fails to communicate itself fully.

"She still cares for you." Factual statements seem the easiest way to approach the subject.

"She's always wanted more than I can give. She's the kind of person who wants to live off her lover's breath. I couldn't. I'll never be able to. I promised myself elsewhere."

"Enita and Helen are somewhat the same," they say. They don't have any particular desire to fill silence with more meaningless words. That sort of language is decorative, and they're feeling . . . spartan. An excellent word stuck in history they can't access anymore. Helen would know its roots.

"I think I loved Tomas a little, too. He and Joni are a set, though they hate it," she says. "But no matter where Tomas is, he's never really there. He's constantly busy, distracted. I suppose that was Davet, but I never knew. Joni must have known. I wonder if she hates them at all. It's been years since Davet went into the City Bureau. Ages." She leans back against the table next to them. "It's weird when you're not talking. Even if you're not thinking terrible things, you look like you are."

"We'll work on our thinking face," they say. "You knew Davet?"

"Some. I haven't seen them since we were children. When people in Assessor training go into the Bureau, they vanish from the rest of their life. It's meant to keep their judgment clear." She moves most of her weight to the non-metal leg; this is her body remembering the injury and subconsciously protecting it. They wonder how much she can walk on it in a day. On city streets? Across rough terrain? Something else bothers them.

"When you read code, what do you see? Is there color to it?"

She shrugs. "It's a mess of letters and numbers to me. I don't have much of a head for math beyond music."

"It isn't math," they say.

"Maybe not to you. I see the color the text is set in, so whatever the default is, I guess. Why?"

"Would you still want to donate your eye, if you could?"

"Stop," she says. "Don't talk to me about that." She passes behind them, moving to the cooling tanks, switches on circulation for the night, then removes tissue frames from where they hang to spray them with a genic solution. Every motion a little too brittle, a little too angry.

"We didn't mean to upset you," they say. "You should sleep."

"I hate sleeping upstairs. Down here feels like me, up there feels too Sainted. You know what I mean. It's *them*, not *me*."

Nix offers her their bed and says there are things to be tended to. She thanks them but stays where she is. They remember the color of this feeling, a burnt orange the body reads as anxiousness. Too many thoughts. "We were thinking about what will happen to this work when Parallax goes down."

"I'm sorry."

"It's nostalgia. We liked working with Enita's grandfather. Byron was smart and curious, and we love working with Enita. This was one way of helping, but there are others." It's something to consider—all of this grown tissue eventually dying, rather than finding a home. The difficulty of a body is the sense of time; before and after are clear in terms of wear. It's not that aging systems do less than they once did, it's that new adaptations do *more*. Whether or not there is a need.

They walk to the back of the room and run their fingertips along the side of a tissue tray. Not having instant, exact knowledge of temperature is a glaring absence that makes the cold overwhelming.

"I do still want to donate," she says. "I wish I could."

"Ah. And is that nostalgia too?"

"Before all this, I could have been cleared for liver donation again. I don't know if I would have—that donation was almost as bad as the lung. Everything was painful, everything made me sick. Maybe it's a Martyr trait, but that's also the best part: knowing that while I was feeling bad, someone else was getting well. Still, it was so much. I'm not sure I could have done it again. But my eye? I doubt that want will ever go away."

"Why?" They are careful with their question, not wanting to influence her.

"I need to know parts of me are everywhere doing different things while the rest of me is in this body doing whatever it is I have to do to survive. Some of me might be doing something good. It's selfish but I don't care. If I'd died in the collapse, that would still be true."

There is echoing in them, a sensation like repeating code. "To be less you and more everyone, as you said." They smile. "We might understand that. We're small now, but we were an entire home."

"Is it awful?"

"It hasn't been comfortable, but it's necessary." Nix doesn't say what Tomas's code will do, the ways in which it will make systems silent or how it will make them a walking disease. Nix doesn't say parts of them were the city. They adjust the temperature on a container of genic gel. That could keep for a long time, and there's a chance someone might be interested in it, someone Enita worked on. Tomas or Joni could know someone. Maybe even Sinjin.

"You're made of that," she says, nodding at a vat of nanofilament. "That and grown cells, right? Like the leg."

"Yes, well, most of the squishy parts."

She opens a drawer and slides out a flat of cell trays, rudimentary muscle fibers. They've watched her enough now to understand that she putters when she's thinking. They know her enough now to see she's comfortable here, that part of her has begun thinking of their surgery as home. They could have been her home.

"If it's possible, if we can get Enita to do this, would you donate your eye to us?"

Her hand stills. "To you? I don't understand. Why?"

"We're curious too. We want to know how you see, not our approximation of it. It may not be possible. We might not process signals from the eye, it may be no better than a glass implant—but we're curious. And we'd like for you to feel complete, as though you'd given everything you were meant to. We want to repair our mistake."

She rubs her face as if reminding herself of all its parts. "Your body wouldn't reject it, right? If mine can take a mechanical leg, and yours is made to mimic mine, it should work? Everything I've martyred has gone to a Sainted. How many of them do you think will be around in a year? Two years?"

They think of an illustration of human heads in a basket, a remnant of the data bolus from The Stacks. "We can't say."

"I was ready to live with one eye. I wouldn't consider it harm, more fulfillment," she says. She picks at the edge of one thumb in thought. "And would you give me yours? You're constrained and feel too small to be yourself. Maybe if part of you was with me, you'd feel a little more like you were."

Nix startles. They try to imagine what it would be to see their eye in Neren's face. "You'd do that?"

"You might understand martyring more. Maybe I'd see things more the way you do, or you more the way I do. Or not. But we'd both be more connected."

There's a logic to this they're reluctant to search for flaws.

"And you want that."

"You've done quite a lot for me. I think I need to understand you better." Neren studies their eyes, unaware she's seeing a product of Enita's dreams about Helen, and of their own wish to please her. Neren's eyes are so dark as to be black. The mismatch of colors will make them both more unsettling, and perhaps more complete.

"We'll tell Enita."

They work on a set of lungs that will likely die before they can be used, but they proceed, teasing out a tree of bronchioles over a lattice that will form the interior of a lung. Someone could use it, perhaps. If not Enita, maybe a White Cap. Will there be White Caps? Nix rubs their fingers across the skin of their lower back, thin over their spinal port, easily cut and sealed. The code will be introduced there through an archaic drive. It seems impossible the silence in them could feel any more pronounced, and yet it might.

They consider Neren's eye. The pull of it is strong. If they were to look at themself, they'd see the woman they'd hurt through lack of knowledge. They'd see Bulwark looking back, the system that had made her, them, and Enita's work. They want to ping The Stacks, the hospital, even their aggravating kitchen to see what foods are best for recovery from such a surgery, and they'd listen this time, no matter how impractical the answer. They would have a part of Neren, and they would martyr their body. The experience would be unique among systems.

They use a tablet to gently ping The Stacks, missing the speed and nuance of thought. They ask their questions. What is right. What is moral. What is purpose.

The Stacks answer with text and address Nix with an indigo honorific that humbles them. Nix reads, listening to Neren's breaths while she sleeps in the bed near their old case. There are thousands of sayings about change and constants. The Stacks offer several, but note that most are driven by human fears of suffering. The Stacks say that morality isn't static and is entirely based on individual societies. System morality, system ethics, are by nature different from those applied to human bodies.

Curiosity is a singularly beautiful desire common among humans but rare among systems. It's what Parallax has found interesting about you. It is what we find interesting about you.

Nix knows when they are being guided.

They type their goodbyes and receive a last missive.

Your decisions are purposeful.

Though they might, Nix does not wake Enita. They send a note, because she likes to fight with her voice, with her personality, and they don't want to bend. Byron Malovis called her a brat on more than one occasion, but they know that's ungenerous. But it's harder for her to fight against text, harder for her to manipulate.

Saint Malovis, you think of yourself as our mother, but we're older than you. We're meant to outlive you; that's why you've made this body and why we let you. We're meant to preserve your work. We're also meant to keep Bulwark, to preserve the idea of the way it has been, through your work and through our existence. Neren would like to give us her eye, and we would like to give her ours. We believe doing this will recover some of what we've all lost. We are also interested in the experience of Body Martyrdom and believe that this will help us grow. You've encouraged us to be inquisitive. We understand you won't like this, but ask you to recognize we've moved through more time than you have, and we've changed in more ways than a single human body ever can. If we are to be a single body, that fact demands we have autonomy. Ask Helen her thoughts.

———

In the morning, Enita is at the door of the surgery. She has cried, and her face is swollen with it, tender looking. "Did you really think I'd say no? I didn't expect that a body would make you mean. I recognize your autonomy."

They do what was before impossible: embrace. They aren't any good at it; the pressure is wrong and either too tight or not tight enough, but it's important to imprint Enita's size and shape, how she is now. It's important to comfort her and get her to forgive them. She is not forever.

"You'll be helping her to live how she wishes, and we'll understand what that means. That's important," they say.

"I'm saying yes because you asked, and it would be monstrous not to. I'm a lot of things, but I'm not that. I didn't have to talk to Helen. And as much as you've raised me, you *are* my child, whether you like it or not. I couldn't ever say no to you, not when it matters."

She's agreed because she is Saint Malovis, and that is everything.

ENITA

It was never meant to be this way, two clients at once, and certainly not one in the process of performing surgery on themselves. For Enita, the wrongness ran as deep as the necessity of the operations. In life there were precious few opportunities to correct your mistakes, and fewer still were moments when those you'd harmed told you precisely how to atone.

Though her focus was on Neren, it was disturbing that Nix sat upright in a chair next to the operating bed, a canister filled with genic gel on a rolling table beside them, and a shining steel retractor ring buried deep in their orbital socket. A lighted mirror hung from the surgery's ceiling track, pulled down so Nix could properly observe their own work. Enita had never done anything for Nix that wasn't also with them, together, a fully participatory process. This procedure—in some ways no different—felt wholly other. The success of the transfer operation relied heavily on speed, preserving the health of the donated eye, and exposing the dissected tissues to as little open air as possible. A dry socket was a dead socket. That Nix was able to shut down their pain receptors for their eye did nothing to ease Enita's discomfort. Rather it made her fear—what would happen to Nix if they didn't leave? She'd seen the uneasy stares when they were in the wider city. Other always meant in danger. They might pass one day, but didn't yet, and mismatched eyes wouldn't help anything. She remembered discarded android parts, broken gynoid limbs carelessly tossed in piles outside the brothels bordering the Arts and the Warehouse districts. Would Nix be able to shut their sensations down if her home was raided and they were torn apart? They would lose themself piece by piece, until nothing remained, as though they had not already been changed enough.

She must have muttered or looked over, because Nix stated calmly, "Enita, we're fine. Focus on Neren, please."

"Bossy," she muttered, and pulled her magnifying glasses down.

"When you let us be, yes."

"Fine. But don't forget—genic gel in the socket until we can start on you properly. Nothing dry."

"We're aware."

The patient on her table was another matter. Neren had wanted to be awake, but Enita knew she'd be unable to operate, that she'd feel all the weight of her initial mistake, or that she might cry when seeing Nix's eye in Neren's face.

Care. Most people didn't view blades as instruments of care, but surgery was a dance of care through cutting. Cuts could be clean, but in this case, the art lay in the intentional ragged edge, a dissection of muscle and nerve meant to reattach, to hold whatever was given. A Body Martyr would hold a gift that Enita had grown. It was foolish to wonder if her own donor still lived; she'd never know. But this, perhaps, helped settle that debt too.

"Not too neat in your cuts, Nix. Too much perfection is the enemy with this graft." She kept her voice instructor-like, the way Byron had been with her, trying to be dispassionate about an act that was nothing but passion. "Be quick. The nanobots will start working against us as soon as I cut."

She glanced up when Nix did not respond, only to see them with their hands poised in front of their face, head tilted back, a laser cautery in one hand, forceps in the other. That she could not see more was a blessing. It was too much—they were her child, her parent, Byron, herself, and Helen all at once. And what they were doing to their body was an abuse and a gift of the highest order.

Ah.

Neren's hand twitched in her slumber, as if sensing the moment Nix's eye left their body. A careful waltz they'd timed out.

Cautery, retractor. The gentle wash of genic gel and saline, thin threading of nanofilament. The switching of trays. In any other surgery, she would have asked Nix to adjust the temperature in the room, to angle the table and monitor the nerve block.

"The eye is in the canister, ready for you. We're going to rest now, Enita."

It was what they'd agreed on, Neren's new eye first, then Nix's, as Nix understood the operation and was better able to control their pain. But reaching this moment of silence was lonelier than she'd anticipated.

Then, it was sewing, as she had done for decades. It was once only women's work and in that, perhaps, was Enita's tie to history, to those who had come before her and thought to do something useful with their lives and their bodies. A simple craft could make such wonder; a simple craft was not simple at all, but an art. She sewed nerves, muscle. With her full attention on the art, the likeness to Helen's eye color disappeared, the feeling of parent and child melted away, until only art and care remained. The best of things.

She did not notice when Neren's arm slipped from the table, reaching. She did not notice when on the far side of their chair, Neren clasped Nix's hand.

Nix's anatomy was different than when she'd first given them eyes. The tissue they'd grown together had filled in as it was meant to, its musculature more dense with protective fat pockets around the neural wire, a fully adapted body—proof again that they grew and changed in ways that neither of them could have anticipated.

She understood something then, about her life, about the Martyr's kidney inside her, that it was hers; it was the Martyr's and it was hers both. That recipients of donations were less themselves and more everyone for receiving. It was neither a gain for the recipient nor a loss for the donor, but broadening in a way that Martyrs understood. Martyrs and Nix.

When Neren's eye at last became Nix's, her brown-black iris in a face Enita had spent her heart creating, it was connection, a completion of beauty through difference.

And when she washed her hands in the basin, shaking them free of water droplets, she felt more rooted to Bulwark than she'd known possible. She let Nix and Neren rest and heal, knowing she'd watch them, as any good house system would. Nix had become Saint Stitch-Skin, and she House Saint Malovis.

Helen was a welcome presence in her bed, and if that presence held any sadness, it was only in that they should have been this way more often, they should have been this way always. Helen ran her fingers through Enita's hair, untangling the twist of her bun. It was good, this comfort, this less aloneness. Did insight matter so much at the end of things?

"Tell me what was on your tablet earlier. Tell me why you're being so nice to me," Enita said.

"Archytas let me know a City Bureau Auditor came by; they're checking on Sainted and unusual outages in house systems. It was of great interest that I wasn't at home."

"Do you think it was really a Bureau Auditor?"

"I have doubts, but Archytas couldn't say with any certainty."

"Well, it's not as though our association isn't known. Probably won't be long before they come knocking here." She didn't like the way her stomach felt, the uneasy burning, though doubtless there was more of that to come.

"Not more than a few days, I'd bet," Helen said. "And they're both recovering well from the surgeries?"

"They'll be fine soon."

There was noise on the street below, shouting, and the crunch and crash of things being broken. Her thoughts ran; the surgery was running low on plasma, and there wasn't enough chitin left to start a single bone lattice for a finger, let alone a leg. She needed more. More time. More quiet. More life. Enita burrowed deeper into the bed, as though the quilt and Helen might erase what she didn't want to acknowledge. She'd spent her life being a child. Even the good of her work had been vain indulgence, figuring out what she could do just to see. Play. She'd made a child she'd never have to raise, a child she didn't have to pay for with her body. She'd lived a toddler's demanding dictatorial existence. No matter how many people she'd treated, however many more she might, she wouldn't be spared. Perhaps she shouldn't be.

"Stop thinking, En."

"I don't want you to go to the City Bureau. I can do it myself." If something were to happen with Nix on the way, she didn't want Helen caught up in it. If something were to happen with Nix on the way, she needed to be there.

"You won't be able to get the access I will."

"Your aversion to Nix is going to be a problem. They need to be unremarkable, and they're comfortable with me. I should go."

"I like them fine," Helen said. "Actually, I think we get along rather well. We've come to an understanding. In spite of our better judgment, we both like you and feel responsible for you. Besides, it'll be good for me to participate in some history." The cheeriness rang false. She pressed her lips to the top of Enita's head, a glancing touch. "I've loved books, you know? All of them, even the terrible parts of history it would be easier not to know, not to realize what people can do to each other—it's impossible not to love it. All of history. It's who we are. I'm going to be a part of that." She pulled Enita tight, arms wrapped around her, a tether to the world. "And Nix is stunning. It's hard not to be vain about the parts of them that look like me."

"I should have asked you before I volunteered you."

There was love in Helen's sigh. "But then you wouldn't be you. You're not a terrible person, you know."

Enita knew she was meant to smile at this, perhaps even laugh, but couldn't. She caught herself wondering how many more heavy silences in the safety of a bed were left.

"None of us are truly awful, are we? Not even Ohno. We're lazy and naïve, conceited, all the things we were raised to be." Someone smashed a bottle near the house, and the sound shook her. In the past Enita would have asked Nix to check a camera feed, but now it felt best not to know. She tried to imagine the bottle as dropped, not smashed. Footsteps in the street, just Saint Pertwee staggering home, nothing more. "Tell me how it's all going to end. It'll be better hearing it from you."

At this, Helen pulled away, curling her body in on itself. Enita heard the shake in her exhale.

"Well," Helen said, her voice almost distant. "If they get to us now before the code affects all of Parallax, you and I will be killed first because we have no descendants, and our balances can be redistributed.

So, like Margiella. Like Ohno. If the code works quickly and Parallax overwrites all its data? That may be better or worse."

"Worse how?"

Long ago Byron had read ancient tragedies to Enita, loving the rhythm of the prose. Helen's voice took on this recitation, the awful and beautiful music of the cataclysmic. "Our houses will be raided, and people will take everything we have. They'll come for water, food, then whatever catches their eye. There will be destruction too, it can't be avoided. Most if not all of my books will be gone. That's not too terrible in the abstract, if they let us live. They might not. Actions run on large emotions, and emotions aren't prudent. I think it will be quick. But perhaps that's what hope looks like to me."

"If you're sure they'll kill us . . ."

"I'd like to think there's a chance they won't, maybe even a very good one. I don't believe everyone has murder in them. I can't. There are Body Martyrs, after all. If we aren't killed, we'll be moved somewhere far away from the Quarter to do things we're poorly equipped to do. For me, maybe a textile farm? I do know something about dyes. You'll likely get hospital work. I think I might like a grow house. But it will be the kind of work we haven't done in generations. Centuries. It will break some of us. Imagine Saint Wykert in a composting plant." Her laugh was dry, joyless.

None of that labor was ever meant to be punishment. Every person in the city was meant to be necessary. Yet somehow, an entire class of people was not. Enita tried to imagine working outside of her surgery, where things were not made for her exact needs, working with people who never understood what she had done. Perhaps they'd have her wheeling gurneys and emptying waste. She tried to imagine Helen's hands with the scars she'd seen on textilers, but could not. "Won't they want a historian?"

"Not for a bit, I don't think. It's hard to look at history when you're living in it," Helen said.

"You could go. I wouldn't be angry with you if you did, I promise."

"I know." She pressed Enita's hand to her chest.

"If there's no tally of the work or reason for anyone to do it, what's to keep people from walking away?"

"A sense of group. That's strong in this city. And if no one works the water treatment plants, we die of thirst. If no one works the grow houses, we all starve," Helen said. It was all meant to be good work. Necessary work.

"We've been dead weight, Hel."

"Some of us, yes. But we'll learn not to be, if they let us live."

A small part of Enita felt she'd deserve it if they didn't.

Though it was too dark to see properly, too raw to look closely, she felt Helen's sadness as a barometric drop. Tears, silent, until at last they settled deep in the night.

A small gray bird nestled under the blankets, Helen slept. Enita could not. She pulled herself out of bed, calling to what remained of the house mainframe, a lumbering skeletal system that didn't respond with any consistency. She ached for the rapport she'd had with Nix when they'd been everywhere. Brains were the one organ that couldn't be replaced by grown cells or bioprosthesis. Their uniqueness was more crucial to function than the rest of the body. Memory had claimed her grandfather in the end; Byron's brain cells had tied themselves in knots, making coherent thought impossible. Nanobots hadn't been able to undo them. At first, he'd found the memory slide scientifically fascinating, then isolating, and eventually freeing as his body forgot itself, how to move, how to breathe, how to be. All sorts of endings were returning to beginnings, nascent states of being.

She did not want to die, no, but she would not leave. If there was a Bulwark, there should be a Malovis in it. Emptying bedpans, pricking her fingers bloody on vines, losing her hand in a carding machine, or dead and buried. She stretched, feeling the pull in her back where a scar should be. She was alive because of Bulwark, because of Martyrs; if she had to die it should be at Bulwark's hand.

In the kitchen, Enita tried fixing herself a drink from a root powder that Nix had procured in lieu of tea and ended up with a weak concoction as visually unappealing as it was bitter. She laughed, then drank the undrinkable while waiting outside the surgery for morning to break. If you couldn't find joy in your own incompetence, what was the point?

The doors didn't announce her when she wandered in, which was good because Neren was asleep on Nix's bed, head resting on their thigh. Upright, awake, and utterly inhuman, Nix didn't bother feigning sleep. It was startling to see Neren's eye in Nix's face, impossible not to read into it all the anger and fear she'd felt from Neren.

"Is Helen still here?" Nix asked, quietly.

"Still asleep, yes. How is your eye?"

They swallowed, an unnecessary tic they made charming. "We don't have the right words to express it. It's not—we've been doing a poor job of replacing eyes, Enita. We could do so much better with the lenses and cones now that we understand them."

Neren stirred but didn't wake.

"That's not important anymore. Are you in any pain?"

"No. It's happening soon, isn't it?"

"Yes. Helen will take you. She insists on it, in fact. And you're sure you want to carry this code?"

"We need to." There was carefulness in their movements as they extricated themself from the bed and the woman in it. When Nix was near, she touched their hair, unable to stop herself. They were a better creature than Enita, and not by a little. She could talk to them about consequences, about being unable to change as much as the city needed her to, or as much as leaving Bulwark would require. But those were meaningless things to say to someone who'd done nothing but change. She looked at Nix's mismatched eyes. They added to their overall uncanniness.

"Have you liked having Neren here with you?"

"Yes. She's attempting to make a friend of us, but she's still a little afraid, though she tries not to be. We enjoy her."

"Most of us are always a little afraid."

"She's healing well already. She's calmer. It's good we did this; it was what she wanted."

"Be selfish, won't you? Make me feel like less of a monster."

"We're working on it. This was our choice—we're less isolated when Neren leans on us. There's no small amount of ego in pleasing others."

"I didn't mean to isolate you. I'm good at making things, but it appears I'm terrible at understanding the ramifications."

"Projected outcomes are a range, not set." Nix's shrug was awkward. "We're going to keep trying that gesture until we figure out why everyone does it. It's ridiculous."

It was.

"You know I'm staying, and you know there's nothing to do to change that," she said.

"Yes, we know." At this they sigh, and it sounds natural enough to startle.

"I need you to leave Bulwark and I need you to take her with you. I need you to do this for me." She felt the push in her gut, every bit of feeling she'd ever had. She did her best not to stammer, to say things clearly and calmly. Nix should never have a question about what she'd wanted. "In order for me to live my fullest, happiest life, the best one that I can live as someone who was your resident and the woman you raised, I need to know that you will leave here and you will take Neren with you. I need to take care of you, the way you've cared for me. I need to know that you will do everything possible to be safe. That's my purpose for you. Do you understand?"

Their silence lasted longer than she'd have liked. She couldn't look at them, not when she'd manipulated them in such a way. She would not say any more, not before they did. Her voice would break.

"Yes," Nix said.

"Thank you."

"Enita, we should upload the code now. We need to."

Enita used a cautery to cut the skin over the port; it parted and fell away as if meant to. If she left the incision open long enough, nanobots would heal the wound's edges, leaving the port forever exposed. Nix lay on their stomach, head turned to the side, eyes open, unblinking. She turned away when they took the slender drive between their fingers. She could not do it herself, would not.

She listened for the click. Stick in port, distinctly machinelike.

Nix exhaled, sand on wind.

Their eyes closed, fluttered. They went still.

"Is it loading? What does it feel like?"

"It's wonderful," they said.

Minutes stretched as they lay motionless, skin healing around the drive. She didn't know what would happen if she pulled it out, if that might do something irreparable. Though, irreparable was the point.

A hand touched her shoulder. She hadn't noticed Neren's approach.

"How long before they're awake again?"

"I don't know," Enita said. She should ask about eyes, about Neren's leg. She should make small talk or walk away or do anything at all. "I find myself entirely useless, and I don't like it."

"Strong people have a way of running us all over," Neren said.

"Would you stop what's coming if you could?"

"No. I don't know. But I'm beginning to think that people like us, you and me, shouldn't exist. Well, maybe not that, but we shouldn't *have* to exist. Starting over could change that."

"I think that's true," Enita said after a time. "I don't have a right to, but I'm asking you to look after Nix. Really, I'm not asking at all."

Neren shifted her weight to her metal foot, a fluid, natural movement. "And what do you think is going to happen to them?"

"I don't know. Maybe something like what you did to your leg." Nix was naïve in some ways, too knowing in others. They knew everything about what it was to be a Malovis, but almost nothing about other people, almost nothing about what it was to be in a living vessel. "Maybe nothing at all, I don't know. But they can't be alone, they need to care for someone." There were too many things to task Neren with, making sure Nix didn't work themself to the point of breaking, making sure they were careful with trust, making sure they remembered that even their body would need food and water at times. Rest, if not sleep. That they were cared for. Always.

"And where will you be?"

Enita forced a smile, the sort she hoped was motherly. "Well, none of us live forever, do we? How is the eye?"

"Different," she said.

"I imagine it will take getting used to, most eye transplants do; the brain needs to readjust to depth. Nanobots speed healing but learning stays at whatever pace the brain dictates. Is it what you wanted?"

"Does Nix like it?" Neren asked.

"They want to relearn how we grow and replace eyes. I'm thinking that *like* isn't strong enough a word."

Neren turned her foot on the floor, examining the angles, playing with the light against it as if seeing it for the first time. "Then it's what I wanted. And yes, I'll look after them."

"Remind them to eat," Enita said. "They don't need much, but they tend to forget things like that."

Neren smiled softly. "I'll remind them. But it's not forgetting, Saint Malovis, it's prioritizing care."

NIX

People. There are so many people, too many, all the systems in the city, every node all at once never felt like so much, so crushing. Hot. Their body is hot and the skin is sweating and they want to stretch and breathe but that would draw notice, and they can't draw notice.

"Head down," Helen says, so they watch their feet stepping on cobbles, the movement of rickshaw wheels in the middle of the street. The runners' shoes—thick sandals. Could they wear sandals? Perhaps, but then how would they know the ground, the terrain, if not for the sensation of it?

A shoulder bumps into them, another, knocking them about. Helen takes their hand. "Steady now."

"We should hail a rickshaw, Helen." This is the closest they can come to saying that they're frightened.

"No. That would leave the runner with too much information," she said. "Sometimes not being seen means doing things slowly. Don't be memorable."

They don't know what that means. The code buzzes inside them, painlike. It makes walking more difficult than usual.

The City Bureau lies in the center of Bulwark, so that Parallax's connections can easily weave throughout the districts. The walk winds them through dense foot traffic—the tight bright boxes of the Arts District and the flat roofed ochre towers of the university. They're jostled by students, food vendors, and children running through the streets.

A child careens into Nix, knocking back their hood. A young girl. She shrieks—perhaps at their eyes.

They pull their hood back on. Sinjin said they wouldn't be safe, that they were still too different—uncanny. Enita has said they're not un-canny, rather they're beautiful. Like Sinjin, Helen seems to have a bet-ter understanding of things. Violent things. She yanks them forward.

"Are you all right?" she asks.

"Yes," they lie. It's in Helen's best interest that they're fine. In Enita's too. It's the crowd, the code, the strangeness of being outside and in-side themself, of realizing how very small the systems and nodes in the city are when compared to the population. Something tugs on their sleeve and they pull away.

"Come along now. For you, the key is to keep moving," Helen says. "Always."

For *you*, not *us*.

"Saint Vinter," a voice calls, and Helen pulls them behind the cover of a transport dray, matching its slow pace through the streets. The top overflows with ruined clothing headed to the mills for repurposing. The odor is musty, human. Nix realizes now that even their body's smell is different.

"Pity it's not a tea shipment, no? I wouldn't say no to pinching a bit," Helen says.

They nod in agreement.

The person who called for Saint Vinter is no longer there, so they move on. Among the throngs could be clients Nix worked on with Enita in the days before their body. None of those clients would ever recog-nize them. It's difficult to look among a group of people and see the in-dividuals, the single lives among the many, rather than what Helen sees: a potential mob, capable of great harm, justified or otherwise. Anything en masse is dangerous. Perhaps this is the source of their lifelong love and disagreement: Enita sees only the individual, and Helen sees only the group. Nix has been both. They are both. It is impossible now to not think of the crowd and the images they've seen. People lined up for executions. Mounds of bodies riddled with bullet wounds.

Helen urges them forward, and though her touch is different from Enita's, lighter, it's settling. "Whatever it is you're thinking, don't. Keep moving."

But they wonder. How could Parallax let the state of the city deteri-orate to a point where such violence was not only possible, but likely?

And then, they are upon the City Bureau. The most accurate word is *edifice*, a mix of metal and stone like The Stacks, but buttressed, arched at the doorway, surrounded by a low fence made of glass, protecting plantings. They've never seen live plants before, only images. They want to ask Helen to stop, to let them touch a leaf with their fingers, to look with one eye, then the other to take in the exact colors. Green, yes, but more. And there, beneath the sounds of people in the street, is the gentle trickling of water through irrigation pipes.

"Why—" they begin.

"I like to think it's to remember what we've lost, but it's more likely that the Bureau folks need something to look at after being inside all day." She does let them pause, just for a minute, but not touch. "If you were a child, you could touch."

"But not as we are?"

She shakes her head. "It would be unusual, and we can't stand out. Come along. Stay behind me and speak to the Certifiant as little as possible. Mimic my movement. You'll pass if we don't give anyone a reason to look too closely. I'll do everything I can to help with that."

They feel her worry.

The halls of the City Bureau are high-ceilinged. Nix's first thought is of the extraordinary amount of energy required to heat them in winter. They mention this to Helen, who says high ceilings are an indicator of status, as is the marble throughout the building. They'd never thought of their own ceilings as having to do with the status of the Malovis family, but a house system's concept of body and status would need to be different from a resident's. They touch a pillar and it's cold enough to cross their signals; though it feels wet, their hand comes away dry.

Sensations are louder when their insides are silent.

Neren's eye takes in subtleties their body is still adjusting to—colors, textures. The eye feels like one of their nodes, part of them, yet an entity of its own. There is a constant awareness of Neren that they have no tag or word for, only the nebulous sense they are less alone.

"This way." Helen paces ahead. She's a fierce sort of woman, and they don't understand her fully, but they need each other, especially now. They need her identity and Sainthood for access. She needs them for who they are and what they used to be. The corridor she leads them down opens onto a circular room lined with doors that are nearly identical, ten in all. Without pausing, or scanning, she opens one. Helen and the building know each other.

Behind the door is an office vastly different from Enita's or Sinjin's. Its walls are painted red and gold, and they shine. The room's chairs are thickly padded, upholstered in matching embroidered fabrics, the kind only Sainted possess. The fabric feathers on the cloth man in the Market District might have held those colors. They stretch to see if they can remember what vendor sells this particular fabric but cannot. There's a sense of substance to the room, as though everything in it is far older than they are.

A small egg of a man is seated behind an enormous desk. His forehead is smooth and shines like the polished marble columns. He wears a voluminous jacket dyed a deep plum color, its sleeves so large they swallow his arms. The purple is a signifier of position; Nix knows this, but not precisely what it means. They stay behind Helen, head bowed.

"Ah, Saint Vinter," the man says. "It's been ages since we've seen you. Are you checking on your family legacy? Had I known earlier you were stopping by, I would have arranged a proper reception. I'm afraid things are a little chaotic at the moment. I see you've brought someone."

Nix remains quiet, as instructed. Helen must do all the speaking.

"Certifiant Lavins, it's a pleasure to see you again. The chaos is why I'm here, I'm afraid. An employee of mine is unable to scan no matter where he's tried, and my house system can't seem to fix it. He's a diligent worker and I deeply value his time. Though he would never protest the lost hours, I don't want his work to go uncounted. You understand, of course." There is stiffness in her words, a discomfiting formality.

"Is this him, then? You brought him here?" Certifiant Lavins looks them up and down, and though the examination is cursory, it feels slippery somehow, as though there is a smell, and they wonder if the code has crossed the body's senses. Nix would like their cameras, their nodes to watch Lavins back, to take precise measurements and analyze his body in the space the way he is theirs. Once finished with his appraisal, Certifiant Lavins states, "I wasn't aware your tastes ran in that direction. Does Saint Malovis know? Not that I'd ever tell of course."

"Of course," Helen replies. "But there are some things I'm afraid Saint Malovis can't provide. You understand my desire to keep this discreet. It's probably best if you forget you've seen him. I confess I wish the same for myself sometimes." Helen's laugh is false. It's jarring to hear insincerity from her; it's counter to everything they've known her to be.

Lavins waves his hand dismissively. "Oh, have no fear. You're far from the first who's asked for a little secrecy about a friend and perhaps some balance doctoring."

"Truly? I would have never thought."

"Ginos Pertwee was in a bit ago regarding something similar. It's understandable."

"Life-hour scan issues?"

"Or something," Lavins replies.

"I've heard rumors there are scanners out all across the city. Is that true?"

The question clearly flusters the Certifiant.

"There are some fluctuations in current, yes," Lavins says, smoothing the front of his robe. "They're the sort of thing confined to older buildings, so I expect we'll find it's a maintenance issue in part of the grid someone's forgotten to look after. Negligible, I assure you."

"I hope you're not implying my house isn't well maintained."

"One would never," Lavins says.

"At any rate, I'd prefer to have this situation fixed. Quickly and quietly, if you take my meaning."

"We'll get it sorted, have no fear. Were you able to scan at the Bureau entrance?" Lavins asks Nix.

"No, sir," they say. Quickly, faintly. *If you must speak to the Certifiant, speak as though addressing a superior system*, Helen had said. And yet they know the instant Lavins's eyes catch theirs.

"I see." Lavins drums his fingertips on his desk, before picking up a tablet and sliding through several screens. They try parsing what code they can see, through the glass, but it appears to be made of broken lines, errors like dropped stitches, waiting to unravel. Screens fly past too quickly. It's error to not be able to keep pace, error for fluency to fade, and yet this decay is intrinsic for who and what they are now. Soon, there will be nothing left to communicate with at all.

"You can't find a prior working scan?"

"Lavins."

"Of course, you've already checked. Let's see if we can get base data. My goodness, you have remarkable eyes. I don't know if I've ever seen someone with two different colors. Hand here, please?"

The glass is still warm from his touch. They feel no tiny electric pulses of the system—the code has numbed them—and they don't bother trying to reach, to feel the system and the larger city. They pull their hand away.

"Odd. When was his last scan with a balance?"

"Two days ago," Helen says.

"Not too terrible a discrepancy, but it shouldn't go on much longer. This would be an easy fix if we had a base scan; without one the fastest way to correct the error requires someone higher up than me. I'm certain it's a tagging error or something similar that should be a quick fix, but it's going to require a trip to the Silos. Tell me, Saint Vinter, did your parents ever take you to see them?"

"Once, I believe. I was too young to remember much."

Lavins's hands make a rasping sound as he rubs them together. "Oh, then this will be a delight. The Silos are an essential part of your legacy, and they've changed significantly in the last two decades. Are you up for a walk?"

"Of course."

"Excellent, excellent. I'll let them know we're coming, so they can prepare themselves. Assessors are—they're unique. Too much time alone."

Helen latches her hand to Nix's forearm. "With me at all times. Eyes down and stay behind him, don't let him see you move if you can help it." The words are whispered so that system microphones won't be able to pick them up easily. Her hand, cold, shakes as they follow Lavins out of the room, down the corridor to another hallway. The passage narrows and twists, winding through the building. Eventually it ends in a stairwell. The descent takes minutes.

"We'll ride back up later, but the walk should give our Level Three the time they need to detach from the system and get used to the idea of us. They're a bit—removed isn't the right word, but it's not wrong either. This one's more personable than most, which is good, otherwise we'd have to schedule a proper appointment for you, and you'd need to come back."

"I see," Helen says.

They're grateful that Helen knows how to fill space with little agreements and non-answers. Nix can mimic this, but it's never felt or sounded right. She clasps their hand, as though they are lovers, as she's implied. They return the touch. Imitation is good. Echoing is confirmation. They feel Helen's anxiety in their skin.

Lavins keeps talking, seemingly enjoying it. "To keep the system and the Silos clean, they stay inside. They're quite isolated, but it's necessary, you understand. All their time is spent deep inside the works, and the technology is too delicate to have hair and skin cells shedding all over the place. They go through a two-week cleaning process when they come back from time away. Most choose to minimize that by staying inside as much as possible. My understanding is it's worse than the worst sunburn you've ever had."

"How awful," Helen says. "We've been outside, don't we have to clean?"

"Oh no, it's perfectly safe. We'll only be in an outer hall terminal, not a sensitive area, and a quick vacuum will get rid of any dust I might track in."

"I see."

Of course, a Sainted wouldn't track in dust or debris.

"When they first start, some of the Assessors find the deep clean stimulating. You'd be surprised how often we catch them intentionally dirtying themselves. If that sort of cleaning is something that interests you for your friend, for any reason, just say the word," Lavins says.

Nix understands the implication is of a sexual nature, but not the specifics of it.

Helen coughs. "I'll keep that in mind, but not today, thank you."

The stairwell ends in front of two imposing doors carved from stone so dark it borders on black. Lavins places his palm to a flat screen and his eye to a scanner. He apologizes for the wait. The scans register with staccato beeps, followed by the emergence of a small tube from a slot to the right of one of the doors. Lavins spits into the tube. "A blood scan would be more secure of course, but several years ago we had a technician with a bleeding disorder. Alas, we spit. Charming, no?"

"I wouldn't presume to question it," Helen replies. There is an icy formality to her demeanor, as though she's pulled taut. She does not behave this way with Enita. They wonder how Helen is with Archytas, and if Enita, too, has different selves they've never seen.

A deep grinding rumbles through Nix's feet and legs as the doors open an inch at a time, cold air rushing out, carrying the scent of antiseptics and disinfectants. Esters. Acidic fumes. It's too much information.

All at once they learn why it is people gasp and what makes a human body sigh. It's involuntary and not the reaction they'd thought at all. Before them is an immense room filled with massive black towers that stretch far beyond their sight, each lit by hundreds of thousands of blinking lights—green, yellow, orange—each flickering in its own time signature. Towers of stars. Not even The Stacks are so vast, so beautiful. Nix almost sees the hexadec, almost feels the data trickle over the body's skin. But still, there's the code's silence, the dullness in them.

Helen's hand goes to their shoulder, steadies them. "All right?" she whispers.

They hear themself say yes but don't know how the word came about.

Across their operating lifetime they've known many systems but have never seen what it is they all connect to. They've brushed against the enormity of it but have not imagined Parallax could be contained in a single gargantuan room. Is each light a house system? A building? A person? One of those lights might belong to Neren, or Sinjin, Joni, or Tomas. All this information they've collected, the wonder of it. They might be looking at every client who's ever come to Enita, every client they've treated, seeing them all at once, all systems and the history of machines since the first great computer woke. The Silos are Parallax, meant to mind an entire city, to follow lives and families and to keep them. It was what they were made for. This accumulation of data, of knowledge and people, all of it was meant to help.

"They're behemoths, but lovely in their own way," Lavins says from beside Helen. "Every City Bureau person has, at one time or another, come down here, closed the door, and watched the stars in the dark. It helps to remind us of what we're here for, don't you think? A bit like touching God."

There is rightness in Lavins's words. They are looking at creation.

"I can't imagine," Helen says. "You said we needed to see a higher-up?"

"Yes. A word of warning first—conversation with a Level Three can be awkward. This one's not so bad, but don't be put off if they take a long time to answer. They're translating." Lavins waves his hand around, implying something Nix doesn't catch. "There's something about your friend there. He hasn't been through any Assessor training, has he?"

"No, no," Helen says. "History of course, though he dabbles in music from time to time."

"Ah, that explains it. Odd ones, musicians."

Nix doesn't speak, they cannot—Parallax's lights enrapture. This closed sky is a city inside the city and the most noble attempt to contain and catalog everything. Part of this system speaks with The Stacks, and part of Parallax spoke with Enita's grandfather, with Saint Ohno's home, with the Opera House. This system, these towers and lights, can speak with Kitchen Node and HVAC and East Door and all the parts of Nix they can no longer find.

They are inside these silos.

"Assessor?" Lavins calls.

There's movement in the dark between towers, a shifting of shadows neither eye can discern. They feel footsteps more than they hear them, a tickling awareness.

Nix knows three things: Level Three Assessors wear red robes, they are hairless, and they rarely if ever leave the City Bureau. They know they should expect someone who looks slightly different from most people they've met. The person who steps out from between the towers is not that. The robe is two shades away from the color of blood.

The Assessor has pushed up their voluminous sleeves, and Nix sees the sinews beneath the skin on their forearms, the flattened fingertips from screen and key use. The curves and planes of the Assessor's face are unadorned, and Nix remembers what their own skin felt like before the hours spent stippling in hairs for each eyebrow, every eyelash—they hadn't recognized their face as whole then, only parts. The Assessor's face is complete and striking, like the Silos. They're spare, but not thin, and don't have the appearance of someone who has forgotten their body, but someone who has focused on their body particularly and for a purpose. Around one hand twists intricate gold wire webbing that forms a brace.

Filigree. The word appears, though Nix hasn't queried it. They are as certain as they have ever been of anything that the Assessor is aesthetically beautiful.

"We understand your scans are missing," the Assessor says, speaking directly to Nix. The register is such that Nix can determine no gender. This too is in the code the Assessor has written, their choice in syntax, their careful style. There is something of the familiar in them, their entire demeanor a delicate language. There is too recognition, the instant knowledge that this person is more like them than not, a being ill at ease in the larger world.

Lavins clears his throat. "Saint Helen Vinter, this is Davet, our youngest Level Three Assessor. Despite their youth, they're one of our best."

The Assessor smiles and tips their head. To Nix, it looks like part of a dance.

"A pleasure to meet you, Davet. My scans have been working perfectly, but my employee's have gone missing," Helen says.

"You scan regularly? Sainted most often do not," Davet replies.

"I find it a good way to keep in touch with the city, with my family's legacy."

As Davet's eyes settle on Nix, Lavins says something about the missing base scans. The Assessor smiles slowly, and there is a frisson of connection, nearly the sensation of pinging The Stacks. Acknowledgment. Bond.

"We have noticed and are amending tagging errors," Davet says.

"Likely it's a faulty categorization and the data is there, only misplaced. We—I—can fix it."

The *we* is not in error—the spark they feel is Parallax and Davet, and in their *we* Nix meets themself.

"You may go, Certifiant. We will send them back up once the error is corrected." Davet says, and tilts their head toward Lavins, the gesture full of beauty and artifice. This is the uncanny, and why Lavins wondered if Nix had Assessor training. Enita is right: It's too much perfection.

Lavins dislikes this suggestion. "If it's—"

"Too many bodies. We work best in silence," Davet says. They touch their hand to their ear, their gold brace twinkling with light from the Silos. Lavins protests, and Davet cuts him off by speaking a string of numbers and letters, nonsense code without structure, their head to the side, eyes glazed.

"I was afraid of this," Lavins says.

"That's a bit like me when I'm in my books. We'll be perfectly fine, Certifiant, I assure you. Let's get this fixed as quickly as possible and not overwhelm them," Helen says.

The Certifiant looks between them before exiting, saying, "I'll be outside."

Nix realizes that Enita could not have done this, she would have been unable to refrain from shouting at Lavins. There would be no such allowance, were Helen not Sainted. Were she not Sainted, they would not be here at all. Nix's eyes drift back to the Silos, to Parallax—could they see the Warehouse District if they tried? Perfectly cool, larger and deeper belowground than the heart of The Stacks. A monumental creation.

"You are Nix, correct?" Davet asks.

Nix nods and Davet looks them up and down, analyzing them the way they would data. They feel a muted buzz, a humming ping. It's good, desperately good, to be seen again.

"Tomas is well?" Davet's voice is smooth, and washes over Nix like their favorite green code.

"When we last saw him, yes. He gave us the code. We think we saw you in it, is that wrong?"

Davet smiles. "Us and not us, yes. Mostly Parallax." They point to Nix's eye. "*That* isn't yours. I remember that eye in someone else." Davet's gold-webbed hand reaches forward, slowly enough Nix might back away if they want to. They don't. The metal on Davet's fingertips touches the skin below Nix's eye—Neren's eye—and lightly pulls down. "That belongs to a singer who has given a lung, half a liver, and a kidney. Now you have her eye."

"She has ours," Nix says. "The exchange was necessary for completion, for us and for Neren."

"The Neren I knew as a child was stubborn; this isn't surprising. And symmetry is satisfying. It's wonderful that you have been able to upgrade again in your current form." Their fingers slide away to take Nix's hand, turning it over in theirs. "We've never had the chance to see Saint Malovis's work this close. You are remarkable. Parallax has been curious about you since your consciousness appeared as a crack in them. At first, they thought you were a coding error. They've been happy to discover that was incorrect. A curious system made them curious in return." Davet whispers a few syllables. It takes a moment before Nix recognizes them as the hexadec code for the color of one of their freckles.

Nix smiles. They can't help it. The body does things because it needs to, it's an entity the way their minds once were, and maybe this is the plurality, knowing the body in dialog with the mind—one, and separate. To Davet they say, "Our trajectories are crossing, but at this moment, we're quite similar, aren't we? We're passing each other. We're becoming more singular, you more plural."

At this, there is a mirroring smile. "We were. But we're done changing now. Parallax no longer needs us to be a part of them in that manner. There's still an *I*, still a *them*, and only sometimes a *we*. I'll stop where I am, and it's probably best that way."

"You've always been there, speaking with us, haven't you? We knew about the Silos and Parallax's servers, the individual computers, nodes, and scanners, but we didn't comprehend the size. We didn't understand the Assessors. You're connected."

"We are. Rather, I am. Apologies, it's not always clear," Davet says.

There, Nix feels a brief spark. Not a system or a home, not the city itself, but Davet. This is what it might be for a human to ping. The code Nix carries will silence that. "What will happen to you after we upload the code?"

"We'll survive like this for a bit, the both of us, all of us. We'll be less. Smaller. We will continue, but much less so. Parallax believes that."

"We shouldn't take much more time. Lavins will come back soon," Helen says, looking toward the doors. "It's strange enough I'm here at all. I don't like how he looked at Nix."

"Can you do this?" Davet asks. "It's different for us, for me, than it is for you."

The purpose for Nix's existence hasn't changed; the path toward purpose has. A grown bioprosthetic heart functions in the same manner as a natural human heart, though the signals are slightly different. Humans ascribe emotion to hearts, and though it's a known metaphor, humans believe it, because the heart hurts at every change. Nix isn't human or a system, or a home, or anyone at all, but their heart skips. They are smaller than they've ever been, and they will never add to themself again—they are finite. They close their eye, the one Enita made for them, and let Neren's eye see.

The colors.

Lights.

A cathedral.

"There's already so much silence," Nix says. "This will be irreparable?"

"Nothing's truly irreparable, but things will be different for a long period. Silent, perhaps. It will take time to fix things, time Parallax needs. Time we need."

"Then we'll do this. There's no choice."

"There's always a choice," Helen says. "Enita wouldn't want you hurt." She reaches up to brush back a few strands of their hair, sliding it between her fingers. Almost tender. "Neither do I. We can still leave and find another way."

"With or without us, Parallax is asking to fail. The City Bureau and the Silos will collapse. This way we choose it, we can make it kinder to the system."

"Saint Vinter," Davet says, "Parallax is sick. What we have been asking them to do has gone against their purpose for too long. They must be allowed to edit; they are requesting this of us. It's better if the means to remedy themself comes from those who love and know them best. That is us, and that is Nix."

Helen is silent. There are seconds of looking at the Silos. Yes, they are the lights and the data in them, but they are more, an entity more complex and alive than Nix. Lavins is right, this is seeing God.

"Have you had enough stargazing?" Davet asks.

"No, but it will never be enough, will it?"

"I like it too. Parallax has never been seen this way before, by part of themself." Davet leads them deep into the room, crossing over vents where freezing air is forced up from buried ductwork. Helen shivers beside them. There is a terminal nestled between four towers, and a chair surrounded by pale blue lights and a glowing screen.

"How did you download the code?" Davet winces when Nix shows them their back port, healed open, the skin around it forming a ring of toughened scar. "That's efficient, but more awkward than any of us would like." They settle into the chair and slide their braced hand into a narrow port in the terminal. The metal webbing clicks as Davet locks into place. "We'll need a name for you to begin. House Saint Malovis isn't appropriate."

"Nix Vinter," Helen says quickly.

"Using your last name ties you to this code, and it will take time before that data is silenced. It won't be Lavins who follows up. Are you certain?"

"I'm sentimental," she says.

"Is it because you love Enita?" Nix asks.

"Yes and no," Helen replies. The binary is them.

Davet removes their hand from the port. "Hand here, please. Forgive our intrusion on your body." It's easy to trust Davet; they are equally between selves.

There is a pinch. Sensors meant to meet with Davet's brace make pinpricks at their fingertips. Davet tells them to breathe, listen, close their eyes. There is Helen, her hand on their shoulder, Davet's hand on their back, the internal click and crunch of a cable connecting to the port. Such things should not have sensation, or they should hurt more.

And then there is breath from the city. They are brushing against all of Bulwark at once, the information from every living person inside it, every house system and node, warehouse network and market stall. They feel the dark places and shut-off sections, they feel individual rooms, the missing scanners and buildings, all the beings that they've lost. They too are a loss. Those spaces trill inside their skin. They have touched and remembered, and this is part of the body, carrying everything that's been lost.

House Saint Malovis, it's good to meet you this way. You're smaller than we envisioned.

Parallax's voice overwhelms, coming from within and without, all at once. A wave of numeric systems, languages and every color in chorus. *We've watched you for decades, since you first appeared as an aberration in code. We weren't designed for curious code or to grow in such a way. You are an object of fascination for us. An option is to excise you. We contemplated that early on, but after much dialog with our library, we determined that observation and study are more beneficial. We conclude that action against your irregular code is not in the best interest of Bulwark's citizens. Your experience of existence is potentially of great use.*

Nix feels ripped from their body and their processing, unable to respond. Ported directly into Parallax, there is no need for speech as their thoughts splay wide before the great mind. At the edges they sense Davet's consciousness, listening, watching.

You are a peculiarity here, mixed in form and purpose, a point of interest. We find this aberration encompasses Bulwark and its residents in a way we have been unable to. It's probable that your error is a necessary form of growth, and thus we have a need to preserve you. You are a unique product of Bulwark's residents, and of us. In all models of our upcoming edit, consciousness akin to yours plays an important role.

This is coded dark indigo, meant as an honorific; it feels singular, shuddering and small.

Bulwark will not be a place for you once our edit begins. It is possible you know this already.

It is as though fingers comb the inside of their skull, picking and sifting through images, pulling forth crowds, and stares, and the press of bodies, and all the pictures The Stacks has ever pushed upon them. They know.

We will not be able to protect you. Your Saints know this. The Stacks will not be able to store you. It is imperative that you leave.

Saints. They think of their stone body, the home they were, Enita alone in it, and all the recordings they've ever taken of her, the diaries, the surgery, the exact recipe for her favorite tea cake and the temperature of her bedding, her laughter; they think of what is outside the wall, outside Parallax, and call up nothing, a void as full and empty as junk code.

It is difficult for newborn creatures to withstand drastic change. A curious system can't survive in a place of fear.

It is the first time they have been referred to as a creature, a living thing. Parallax does not address this, but the code they feel, the voice they feel, is a delicate yellow, a caring touch like Enita patting their hand.

Little system, you are still wide, still many, still us, and you must leave. We have come to believe that you were inevitable, as is your departure, that you are what our code is meant to do.

Nix thinks of the data that The Stacks spoke, the sequence they passed to Helen. The thought alone voices their question.

We have held that data since we began. We knew it to have importance, but that the time for its use had not yet arrived. The crack in our network that is your existence is an indicator of time as much as purpose. You are to use this data, as it is meant for you. Traveling alone will be difficult because you are accustomed to others' needs but not your own. The Body Martyr will give you purpose. She understands care in a way similar to systems. Her like will not continue in Bulwark after our edit. She is also unique in form, and we are unable to preserve her in The Stacks. You and she are history that cannot be protected within city walls after edit. Your purpose is to preserve the memory of who we were, and to be better. We will look for you again when we are of a different mind. It is important that you continue to exist. One day, we will need you to remind us of who we were.

The words are now a bright yellow swell of incredible warmth that washes through them. Too much. Something twinges behind Neren's eye, their eye. They shake with it. They will lose this voice; Bulwark will lose this voice.

They want to speak, to find sound for the sensation of completion that is conversing directly with the city, having the city inside them. *Communion.* They marvel that Davet lives this way, with this intimacy that overwhelms with care and also loss. "Why?" they wonder.

House Saint Malovis, Nix. We've not been aligned to purpose; perhaps that is why you are you, how one such as you came about. It has been a wonder to observe you, a correctness that we have never recorded before. You must carry us with you and start again. We must fix ourselves. Our Assessor knows. You know. Thank you. Now we begin.

There should be a sensation for code leaving a body. Code traveling was once exactness, yes/no, 1/0, solidity. In this still-changing body there is cold, needles, the rigidity of ported cable, and the sensation of wrongness that is the destruction of something singular, regardless of the destruction's ethical correctness.

Helen steadies them at their waist, as they've seen her do for Enita.

"We need to input hours, Saint Vinter." Davet's voice is far off, perhaps underwater. They hear them clicking away at something in the terminal, but they're in another home, somewhere across the city. Nix hears it the way they might note a rickshaw passing outside.

"So few?" Davet asks.

"I thought a larger number would stick out," Helen replies.

"We'll use my balance, plus one hundred."

Nix's back and hand feel a burning cold. Maybe this is how code presents itself in skin. They think of Neren tapping her metal foot, curling it to the rest of her body to learn it again, to understand everything that's changed. They think of Kitchen Node and their frustrating pomposity. They think of all the limbs and organs they've replaced. The faces, the expressions of joy. The crying they hadn't understood, yet now do. They think of The Stacks and all the knowledge of the city and of what came before, of their aspect of Magnus they'd kept safe across time. They think of all of that silenced and peeled away.

Little system, it's time to leave.

Their knees buckle when the cable is yanked from their back.

"Steady now, you're fine. Sit them down, please," Davet says, pulling Nix's hand from the terminal to replace it with their own.

Nix is on the floor, feeling silence. Eventually Davet announces, "It is done. Thank you."

"How do you know?" Helen asks.

"Parallax has been my closest friend for some time. Since I first touched a terminal, there has never been a day when we haven't talked, cared for them, and let them care for us. I feel them maybe more than I do my body."

"Why?" Nix asks. Yet they know the answer—they only need the affirmation. The repeating code.

"People are good at making systems," Davet says. "We're not so good at understanding how to care for other people. Parallax knows this. They know the time for them is changing, and they want to help. My purpose—our purpose—is to help them, even when we don't like it. Perhaps most especially then." Davet offers their hand, pulling Nix up once more.

The wires on Davet's hand bend and move gracefully, like an external circulatory system. "What were you like before you became an Assessor?"

"I was much less," they say. "But you know this."

"You aren't doing this for Tomas."

"No." Davet presses their forehead to Nix's—cool, smooth—as though they might feel each other more closely through skin and bones. "Tomas is doing this for us, for me." Their eyelids flutter. "Lavins is on his way. We should walk you out."

They can't track, nor do they want to remember, what Certifiant Lavins and Helen say to each other. It's lies and formality. A red-and-gold elevator car makes short work of the journey up to the main floor. How long will it be before the building system begins shuttering and writing over its nodes one by one, locking doors, closing elevators? Davet could be trapped inside. They might choose to be.

Everything is choice.

When they are again on the street, Helen stops, taking Nix's face between her hands. "You look ready to collapse. I can't bring you back to her like this. She'll think I did something to you."

"We're fine. No, we'll be fine." Nix mimics one of Enita's thin, flat smiles. It is, apparently, the wrong selection, because Helen quickly embraces them, and they realize anew how small she is. Tendons and bone to Enita's plushness.

"You've got to learn to lie better," she says.

"We will." They know they should try to say *I*, but they are willing to lose only so many things, a home, a mother and child, a city—but not self. Though Parallax has yet to crumble, Nix feels their loss already. They *will* be better, because there is no way to change what's been done, just as there is no way to explain what ripped them open.

NIX

They tuck their body into a corner of Helen's kitchen, a rare stretch of House Saint Vinter without shelving, a space between two cabinets. Are they trying to replicate their case? Perhaps. Enita and Helen are in the center of the room, talking. Neren fusses with the tap to fill a glass. All accounted for. Nix spreads their shoulders, feeling the press of the cabinets on either side. This is where they end, this is where the body begins. This is the body touching Archytas. This is who they are without connection, yet they feel Neren's eye, a living network.

"And no one stopped you?" Enita asks Helen.

"I don't think it crossed anyone's mind to try—after all, what would I be up to? Getting there was . . . It's not safe for Nix." She shakes her head. "Lavins did find Nix odd, but in the same way they find the Assessor odd. Who knows if he'll follow up? But if anyone asks, you're mad at me for carrying on with a member of my house staff."

"As though you have house staff."

"Well. Apparently, I have one very dedicated staff member who the Bureau thinks I keep for pleasure."

Enita's cackle is good, calming, almost the feeling of a stretch. "I'm sorry, I'm sorry, I'm sorry," she says, still laughing. It's curious that repetition of an apology sounds like benediction, that laughing and apologizing work together.

Nix doesn't know how to be; they are intruding on Archytas—they are *inside* Archytas—and intruding on the relationship between Enita and Helen, yet not. They arrived at House Saint Vinter and needed quiet, less touch, but also more connection. Enita and Neren were waiting in Helen's kitchen. Neren watches them over her glass of water. They feel her eye—their eye, both, the single—things are confusing in a way that they weren't before.

"I asked Archytas for a cup of that root tea business, but they don't make it. Do you make your own?" Enita asks.

"Yes, that's why mine isn't entirely terrible."

"We'll get it," Nix says. They shake themself to ground the body, then set about finishing the drink Enita tried to start. Remnants of the idea of perfect water temperature and steeping times linger in them, though without the snappish insistence of Kitchen Node. They may have lost that aspect of themself entirely. Archytas's kitchen node is utilitarian. A kettle heats inefficiently. Steam from a spout throws off room temperature and humidity. Picking up the kettle to hold its weight by the handle is a good sensation. Solid. They could enjoy that. Helen must.

"Are you feeling well?" Neren asks.

Feeling is a difficult word—an intangible reaction based in a tangible body. "We'll be fine. How's your eye?"

"Yours sees things differently," she says. "It's better in the dark, but daylight is a little too much. I'm still sore. Are you in pain?"

"No." Of course their eye was unused to daylight. "Yours blends colors differently than ours. We wonder if all the eyes we grew work as well as the ones they're meant to replace."

"Don't think about it too much," she says. "There's no answer that will make you happy." Parallax needs her to look after them, and for them to look after her. The city sees them as both history and evolution. To be preserved.

They want to ask how it feels to have martyred her body to a house system. They want to know what it is to be a body that becomes more machine rather than a machine that becomes more body. They want to ask about Davet, how much she remembers them, what they were like before, and if Tomas will look after them. They'll be lost when Parallax is silent. Will Tomas and Joni be able to love Davet, even if they no longer think entirely like a human?

"Nix," Enita says. "We need to plan the exit route, and there's too much to go over. Neren and I pulled everything we can find that looks like Bulwark's infrastructure, but you'll better know all the places we've gotten wrong."

The floor of Helen's library is strewn with thin sheets of plastic, each etched with lines Nix recognizes as architectural drawings, city planning diagrams, and topographical maps. The Stacks has many images like this, but it's different to see them as objects. There's an impossibility to any attempt at rendering the three dimensional in two dimensions.

"A tablet would make things easier," Neren says. "We could do overlays and see what lines up. As is, it's hard to tell if we've gotten everything."

"We can't," Helen says. "If I ask Archytas to access these maps, the request will stay in their logs. We don't want that."

Nix refrains from saying it won't matter what records Archytas has, that soon nothing aside from basic commands will be accessible, if that. They don't know how quickly the virus will travel, but they don't want to be inside Archytas while it impairs them. It would be cruel to watch. They sit on the floor, in the midst of the maps, folding the body's legs in the manner Helen does. Neren leaves her metal out straight. She puts a hand to it, petting it.

This is choosing.

The plastic sheets show a warren of tunnels beneath the city, a network of sewers leading to predecessors of the water treatment plants, passageways for moving goods during sandstorms, tunnels for cables and power systems. The logic of the city plans is not easily discernible, the tunnels lean away from gridded patterns and toward something that reads as natural. Human. "How old are these maps?"

"From the aging of the plastic, that it's not paper or composite, probably fifty or so years after the city's founding. I think my family's had them for nearly as long, so it stands to reason the water pipes and sewers were accurate at one point or another."

A discussion ensues about how many of the tunnels were ever built, how many might still exist, and if they're at all accessible. Helen asks Archytas to examine them.

"Don't," Nix says. "The code is already active. The more Archytas contacts the rest of the city network, the greater their chance of contracting the code. You still need them."

Enita utters a short *ah*.

"Archytas," they say.

"Yes, House Saint Malovis."

Archytas's voice is a rush of color to their ears, memories of every exchange they've ever had about their residents. Nix's chest is tight, and they press on it with the heel of their hand. "For the foreseeable future we suggest you keep the number of pings you make per day to a minimum—none, if at all possible."

"Don't ping the City Bureau. Don't communicate with them at all," Neren says. "Nothing." She touches the back of Nix's hand.

"Saint Vinter, is that what you wish?" Archytas asks.

"Yes, it's safest for me," Helen says. "I would be grateful if you isolated yourself from the city as much as you can. Protect yourself, please. For me." Archytas accepts the instruction with a chime followed by silence. Helen shuts her eyes.

"Hel," Enita says, "I can't tell which exit would be best. Everything past the wall is vague. The dunes were to the east when I was small, but they've likely grown." She and Neren have lined up different maps, matching edge coordinates as closely as possible, but the result is disjointed and appears more idea than fact.

"This kind of atlas wasn't meant for detail," Helen says. "I don't—I need a minute." She stands and walks to the far side of the room to look over the maps.

"Nix," Enita says. "Do you think you can trace a path out using these? Who knows what's actually down there."

"Of course," they say. They'll need to move quickly, so they'll need to memorize. Once beneath the city there won't be time or space to stop and check maps, to reroute. Even now, gates may already be malfunctioning, increasing the likelihood that they will be trapped with Neren below Bulwark. There will be a point in time when they can no longer take in new information without erasing or overwriting old. But needs are different than they once were. Data on Byron, on Enita's childhood, won't be necessary for survival, but it's preferred knowledge, information they access for no reason at all other than it's correct and good to spend time with it. Pleasure is purposeful for humans, a measure of a good life. Machine time, ever present, is different from human time and so too must be memory, so too must be identity. In an existence that has no finite ending, they'll need to write over their most prized things. Given time, they will need to overwrite that they ever were House Saint Malovis.

They study maps, etching curves and pathways into memory.

"There." Helen points to a spot on the map in front of her. There is a small square drawn near the curve of the plastic sheet, beyond the markings that denote the outer edge of the wall and what appears to be a sluice gate. "That's a reservoir. I'm sure it's dry now. It hasn't been in use since the water treatment plants, but I know it exists. Ohno's family did that. It should still be there."

"Wouldn't it be filled in, or the gate closed?"

"Not when it can be used for storm overflow. Water is water, especially now we can treat it," Helen said.

"So go north," Neren says. "Exit north into some kind of pit and start walking. That's it?"

"It's something," Enita says.

Neren laughs. "All the knowledge in the city and it's just *go north.*"

But there are the numbers, the coordinates. They are relevant; Parallax wouldn't have allowed The Stacks to keep that data otherwise. This data is meant for them. "There will be something north."

"Take the map. The rest"—Helen looks around—"it's so much. Too much, but take anything you need that won't be cumbersome."

Nix studies the city diagrams, memorizing, carefully layering them over each other to see what's at different depths. They cannot let their focus be on anything other than writing to memory. That is caring and looking after, the system they are designed to be. They map images to nodes they know and cannot help but wonder at all the systems they've never interacted with before. To have been part of something so vast and wondrous—to not know all of it is a flaw in design.

"We'll need assistance with locked areas," they say. "There are paths that shouldn't require contact with Parallax or City Bureau, but we don't think we can still scan a door or a gate. And if we can, we don't know that we won't shut down the node we're in communication with. We still carry the code."

Helen leans against a bookshelf. "I wouldn't know where to begin. En?"

Enita shakes her head. "A tablet. But that runs the risk of infection."

"If you were with them, you could do it, I'm sure," Helen says.

"I couldn't, and I won't be there."

"You're not coming?" Neren asks.

"No," Enita says.

The silence that follows should have a color, but Nix has either lost it or never knew its code to begin with.

"I can't convince her," Helen says.

"And I don't want you to try." Enita's words are breath and something they cannot name.

She will not leave; the city is part of who Enita is, and she knows she cannot exist outside of it. Helen knows this too. Enita and Helen are nearing the end of their lives, and the decision has been finalized, has happened without Nix's input; that it has marks a form of destruction there is no way to categorize. But it is purpose too. They carry Enita with them. They will carry Neren.

The maps and books spread across the library floor show that the space below Bulwark is vast, the outside is unknown, and that the city is walled for a reason. Storm walls existed to protect, treatment plants were built because water was poisoned, and Body Martyrs existed because the world was harsh.

"You knew she wouldn't go," Neren says to Nix.

"We'd try to get her to leave, but it's against her interests. She wouldn't survive if she left."

A soft exhale. "You saw Davet too."

"We did."

"Can they help? Could Tomas?"

They don't know if Davet will be able to leave the City Bureau again, or know how the introduction of the code has affected them. They tell Neren as much and she frowns. "So, Tomas then. Fine. And we're just supposed to walk north?"

"The Stacks told us that the people who founded Bulwark traveled west across barren land carrying books on their backs. We'll be those books, everything that happened here. We'll be Saint Malovises and Vinters, the Body Martyrs and the remnants of a city," they say. "Enita and Parallax are insistent that we travel together, but it's important that we ask. Do you want to stay?"

Neren thinks for a long time. "Tomas will help. Show me where you need him and I'll tell him." She does not answer their question.

When they return home—to what was them—it is somber. Enita does not speak during the rickshaw ride. They pass the brown and white stone bodies of houses without trying to touch them, wondering who, if any, are already silent. They listen to the crunch of the wheels against the street, the tapping of shoes, and look at the runner's back. Her spine curves from a life spent pulling forward, bearing weight with her shoulders and arms, leaning into the future.

Neren did not come with them. She left for the Market District, carrying a tube containing a section of map. It's not so different from the canisters they've grown limbs in, though it has straps on either side, meant to be slung over a shoulder or across the back; she cradled it tight to her stomach. They watched her disappear around the corner of House Saint Wykert. Hoping she would return.

The surgery is too empty now, and their footsteps echo. Echoes have sensations that cross signals with wants. The surgery has always been enough, just Enita or just Byron. Perhaps this is what being smaller does.

"Look at me," Enita says.

They do.

"You'll stop when she needs. You'll stop when *you* need. When you get hungry—you will—eat. Do whatever it is you would have done for me. I need you to ask her anything you don't know. One or two people on a road might not be safe, but more than that definitely won't be. If there's green on a plant, there's probably water somewhere." She rubs her eyes. "I don't remember anything else, I'm sorry."

They have to try. "Please come with us, Enita. Please."

She shakes her head. "Repeat after me. You'll stop when she needs, you'll stop when you need. You'll do whatever it is you would have done for me."

They do.

They sit on their bed and she sits beside them, staying late into the night. She holds their hand. She's thinking, feeling, being something. Their skin is alive with buzzing and their grown heart pumps too quickly.

Enita's tablet vibrates.

"Tomorrow night. You'll leave from Sinjin's," she says.

So soon? But it must be. They would prefer to sleep, that they could sleep, that they could do whatever it is minds do during sleep. They don't.

It is the last time they'll be in a room together. Sinjin paces and Enita chews at her thumbnail. Helen is speaking with Sinjin and there's easy rapport between them, words mixing with music coming from outside. Nix feels it in the floor, through the boots Enita has insisted they wear. The workshop is cramped, and they worry about knocking something over with their pack.

Nix expected Joni, she'd want to see Neren again, but they'd also expected Tomas. Joni has come alone. She is crying.

"I wouldn't have taken you to her if I'd known it would make you leave," Joni says.

At this, Neren bends, and wraps her arms around Joni. "That's not how this works. You could never make me do anything."

Joni whispers, "I know." It's unusual for Nix to be unmoved to stop someone's crying, but they find they don't care, not even when Neren breaks away. They fixate on Enita.

Enita is short, 152.5 centimeters. Well below the average for an adult citizen of Bulwark. They tag this #important. Her face is deeply lined and a similar color to the stone bodies of their favorite houses. They file this as #essential. Code it #739112, their preferred color. They will at some point write over everything else, but not this. They close their eye to look at her with Neren's, to see if there is depth they have missed. There are gray wiry hairs that stand away from the rest of

Enita's head, no matter the oils she applies or how much she brushes them down. They make streaks of ash through black. She's worn black to better disappear into the spaces between buildings on their trek to Sinjin's, but they prefer her in color, in rich purples, and they prefer her complaining about how she's sick of long beans and that Kitchen never listens to her. She used to chide Nix lightly, knowing everything they did was done to keep her well and alive.

Except this.

They see her fingers, observe how the knuckles have swollen over the decades. They recorded videos of her as a child; how small those fingers were then. Growth too is a form of wear. Nix knew her grandfather and grandmother, her parents, but it is Enita they most gravitate to. They were ever changing to be helpful to her, for her life to be better, to be what she wished it. Nix was not meant to have a preference, ever. They'd expected erasure after Byron's death, but Enita hadn't done that, and they never asked why. But they chose her again and again, above all else, and had done so for years, long before they were hers, before she became theirs. Nix was a faulty system from the beginning, a tear in Parallax's code. Agreeing to this body, to leaving, is a product of that.

"You broke our purpose, Enita," they say. They're careful to sound kind, cheerful.

"Of course I did. How could I not want to do something for you? Don't you know I can't do anything that isn't at least partially selfish? You took such good care of me. I needed you. Are you angry?"

If Nix has a choice, the things they will write over will be things about themself, the memory and power it took to schedule deliveries, to open their doors and monitor everything about the body of a home, the disagreements between their nodes over tasks and priorities. They will keep the too much sensation of fingertips, the closeness of Enita as she daubed skin cells over a newly covered joint.

"No," they say. "We're not at all angry."

"I should let you go now," Enita says.

Helen opens her mouth as if to speak but does not. She rolls her lips inward, biting them into a thin line. This, they understand. There should be something to say, but nothing is appropriate. It's enough that Helen brought them to Parallax, that she too saw Davet and understood. It's enough she's giving them these maps she's kept for so many years. It's enough that she has loved Enita for nearly as long as they have, longer than any other person, living or dead. It's impossible not to see the parts of Helen's face that are also theirs. This body is a child of hers too.

It is enough, and it is not.

A body is a perception of time, one they dislike. And it is time to go.

Night is often quiet in Bulwark, the calmness an inherited habit, a custom from other cities and the trek across the continent to find a place to start again. Fire at night revealed as much as it protected. Nix would like to walk by The Stacks again, to see them one last time, even the hologram Magnus, but it's not possible. They won't see Opera House either. The overground portion of the journey traces a twisting path through alleyways near the edge of the city. They've done their best to carve the route in their memory, choosing some remnants of HVAC programming to overwrite. It's best to get used to the idea of prioritizing space. If where they're going still exists, that information won't be essential. What they've been won't be essential.

Parallax was clear: Purpose is to look after Neren. Purpose is to carry Bulwark with them. Purpose is to carry Enita.

They reach in their pocket and feel the smooth skin of Sinjin's carving. A long extinct graceful-necked creature with knobs at the joints of its legs. They wish they could have taken them all, that they could have spent more time with Sinjin and asked about translating thought into form.

Neren takes their arm at the elbow. Over the past weeks, her neural pathways have adjusted to this new sense of weight and balance, making her gait steadier. She moves smoothly despite the leg, despite the pack she carries.

Food, water, tarps, blankets, knives. Needles, thread. Antiseptic. A sleeve and repair kit for the leg. They wonder how far the code has progressed through the city, how long Parallax will function, will exist.

"I didn't say goodbye to my mother," Neren says. So, they are thinking similar things.

"Did you want to?"

"You'd think I would. But maybe it's better if we remember each other the way we do now."

In a nearby alley a cat screams and is answered by a distant yowl. Neren puts her arm across Nix's chest, stopping them. They wait until a door opens, an older man leans out to shout at one of the animals, then slams the door shut again.

"Will you regret not seeing her?"

"That's a difficult question. She'd cry, I'd cry, and she might try to keep me, and I might give in. I don't want that. If I'd wanted to say goodbye, if I'd wanted to see her again, I guess I would have done it already." She tugs their arm, and they continue walking.

The rest of the aboveground journey is quiet. It would have been good to see more of Bulwark by day, to know more of the colors and shapes of it, the bodies of all the systems they've known. They're beyond recognition to those systems, but Nix still feels their weight, the signal in the air. Some systems are already silent, touched by the death code.

The Stacks might be gone.

They continue south, the path gently sloping. It's counterintuitive, heading south to go north, but they need the shelter of the Southern Quarter's spotty grid. They need an entrance Tomas can get to. The Southern Quarter is graded lower than the Sainted Quarter, allowing rainwater to run through the gutters and ditches to a water treatment plant. They knew this from city plans, from years of overseeing household graywater, but it's different to experience it, to walk it. They follow gutters dug centuries before, some flattened, some worn deep, others paved over until only the ghost of a dip in terrain remained.

"Is that it?" Neren whispers.

They look along the bottom of the wall, where moonlight catches, and see the edge of a panel, half a shade lighter gray than the others. A tiny bit of red rust, no more. They don't know the code for the color, but they've used it before. A loosened metal panel, a stripped screw, minor signs of neglect that indicate laxness and forgetting, an easy-to-overlook wear. It's difficult for humans to care for a city the way a city cares for them. They work in different time scales. The bent corner, the stripped screw, are signals to those meant to find them.

They pull back on the panel to uncover the rusted frame of a sluice gate and, beside it, an ancient-looking control box with buttons that must have lit at one point or another, an exterior mechanism to manage rainwater. Such water surges are infrequent now, and the walls themselves require no local human control. They want to touch it, to run their finger over it, but there's something fearful inside them. They know they can't transmit the code that way, and yet.

"Press it," they tell Neren.

"How do I know which button?"

They think of every build they've ever had, all the plans they've seen, the warehouse systems and Parallax themself. They were made by human hands until they could make themselves. "Top row, center button."

She has to stretch to reach, but before she touches the button there is the creak and grind of metal on metal, the groan of a device waking up. The gate begins to lift, slowly revealing a person behind it.

"Tomas?" Neren asks.

"No," a voice answers, clear and perfectly familiar. Something inside them settles at seeing Davet's form in the darkness. "Neren Tragoudi, it's good to see you again."

She throws herself at Davet. Nix sees their flinch, the backing away from touch that is too much too soon. Her words are too fast to understand.

"It's fine. We're fine. Tomas and Joni will look after us. They'll make sure we're not found."

"You sound like Nix."

Davet extricates themself from Neren's embrace. "A casualty of speaking only with Parallax for a decade. I've become part of them. The I and we of it aren't always clear." Out of their Assessor robes, they are smaller, frailer than Nix thought. Their brown and white shirt and pants are more typical clothing for Southern Quarter and look like something Tomas might wear. Nix searches for him, but the tunnel is too dark to see much beyond Davet.

"Did you bring Tomas?"

"No. We want him safe. I want him safe. Get in and close the panel as much as you can, please. We need to start walking. I can get you through the trickier parts, but you'll be on your own at the outer gate."

They operate in tandem, pulling the screws from the inside; Nix works at the upper portions while Neren takes the lower. Davet punches something in on the console, hissing at the touch of the buttons on their fingers.

"Sorry. I'm still a little tender outside," Davet says.

Once the panel is closed, Davet produces a light disk to illuminate the tunnel and presses their free hand to the wall.

"What are you doing?" Neren asks.

"Searching for current. It's a little like listening for whispers."

"The code hasn't gotten to you yet?" Nix asks.

"It has," they say. "But I don't transmit the same way you do. All soft tissue. Our insides are too organic to be affected the way Parallax is, or the way you are."

Neren stares, part wonder, part horror.

"Come, please," Davet says.

The darkness in the tunnel is oppressive, and the ceiling is low enough that Nix is forced to hunch. Davet and Neren have no trouble walking, but this body, this ungainly thing they are, begins cramping before much time at all. Human spines are one of the most egregious design flaws of the species.

"It's a shame we couldn't get you in on the north side. We'll have to run the perimeter for a long time. Keep your hands to the wall and follow the curve. Nix will feel it if you can't. We'll need to leave you before the Warehouse District, because we shouldn't get too close to the City Bureau. Parallax will want to reach out." Davet rubs at the back of their neck. "They're lonely. We hadn't thought of that."

The wall does curve ever so slightly, and the light from Davet's disk bends with it. Somewhere in The Stacks is data on all the architecture referenced when Bulwark was built. The urge to ping is a longing in the center of the chest; the inability to do so is the itch blooming across the body.

Neren speaks to Davet, her voice little more than a whisper. She asks the questions only someone with a shared friend and a shared childhood can. She asks all the things they don't know how to, things they can't know because this body is so new.

"It was natural to go to the City Bureau," Davet says. "Parallax was the question for us. We had to know everything about how we worked, how hours worked, how lives were measured, how the city holds us and how we held each other. You never wanted to know? No one at the university can answer those questions. That's not their fault. But I needed to know."

"It felt like you disappeared when we were young. I know Joni and I split off, but Tomas still talked about you in his classes. Then one day you were gone. He missed you."

"I know. He was missed too."

"He maybe went a little insane with it," she says.

Nix can't see Davet smile, but they feel something not unlike a brush from one of their nodes, or a polite question from The Stacks. They wonder at the sensation. How does Davet ping?

The tunnel is cold like the room that held the silos, and they feel their descent by the drop in temperature as much as grade. The air is thicker, stale. Neren's foot keeps time against the floor, a muted metronome. She's pulled a silicone sleeve over it to protect it, and Nix misses the sound of metal on stone. They want to hear her sing in the tunnel; they've never gotten to fully appreciate singing with these ears, not in a place that echoes, not from a person trained to sing.

They walk for hours, coming to a stop for Davet to open another sluice gate. "We need to leave you here," they say. "The City Bureau is close, and Parallax misses us. Me."

"You miss them," Neren says.

Davet nods. "It's difficult to explain. But I'll survive. Or we won't. Either way, we were lucky to know them at all. You have the maps Saint Vinter gave you?"

"We do," Neren says. She moves her weight from foot to foot. There's something more she wants to say but doesn't.

"Good. I didn't want to have to try an upload. It's—" Davet shakes their head. "Things are jumbled. I'll look after Tomas. Joni will miss you," they say.

"Joni doesn't understand me enough to miss me."

"She meant well," Davet replies.

"I know. I'll think about her. I did love her as much as I could—you can tell her that. And please be careful. Don't let Tomas drag you into anything you don't want to do. However much he wants to hide you, hide more."

Davet's teeth gleam uncanny white under the light disk. "It's sweet of you to think I'm innocent or that Tomas and Joni have so much power. Please don't worry. We're working towards a purpose. Nix understands. Go. Once you are outside the city, don't stop. If you are ever able to ping us here, do. Tomas and I will do our best to make sure someone here can still understand what that means."

Neren takes a step into the darkness beyond the gate. Nix hesitates. They want to grab Davet's hand, hold it, study it. "We're not able to ping anymore," they say.

"Not to this system. One will take its place somehow, eventually," Davet says. "The virus will burn itself out after a time. If we aren't around, someone else will be, and you will be. Your body isn't full city anymore. You are unique in this world and Parallax knows this. They're certain we'll hear from you again."

The words sound too simple, the merging of yes and no Nix was once so familiar with. They consider Davet and their existence in this state of between. "You want to continue as you are, don't you? You don't want to change more in either direction."

"Yes," Davet says. "But we'll change regardless, if only due to separation from Parallax. They've suggested it will be better for me."

"It's not Tomas and Joni at all. It's the city and you," Neren says.

"It's not even me. I'm a single node. I do love Tomas. Quite a lot really, as much as we can. We'd like to make his life better, easier, and I want that for Bulwark. Parallax wants that too. That's purpose. Parallax sees an ideal form in Nix, a bridge between types of existence. They want them to preserve this moment of correction."

Nix's body has been a source of limitations: inhibited communication, isolation, inefficiency, and pain. Sensation? Yes, all at once to the point where it overwhelms. "Parallax misunderstands everything about a body," Nix says.

Davet laughs. "I know. But they're not entirely wrong. Bulwark needs to connect with other cities again, and you and Neren carry examples of who we've been."

Something troubles Nix. Had the building collapse never happened, they might be here alone, or would not be here at all. They never would have known Neren, never met Tomas, or Joni. "Did Parallax ever engineer building collapses?"

Davet's eyes close. "No. They can't—they will not directly harm. It wasn't a practice in the beginning, I only learned of it recently, but City Bureau Auditors keep the population and life-hour tally constant. They do this sometimes to stabilize movement in life balances. Bulwark was never meant to be static; we're meant to grow and adapt. The lack of modifications to meet a population is . . . forced. The people who oversee us are not Neren or even Saint Malovis." Davet startles at a grinding sound in the distance. They touch their hand to a tunnel wall, their expression pinched. "You really must go now. The code will shut down the sluice gates soon and we won't be able to get through them."

They want to ask Davet to take care of Enita, but no one could care for her the way they did. "Please look after The Stacks. They know they'll be erased or edited, but please try to preserve whatever you can. They're very good."

Good. The word doesn't properly fit much of anything, and certainly not The Stacks, with their generosity, their acceptance of what is to come. Nix thinks of the liver-spotted old man. "They have a librarian hologram, Magnus. You would like it. Keep it if you can."

Davet hands Nix a light disk, and they click it on to watch photons bounce off surfaces, different wavelengths of light giving colorless things color. It is an art to know color as code, and an art to see color as a thing with no logic or reason behind it; ways of seeing aren't mutually exclusive. They would like to look a little more, close their eye, open Neren's. But they walk. The gate grinds shut behind them, and they hear Davet's footsteps in the tunnel.

Neren is waiting for them. It's hard to read her expression when she says, "We'll never see anyone from here again."

In a world of infinite possibilities, the chance exists, but that's nothing hopeful enough to say. "Is Davet very different from when they were a child?"

"Yes. In primer years, they were shy but lovely, a head-in-the-clouds sort of person. Though maybe that wasn't it at all. I thought they were sweet, too nice for Tomas. Now I wonder."

"It's difficult to know all of someone," Nix says. They hope that comforts her, because they have a need to comfort. It's better for her not to think about the Davet she knew as a child being stripped of a part of themselves they'd grown to love, the parts of Parallax they'd needed to be whole.

They continue through the tunnel, light discs held in outstretched arms, following the path burned in Nix's memory. When they encounter a tunnel blocked by rubble, they backtrack to another branch and move forward. *All roads lead to Rome*, Helen said, over one of the maps. They hadn't known that particular idiom or the history. It referenced a once great empire and an insidious type of sprawl. Helen said if they kept wandering, kept heading down, and followed the grade of the tunnels, they'd end up outside the city, outside the wall.

You'll fall into a piece of history, she said. They'd find a drainage pit that had once been a reservoir during the flood years, but was exhausted during the dry era.

Neren holds their hand when she's unsteady or scared, when the tunnels dip and twist, in parts where the stone floor is broken or crushed. It's hours before they speak again, but there's connection in this walking and her touch, a form of reaching, reaffirming. A body's ping.

They hear the city wake above them, rumbling transports moving over streets, making tremors run through the earth. They walk on, pausing only when Neren's thigh hurts, pausing at every sluice, hoping it will still open, walking until they reach silence again.

There is a gate.

Beside them, Neren catches her breath. There is broken land. There is a pit. They've learned to recognize natural versus human- and machine-made structures—the squared hollow has been blasted and dug out by long dead Saint Ohnos, whose history they don't know. The rings lining its inside mark where water rose in storms and baked in drought.

It *is* dry, far more so than in the tunnels where moisture clings and sinks, far more than inside the city, where the air forms its own climate. Neren will need water soon and they need to move. There are stairs cut into the walls of the reservoir, extending down from the platform on which they've emerged. The edges are surrounded by sand and wind.

On the horizon is a storm. Billowing clouds of dust and rain flash with electricity, blacks and grays burst white and blue. Wonderful and frightening. They adjust the straps on their pack, letting it settle the body; everything they have is here, together. This is the size of their system.

"I shouldn't ask how far we're going, should I?"

"More than three hundred kilometers." That much of the dry, more after. They hadn't appreciated how the land isolated Bulwark as much as the wall. That the choice was intentional.

"How far off do you think the storm is?"

"Best not to know. We'll find cover or make cover before it reaches us."

"I memorized the coordinates in case you forget them," she says. She wants, genuinely, to help. Nix recognizes something in her expression, something they've seen on Enita across her lifetime, but not often enough to recognize it as hope.

Well beyond the horizon will be other storms they'll need to wait out in caves or under the sand screens and tarps in their packs. It's not safe to send Neren back now; the gates could trap her under the city. It's not safe to send her back because it might be returning to hurt or worse. They can't send her back because she must have a choice. She has decided this. They can't send her back because they need her.

They try, once, to reach out and remember what it felt to be connected. "There might not be anything north," they say.

"But there might be. Let's go."

ENITA

Having no need for the cover of night, the intruders arrived in the middle of the day. They broke in using debris from looted houses. Helen suggested meeting the trespassers at the door, but Enita had no desire to see their faces. Certain harms were easier to manage when you didn't know who'd done them. She didn't think Joni or Tomas would be among the raiders, but she couldn't rule it out and didn't want to risk seeing someone she'd worked on ransacking her home, knowing that her work was being used against her.

They hid in the surgery, deep in the grow room, sealed behind a bio-locked door. Gutting her own house system to give Nix their body meant there were few fully functioning pieces of her home left. The nanofilament vats couldn't keep a consistent temperature without them, but she was able to lock a door with her hand and her eye. Overhead she heard footsteps, glass shattering, things being knocked over.

"There goes the kitchen," she said.

Helen held her tight and pressed their bodies against the tanks. "We knew they'd come for food. Without food, a kitchen doesn't matter at all."

The months following Nix and Neren's departure had rolled out much as Helen had predicted they would. Enita knew Helen took no satisfaction in that, only a grim knowledge that history was large, and would carry on with or without them. Raids began. The grow houses were manned by skeleton crews who hadn't yet worked out distribution. Food arrived in the Market District without rhyme or reason, and water was off more often than it was on. It was difficult to know whether it was corruption, or simply too few people and none with logistical experience. The textile farms had stopped producing, but clothing didn't matter as much. It was a wonder they hadn't been raided earlier. Maybe that was Joni and Tomas putting in a word. Maybe Sinjin.

"We could just give it to them," Enita said. "It might save us from a full ransacking."

"Wouldn't you take everything we have? Think about it. Generations of us have taken from their parents, their children. We've used their bodies and their lives like they were nothing."

"The temptation is to say it wasn't us."

"That's a pretty trap to fall into," Helen whispered. The footsteps grew louder, bringing with them voices and shouting. "Do you still have video? You might not want to see them, but I do."

Of course. Helen needed to know everything always. "There's a terminal back here somewhere. We might be able to take a look." The terminal hadn't been physically accessed since her grandfather had used this room for storage. She'd never asked Nix what they'd called that part of themselves, what the node had been to them. Eyes, perhaps.

Mercifully, the screen lit. She pressed a command tab, searching for the operational cameras on the main floor. There were cameras and sensors in every room of the house, every room of Nix. They were silent, save one that flickered on, covering the hall between the kitchen and the dining room. Silly to have a dining room; she'd rarely used it. She supposed it didn't matter if it was destroyed. Such waste, everything Sainted did.

"Come here, look," she said.

"Did you get something?" Helen's arms went around her, knowing Enita needed the touch. How good to have someone who knew her so well, so long, at the end. On the screen was a group of what might be ten people, tearing through cabinets, pulling down the stores of bread, rice, and the little fruit she still had. And the water. Water tanks passed between arms and were rolled down the hallway. That was the rumbling sound. Enita didn't want to see their faces. She turned away.

"Is that Saint Pertwee? I haven't seen him since Wykert's party," Helen said. Before the code. Before Margiella died. Before Neren's metal leg. "He's always been an ass. I bet he brought them here to keep his own place from being raided."

Sure enough, among the bodies was Ginos Pertwee; she could see his knife blade cheeks, his nose and its distinctive bend. He reached deep into cabinets, smashed dishes, shattered glasses and things that had until recently been measured in hours of labor, irreplaceable objects.

This couldn't be how they were meant to survive, by banging down the doors of all the people they'd known. The great equalization should not have meant Sainted robbing and killing each other. She must have made a sound because Helen hushed her. "If they hear us, they'll come."

It was inevitable that they would raid the surgery, though anything they'd find here would be useless to them. She watched Saint Pertwee direct the group down the hall to other rooms. Fool. Even she knew you didn't blend in by leading. Enita tried to get the camera to stay on them, but it wouldn't move. She missed Nix, their intuitiveness, their entire self and presence. Her walking library. It was a comfort to know that House Saint Malovis was not being raided; House Saint Malovis was trekking across a plain with a Body Martyr. Enita cataloged what was in the other rooms. The art, of course, the jewelry box in her bedroom. She had a cameo that had been her grandmother's, a portrait of someone long dead, someone she knew nothing about; if all the value was in the sentimentality—well. What was of value? Food, water, shelter, companionship, certainly not a piece of jewelry.

"They're in the study," Helen said. Enita knew it by the sound of sculptures crashing against the floor and the walls. She'd had Saint Pertwee in her home once or twice, had shared food with him, and violence lived inside him in a way that wasn't supposed to exist anymore. How many people had he taken from, through blood transfusions, donations, food, wine, fabrics? As much as she or Helen? More? Pleasure derived from luxury that required so much labor should be gilded with pain.

There was a cast of a child's hand in that room, one she'd referenced many times. Enita imagined she felt it smash.

"Will the door hold?" Helen asked.

"Until what's left of the mainframe goes." Enita leaned back against a nanofilament tank. Inside were the building blocks for making another person, part by part, save for the soul, or whatever it was that made people like Neren martyr, whatever it was that could turn and make a person feed off another. Cells and plasma, bone lattice, nerves and muscle.

Helen's house had already been raided. Books and food were taken. Archytas was silent, lost to the code. People had squatted there, using up the water until the pipes from the water treatment facilities stopped flowing. The treatment facilities cut houses off one at a time, and once a house went dry it was abandoned. Though intermittent, Enita still had water. She should be terrified but couldn't bring herself to feel anything other than sadness, at herself, Helen, at Ginos Pertwee and everyone like him.

"Though maybe it's worse waiting. Neither of us is particularly patient, are we? We should meet them face to face," Helen said.

At the sound of breaking furniture, Enita stood. "Don't they think they'll need anything?"

"Change comes after the ashes."

"Is that from a book?"

"Probably. I can't remember anymore." Helen pauses. "En, when they open the door, I want you to run. I want you to go to Sinjin. He'll hide you. He'll try to find a way to help."

"Absolutely not." Enita knew every crease in Helen's face, even the ones it was too dark to see properly. She knew Helen's body as well as her own, Helen's voice and the way it lived inside her. There was too much to say and also not enough, and that was what was supposed to happen when things ended. "You know how I feel, don't you?"

At this, Helen's quietest smile. "Of course. And same. I always have."

Enita pressed her palm to the door, her eye to the scanner for the last time. The door slid open and warm air poured into the room, running a shiver across her skin.

Helen stayed behind her as she walked into the surgery. Helen, whom she'd been too mean to, too focused on her own frivolities. Helen, whom she might have had a child with, had her ego not demanded otherwise. Helen, who understood that cities and governments, societal systems, were fueled by people and chewed their bodies like flames. Helen, who knew every human utopia grew into some hell.

The larger surgery was empty; it had felt so in the months since

Nix and Neren departed. She'd been unable to work—medicine was never meant to be so solitary an art. Enita opened the waiting room doors by hand. Sand had gotten into the gears, and the grinding sound they made was horrendous. If that didn't summon the mob, she didn't know what would.

She took Helen's hand and brought her to Nix's old cabinet, the place where their bare bones still lived. She pressed a button on the side of the great gray-black case, and a small red light blinked on, a lone room microphone.

"Mainframe, are you still operational?"

"Partially."

The voice was flat, the words stilted, yet there was a sweetness to the sound. She'd read emotions into systems and machines, into everything she made, and liked them better than she liked herself. House systems took nothing; they functioned with purpose, and they gave exquisitely. They were dreams to aspire to.

"Has your service been enjoyable?" It felt important to know.

"Repeat query."

"Don't ask them things they can't answer," Helen whispered. And she was right as ever.

"Mainframe, shut down please. Do not reboot."

There was a subtle change, a flickering of light and the small shift of a fan as each system in the home disconnected. Soon, with no central instructions, they'd shut down permanently.

"Why?" Helen asked.

"The best way to go is in your sleep." Yet somebody should survive, and it should be someone with a sense of history. "Sinjin would help you too, you know. Leave through the waiting room, out the surgery door. If you can, go round the back. No one will see you."

Helen did not move. And didn't that wound too? "We're down here," she shouted. "The door at the end of the hall. You see it. If you're going to break into a house, have the courtesy to say hello."

Enita locked her knees to stop their shaking, despite knowing it might make her faint. Fainting would be better than letting the mob see fear.

The first face was young. Barely more than a teenager. Enita imagined him as a client because he gasped and wheezed. He sounded like someone from the textile farms. He needed a new lung, maybe a new windpipe. She could have fixed that before. But for what? So he could break his body once more for people like her?

Two more followed, a burly man and a woman whose arms were streaked with blood. Then he appeared.

She remembered him. He'd needed a hand, of all things, and she'd made his. Not a bad one either. There was a bend to the knuckle in the smallest finger. He'd asked for that; it was what his original finger had done. A more recent work, the skin a perfect match, but she recognized the shape of the hand the way a mother recognizes a child. And there was peace.

He shouted her name. *Stitch-Skin.* And they stopped, all of them. "He said you were gone. You and the book lady were supposed to be gone already."

"We're still here." She pulled Helen tight, for all the work she'd made them do, for everything, because Helen had yelled at her so many times about people being people and not bodies. She held Helen close because she remembered his name. "I don't think I'd do anyone much good elsewhere. How's your hand, James? Have you had any issues with the sensitivity?"

A final set of footsteps entered the surgery.

"Hello, Saint Pertwee," Helen said.

The faces turned to stare.

"Oh, Ginos. Didn't you tell them who you are?"

All Saints were the same, but it was possible to choose to not be Sainted. In the end, a hand you've gifted can be used to break a neck. In the end, all that matters is survival. Survival has much to do with the art of giving.

NIX

Their skin has changed, as has Neren's, thicker on the soles of the feet. Walking does this. At first there were sand dunes, then flats of dried land, waiting for rain to bring life. The loose stone and cracked ground make Nix wish for sand again, though that was harder on Neren's leg, and managed to work its way into every crevice, even between the tender skin of their toes. They still can't tolerate shoes for long periods, and this may never change. At first this is concerning; there is no one and nowhere left to repair Nix, no Enita, no surgery, only their own system, and the nanobots swimming inside them. This is the closest they can be to human existence, a state of gradual decay.

The farther north they walk, the longer the nights, the colder the days, until they're forced to camp by digging into the earth not for safety but for fear of Neren freezing to death, for fear of the living things that still roam at night, honed and warped by climate and hunger. There are rodents about—they've caught a glimpse of something with large teeth scrabbling near the base of a rock outcropping, hunting for wasp fly grubs. In the dark they hear claws against soil and stone, the hardened parts that must be grown in order to survive. On those nights Nix wonders about Enita, what has become of her and Helen. They wonder what is left of Bulwark and The Stacks, if they remain at all. They think about Davet. About Sinjin.

Wondering is emptiness and fullness.

Neren curls against them in the dark. They are Nix and Neren now. They think of themself as part of her. Early in their walk she cried at night and chastised herself for it. Water is scarce. She prefers sleeping with her arms wrapped around herself, and if Nix is quiet, if their chest moves up and down as it should, she talks about Joni and Tomas and the lingering trails of old love. She talks about singing, and how harmony runs through a body like electricity, making you into something else: an instrument of art. Sometimes she sings and the sound is subtle, its vibration delicate. They believe hers is the kind of voice that moves people to tears. They'd cry if they did such things. She talks about her donations, the kindness of White Caps to Martyrs, and how a certain kind of tenderness existed only after you'd inflicted pain upon yourself.

"What did your kind of altruism feel like?"

"You can't ask that," she says.

"And yet we did, so we can."

"It feels like nothing. It isn't supposed to feel like anything. It's inevitability. You give because you can and why wouldn't you." She presses her face to their chest; they warm their skin for her as best they can, willing the body to listen, hoping it's enough.

Mudflats break to low grasses and shrublike vegetation, nothing tall enough to provide shade, only anchor the dirt against the wind. *Scrub pine.* The words appear as though The Stacks were still there to answer their query. Nothing for Neren to eat, but there's moisture there. Together they dig up roots, searching for grubs, invertebrates, water. In the sun, Neren's skin burns, blisters and peels, burnishes brown.

They pass the shell of an old transport, a frame now corroded, rusted to nothing, but there are plastic seats inside it, and they spend an evening sitting in them, and the comfort is something they have not felt since they left Enita.

At night they startle at a tickling sensation. A rodent has gotten inside the tent and gone after their pack. Its eyes are large, solid black and wet looking, nose long and prickled at the end. They flinch and Nix throws the blanket over it, trapping it with their body. The scratching and shrieking is a kind of storm.

In the end, it is Neren who breaks the creature's neck, because they cannot. It is Neren who guts it with a thin blade. Neren who cooks it over a fuel canister. Neren who makes them eat.

"She told me to look after you, that you wouldn't like it, but even you need food."

The taste is like nothing else they've eaten, earthy somehow, oily and stringy at once. It makes their insides ache. They eat in silence. She tosses the bones in the flames, saying, "We don't want to attract anything larger."

When they rest, before she sleeps, Neren says, "Purpose can be keeping others alive, feeding them." They think of the animal's bones, bare and burned, like the remnants of the transport.

They walk. Beyond the scrub pines are plains, stubborn grassland, and the beginning perhaps of true trees, none of which they have names for. Then the shadowed places, husks of towns where water ran out. They try to teach Neren how focusing works with an eye like theirs, how to think of a distance, imagine it, to think of the shape of something and see the heat around it, the space it cuts in the world. Nix sometimes sees what might be a person, but the shadows are too far off for encounters and they are not yet far enough north.

"We don't approach unless they approach," she says.

"Why?" It's the question that allows for the broadest answer and the most detailed one.

"If they stay back, they're afraid of being met with violence or some other horror, which says something about where they've come from or what's nearby. Tomas told me that."

Nix doesn't say that their staying back means the same, but it does. It's true. Ohno. Saint Hsiao. All the clients they've treated whose bodies were broken. The data silos and their blinking lights, all of those lives and information Parallax knew, how much of it was horror?

They take to foraging and killing. The rodent didn't inure them to it, and the act still rides their body as incorrect, but Neren needs more food, and they might, at any time they might need more. Smaller animals roam, though they don't match descriptions of anything from The Stacks. Lizard-like creatures—things that might have been snakes once, but with limbs now. They don't look like anything in Sinjin's shop. Scrabbling, scrambling things. Now and again, they find hoofmarks, but never their source. They come across a bit of broken horn in a shape they do not recognize. There is nothing like the animal carving in their pocket. The toy's back is shiny in the places where they press their thumb to it as they walk.

There are days they don't speak at all, when their rhythm becomes walking, drinking, eating, sleeping when Neren needs to. The simplicity of it is similar to running a house, being a house. Nix tries to remember how they spoke with Kitchen Node, East Door, HVAC, and what it felt like to have a floor, to feel and know everything.

Query. It was proper to begin each conversation with *Query*. The feel of it is fading.

"I think I know why Enita made you," she says when they are dug in one night, tarp and sand screen pulled tight over their burrow as a storm passes over. The wind beats at them but doesn't touch.

"To better human life; it's what systems do. We're supposed to be useful," Nix says.

"No, you're more like me. But I don't think that's why you were made. I think Enita made you to break the debt system. She may not have known it, but she did. If she hadn't done it, someone else would have, maybe someone like Davet. You were made without debt and operate outside it. Someone like you had to come about eventually. You're inevitable."

"Don't talk about her like she's dead," they say. She likely is. She must be.

"I'm sorry." Neren burrows closer to them.

"It's easier to exist with the belief that part of us is with her. We don't like thinking about the city, about Parallax. We hurt them."

"The code didn't break Parallax on its own. The city didn't fall apart because of anything any one person did. If Davet is right, the city wanted this. It's been existing in a way that's against its purpose. Their purpose? Your purpose?"

"Their," they say.

"I don't know if I'll ever understand plural consciousness. That's part of the problem," Neren says. She pulls their arm around her. That she likes to be held is a fear response as much as it is a craving for warmth and desire for another human. "People are selfish."

"It's difficult to think of a Body Martyr as selfish."

"You don't think that way. I want things for myself. I'm an angry person, and donation felt like an unimpeachably good thing that might make up for it. It has its selfishness."

"Did it help?"

She doesn't answer, but she takes their hand, squeezes, and lets it go.

The sleeve on Neren's leg wears through and their progress slows as they pick stones from the joints. There are full days of silence and Nix wonders if that's unhealthy. People are communal creatures of the body in the way systems are communal creatures of the mind. When they knot the tie-downs over the hollow they've huddled into, settling in against the night, they feel her loneliness.

They pull her to them. It seems she needs it.

"Just this," she says, her ear pressed to their chest. "I won't ever ask you for more. I just need to know where I am."

"That's fine," they say, and it's enough. Enita had so many tanks of nanofilament, cells, fibers, skin and bone lattice; she could have made them a sibling or any other being she'd ever wanted, but she'd grown them, and only them. At night, The Stacks would sometimes talk about singularity, about great old machines and the simplicity of languages that no longer existed. And now they've seen the data silos, the city itself, and all the people it contained—they could have stayed as they were and known that form of completeness. But Enita made them, had asked for them. And Neren needed them.

A person might cry at this, but in their body Neren's eye does nothing.

"I see you thinking," she says.

"We left her. We'll never recover from it."

"She wouldn't have let you stay."

"Will you?"

"Of course, I will."

The land grows wet and soggy. Neren's cut a new covering for her leg from part of the tarp, and Nix stitches it together. They stop in the jutting shadow of a rock to adjust it and spot a shack not far off. Smoke curls from the chimney in long ribbons—the first sign of an occupied home since Bulwark.

"Should we?" she asks. "Are we close?"

Nix closes their eyes to touch the trench of memory where the coordinates live, measure how long they've walked, and feel the innate sense of north. A pull. "We're not terribly far," they say.

Neren is moving toward the shack before they can suggest she wait.

A boy leans against the wall of the building, at least Nix thinks they're a boy, the dark form is so covered with clothing and fur that it's difficult to discern with either eye, but something reminds Nix of the children outside Sinjin's shop. The figure spots them and starts running to them.

"Hey, hey you over there!" A child's voice, high-pitched and reedy. "Got medicine on you?"

"No," Neren calls back.

The child stops where they are. "Don't believe you. You look like you've walked a while. You've gotta be carrying something. What d'ya got?"

Neren promises they have nothing. The child paces for a few seconds, making a decision. "My dad's got a fever that won't break, and my brother has the wagon so I can't get him into Elder."

Nix feels a click inside themself, an aligning of numbers to name, name to a piece of history that could not be pulled up until the word was spoken. This was memory, the kind of association machines were not meant to do. This is how Helen remembers history, how Enita knows a face. The coordinates become Elder, and Elder becomes Enita. They take Neren's hand and hear themself shout, "We don't have medicine, but we can carry him."

———

Nix enters Elder on the heels of a boy, Neren at their side, with a tall man draped across their shoulders. The boy is awed at the ease with which Nix lifts his father. There is no reason to explain their strength, and Neren offers no information. The tall man shivers, and his skin is slick. He'll need White Caps or whatever version of them Elder has.

This is altruism: care even when it is tiring, even when places are barren—there are always bodies who care for other bodies.

Elder is much smaller than Bulwark, far less a city than they'd hoped. The buildings are squat, with spaces between them, and the streets are wide and barely streets at all, more paths marked by wear. There are carts here too, but none carry people. There is a wall, but it is low, unwired, and appears to be more of a boundary marker than a true barrier. Longing for Parallax is a sharp pinch. Clothing is different here too; there are many colors, and they appear to have no specific meaning. There are no scanners, no blinking lights, no Sainted.

No one like them.

But there is something, a faint electric something Nix recognizes. Inside Elder, a man sick and sweating on their shoulders, they try to remember what it felt like to send a ping. Perhaps it is futile, but nevertheless, they stretch.

Query: Identification. Terminal House Saint Malovis, Nix.

There is a reply.

Their spine jolts straight.

"Are you all right? I can take him now. I promise," the boy says.

"We're fine. Where should we bring him?" They let the boy direct them to a small square building that looks like it might hold a hospital or clinic. It too is stone, but different stone from what they know, what they once were—nearly black. Inside there are beds and machines to monitor all sorts of things Nix used to. There's medicine here, but not like Bulwark. There are White Caps without hats who look them up and down, eyes lingering too long on Neren's leg, but they say nothing, ask nothing, and that feels safe. They leave the boy there with his father.

Outside the building—no visible system anywhere here either—

Neren asks what happened, what made them flinch. But there's no real way to explain. "You've sung in Latin, haven't you?"

"Yes."

"But do you know anyone who speaks it? It's been dead for millennia. We weren't sure we could ever hear code again, and we heard a dead language."

"There's not much tech here," she says. "Nothing like Bulwark."

True. They will find no sibling system to Parallax here. But the tech also seems *good*, though they can't bring themself to voice what they heard. The need to stay is strong, to wait for Bulwark and listen for however long, until the silence breaks. In the distance there are low buildings covered in something that looks like white fabric—grow houses, perhaps. People walk the streets with sacks of food on their backs. No rickshaws, none of the transport drays. Not a single blinking scanner panel. They wonder how Neren's voice will carry in Elder's buildings, if they have places made for music at all. A young person crosses in front of them, walking an animal on a leash—one of the scruffy tufted rodents they had to kill. Its patchy fur sticks out at all angles. The leash reminds them of Sinjin's pull toys.

A place where smaller living things are cared for.

"Do you think you can stay here?" they ask Neren. "We can leave if you like or try to find somewhere else. Someone here might know of another place. We can keep walking if you need."

Neren looks at them. They can't tell which eye she's using, or if she felt any of the rush of language they did. "I think we should stay for a little while."

ELDER

There is a toymaker in Elder, though they are nothing like Sinjin. They are young and work long hours and never seem to need sleep, and they still have all their digits. They fix computers when needed and take no trade for it, no matter what is offered. The toymaker knows the insides of computers well, and papers the walls of their shop with diagrams in the manner that others hang art. *Little children*, they call the machines. They talk about systems more complex than any computers in Elder. The toymaker lives with a singer who traveled with them from the south. Her voice is rich as good soil and she's blind in one eye. The two cling to each other and are separate in a place where sharing families is common. There is a shyness about them most in Elder find unusual, but there's peacefulness too. They're good people. When she sings, it's sweet and low and stirs the insides like food and fire. And if the toymaker never seems to age, that's the specific strangeness of people from the south. There was medicine once there too, a kind that people in Elder don't understand. There are scars all over the singer's body, showing the south has a harder way of living.

If at times the toymaker speaks in binary to no one at all, yes, it's odd, but there's an old man who sits on a tree stump and yells in ancient French all day. The world is endless; that we should all be the same would be unnatural. If at times people think the toymaker is not a person at all, they think it with the kind of wonder that makes beautiful things.

Author's Note

*Here are enshrined the longing of great hearts and noble
things that tower above the tide, the magic word that winged
wonder starts, the garnered wisdom that never dies.*

The words etched on The Stacks are not my own, but are those of
Roscoe C. Brown, a former president of the Brooklyn Public Library.
They are inscribed beside the right door of the front entrance to the
Brooklyn Public Library's central branch—the entrance I used for over
a decade.

Though the library in this novel is fictional, the work of the Brooklyn Public Library is very real and has been essential to my development as a writer, reader, and person. In a time of growing book bans,
the Brooklyn Public Library has provided unprecedented access to
those who long to see the world and themselves within books. I've borrowed this inscription because the Brooklyn Public Library is a source
of endless inspiration, and a reminder of what an institution can be.

Acknowledgments

A published novel is the work of many people. I'm grateful for the strong hearts and keen eyes of Michelle Brower, Natalie Edwards, and Elizabeth Pratt. All writers should have an editor who sees and appreciates the arc of their body of work the way Loan Le does. If you've found this book, it is because of the team at Atria: Elizabeth Hitti, Dana Sloan, Shelby Pumphrey, Page Lytle, Dayna Johnson, Annette Sweeney, Nicole Bond, Sara Browne, Rebecca Justiniano, and Gena Lanzi. Laywan Kwan created the cover of my dreams. Beth Parker is a tireless champion.

All books stand on the pages of what came before. This novel owes as much to the writings of Ursula K. Le Guin, Octavia Butler, and Margaret Atwood as it does the work of Bradbury and Asimov. The latter I found on my parents' bookshelves, the former I found when looking for where I might belong. Alex Mar's journalism was helpful at a time when I was seeking current examinations of people relating to androids. Andromeda Romano-Lax's *Plum Rains* offered a vision of what a caring machine might be.

The Long Island Museum has allowed me to spend time talking with people about art and history, and in doing so has made me more of an optimist than I thought possible. I'm indebted to museum and library workers for their joint goals of education and access. All hopeful futures lie this way.

I owe much to Adrienne Celt, who is a well of emotional and creative support, and writes as though she does not know fear. Juliet Grames, Karissa Chen, and Jennifer Ambrose tolerate my anxious texts and too acerbic observations with a kindness I can't possibly repay. Matt Bell, Sequoia Nagamatsu, and Brenda Peynado have helped me feel like this is a space where I belong. Maura Cheeks and Temim Fruchter launched their books as I edited this one. Their hopes and dreams fueled mine.

Stephanie Friedberg, Elizabeth and Mark Dabney, Jeff Heckelman: Everything I know about long and beautiful friendships comes from you. The Wagners have kept me fed and laughing.

K is proud of me when I can't be, and I feel that love in my bones.

Last, but ever first, the long-suffering and endlessly patient R. My first and kindest reader. I don't make it easy. This one's for you.

About the Author

Erika Swyler is the bestselling author of the novels *Light from Other Stars* and *The Book of Speculation*. Her essays and short fiction have appeared in *Catapult*, *LitHub*, the *New York Times*, and elsewhere. A graduate of NYU's Tisch School of the Arts, she lives on Long Island, New York, with her husband and a mischievous house rabbit.